SHE WAS PRIESTESS-RULER . . .

in a world of humanoid aliens. Yet she was as human as he was, though their star-nations had been bitter enemies for two thousand years.

"Welcome to my world, Kurt Morgan," she said. "We seem to be humanity's orphans in this limb of nowhere. Kta t'Elas came and begged for your freedom. I told him you were not to be trusted."

"I swear to you, I have no ambitions, only to stay alive," Kurt answered.

"I hope you remember that, when you grow more comfortable. Remember that you came here with nothing, and that you begged any terms I would give you. I reserve the right to collect on this debt. You are here on tolerance and I will try you. I am sending you to Kta, putting you in his charge for two weeks . . ."

Kurt was beset with new doubts. It was not the way he had known the Hanan enemy, and he began to fear some subtlety, a snare laid for someone. Or perhaps loneliness had its power even on the Hanan, destructive even of the desire to survive. And that thought was no less disquieting in itself . . .

C.J. CHERRYH
THE ALLIANCE-UNION UNIVERSE

The Company Wars
DOWNBELOW STATION

The Era of Rapprochement
FORTY THOUSAND IN GEHENNA
MERCHANTER'S LUCK

The Chanur Novels
THE PRIDE OF CHANUR
CHANUR'S VENTURE
THE KIF STRIKE BACK
CHANUR'S HOMECOMING

VOYAGER IN NIGHT
PORT ETERNITY

The Mri Wars
THE FADED SUN: KESRITH
THE FADED SUN: SHON'JIR
THE FADED SUN: KUTATH

SERPENT'S REACH

Merovingen Nights (Mri Wars period)
ANGEL WITH THE SWORD

Merovingen Nights—Anthologies
FESTIVAL MOON (#1)
FEVER SEASON (#2)
TROUBLED WATERS (#3)
SMUGGLER'S GOLD (#4)

The Age of Exploration
CUCKOO'S EGG

The Hanan Rebellion
BROTHERS OF EARTH
HUNTER OF WORLDS

C.J. CHERRYH
BROTHERS OF EARTH

DAW BOOKS, INC.
DONALD A. WOLLHEIM, PUBLISHER

1633 Broadway, New York, NY 10019

FIRST PRINTING, OCTOBER 1976

6 7 8 9

PRINTED IN THE U.S.A.

C.J. CHERRYH
BROTHERS OF EARTH

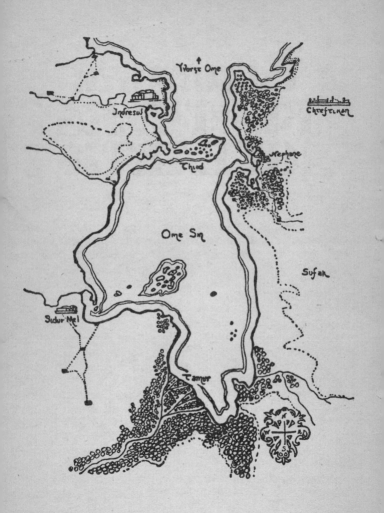

I

Endymion died soundlessly, a man-made star that glowed and quickly winked out of existence.

Kurt Morgan watched her until there was no more left to see, eyes fixed to the aft scanners of the capsule. When it was over, he cut to forward view and set his mind on survival.

There had been eighty men and women on *Endymion*, seventy-nine of them now reduced to dust and vapor, one with the ship and indistinguishable from its remains. Two minutes to sunward was another cloud that had been the enemy, another hundred individuals, the elements that had been life from a score of worlds borne still on collision course, destroyer and destroyed.

No report of the encounter would go back to Central. There was no means to carry it. The Hanan planet of origin, Aeolus, was no more than a cinder now, light-years distant; and *Endymion* in pursuing the Hanan enemy had given no reference data to Command. They had jumped on their own, encountered, won and perished at once; the survival capsule had no starflight capability.

A nameless star and six uncharted worlds lay under the capsule's scan. The second was the most likely to support life.

It grew larger in his scanners over the course of seven days, a blue world wreathed in swirling cloud and patched with the brown of land. It had a large, solitary moon. In all particulars it read as an Earth-class planet, one the Alliance would have sacrificed a hundred ships to win—which they had already won if they could have known it.

The feared Hanan retaliation did not materialize. There were no ships to threaten him. The world filled the scanners now. Kurt vacillated between euphoric hope and hopeless fear—hope because he had planned to die and it looked as if he might not; and fear, because it suddenly dawned on him that he was truly alone. The idea of a possible enemy had kept him company until now. But *Endymion* had run off the edge of the charts before she perished. If the Hanan were not here, then there were no other human beings this far from Sol Center.

That was loneliness.

Absolute.

The wedge-shaped capsule came in hard, overheated and struggling for life, plates shrieking as they parted their joinings. Pressure exploded against Kurt's senses, gray and red and dark.

He hung sideways, the straps preventing him from slipping into the storage bay. He spent some little time working free, feverish with anxiety. When he had done so he opened the hatch, reckless of tests: he had no other options.

Breathable. For a time after he had exited the ship he simply stood and looked about him, from horizon to horizon of rolling wooded hills. Never in all his planetfalls had he seen the like of it, pure and unspoiled and but for the stench of burning, scented with abundant life.

He stood there laughing into the sun with the tears running down his face, and shut his eyes and let the clean wind dry his face and the coolness of the air relieve the stifling warmth that clung to him.

The land began to descend perceptibly after the forests: a long hill, a rocky bow of land, a brief expanse of beach on an unlimited expanse of sea. The sun was low in the sky before he had found a way down from the high rocks to that sandy shore.

And there he dropped his gear on the dry sand and gazed out entranced, over a sea bluer than he had ever seen, and greener than the hills, colors divided according to the depth. Isles lay against the horizon. The sand was white and littered with the refuse of the sea, bits of wood and weed, and shells of delicate pinks and yellows, in spiked and volute shapes.

Delighted as a child, he bent and dipped his hands into the water that lapped at his boots, tasted the salt of it and spat a little, for he had known what a sea ought to be, but he had never touched one or smelled the salt wind and the wrack on the beach. He picked up a stick of driftwood and hurled it far out, watched it carried back of him. Something within him settled into place, finding all the home-tales of his star-wandering folk true and real, even if it was in such a place as this, that man had never touched.

He waded at the edge a while, barefoot, careful of stepping on something poisonous, and used a stick to prod at things that lived there. But the daylight began to fade, so he could no longer see things clearly, and the wind became cold; then he began to reckon with the coming night, and gathered a great supply of driftwood and made a fire.

It was the dark that was terrible, lonely as the space between stars. He had seen birds that day, too high to distinguish; he had seen the shells of mollusks and nudged at things that scuttled off into deeper water; and several times he had startled small creatures from the high grass and sent them bounding off, quickly invisible in the brush and weeds. Nothing yet had threatened him, and no cries disturbed the night. But his mind invented images from a score of worlds. He started at every sound. The water lapped and sucked at the shore, and small scavenger crustaceans sidled about beyond the circle of firelight, seeking food.

At last he rose up and put a great deal of wood on the fire, then curled up as closely as he could before he abandoned himself to sleep.

Pebbles grated. Sand crunched. Kurt lifted his head and strained his eyes in the dying glare of the fire. Beyond it a dark dragon head rode the waters, rocking with the motion of the sea.

He scrambled for his gun, was hurled flat by sinuous bodies that hit his back, man-sized and agile. He spat sand and rolled and twisted, but a blow exploded across the side of his head, heavy with darkness. He went down again, fading, aware of the bite of cords, of being dragged through water. He choked in the brine and went out altogether.

He was soaking wet, facedown on a heaving wooden surface. He sprang up, and was tripped and thrown by a chain that linked his ankles together around a wooden pillar; when he twisted over to look up, he could make out a web of ropes and lines against the night sky, a dragon head against the moon. It was a wooden ship, with a mast for a single sail.

Men's voices called out and oars splashed down, sweeping in unison; the motion of the ship changed, steadied, —and with a rustle and snap of canvas the great square sail billowed out overhead, men hauling to sheet it home. Kurt stared up in awe as the swelling canvas blotted out the sky and the deck acquired a different feel as the wind sped the ship on her way.

A man crowded him. Kurt scrambled up awkwardly, the chain keeping his feet apart around the mast. Others were close to him. He saw in the dim light the same structure repeated in every curious face; wide cheeks, flat noses, well-formed, with flaring nostrils; the eyes large and dark, brows wide and heavy, slightly tilted on a plane with the high cheekbones—the faces of wise children, set in a permanent look of arrogant curiosity; but the bodies were those of men, tall and slim and muscular.

They did not touch him. They looked. And finally one spoke to them with authority and they dispersed. Kurt sank down again, sick and trembling, not alone with the chill of the wind. One returned, and gave him a warm cloak for his comfort, and he clutched that about him and doubled up. He did not sleep.

No one troubled him until the first light brought color to things. Then a man set a bowl and cup beside him on the boards, and Kurt took the warm food gratefully, and drank the hot, sweetened tea.

In the growing daylight he found the men of the ship not unpleasant to look upon. They were brown- to golden-skinned, with black hair. They moved about the tight confines of the ship with amiable efficiency, and their laughter was frequent and not unkind among themselves. Kurt soon began to know some of them,—the one who had brought him the food, the gruff elder man who relayed the orders of a narrow-eyed young officer; and he thought the name of the boy who scurried around on everyone's errands must be Pan, for that was the word others shouted when they wanted him.

They were cleanly, proud folk, and they kept their ship well ordered; human or not, they were a better crew than some lots of *homo sapiens* he had managed.

Fed and beginning to be warmed by the daylight, Kurt had only begun to achieve a certain calm in his situation, when the young officer approached him and had the chain removed. Kurt rose carefully, avoiding any appearance of hostility, and the man nodded toward the low cabin aft.

He let himself be directed below, where the officer opened a door for him and gestured him through.

Another young man was seated at a low writing table, on a chair so low he must cross his ankles on the floor. He spoke and Kurt's escort left him and closed the door after; then he gestured, offering Kurt to sit too. There was no chair, only the woven reed mat on which he stood. With ill grace Kurt settled cross-legged on the mat.

"I am captain of this ship," said the man, and Kurt's heart froze within him, for the language was Hanan. "I am Kta t'Elas u Nym. The person who brought you in is my second, Bel t'Osanef." The accent was heavy, the forms archaic; as *Endymion*'s communications officer, Kurt knew enough to make sense of it, although he could not identify the dialect.

"What is your name, please?" asked Kta.

"Kurt. Kurt Morgan. What *are* you?" he asked quickly, before Kta could lead the questions where he would. "What do you want?"

"I am nemet," said Kta, who sat with hands folded in his lap,—he had a habit of glancing down when beginning to speak. His eyes met Kurt's only on the emphasis of questions. "Did you want that we find you? Was the fire a signal asking help?"

Kurt remembered, and cursed himself.

"No," he said.

"Tamurlin are human like you. You camp in their land like a man in his own house,—careless."

"I know nothing of that." Hope surged wildly in him. Kta's command of human speech found explanation—a Hanan base onworld, but something in the way Kta spoke the word *Tamurlin* did not indicate friendship between that base and the nemet.

"Where are your friends?" Kta asked, and took him by surprise.

"Dead, —dead. I came alone." .

"From what place?"

Kurt feared to answer and did not know how to lie, but Kta shrugged, and from a decanter on the table beside his desk he poured drink into two tiny porcelain cups.

Kurt was not anxious to drink, for he did not trust the sudden hospitality; but Kta sipped at his delicately and Kurt followed his example. It was thin and fruit-tasting, and settled in the head like fire.

"It is *telise*, said Kta. "I offer to you tea, but *telise* is more warming."

"Thank you," said Kurt. "Would you mind telling me where we're going?" But Kta only lifted his small cup slightly as if to say they would talk when they were finished; and Kta took his patient time finishing.

"Where are we going?" Kurt repeated the instant Kta set his cup aside. The nemet's short brows contracted slightly.

"My port. But you mean—what is there for you in my port? We nemet are civilized. You are civilized too, not like the Tamurlin. I see this. Please do not have fear. But I ask: why came you?"

"My ship—was destroyed. I found safety on that shore."

"From the sky, this ship. I am aware of such things. We have all seen human things."

"Do you fight the Tamurlin?"

"Always. It is an old war, this. They came,—long ago. We drove them from their machines and they became like beasts."

"Long ago."

"Three hundreds of years."

Kurt kept his joy from his face. "I assure you," he said, "I didn't come here to harm anyone."

"Then we will not harm you," said Kta.

"Am I free, then?"

"In day, yes. But at night—I am sorry. My men need secure rest. Please accept this necessity."

"I don't blame you," said Kurt. "I understand."

"*Hei yth,*" said Kta, and joined his fingertips together before him in what seemed a gesture of gratitude. "It makes me to think well of you, Kurt Morgan."

And with that, Kta turned him out on the deck at liberty. No one offered him unpleasantness, even when his ignorance put him in the way of busy men. Someone would then gesture for him to move—they never touched him—or politely call to him: "*Umanu, o-eh,*" which he thought was his species and a request to move. And after a part of the day had passed and he decided to imitate the crew's manner of bows and courteous downcast looks, his status improved, for he received bows in return, and was called "*umanu-ifhan*" in a tone of respect.

But at night the young officer Bel t'Osanef came and indicated he must take his place again at the mast. The seaman who performed Bel's order was most gentle in applying the chain, and came back afterward to provide him a blanket and a large mug of hot tea. It was ludicrous. Kurt found the courage to laugh, and the nemet seemed also to understand the humor of the situation, and grinned and said, "*Tosa, umanu-ifhan,*" in a tone which seemed kindly meant.

His hands left free, he sipped his tea at leisure and finally stretched out at such an angle that he did not think anyone would trip over him in the dark. His mind was much easier this night, though he shuddered to think what might have become of him if not for the nemet. If Kta's Tamurlin were indeed fallen Hanan, then he had had an escape close enough to last a lifetime.

He would accept any conditions of the nemet rather than fall to the Hanan: and if Kta spoke the truth and the Hanan were powerless and declined to barbarism, then he was free. There was no more war. For the first time in his imagination, there was no more war.

Only one doubt still gnawed at the edges of his mind: the

question of why a modern Hanan starship had run from the destroyed world of Aeolus to this world of fallen humans.

He did not want to think on that. He did not want to believe Kta had lied, or that the gentleness of these people hid deception. There was another explanation. His hopes, his reason for living insisted upon it.

In the next two days he walked the deck and scanned the whole of the ship for some sign of Hanan technology, and concluded that there was none. She was wooden from stem to stern, hand-hewn, completely reliant on wind and oars for her propulsion.

The skills by which these men managed their complex vessel intrigued him. Bel t'Osanef could explain nothing, knowing only a handful of human words. But when Kta was on deck, Kurt questioned him earnestly; when the nemet captain seemed finally to accept that his interest was unfeigned, he tried to explain, often groping for words for objects long-vanished from human language. They developed between them their own patois of Hanan-Nechai, Nechai being Kta's own language.

And Kta asked about human things, which Kurt could not always answer in terms Kta could understand. Sometimes Kta looked puzzled at human science and sometimes shocked, until at last Kruk began to perceive the disturbance his explanations caused. Then he decided he had explained enough. The nemet was earthbound; he did not truly conceive of things extraterrestrial, and it troubled his religion. Kurt wanted least of all for the nemet to develop some apprehension of his origins.

A third day passed in such discussions, and at the dawn of the fourth, Kta summoned Kurt to his side as he stood on the deck. He had the look of a man with something definite on his mind. Kurt approached him soberly and gave a little bow of deference.

"Kurt," said Kta, "between us is trust, yes?"

"Yes," Kurt agreed, and wondered uneasily where this was tending.

"Today we go into port. I don't want shame for you, bringing you with chains. But if I bring you in free, if then you do hurt to innocent people, then I have responsibility for this. What must I do, Kurt Morgan?"

"I didn't come here to hurt anyone. And what about your people? How will they treat me? Tell me that before I agree to anything."

Kta opened his hands, a gesture of entreaty. "You think I lie to you these things?"

"How could I know? I know nothing but what you tell me. So tell me in plain words that I can trust you."

"I am of Elas," Kta said, frowning, as if that were accustomed to be word enough; but when Kurt continued to stare at him: "Kurt, I swear this beneath the light of heaven, and this is a holy word. It is truth."

"All right," said Kurt. "Then I will do what you tell me and I won't cause trouble. Only what is the place where we're going?"

"Nephane."

"Is that a city?"

Kta frowned thoughtfully. "Yes, it is a city, the city of the east. It rules from Tamur-mouth to the Yvorst Ome, the sea of ice."

"Is there a city of the west?"

The frown deepened. "Yes," he said. "Indresul." Then he turned and walked away, leaving Kurt to wonder what he had done to trouble the nemet.

By midday they were within sight of port. A long bay receded into the shoreline, and at the back of it was a great upthrust of rock. At the base of this crag and on its gently rising side were buildings and walls, hazy with distance, all the way to the crest.

"*Bel-ifhan,*" Kurt hailed Kta's lieutenant, and the narrow-eyed officer stopped and bowed, although he had been going elsewhere in apparent haste. "*Bel-ifhan, taen Nephane?*"

"*Lus,*" Bel agreed and pointed to the promontory. "*Taen Afen, sthages Methine.*"

Kurt looked at the crag Bel called Afen, and did not understand.

"*Methi,*" said Bel, and when he still did not understand, the young officer shrugged helplessly. "*Ktas unnehta,*" he said. "*Ktas, uleh?*"

He left. They were going in. Somewhere aft, Bel shouted an order and men ran to their stations to bring in the sail, hauling it up to the yard. The long oars were run out and they dipped together, sweeping the ship toward the now visible dock at the foot of the cliffs, where a shoreside settlement nestled against the walls.

"Kurt."

Kurt glanced from his view of the bay to the face of Kta, who had joined him at the bow.

"Bel says you have question."

"I'm sorry. I tried to talk to him. I didn't mean he should bother you. I wasn't that important."

The nemet turned one hand outward, a shrug. "Is no difficulty. Bel manages. I am not necessary. —What think you of Nephane?"

"Beautiful," Kurt said, and it was. "Those buildings at the top—Afen, Bel called it."

"Fortress. The Fortress of Nephane."

"A fortress against what enemy? Humans?"

Again a little crease of a frown appeared between Kta's wide-set eyes. "You surprise me. You are not Tamurlin. Your ship destroyed, your friends—dead, you say. But what want you among us?"

"I know nothing. I'm lost. I've trusted you. And if I can't trust your given word, then I don't know anything."

"I don't lie, Kurt Morgan. But you try hard not to answer my question. Why do you come to us?"

A crowd was on the docks, gaily colored clothing a kaleidoscope in the sunlight. The oars rumbled inboard as the ship glided in, making conversation impossible for the moment. Pan was poised near them with the mooring cable, ready to cast it to the men at the dock.

"Why," asked Kurt, "do you think I should know my way in this world?"

"The others, they knew."

"The . . . others?"

"The *new* humans. The—"

Kta's voice trailed off, for Kurt backed from him. The nemet suddenly looked frightened, opened his hands in appeal to him. "Kurt," he protested, "wait. —No. We take—"

Kurt caught him by surprise, drove his fist to the nemet's

jaw and vaulted the rail, even as the ship shuddered against the dock.

He hit the water and water went up his nose at the impact, and again when something hit him, the gliding hull of the ship itself.

Then he made himself quit fighting and drifted, wrapped in the darkening green of the sea, a swift and friendly dark. It was hard to move against the weight of the water. In another moment vision and sense went out together.

He was strangling. He gasped for air and coughed over the water mingling with it in his throat. On a second try he drew a breath and heaved it up again, along with the water in his stomach, twisting onto the stones over on his belly while his insides came apart. When he could breathe again, someone picked him up and wiped his face, cradling his head off the stone.

He was lying on the dock, the center of a great crowd of nemet. Kta held him and implored him in words he could not understand, while Bel and Val leaned over Kta's shoulder. Kta and both the other men were dripping wet, and he knew that they must have gone in after him.

"Kta," he tried to protest, but his raw throat gave out only a voiceless whisper.

"You could not swim," Kta accused him. "You almost die. You wish this? You try to kill yourself?"

"You lied," Kurt whispered, trying to shout.

"No," Kta insisted fervently. But by his troubled frown he seemed at last to understand. "I didn't think you are enemy to us."

"Help me," Kurt implored him, but Kta turned his face aside slightly in that gesture that meant refusal, then glanced a mute signal to Val. With the big seaman's help, he eased him onto a litter improvised out of planks, though Kurt tried to protest.

He was in shock, chilled and shivering so he could hardly keep from doubling up. Somewhere after that, Kta left him and strangers took charge.

The journey up the cobbled street of Nephane was a nightmare, faces crowding close to look at him, the jolting of the litter redoubling his sickness. They passed through

massive gates and into the Afen, the Fortress, into triangle-
arched halls and dim live-flame lighting, through doorways
and into a windowless cell.

Here he would have been content to live or die alone, but
they roused him and stripped the wet clothing off him, and
laid him in a proper bed, wrapped in blankets.

There was a stillness that lasted for hours after the illness
had passed. He was aware of someone standing outside the
door, someone who never left through all the long hours.

At last—he thought it must be well into another day—the
guards brought him clothing and helped him dress. From
the skin outward the clothing was strange to him, and he
resented it, losing what dignity he had left at their hands.
Over it all went the *pel*, a long-sleeved tunic that lapped
across to close in front, held by a wide belt. He was not
even permitted to lace his own sandals, but the guards
impatiently took over and, having finished, allowed him a
tiny cup of *telise*, which they evidently thought sovereign for
all bodily ills.

Then, as he had dreaded, they hailed him with them into
the A-shaped halls of the upper Afen. He gave them no
trouble. He needed no more enemies than he had in Nephane.

II

A large hall was on the third level. Its walls were of the same irregular stone as the outer hall, but the floor had carpets and the walls were hung with tapestries. The guards sent him beyond this point alone, toward the next door.

The room beyond the threshold was of his own world, metal and synthetics, white light. The furnishings were crystal and black, the walls were silver. Only the cabinet at his left and the door at his back did not belong: they were carved wood, convolute dragon figures and fishes.

The door closed softly, sealing him in.

Machinery purred and he glanced leftward. A woman in nemet dress had joined him. Her gown was gold, high-collared, floor-length. Her hair was amber, curling gently. She was human.

Hanan.

She treated him with more respect than the nemet, keeping her distance. She would know his mind, as he knew hers; he made no move against her, would make none until he was sure of the odds.

"Good day, Mr. Morgan—Lieutenant Morgan." She had a disc in her fingers, letting it slide on its chain. Suddenly he missed it. "Kurt Liam Morgan. Pylan, I read it."

"Would you mind returning it?" It was his identity tag. He had worn it since the day of his birth, and it was unnerving to have it in her hands, as if a bit of his life dangled there. The considered a moment, then tossed it. He caught it.

"We have one name," she said, which was common knowledge. "I'm Djan. My number—you would forget. Where are your crewmates, Kurt Morgan?"

"Dead. I've told the truth from the beginning. There were no other survivors."

"Really."

"I am alone," he insisted, frightened, for he knew the lengths to which they could go trying to obtain information he did not have. "Our ship was destroyed in combat. The life-capsule from Communications was the only one that cleared on either side, yours or ours."

"How did you come here?"

"Random search."

Her lips quivered. Her eyes fixed on his with cold fury. "You did not happen here. Again."

"We met one of your ships," he said, and his mouth was suddenly dry; he began to surmise how she knew it was a lie, and that they would have all the truth before they were done. It was easier to yield it, hoping against expectation that these Aeolids would dispose of him without revenge.

"Aeolus was your world, wasn't it?"

"Details," she said. Her face was white, but the control of her voice was unfaltering. He had respect for her. The Hanan were cold, but it took more than coldness to receive such news with calm. He knew. Pylos also was a dead world. He remembered Aeolus hanging in space, the glare of fires spotting its angry surface. Even an enemy had to feel something for that, the death of a world.

"Two Alliance IST's penetrated the Aeolid zone with thirty riders. We were with that force. One of your deepships jumped into the system after the attack, jumped out again immediately when they realized the situation there. We were nearest, saw them, locked to track—it brought us here. We—fought. You monitored that, didn't you? You know there were no other survivors."

"Keep going."

"That's all there is. We finished each other. We suffered the first hit and my station capsuled then. That's all I know. I had no part in the combat. I looked for other capsules. There were none. You *know* there were no others."

An object was concealed in her hand. He caught a glimpse

of it as her hand moved by her many-folded skirts. He saw her fingers close, then relax. He almost took the chance against her then, but she was Hanan and trained from infancy: her reflexes would be instant, and there was the chance the weapon was set to stun. That possibility was more deterrent than any quick oblivion.

"I know," she said, "that there are no other ships, that at least." Her tone was low and mocking. "Welcome to my world, Kurt Morgan. We seem to be humanity's orphans in this limb of nowhere,—there being only the Tamurlin for company otherwise, and they're not really human any longer."

"You're alone?"

"Mr. Morgan. If something happens to me at your hands, I've given the nemet orders to turn you out naked as the day you were born on the shore of the Tamur. The other humans in this world will know how to deal with you in a way humans understand."

"I don't threaten you." Hope turned him shameless. "Give me the chance to leave. You'll never see me again."

"Unless you're the forerunner of others."

"There are no others," he insisted.

"What security do you give me for that promise?"

"We were alone. We came alone. There was no way we could have been traced. There were no ships near enough and we jumped blind, without coordinates."

"Well," she said, and even appeared to accept what he said, "well, it will be a long wait then. Aeolus colonized this world three hundred years ago. But the war—the war— Records were scrambled, the supply ship was lost somehow. We discovered this world in archives centuries old on Aeolus and came to reclaim it. But you seem to have intervened in a very permanent way on Aeolus. Our ship is gone: it could only have been the one you claim to have destroyed; your ship is gone—you claim you could not be traced; Aeolus and its records are cinders. Exploration in this limb ceased, a hundred years ago. What do you suppose the odds are on someone chancing across us?"

"There there is no war. Let me leave."

"If I did," she said, "you might die out there: the world has its dangers. Or you might come back. You might come back, and I could never be sure when you would do that. I would have to fear you for the rest of my life. I would have no more peace here."

"I would not come back."

"Yes you would. You would. It's been six months—since my crew died here. After only that long, my own face begins to look strange to me in a mirror; I begin to fear mirrors. But I look. I could want another human face to look at,—after a certain number of years. So would you."

She had not raised the weapon he was now sure she had. She did not want to use it. Hope turned his hands damp, sent the sweat running down his sides. She knew the only safe course for her. She was mad if she did not take it. Yet she hesitated, her face greatly distressed.

"Kta t'Elas came," she said, "and begged for your freedom. I told him you were not to be trusted."

"I swear to you, I have no ambitions,—only to stay alive, I would go to him—I would accept any conditions, any terms you set."

She moved her hands together, clasping the weapon casually in her slim fingers. "Suppose I listened to you."

"There would be no trouble."

"I hope you remember that, when you grow more comfortable. Remember that you came here with nothing, with nothing—not even the clothes on your back; and that you begged *any* terms I would give you." She gazed at him soberly for a moment, unmoving. "I am out of my mind. But I reserve the right to collect on this debt someday, in whatever manner and for however long I decide. You are here on tolerance. And I will try you. I am sending you to Kta t'Elas, putting you in his charge for two weeks. Then I will call you back, and we will review the situation."

He understood it for a dismissal, weak-kneed with relief and now beset with new doubts. Alone, presented with an enemy, she did a thing entirely unreasonable: it was not the way he had known the Hanan, and he began to fear some subtlety, a snare laid for someone.

Or perhaps loneliness had its power even on the Hanan, destructive even of the desire to survive. And that thought was no less disquieting in itself.

III

To judge by the size of the house and its nearness to the Afen, Kta was an important man. From the street the house of Elas was a featureless cube of stone with its deeply recessed A-shaped doorway fronting directly on the walk. It was two stories high, and sprawled far back against the rock on which Nephane sat.

The guards who escorted him rang a bell that hung before the door, and in a few moments the door was opened by a white-haired and balding nemet in black.

There was a rapid exchange of words, in which Kurt caught frequently the names of Kta and Djan-methi. It ended with the old man bowing, hands to lips, and accepting Kurt within the house, and the guards bowing themselves off the step. The old man softly closed the double doors and dropped the bar.

"Hef," the old man identified himself with a gesture. "Come."

Hanging lamps of bronze lit their way into the depths of the house, down a dim hall that branched Y-formed past a triangular arch. Stairs at left and right led to a balcony and other rooms, but they took the right-hand branch of the Y upon the main floor. On the left the wall gave way into that same central hall which appeared through the arch at the joining of the Y. On the right was a closed door. Hef struck it with his fingers.

Kta answered the knock, his dark eyes astonished. He gave full attention to Hef's rapid words, which sobered him greatly; then he opened the door widely and bade Kurt come in.

Kurt entered uncertainly, disoriented equally by exhaustion and by the alien geometry of the place. This time Kta offered him the honor of a chair, still lower than Kurt found natural. The carpets underfoot were rich with designs of geometric form and the furniture was fantastically carved, even the bed surrounded with embroidered hangings.

Kta settled opposite him and leaned back. He wore only a kilt and sandals in the privacy of his own chambers. He was a powerfully built man, golden skin glistening like the statue of some ancient god brought to life; and there was about him the power of wealth that had not been apparent on the ship. Kurt suddenly found himself awed of the man, and suddenly realized that "friend" was perhaps not the proper word between a wealthy nemet captain and a human refugee who had landed destitute on his doorstep.

Perhaps, he thought uneasily, "guest" was hardly the proper word either.

"Kurt-ifhan," said Kta, "the Methi has put you in my hands."

"I am grateful," he answered, "that you came and spoke for me."

"It was necessary. For honor's sake, Elas has been opened to you. Understand: if you do wrong, punishment falls on me. If you escape, my freedom is owed. I say this so you will know. Do as you choose."

"You took a responsibility like that," Kurt objected, "without knowing anything about me."

"I made an oath," said Kta. "I didn't know then that the oath is an error. I made an oath of safety for you. For the honor of Elas I have asked the Methi for you. It is necessary."

"Her people and mine have been at war for more than two thousand years. You're taking a bigger risk than you know. I don't want to bring trouble on you."

"I am your host fourteen days," said Kta. "I thank you that you speak plainly; but a man who comes to the hearthfire of Elas is never a stranger at our door again. Bring peace with you and be welcome. Honor our customs and Elas will share with you."

"I am your guest," said Kurt. "I will do whatever you ask of me."

Kta joined his fingertips together and inclined his head. Then he rose and struck a gong that hung beside his door, bringing forth a deep, soft note which caressed the mind like a whisper.

"I call my family to the *rhmei*—the heart—of Elas. Please." He touched fingers to lips and bowed. "This is courtesy, bowing. *Ei,* I know humans touch to show friendliness. You must not. This is insult, especially to women. There is blood for insulting the women of a house. Lower your eyes before strangers. Extend no hand close to a man. This way you cannot give offense."

Kurt nodded, but he grew afraid, afraid of the nemet themselves, of finding some dark side to their gentle, cultured nature—or of being despised for a savage. That would be worst of all.

He followed Kta into the great room which was framed by the branching of the entry hall. It was columned, of polished black marble. Its walls and floors reflected the fire that burned in a bronze tripod bowl at the apex of the triangular hall.

At the base wall were two wooden chairs, and there sat a women in the left-hand one, her feet on a white fleece, as other fleeces scattered about her feet like clouds. In the right-hand chair sat an elder man, and a girl sat curled upon one of the fleece rugs. Hef stood by the fire, with a young woman at his side.

Kta knelt on the rug nearest the lady's feet, and from that place spoke earnestly and rapidly, while Kurt stood uncomfortably by and knew that he was the subject. His heart beat faster as the man rose up and cast a forbidding look at him.

"Kurt-ifhan," said Kta, springing anxiously to his feet, "I bring you before my honored father, Nym t'Elas u Lhai, and my mother the lady Ptas t'Lei e Met sh'Nym."

Kurt bowed very low indeed, and Kta's parents responded with some softening of their manner toward him. The young woman by Nym's feet also rose up and bowed.

"My sister Aimu," said Kta. "And you must also meet Hef and his daughter Mim, who honor Elas with their service. *Ita, Hef-nechan s'Mim-lechan, imimen. Hau.*"

The two came forward and bowed deeply. Kurt responded, not knowing if he should bow to servants, but he matched his obeisance to theirs.

"Hef," said Kta, "is the Friend of Elas. His family serves us now three hundred years. Mim-lechan speaks human language. She will help you."

Mim cast a look up at him. She was small, narrow-waisted, both stiffly proper and distractingly feminine in the close-fitting, many-buttoned bodice. Her eyes were large and dark, before a quick flash downward and the bowing of her head concealed them.

It was a look of hate, a thing of violence, that she sent him.

He stared, stricken by it, until he remembered and showed her courtesy by glancing down.

"I am much honored," said Mim coldly, like a recital, "being help to the guest of my lord Kta. My honored father and I are anxious for your comfort."

The guest quarters were upstairs, above what Mim explained shortly were Nym's rooms,—with the implication that Nym expected silence of him. It was a splendid apartment, in every detail as fine as Kta's own, with a separate, brightly tiled bath, a wood-stove for heating water, bronze vessels for the bath and a tea set. There was a round tub in the bath for bathing, and a great stack of white linens, scented with herbs.

The bed in the main triangular room was a great feather-stuffed affair spread with fine crisp sheets and the softest furs, beneath a sunny window of cloudy, bubbled glass. Kurt looked on the bed with longing, for his legs shook and his eyes burned with fatigue, and there was not a muscle in his body which did not ache; but Mim busily pattered back and forth with stacks of linens and clothing, and then cruelly insisted on stripping the bed and remaking it, turning and plumping the big brown mattress. Then, when he was sure she must have finished, she set about dusting everything.

Kurt was near to falling asleep in the corner chair when Kta arrived in the midst of the confusion. The nemet surveyed everything that had been done and then said something to Hef, who attended him.

The old servant looked distressed, then bowed and removed a small bronze lamp from a triangular niche in the west wall, handling it with the greatest care.

"It is religion," Kta explained, though Kurt had not ventured to ask. "Please don't touch such things—also the *phusmeha*, the bowl of the fire in the *rhmei*. Your presence is a disturbance. I ask your respect in this matter."

"Is it because I am a stranger," Kurt asked, already nettled by Mim's petty persecutions, "or because I'm human?"

"You are without beginning on this earth. I asked the *phusa* taken out not because I don't wish Elas to protect you, but because I don't want you to make trouble by offending against the Ancestors of Elas. I have asked my father in this matter. The eyes of Elas are closed in this one room. I think it is best. Let it not offend."

Kurt bowed, satisfied by Kta's evident distress.

"Do you honor your ancestors?" Kta asked.

"I don't understand," said Kurt, and Kta assumed a distressed look as if his fears had only been confirmed.

"Nevertheless," said Kta, "I try. Perhaps the Ancestors of Elas will accept prayers in the name of your most distant house. Are your parents still living?"

"I have no kin at all," said Kurt, and the nemet murmured a word that sounded regretful.

"Then," said Kta, "I ask please your whole name, the name of your house and of your father and your mother."

Kurt gave them, to have peace, and the nemet stumbled much over the long alien names, determined to pronounce them accurately. Kta was horrified at first to believe his parents shared a common house name, and Kurt angrily, almost tearfully, explained human customs of marriage, for he was exhausted and this interrogation was prolonging his misery.

"I shall explain to the Ancestors," said Kta. "Don't be afraid. Elas is a house patient with strangers and strangers' ways."

Kurt bowed his head, not to have any further argument. He was tolerated for the sake of Kta, a matter of Kta's honor.

He was cold when Kta and Mim left him alone, and crawled between the cold sheets, unable to stop shivering.

He was one of a kind, save for Djan, who hated him.

And among nemet, he was not even hated. He was inconvenient.

Food arrived late that evening, brought by Hef; Kurt dragged his aching limbs out of bed and fully dressed, which would not have been his inclination, but he was determined to do nothing to lessen his esteem in the eyes of the nemet.

Then Kta arrived to share dinner with him in his room.

"It is custom to take dinner in the *rhmei*, all Elas together," Kta explained, "but I teach you, here. I don't want you to offend against my family. You learn manners first."

Kurt had borne with much. "I have manners of my own," he cried, "and I'm sorry if I contaminate your house. Send me back to the Afen, to Djan—it's not too late for that." And he turned his back on the food and on Kta, and walked over to stand looking out the dark window. It dawned on him that sending him to Elas had been Djan's subtle cruelty; she expected him back, broken in pride.

"I meant no insult," Kta protested.

Kurt looked back at him, met the dark, foreign eyes with more directness than Kta had ever allowed him. The nemet's face was utterly stricken.

"Kurt-ifhan," said Kta, "I didn't wish to cause you shame. I wish to help you,—not putting you on display in the eyes of my father and my mother. It is your dignity I protect."

Kurt bowed his head and came back, not gladly. Djan was in his mind, that he would not run to her for shelter, giving up what he had abjectly begged of her. And perhaps too she had meant to teach the house of Elas its place, estimating it would beg relief of the burden it had asked. He submitted. There were worse shames than sitting on the floor like a child and letting Kta mold his unskilled fingers around the strange tableware.

He quickly knew why Kta had not permitted him to go downstairs. He could scarcely feed himself and, starving as he was, he had to resist the impulse to snatch up food in disregard of the unfamiliar utensils. Drink with the left hand only, eat with the right, reach with the left, never the right. The bowl was lifted almost to the lips, but it must never touch. From the almost bowlless spoon and thin skewer he kept dropping bites. The knife must be used only left-handed.

Kta was cautiously tactful after his outburst, but grew less so as Kurt recovered his sense of humor. They talked, between instructions and accidents, and afterward, over a cut of tea. Sometimes Kta asked him of human customs, but he approached any difference between them with the attitude that while other opinions and manners were possible,— they were not so under the roof of Elas.

"If you were among humans," Kurt dared ask him finally, "what would you do?"

Kta looked as if the idea horrified him, but covered it with a downward glance. "I don't know. I know only Tamurlin."

"Did not—" he had tried for a long time to work toward this question,—"did not Djan-methi come with others?"

The frightened look persisted. "Yes. Most left. Djan-methi killed the others."

He quickly changed the subject and looked as if he wished he had not been so free of that answer, though he had given it straightly and with deliberation.

They talked of lesser things, well into the night, over many cups of tea and sometimes of *telise,* until from the rest of Elas there was no sound of people stirring and they must lower their voices. The light was exceedingly dim, the air heavy with the scent of oil from the lamps. The *telise* made it close and warm. The late hour clothed things in unreality.

Kurt learned things, almost all simply family gossip, for Djan and Elas were all in Nephane that they both knew, and Kta, momentarily so free with the truth, seemed to have remembered that there was danger in it. They spoke instead of Elas.

Nym had the authority in the household as the lord of Elas; Kta had almost none, although he was over thirty (he hardly looked it) and commanded a warship. Kta would be under Nym's authority as long as Nym lived; the eldest male was lord in the house. If Kta married, he must bring his bride to live under his father's roof. The girl would become part of Elas, obedient to Kta's father and mother as if she were born to the house. So Aimu was soon to depart, betrothed to Kta's lieutenant Bel t'Osanef. They had been friends since childhood, Kta and Bel and Aimu.

Kta owned nothing. Nym controlled the family wealth, and would decide how and whom and when his two children must marry, since marriage determined inheritances. Property passed from father to eldest son undivided, and the eldest then assumed a father's responsibility for all lesser brothers and cousins and unmarried women in the house. A patriarch like Nym always had his rooms to the right of the entry, a custom, Kta explained, derived from more warlike times, when a man slept at the threshold to defend his home from attack. Grown sons occupied the ground floor for the same reason. This room that Kurt now held as a guest had been Kta's when he was a boy.

And the matriarch, in this case Kta's mother Ptas, although it had been the paternal grandmother until quite recently, had her rooms behind the base wall of the *rhmei*. She was the guardian of most religious matters of the house. She tended the holy fire of the *phusmeha,* supervised the household and was second in authority to the patriarch.

Of obeisance and respect, Kta explained, there were complex degrees. It was gross disrespect for a grown son to come before his mother without going to his knees, but when he was a boy this difference was not paid. The reverse was true with a son and his father: a boy knelt to his father until his coming-of-age, then met him with the slight bow of almost-equals if he were eldest, necessary obeisances deepening as one went down the ranks of second son, third son, and so on. A daughter, however, was treated as a beloved guest, a visitor the house would one day lose to a husband; she gave her parents only the obeisance of second-son's rank, and showed her brothers the same modest formality she must use with strangers.

But of Hef and Mim, who served Elas, was required only the obeisance of equals, although it was their habit to show more than that on formal occasions.

"And what of me?" Kurt asked, dreading to ask. "What must I do?"

Kta frowned. "You are guest, mine; you must be equal with me. But," he added nervously, "it is proper in a man to show greater respect than necessary sometimes. It does not hurt your dignity; sometimes it makes it greater. Be most polite to all. Don't—make Elas ashamed. People will watch you—thinking they will see a *Tamuru* in nemet dress. You must prove this is not so."

"Kta," Kurt asked, "—am I a man—to the nemet?"

Kta pressed his lips together and looked as if he earnestly wished that question had gone unasked.

"I am not, then," Kurt concluded, and was robbed even of anger by the distress on Kta's face.

"I have not decided," Kta said. "Some—would say no. It is a religious question. I must think. —But I have a liking for you, Kurt, even if you *are* human."

"You have been very good to me."

There was silence between them. In the sleeping house there was no sound at all. Kta looked at him with a directness and a pity that disquieted him.

"You are afraid of us," Kta observed.

"Did Djan make you my keeper only because you asked, or because she trusts you in some special way—to watch me?"

Kta's head lifted slightly. "Elas is loyal to the Methi. But you are guest."

"Are nemet who speak human language so common? You are very fluent, Kta. Mim is. Your—readiness to accept a human into your house—is that not different from the feelings of other nemet?"

"I interpreted for the *umani* when they first came to Nephane. Before that, I learned of Mim, and Mim learned because she was prisoner of the Tamurlin. What evil do you suspect? What is the quarrel between you and Djan-methi?"

"We are of different nations, an old, old war. Don't get involved, Kta, if you did only get into this for my sake. If I threaten the peace of your house—or your safety—tell me. I'll go back. I mean that."

"This is impossible," said Kta. "No. Elas has never dismissed a guest."

"Elas has never entertained a human."

"No," Kta conceded. "But the Ancestors when they lived were reckless men. This is the character of Elas. The Ancestors guide us to such choice, and Nephane and the Methi cannot be much surprised at us."

*   *   *

The nemet's lives were uniformly tranquil. Kurt endured a little more than four days of the silent dim halls and the hushed voices and the endless bowing and refraining from untouchable objects and untouchable persons before he began to feel his sanity slipping.

On that day he went upstairs and locked the door, despite Kta's pleas to explain his behavior. He shed a few tears, fiercely and in the privacy of his room, and curtained the window so he did not have to look out upon the alien world. He sat in the dark until the night came, then he slipped quietly downstairs and sat in the empty *rhmei*, trying to make his peace with the house.

Mim came. She stood and watched him silently, hands twisting nervously before her.

At last she pattered on soft feet over to the chairs and gathered up one of the fleeces, and brought it to the place where he sat on the cold stone. She laid it down beside him, and chanced to meet his eyes as she straightened. Hers questioned, greatly troubled, even frightened.

He accepted the offered truce between them, edged onto the welcome softness of the fleece.

She bowed very deeply, then slipped out again, extinguishing the lights one by one as she left, save only the *phusmeba,* that burned the night long.

Kta also came out to him, but only looked as if to see that he was well. Then he went away, and left the door of his room open the night long.

Kurt rose up in the morning and paused in Kta's doorway to give him an apology. The nemet was awake and arose in some concern, but Kurt did not find words adequate to explain his behavior. He only bowed in respect to the nemet, and Kta to him, and he went up to his own room to prepare for the decency of breakfast with the family.

Gentle Kta. Soft-spoken, seldom angry, he stood above six feet in height and was physically imposing; but it was uncertain whether Kta had ever laid aside his dignity to use force on anyone. It was an increasing source of amazement to Kurt that this intensely proud man had vaulted a ship's rail in view of all Nephane to rescue a drowning human, or sat on the dock and helped him amid his retching illness.

Nothing seemed to ruffle Kta for long. He met frustration by retiring to meditate on the problem until he had restored himself to what he called *yhia,* or balance, a philosophy evidently adequate even in dealing with humans.

Kta also played the *aos,* a small harp of metal strings, and sang with a not unpleasant voice, which was the particular pleasure of lady Ptas upon the quiet evenings,—sometimes light, quick songs that brought laughter to the *rhmei,* —sometimes very long ones that were interrupted with cups of *telise* to give Kta's voice a rest,—songs to which all the house listened in sober silence, plaintive and haunting melodies of anharmonic notes.

"What do you sing about?" Kurt asked him afterward. They sat in Kta's room, sharing a late cup of tea. It was their habit to sit and talk late into the night. It was almost their last. The two weeks were almost spent. Tonight he wanted very much to know the nemet, not at all sure that he would have a further chance. It had been beautiful in the *rhmei,* the notes of the *aos,* the sober dignity of Nym, the rapt face of lady Ptas, Aimu and Mim with their sewing, Hef sitting to one side and listening, his old eyes dreaming.

The stillness of Elas had seeped into his bones this night, a timeless and now fleeting time which made all the world quiet. He had striven against it. Tonight, he listened.

"The song would mean nothing to you," Kta said. "I can't sing it in human words."

"Try," said Kurt.

The nemet shrugged, gave a pained smile, gathered up the *aos* and ran his fingers over the sensitive strings, calling forth the same melody. For a moment he seemed lost, but the melody grew, rebuilt itself in all its complexity.

"It is our beginning," said Kta, and spoke softly, not looking at Kurt, his fingers moving on the strings like a whisper of wind, as if that was necessary for his thoughts.

There was water. From the sea came the nine spirits of the elements, and greatest were Ygr the earthly and Ib the celestial. From Ygr and Ib came a thousand years of begettings and chaos and wars of elements, until Las who was light and Mur who was darkness, persuaded their brother-gods Phan the sun and Thael the earth to part.

So formed the first order. But Thael loved Phan's sister Ti, and took her. Phan in his anger killed Thael, and of Thael's ribs was the earth. Ti bore dead Thael a son, Aem.

Ten times a thousand years came and passed away.
Aem came to his age, and Ti saw her son was fair.
They sinned the great sin. Of this sin came Yr,
Yr, earth-snake, mother of all beasts.
The council of gods in heaven made Aem and Ti to die,
and dying, they brought forth children, man and woman.

"I have never tried to think it in human terms," said Kta, frowning. "It is very hard."

But with a gesture Kurt urged him, and Kta touched the strings again, trying, greatly frustrated.

"The first beings that were mortal were Nem and Panet, man and woman, twins. They sinned the great sin too. The council of gods rejected them for immortality because of it, and made their lives short. Phan especially hated them, and he mated with Yr the snake, and brought beasts and terrible things into the world to hunt man.

The Phan's sister Qas defied his anger,
stole fire, rained down lightning on the earth.
Men took fire and killed Yr's beasts, built cities.
Ten times a thousand years came and passed away.
Men grew many and kings grew proud,
sons of men and Yr the earth-snake,
sons of men and inim that ride the winds.
Men worshiped these half-men, the godkings.
Men did them honor, built them cities.
Men forgot the first gods,
and men's works were foul.

"Then a prophecy came," said Kta, "and Phan chose Isoi, a mortal woman, and gave her a half-god son: Qavur, who carried the weapons of Phan to destroy the world by burning. Qavur destroyed the godkings, but Isoi his mother begged him not to kill the rest of man, and he didn't. Then Phan with his sword of plague came down and destroyed all men, but when he came to Isoi she ran to her hearthfire and sat down beside it, so that she claimed the gods' protection. Her tears made Phan pity her. He gave her another son, Isem, who was husband of Nae the seagoddess and father of all men that sail on the sea. But Phan took Qavur to be immortal; he is the star that shines in morning, the messenger of the sun.

"But to keep Nae's children from doing wrong, Phan gave Qavur the *yhia* to take to men. All law comes from it. From it we know our place in the universe. Anything higher is gods' law; but that is beyond the words of the song. The song is the *Ind*. It is sacred to us. My father taught it to me, and the seven verses of it that are only for Elas. So it has come to us in each generation."

"You said once," said Kurt, "that you didn't know whether I was man or not. Have you decided yet?"

Kta thoughtfully laid aside the *aos*, stilled its strings. "Perhaps, said Kta, "some of the children of Nem escaped the plague; but you are not nemet. Perhaps instead you are descended of Yr, and you were set out among the stars on some world of Thael's kindred. From what I have heard among humans, the earth seems to have had many brothers. But I don't think you think so."

"I said nothing."

"Your look did not agree."

"I wouldn't distress you," said Kurt, "by saying I consider you human."

The nemet's lips opened instantly, his eyes mirroring shock. Then he looked as if he suspected Kurt of some levity, and again, as if he feared he were serious. Slowly his expression took on a certain thoughtfulness, and he made a gesture of rejection.

"Please," said Kta, "don't say that freely."

Kurt bowed his head then in respect to Kta, for the nemet truly looked frightened.

"I have spoken to the Guardians of Elas for you," said Kta. "You are a disturbance here, but I do not feel that you are unwelcome with our Ancestors."

Kurt dressed carefully upon the last morning. He would have worn the clothes in which he had come, but Mim had taken those away, unworthy, she had said, of the guest of

Elas. Instead he had an array of fine clothing he thought
must be Kta's, and on this morning he chose the warmest
and most durable, for he did not know what the day might
bring him, and the night winds were chill. So it was cold in
the rooms of the Afen, and he feared he would not leave it
once he entered.

Elas again began to seem distant to him, and the sterile
modernity of the center of the Afen increasingly crowded
upon his thoughts, the remembrance that, whatever had
happened in Elas, his business was with Djan and not with
the nemet.

He had chosen his option at the beginning of the two
weeks, in the form of a small dragon-hilted blade from
among Kta's papers, where it had been gathering dust and
would not be missed.

He drew it now from its hiding place and considered it,
apt either for Djan or for himself.

And fatally traceable to the house of Elas.

It did not go within his clothing, as he had always meant
to carry it. Instead he laid it aside on the dressing table. It
would go back to Kta. The nemet would be angry at the
theft, but it would make amends, all the same.

Kurt finished dressing, fastening the *ctan,* the outer cloak,
upon his shoulder, and chose a bronze pin with which to do
it, for his debts to Elas were enough, he would not use the
ones of silver and gold which he had been provided.

A light tapping came at the door, Mim's knock.

"Come in," he bade her, and she quietly did so. Linens
were changed daily throughout the house. She carried fresh
ones, for bed and for bath, and she bowed to him before she
set them down to begin her work. Of late there was no
longer hate in Mim's look: he understood that she had had
cause, having been prisoner of the Tamurlin; but she had
ceased her war with him of her own accord, and in consideration of that he always tried especially to please Mim.

"At least," he observed, "you will have less washing in
the house hereafter."

She did not appreciate the poor humor. She looked at
him, then lowered her eyes and turned around to tend her
business.

And froze, with her back to him, facing the dresser.

Hesitantly she reached for the knife, snatched at it and faced about again as if uncertain that he would not pounce on her. Her dark eyes were large with terror; her attitude was that of one determined to resist if he attempted to take it from her.

"Lord Kta did not give you this," she said.

"No," he said, "but you may give it back to him."

She clasped it in both hands and continued to stare at him. "If you bring a weapon into the Afen you kill us, Kurt-ifhan. All Elas would die."

"I have given it back," he said. "I am not armed, Mim. That is the truth."

She slipped it into the belt beneath her overskirt, through one of the four slits that exposed the filmy *pelan* from waist to toe, patted it flat. She was so small a woman: she had a tiny waist, a slender neck accentuated by the way she wore her hair in many tiny braids coiled and clustered above the ears. So little a creature, so soft-spoken, and yet he was continually in awe of Mim, feeling her disapproval of him in every line of her stiff little back.

For once, as in the *rhmei* that night, there was something like distress, even tenderness in the way she looked at him.

"Kta wishes you come back to Elas," she said.

"I doubt I will be allowed to," he said.

"Then why would the Methi send you here?"

"I don't know. Perhaps to satisfy Kta for a time. Perhaps so I'll find the Afen the worse by comparison."

"Kta will not let harm come to you."

"Kta had better stay out of it. Tell him so, Mim. He could make the Methi his enemy that way. He had better forget it."

He was afraid. He had lived with that nagging fear from the beginning, and now that Mim touched nerves, he found it difficult to speak with the calm that the nemet called dignity. The unsteadiness of his voice made him greatly ashamed.

And Mim's eyes inexplicably filled with tears—fierce little Mim, unhuman Mim, that he could have thought interestingly female to Kurt but for her alien face. He did not know if any other being would ever care enough to cry over him, and suddenly leaving Elas was unbearable.

He took her slim golden hands in his, knew at once he should not have, for she was nemet and she shivered at the very touch of him. But she looked up at him and did not show offense. Her hands pressed his very gently in return.

"Kurt-ifhan," she said, "I will tell lord Kta what you say, because it is good advice. But I don't think he will listen to me. Elas will speak for you. I am sure of it. The Methi has listened before to Elas. She knows that we speak with the power of the Families. Please go to breakfast. I have made you late. I am sorry."

He nodded and started to the door, looked back again. "Mim," he said, because he wanted her to look up. He wanted her face to think of, as he wanted everything in Elas fixed in his mind. But then he was embarrassed, for he could think of nothing to say.

"Thank you," he murmured, and quickly left.

IV

All the way to Afen, Kurt had balanced his chances of rounding on his three nemet guards and making good his escape. The streets of Nephane were twisting and torturous, and if he could remain free until dark, he thought, he might possibly find a way out into the fields and forests.

But Nym himself had given him into the hands of the guards and evidently charged them to treat him well, for they showed him the greatest courtesy. Elas continued to support him, and for the sake of Elas, he dared not do what his own instincts screamed to do: to run,—to kill if need be.

They passed into the cold halls of the Afen itself and it was too late. The stairs led them up to the third level, that of the Methi.

Djan waited for him alone in the modern hall, wearing the modest *chatem* and *pelan* of a ne. ¿ lady, her auburn hair braided at the crown of her head, laced with gold.

She dismissed the guards, then turned to him. It was strange, as she had foretold,—to see a human face after so long among the nemet. He began to understand what it had been for her, alone, slipping gradually from human reality into nemet. He noticed things about human faces he had never seen before, how curiously level the planes of the face, how pale her eyes, how metal-bright her hair. The war, the enmity between them—even these seemed for the moment welcome, part of a familiar frame of reference. Elas faded in this place of metal and synthetics.

He fought it back into focus.

"Welcome back," she bade him, and sank into the nearest chair, gestured him welcome to the other. "Elas wants you," she advised him then. "I am impressed."

"And I," he said, "would like to go back to Elas."

"I did not promise that," she said. "But your presence there has not proved particularly troublesome." She rose again abruptly, went to the cabinet against the near wall, opened it. "Care for a drink, Mr. Morgan?"

"Anything," he said, "thank you."

She poured them each a little glass and brought one to him. It was *telise*. She sat down again, leaned back and sipped at her own. "Let me make a few points clear to you," she said. "First: this is my city; I intend it should remain so. Second: this is a nemet city, and that will remain so too. Our species has had its chance. It's finished. We've done it. Pylos, my world Aeolus—both cinders. It's insane. I spend these last months waiting to die for not following orders, wondering what would become of the nemet when the probe ship returned with the authority and the firepower to deal with me. So I don't mourn them much. I—regret Aeolus. But your intervention was timely, for the nemet. That does not mean," she added, "that I have overwhelming gratitude to you."

"It does not make sense," he said, "that we two should carry on the war here. There's nothing either of us has to win."

"Is it required," she asked, "that a war make sense? Consider ours: we've been at it two thousand years. Probably everything your side and mine says about its beginning is a lie. That hardly matters. There's only the *now*, and the war feeds on its own casualties. And we approach our natural limits. We started out destroying ships in one little system, now we destroy worlds. Worlds. We leave dead space behind us. We count casualties by zones. We Hanan —we never were as numerous or as prolific as you; we can't produce soldiers fast enough to replace the dead. Embryonics, lab-born soldiers, engineered officers, engineered followers—our last hope. And you killed it. I will tell you, my friend, something I would be willing to wager your Alliance never told you: you just stepped up the war by what you did at Aeolus. I think you made a great miscalculation."

"Meaning what?"

"Aeolus was the center, the great center of the embryonics projects. Billions died in its laboratories. The workers, the facilities, the records—irreplaceable. You have hurt us too much. The Hanan will cease to restrict targets altogether now. The final insanity, that is what I fear you have loosed on humanity. I do much fear. And we richly deserve it, the whole human race."

"I don't think," he said, for she disturbed his peace of mind, "that you enjoy isolation half as much as you pretend."

"I am Aeolid," she said. "Think about it."

It took a moment. Then the realization set in, and revulsion, gut-deep: of all things Hanan that he loathed, the labs were the most hateful.

Djan smiled. "Oh, I'm human, of human cells. And superior—I would have been destroyed otherwise; efficiently engineered—for intelligence, and trained to serve the state. My intelligence then advised me that I was being used, and I disliked that. So I found my moment and turned on the state." She finished the drink and set it aside. "But you wouldn't like separation from humanity. Good. That may keep you from trying to cut my throat."

"Am I free to leave, then?"

"Not so easily, not so easily. I had considered perhaps giving you quarters in the Afen. There are rooms upstairs, only accessible from here. In such isolation you could do no possible harm. Instinct—something—says that would be the best way to dispose of you."

"Please," he said, rationally, shamelessly, for he had long since made up his mind that he had nothing to gain in Nephane by antagonizing Djan. "If Elas will have me, let me go back there."

"In a few days I will consider that. I only want you to know your alternatives."

"And what until then?"

"You're going to learn the nemet language. I have things all ready for you."

"No," he said instantly. "No. I don't need any mechanical helps."

"I am a medic, among other things. I've never known the teaching apparatus abused without it doing permanent damage. No. Ruining the mind of the only other human accessible would be a waste. I shall merely allow you access to the apparatus and you may choose your own rate."

"Then why do you insist?"

"Because your objection creates an unnecessary problem for you, which I insist be solved. I am giving you a chance to live outside. So I make it a fair chance, an honest chance; I wish you success. I no longer serve the purposes of the Hanan; I refuse to be programmed into a course of action I do not choose. And likewise, if it becomes clear to me that you are becoming a nuisance to me, don't think you can plead ignorance and evade the consequences. I am removing your excuses, you see. And if I must, I will call you in or kill you. Don't doubt it for a moment."

"It is," he said, "a fairer attitude than I would have expected of you. I would be easier in my mind if I understood you."

"All my motives are selfish," she said. "At least in the sense that all I do serves my own purposes. If I once perceive you are working against those purposes, you are done. If I perceive that you are compatible with them, you will find no difficulty. I think that is as clear as I can make it, Mr. Morgan."

V

Kta was not in the *rhmei* as Kurt had expected him to be when he reached the safety of Elas. Hef was, and Mim. Mim scurried upstairs ahead of him to open the window and air the room, and she spun about again when she had done so, her dark eyes shining.

"We are so happy," she said, in human speech. The machine's reflex pained him, punishing understanding.

It was all Mim had time to say, for there was Kta's step upon the landing, and Mim bowed and slipped out as Kta came in.

"Much crying in our house these days," said Kta, casting a look after Mim's retreat down the stairs. Then he looked at Kurt, smiled a little. "But no more. *Ei* Kurt, sit, sit, please. You look like a man three days drowned."

Kurt ran his hand through his hair and fell into a chair. His limbs were shaking. His hands were white. "Speak Nechai," he said. "It's easier."

Kta blinked, looked him over. "How is this?" he asked, and there was unwelcome suspicion in his voice.

"Trust me," Kurt said hoarsely. "The Methi has machines that can do this. I would not lie to you."

"You are pale," said Kta. "You are shaking. Are you hurt?"

"Tired," he said. "Kta,—thank you, thank you for taking me back."

Kta bowed a little. "Even my honored father came and spoke for you, and never in all the years of our house has

43

Elas done such a thing. But you are of Elas. We are glad to receive you."

"Thank you."

He rose and attempted a bow. He had to catch at the table to avoid losing his balance. He made it to the bed and sprawled. His memory ceased before he had stopped moving.

Something tugged at his ankle. He thought he had fallen into the sea and something was pulling him down. But he could not summon the strength to move.

Then the ankle came free and cold air hit his foot. He opened his eyes on Mim, who began to remove the other sandal. He was lying on his own bed, fully clothed, and cold. Outside the window it was night. His legs were like ice, his arms likewise.

Mim's dark eyes looked up, realized that he was awake. "Kta takes bad care for you," she said, "leaving you so. You have not moved. You sleep like the dead."

"Speak Nechai," he asked of her. "I have been taught."

Her look was briefly startled. Then she accepted human strangeness with a little bow, wiped her hands on her *chatem* and dragged at the bedding to cover him, pulling the bed-clothes from beneath him, half-asleep as he was.

"I am sorry," she said. "I tried not to wake you, but the night was cold and my lord Kta had left the window open and the light burning."

He sighed deeply and reached for her hand as it drew the coverlet across him. "Mim,—"

"Please." She evaded his hand, slipped the pin from his shoulder and hauled the tangled *ctan* from beneath him, jerked the catch of his wide belt free, then drew the covers up to his chin.

"You will sleep easier now," she said.

He reached for her hand again, preventing her going. "Mim, what time is it?"

"Late,—late." She pulled, but he did not let her go, and she glanced down, her lashes dark against her bronze cheeks. "Please, please let me go, lord Kurt."

"I asked Djan, asked her to send you word—so you would not worry."

"Word came. We did not know how to understand it. It

was only that you were safe. Only that." She pulled again. "Please."

Her lips trembled, and eyes were terrified, and when he let her hand go she spun around and fled to the door. She hardly paused to close it, her slippered feet pattering away down the stairs at breakneck speed.

If he had had the strength he would have risen and gone after her, for he had not meant to hurt Mim on the very night of his return. He lay awake and was angry, at nemet custom and at himself, but his head hurt abominably and made him dizzy. He sank into the soft down and slipped away. There was tomorrow. Mim would have gone to bed too, and he would scandalize the house by trying to speak to her tonight.

The morning began with tea, but there was no Mim, cheerily bustling in with morning linens and disarranging things. She did appear in the *rhmei* to serve, but she kept her eyes down when she poured for him.

"Mim," he whispered at her, and she spilled a few drops, which burned, and moved quickly to pour for Kta. She spilled even his, at which the dignified nemet shook his burned hand and looked up wonderingly at the girl, but said nothing.

There had been the usual round of formalities, and Kurt had bowed deeply before Nym and Ptas and Aimu, and thanked the lord of Elas in his own language for his intercession with Djan.

"You speak very well," Nym observed by way of acknowledging him; and Kurt realized he should have explained through Kta. An elder nemet cherished his dignity, and Kurt saw that he must have mightily offended lord Nym with his human sense of the dramatic.

"Sir," said Kurt, "you honor me. By machines I do this. I speak slowly yet and not well, but I do recognize what is said to me. When I have listened a few days, I will be a better speaker. Forgive me if I have offended you. I was so tired yesterday I had no sense left to explain where I have been or why."

The honorable Nym considered, and then the faintest of smiles touched his face, growing to an expression of positive amusement. He touched his laced fingers to his breast and inclined his head, apology for laughter.

"Welcome a second time to Elas, friend of my son. You bring gladness with you. There are smiles on faces this morning, and there were few the days we were in fear for you. Just when we thought we had comprehended humans, here are more wonders,—and what a relief to be able to talk without waiting for translations!"

So they were settled together, the ritual of tea begun. Lady Ptas sat enthroned in their center, a comfortable woman. Somehow when Kurt thought of Elas, Ptas always came first to mind,—a gentle and dignified lady with graying hair, the very heart of the family, which among nemet a mother was: Nym's lady, source of life and love, protectress of his ancestral religion. Into a wife's hands a man committed his hearth, and into a daughter-in-law's hands—his hope of a continuing eternity. Kurt began to understand why fathers chose their sons' mates; and considering the affection that was evident between Nym and Ptas, he could no longer think such marriages were loveless. It was right, it was proper, and he sat cross-legged upon a fleece rug, equal to Kta, a son of the house, drinking the strong sweetened tea and feeling that he had come home indeed.

And after tea lady Ptas rose and bowed formally before the hearthfire, lifting her palms to it. Everyone stood in respect, and her sweet voice called upon the Guardians.

"Ancestors of Elas, upon this shore and the other of the Dividing Sea, look kindly upon us. Kurt t'Morgan has come back to us. Peace be between the guest of our home and the Guardians of Elas. Peace be among us."

Kurt was greatly touched, and bowed deeply to lady Ptas when she was done.

"Lady Ptas," he said, "I honor you very much." He would have said—like a son, but he would not inflict that doubtful compliment on the nemet lady.

She smiled at him with the affection she gave her children; and from that moment, Ptas had his heart.

"Kurt," said Kta when they were alone in the hall after breakfast, "my father bids you stay as long as it pleases you. This he asked me to tell you. He would not burden you with giving answer on the instant, but he would have you know this."

"He is very kind," said Kurt. "You have never owed me all of the things you have done for me. Your oath never bound you this far."

"Those who share the hearth of Elas," said Kta, "have been few, but we never forget them. We call this guest-friendship. It binds your house and mine for all time. It can never be broken."

He spent the days much in Kta's company within Elas, talking, resting, enjoying the sun in the inner court of the house where there was a small garden.

One thing remained to trouble him: Mim was usually absent. She no longer came to his rooms when he was there. No matter how he varied his schedule, she would not come; he only found his bed changed about when he would return after some absence. When he hovered about the places where she usually worked, she was simply not to be found.

"She is at market," Hef informed him on a morning that he finally gathered his courage to ask.

"She has not been much about lately," Kurt observed.

Hef shrugged. "No, lord Kurt. She has not."

And the old man looked at him strangely, as if Kurt's anxiety had undermined the peace of his morning too.

He became the more determined. When he heard the front door close at noon, he sprang up to run downstairs but he had only a glimpse of her hurrying by the opposite hall into the ladies' quarters behind the *rhmei*. That was Ptas's territory, and no man but Nym could set foot there.

He walked disconsolately back to the garden and sat in the sun, staring at nothing in particular and tracing idle patterns in the pale dust.

He had hurt her. Mim had not told the matter to anyone, he was sure, for if she had he had no doubt he would have had Kta to deal with.

He wished desperately that he could ask someone how to apologize to her, but it was not something he could ask of Kta, or of Hef; and certainly he dared ask no one else.

She served at dinner that night, as at every meal, and still avoided his eyes. He dared not say anything to her. Kta was sitting beside him.

Late that night he set himself in the hall and doggedly waited, far past the hour when the family was decently in bed, for the *chan* of Elas had as her last duties to set out things for breakfast tea and to extinguish the hall lights as she retired to bed.

She saw him there, blocking her way to her rooms. For a moment he feared she would cry out; her hand flew to her lips. But she stood her ground, still looking poised to run.

"Mim. Please. I want to talk with you."

"I do not want to talk with you. Let me pass."

"Please."

"Do not touch me. Let me pass. Do you want to wake all the house?"

"Do that, if you like. But I will not let you go until you talk with me."

Her eyes widened slightly. "Kta will not permit this."

"There are no windows on the garden and we cannot be heard there. Come outside, Mim. I swear I want only to talk."

She considered, her lovely face looking so frightened he hurt for her; but she yielded and walked ahead of him to the garden. The world's moon cast dim shadows here. She stopped where the light was brightest, clasping her arms against the chill of the night.

"Mim," he said, "I did not mean to frighten you that night. I meant no harm by it."

"I should never have been there alone. It was my fault.— Please, lord Kurt, do not look at me that way. Let me go."

"Because I am not nemet,—you felt free to come in and out of my room and not be ashamed with me. Was that it, Mim?"

"No." Her teeth chattered so she could hardly talk, and the cold was not enough for that. He slipped the pin off his *ctan*, but she would not take it from him, flinching from the offered garment.

"Why can I not talk to you?" he asked. "How does a man ever talk to a nemet woman? I refrain from this, I refrain from that, I must not touch, must not look, must not think. How am I to—?"

"Please."

"How am I to talk with you?"

"Lord Kurt, I have made you think I am a loose woman. I am *chan* to this house; I cannot dishonor it. Please let me go inside."

A thought came to him. "Are you *his*? Are you Kta's?"

"No," she said.

Against her preference he took the *ctan* and draped it about her shoulders. She hugged it to her. He was near enough to have touched her. He did not, nor did she move back; he did not take that for invitation. He thought that whatever he did, she would not protest or raise the house. It would be trouble between her lord Kta and his guest, and he understood enough of nemet dignity to know that Mim would choose silence. She would yield, hating him.

He had no argument against that.

In sad defeat, he bowed a formal courtesy to her and turned away.

"Lord Kurt," she whispered after him, distress in her voice.

He paused, looking back.

"My lord,—you do not understand."

"I understand," he said, "that I am human. I have offended you. I am sorry."

"Nemet do not—" She broke off in great embarrassment, opened her hands, pleading. "My lord, seek a wife. My lord Nym will advise you. You have connections with the Methi and with Elas. You could marry,—easily you could marry, if Nym approached the right house—"

"And if it was you I wanted?"

She stood there, without words, until he came back to her and reached for her. Then she prevented him with her slim hands on his. "Please," she said. "I have done wrong with you already."

He ignored the protest of her hands and took her face between his palms ever so gently, fearing at each moment she would tear from him in horror. She did not. He bent and touched his lips to hers, delicately, almost chastely, for he thought the human custom might disgust or frighten her.

Her smooth hands still rested on his arms. The moon glistened on tears in her eyes when he drew back from her.

"Lord," she said, "I honor you. I would do what you wish, but it would shame Kta and it would shame my father and I cannot."

"What can you?" He found his own breathing difficult. "Mim, what if some day I did decide to talk with your father? Is that the way things are done?"

"To marry?"

"Some day it might seem a good thing to do."

She shivered in his hands. Tears spilled freely down her cheeks.

"Mim, will you give me yes or no? Is a human hard for you to look at? If you had rather not say, then just say 'let me be' and I will do my best after this not to bother you."

"Lord Kurt, you do not know me."

"Are you determined I will never know you?"

"You do not understand. I am not the daughter of Hef. If you ask him for me he must tell you, and then you will not want me."

"It is nothing to me whose daughter you are."

"My lord,—Elas knows. Elas knows. But you must listen to me now, listen. You know about the Tamurlin. I was taken when I was thirteen. For three years I was slave to them. Hef only calls me his daughter, and all Nephane thinks I am of this country. But I am not, Kurt. I am Indras, of Indresul. And they would kill me if they knew. Elas has kept this to itself. But you—you cannot bear such a trouble. People must not look at you and think Tamurlin: it would hurt you in this city; and when they see me, that is what they must think."

"Do you believe," he asked, "that what they think matters with me? I am human. They can see that."

"Do you not understand, my lord? I have been property of every man in that village. Kta must tell you this if you ask Hef for me. I am not honorable. No one would marry Mim h'Elas. Do not shame yourself and Kta by making Kta say this to you."

"After he had said it," said Kurt, "would he give his consent?"

"Honorable women would marry you. Sufaki have no fear of humans as Indras do. Perhaps even a daughter of some merchant would marry you. I am only *chan,* and before that I was nothing at all."

"If I were to ask," he said, "would you refuse?"

"No. I would not refuse." Her small face took on a look of pained bewilderment. "Kurt-ifhan, surely you will think better of this in the morning."

"I am going to talk to Hef," he said. "Go inside, Mim. And give me back my cloak. It would not do for you to wear it inside."

"My lord, think a day before you do this."

"I will give it tomorrow," he said, "for thinking it over. And you do the same. And if you have not come to me by tomorrow evening and asked me and said clearly that you do not want me, then I will talk to Hef."

It was, he had time to think that night and the next morning, hardly reasonable. He wanted Mim. He had had no knowledge of her to say that he loved her, or that she loved him.

He wanted her. She had set her terms and there was no living under the same roof with Mim without wanting her.

He could apply reason to the matter, until he looked into her face at breakfast as she poured the tea, or as she passed him in the hall and looked at him with a dreadful anxiety.

Have you thought better of it? the look seemed to say. *Was it, after all, only for the night?*

Then the feeling was back with him, the surety that, should he lose Mim by saying nothing, he would have lost something irreplaceable.

In the end, he found himself that evening gathering his courage before the door of Hef, who served Elas, and standing awkwardly inside the door when the old man admitted him.

"Hef," he said, "may I talk to you about Mim?"

"My lord?" asked the old man, bowing.

"What if I wanted to marry her? What should I do?"

The old nemet looked quite overcome then, and bowed several times, looking up at him with a distraught expression. "Lord Kurt, she is only *chan.*"

"Do I not speak to you? Are you the one who says yes or no?"

"Let my lord not be offended. I must ask Mim."

"Mim agrees," said Kurt. Then he thought that it was not his place to have asked Mim, and that he shamed her and embarrassed Hef; but Hef regarded him with patience and even a certain kindliness.

"But I must ask Mim," said Hef. "That is the way of it. And then I must speak to Kta-ifhan, and to Nym and lady Ptas."

"Does the whole house have to give consent?" Kurt let forth, without pausing to think.

"Yes, my lord. I shall speak to the family, and to Mim. It is proper that I speak to Mim."

"I am honored," Kurt murmured the polite phrase; and he went upstairs to his own quarters to gather his nerves.

He felt much relieved that it was over. Hef would consent. He was sure what Mim would answer her father, and that would satisfy Hef.

He was preparing for bed when Kta came up the stairs and asked admittance. The nemet had a troubled look and Kurt knew by sure instinct what had brought him. He would almost have begged Kta to go away, but he was under Kta's roof and he did not have that right.

"You have talked with Hef," Kurt said, to make it easier for him.

"Let me in, my friend."

Kurt backed from the door, offering Kta a chair. It would have been proper to offer tea also. He would have had to summon Mim for that. He would not do it.

"Kurt," said Kta, "please, sit down also. I must speak to you—I must beg your kindness to hear me."

"You might find it more comfortable simply to tell me what is in your mind from the beginning," Kurt said, taking the other chair. "Yes or no, are you going to interfere?"

"I am concerned for Mim. It is not as simple as you may hope. Will you hear me? If your anger forbids,—then we will go down and drink tea and wait for a better mind, but I am bound to say these things."

"Mim told me—about most that I imagine you have come to say. And it makes no difference. I know about the Tamurlin and I know where she came from."

Kta let his breath go, a long hiss of a sigh. "Well, that is something at least. You know that she is Indras?"

"None of that possibly concerns me. Nemet politics have nothing to do with me."

"You choose ignorance. That is always a dangerous choice, Kurt. Being of the Indras race or being Sufaki is a matter of great difference among nemet, and you are among nemet."

"The only difference I have ever noticed is being human among nemet," he said, controlling his temper with a great effort. "I would bring disgrace on you. Is that what you care for, and not whether Mim would be happy?"

"Mim's happiness is a matter of great concern to us," Kta insisted. "And we know you would not mean to hurt her, but human ways—"

"Then you see no difference between me and the Tamurlin."

"Please. Please. You do not imagine. They are not like you. That is not what I meant. The Tamurlin—they are foul and they are shameless. They wear hides and roar and mouth like beasts when they fight. They have no more modesty than beasts in their dealing with women. They mate as they please, without seeking privacy. They restrain themselves from nothing. A strong chief may have twenty or more women, while weaker men have none. They change mates by the outcome of combat. I speak of human women. Slaves like Mim belong to any and all who want them. And when I found her—"

"I do not want to hear this."

"Kurt,—listen. Listen. I shall not offend you. But when we attacked the Tamurlin to stop their raids—we killed all we could reach. We were about to set torch to the place when I heard a sound like a child crying. I found Mim in the corner of a hut. She wore a scrap of hide, as filthy as the rest of them; for an instant I could not even tell she was nemet. She was thin, and carried terrible marks on her body. When I tried to carry her, she attacked me—not womanlike, but with a knife and her teeth and her knees, whatever she could bring to bear. So she was accustomed to fight for her place among them. I had to strike her senseless to bring her to the ship, and then she kept trying to jump into the sea until we were out of sight of land. Then she hid down in the rowing pits and would not come out except when the men were at the oars. When we fed her she would snatch and run, and she would not speak more than a few syllables at a time save of human language."

"I cannot believe that," said Kurt quietly. "How long ago was that?"

"Four years. Four years she has been in Elas. I brought her home and gave her to my lady mother and sister, and Hef's wife Liu, who was living then. But she had not been among us many days before Aimu saw her standing before the hearthfire with hands lifted, as Sufaki do not do. Aimu was younger then and not so wise; she exclaimed aloud that Mim must be Indras.

"Mim ran. I caught her in the streets, to the wonder of all Nephane and our great disgrace. And I carried her by force back to Elas. Then, alone with us, she began to speak, with the accent of Indresul. This was the reason of her silence before. But we of Elas are Indras too, like all the Great Families on the hill, descended of colonists of Indresul who came to this shore a thousand years ago, and while we are now enemies of Indresul, we are one religion and Mim was only a child. So Elas has kept her secret, and people outside know her only as Hef's adopted Sufaki daughter, a country child of mixed blood rescued from the Tamurlin. She does not speak as Sufaki, but people believe we taught her speech; she does not look Sufaki, but that is not unusual in the coastal villages, where seamen have—*ei*, well, she passes for Sufaki. The scandal of her running through the streets is long forgotten. She is an honor and an ornament to this house now. But to have her in public attention again—would be difficult. No man would marry Mim; forgive me, but it is truth and she knows it. Such a marriage would cause gossip favourable to neither of you."

Instinct told him Kta was speaking earnest good sense. He put it by. "I would take care of her," he insisted. "I would try, Kta."

Kta glanced down in embarrassment, then lifted his eyes again. "She is nemet. Understand me. *She* is nemet. She has been hurt and greatly shamed. Human customs are—forgive me: I shall speak shamelessly. I do not know how humans behave with their mates. Djan-methi is—free—in this regard. We are not. I beg you think of Mim. We do not cast away our women. Marriage is unbreakable."

"I had expected so."

Kta sat back a little. "Kurt—there could be no children. I have never heard of it happening, and Tamurlin have mated with nemet women."

"If there were," said Kurt, though what Kta had said distressed him greatly, "I could love them. I would want them. But if not, then I would be happy with Mim."

"But could others love them?" Kta wondered. "It would be difficult for them, Kurt."

It hurt. Some things Kta said amused him and some no little irritated him, but this was simply a fact of Kta's world, and it hurt bitterly. For an instant Kurt forgot that the nemet thing to do was to lower his eyes and so keep his hurt private. He looked full at the nemet, and it was Kta who flinched and had to look up again.

"Would they," Kurt said, cruel to the embarrassed nemet, "would children like that be such monsters, Kta?"

"I," said Kta hesitantly, *I* could love a child of my friend." And the inward shudder was too evident.

"Even," Kurt finished, "if it looked too much like my friend?"

"I beg your forgiveness," Kta said hoarsely. "I fear for you and for Mim."

"Is that all?"

"I do not understand."

"Do you want her?"

"My friend," said Kta, "I do not love Mim, but Mim is dear to me, and I am responsible for her as my honored father is. He is too old to take Mim; but when I married, I should have been obliged to take Mim for a concubine, for she is *chan* and unmarried—and I would not have been sorry for that, for she is a most beloved friend, and I would have been glad to give her children to continue Hef's name. When you ask her of Hef, you see, —that is a terrible thing. Hef is childless. Mim is his adopted daughter, but we had agreed her children would remain in Elas to carry on his name and give his soul life when he dies. Mim must bear sons, and you cannot give them to her. You are asking for Hef's eternity and that of all his ancestors. Hef's family has been good and faithful to Elas. What shall I do, my friend? How shall I resolve this?"

Kurt shook his head helplessly, unsure whether Kta thought there could be an answer, or whether this was not some slow and painful way of telling him no.

"I do not know," Kurt said, "whether I can stay in Elas without marrying Mim. I want her very much, Kta. I do not think that will change tomorrow or for the rest of my life."

"There is," Kta offered cautiously, "an old custom—that if the *lechan*'s husband dies and the house of the *chan* is threatened with extinction, then the duty is with the lord of the house nearest her age. Sometimes this is done even with the *lechan*'s husband living, if there are no children after such a time."

Kurt did not know whether his face went very pale or flushed, only that he could not for the moment move or look left or right, was trapped staring into the nemet's pitying eyes. Then he recovered the grace to glance down. "I could even," he echoed, "love a child of my friend."

Kta flinched. "Perhaps," said Kta, "it would be different with you and Mim. I see how much your heart goes toward her, and I will plead your case with Hef and give him my own pledge in this matter. And if Hef is won, then it will be easier to win my lord father and lady mother. Also I will talk to Mim about this custom we call *iquun*."

"I will do that," Kurt said.

"No," said Kta gently. "It would be very difficult for her to hear such words from you. Believe me that I am right. I have known Mim long enough that I could speak with her of this. From her own betrothed it would be most painful. And perhaps we can give the matter a few years before we have concern for it. Our friend Hef is not terribly old. If his health fails or if years have passed without children, then will be the time to invoke *iquun*. I should in that case treat the honor of you and of Hef and of Mim with the greatest respect."

"You are my friend," said Kurt. "I know that you are Mim's. If she is willing, let it be that way."

"Then," said Kta, "I will go and speak to Hef."

*   *   *

The betrothal was a necessarily quiet affair, confirmed three days later at evening. Hef formally asked permission of lord Nym to give his daughter to the guest of Elas, and Kta formally relinquished his claim to the person of Mim before the necessary two witnesses, friends of the family; Han t'Osanef u Mur, father of Bel; and old Ulmar t'Ilev ul Imetan, with all their attendant kin.

"Mim-lechan," said Nym, "is this marriage your wish?"

"Yes, my lord."

"And in the absence of your kinsmen, Kurt t'Morgan, I ask you to answer in your own name: do you accept this contract as binding, understanding that when you have sworn you must follow this ceremony with marriage or show cause before these families present? Do you accept under this knowledge, our friend Kurt t'Morgan?"

"I accept."

"There is," said Nym quietly, "the clause of *iquun* in this contract. The principals are of course Mim and Kurt, and thou, my son Kta, and Hef, to preserve the name of Hef. Three years are given in this agreement before *iquun* is invoked. Is this acceptable to all concerned?"

One by one they bowed their heads.

Two parchments lay on the table, and to them in turn first Nym and then t'Osanef and t'Ilev pressed their seals in wax.

Then lady Ptas pressed her forefinger in damp wax and so sealed both. Then she took one of the *phusmeha,* and with a bit of salt slipped it into the flames.

She uplifted her palms to the fire, intoning a prayer so old that Kurt could not understand all the words, but it asked blessing on the marriage.

"The betrothal is sealed," said Nym. "Kurt Liam t'Morgan ul Edward, look upon Mim h'Elas e Hef, your bride."

He did so, although he could not, must not touch her, not during all the long days of waiting for the ceremony. Mim's face shone with happiness.

They were at opposite sides of the room. It was the custom. The nemet made a game of tormenting young men and women at betrothals, and knew well enough his frustration. The male guests, especially Bel and Kta, drew Kurt off in one direction, while Aimu and Ptas and the ladies likewise captured Mim, with much laughter as they hurried her off.

The bell at the front door rang, faintly jingling, untimely. Hef slipped out to answer it, duty and the normal courtesy of Elas taking precedence over convenience even at such a time as this.

The teasing ceased. The nemet laughed much among themselves, among friends, but there were visitors at the door, and the guests and the members of Elas both became sober.

Voices intruded—Hef,—Hef, who was the soul of courtesy, arguing; and the heavy tread of outsiders entering the hall, the hollow ring of a staff on polished stone, the voices of strangers raised in altercation.

There was silence in the *rhmei*. Mim, large-eyed, clung to Ptas' arm. Nym went to meet the strangers in the hall, Kurt and Kta and the guests behind him.

They were the Methi's men, grim-faced, in the odd-striped robes that some of the townsmen wore, hair plaited in a single braid down the back. They had the narrowness of eye that showed in some of the folk of Nephane, like Bel, like Bel's father Han t'Osanef.

The Methi's guards did not take that final step into the *rhmei,* where burned the hearthfire. Nym physically barred their way, and Nym, though silver-haired and a senior member of the Upei, the council of Nephane, was a big man and broad-shouldered. Whether through reverence for the place or fear of him, they came no further.

"This is Elas," said Nym. "Consider again, gentlemen, where you are. I did not bid you here, and I did not hear the *chan* of Elas give you leave either."

"The Methi's orders," said the eldest of the four. "We came to fetch the human. This betrothal is not permitted."

"Then you are too late," said Nym. "If the Methi wished to intervene, it was her right, but now the betrothal is sealed."

That set them aback. "Still," said their leader, "we must bring him back to the Afen."

"Elas will permit him to go back," said Nym, "if he chooses."

"He will go with us," said the man.

Han t'Osanef stepped up beside Nym and bent a terrible

frown on the Methi's guardsmen. "T'Senife, I ask you come tonight to the house of Osanef. I would ask it, t'Senife,— and the rest of you young men. Bring your fathers. We will talk."

The men had a different manner for t'Osanef: resentful, but paying respect.

"We have duties," said the man called t'Senife, "which keep us at the Afen. We have no time for that. But we will say to our fathers that t'Osanef spoke with us at the house of Elas."

"Then go back to the Afen," said t'Osanef. "*I* ask it. You offend Elas."

"We have our duty," said t'Senife, "and we must have the human."

"I will go," said Kurt, coming forward. He had the feeling that there was much more than himself at issue, he intruded fearfully into the hate that prickled in the air. Kta put out a hand, forbidding him.

"The guest of Elas," said Nym in a terrible voice, "will walk from the door of Elas if he chooses, and the Methi herself has no power to cause this hall to be invaded. Wait at our doorstep.—And you, friend Kurt, do not go against your will. The law forbids."

"We will wait outside," said t'Senife, at t'Osanef's hard look. But they did not bow as they left.

"My friend," Han t'Osanef exclaimed to Nym, "I blush for these young men."

"They are," said Nym in a shaking voice, "*young* men. Elas also will speak with their Fathers. Do not go, Kurt t'Morgan. You are not compelled to go."

"I think," said Kurt, "that eventually I would have no choice. I would do better to go speak with Djan-methi, if it is possible." But it was in his mind that reason with her was not likely. He looked at Mim, who stood frightened and silent by the side of Ptas. He could not touch her. Even at such a time he knew they would not understand. "I will be back as soon as I can," he said to her.

But to Kta, at the door of Elas before he went out to put himself into the hands of the Methi's guards:

"Take care of Mim. And I do not want her or your father

or any of Elas to come to the Afen. I do not want her involved and I am afraid for you all."

"You do not have to go," Kta insisted.

"Eventually," Kurt repeated, "I would have to. You have taught me there is grace in recognizing necessity. Take care of her." And with Kta, that he knew so well, he put out his hand instinctively to touch, and refrained.

It was Kta who gripped his hand, an uncertain, awkward gesture, not at all nemet. "You have friends and kinsmen now. Remember it."

VI

"There is no need of that," Kurt cried, shaking off the guards' hands as they persisted in hurrying him through the gates of the Afen. No matter how quickly he walked, they had to push him or lay hands on him, so that people in the streets stopped and stared, most unnemetlike, most embarrassing for Elas. It was to spite Nym that they did it, he was sure, and rather than make a public scene worse, he had taken the abuse until they entered the Afen court, beyond witnesses.

There was a long walk between the iron outer gate and the wooden main door of the Afen, for that space Kurt argued with them, then found them fanning out to prevent him from the very door toward which they were tending.

He knew the game. They wanted him to resist. He had done so. Now they had the excuse they wanted, and they began to close up on him.

He ran the only way still open, to the end of the courtyard, where it came up against the high peak of the rock on which the Afen sat, a facing wall of gray basalt. It was beyond the witness of anyone on the walk between the wall-gate and the door.

They herded him. He knew it and was willing to go as long as there was room to retreat, intending to pay double at least on one of them when they finally closed in on him. T'Senife, who had insulted—Nym, that was the one he favored killing, a slit-eyed fellow with a look of inborn arrogance.

61

But to kill him would endanger Elas; he dared not, and knew how it must end. He risked other's lives, even fighting them.

A small gate was set in the wall near the rock. He bolted for it, surprising them, desperately flinging back the iron bar.

A vast courtyard lay beyond it, a courtyard paved in polished marble, with a single building closing it off, high-columned, a white cube with three triangular pylons arching over its long steps.

He ran, saw the safety of the familiar wall-street to his left, leading to the main street of Nephane, back to the witness of passersby.

But for the sake of Elas he dared not take the matter into public. He knew Nym and Kta, knew they would involve themselves, to their hurt and without the power to help him.

He ran instead across the white court, his sandalled feet and those of his pursuers echoing loudly on the deserted stones. The wall-street was the only way in. The precinct was a cul-de-sac, backed by the temple, flanked on one side by a high wall and on the other by the living rock.

His pursuers put on a sudden burst of speed. He did likewise, thinking suddenly that they did not want him to reach this place, a religious place, a sanctuary,

He sprang for the polished steps, raced up them, slipping and stumbling in his haste and exhaustion.

Fire roared inside, an enormous bowl of flame leaping within, a heat that filled the room and flooded even the outer air, a *phusmeha* so large the blaze made the room glow gold, whose sound was like a furnace.

He stopped without any thought in his mind but terror, blasted by the heat on his face and drowned in the sound of it. It was a *rhmei,* and he knew its sanctity.

His pursuers had stopped, a scant few strides behind him on the steps. He looked back. T'Senife beckoned him.

"Come down," said t'Senife. "We were told to bring you to the Methi. If you will not come down, it will be the worse for you. Come down."

Kurt believed him. It was a place of powers to which human touch was defilement,—no sanctuary, none for a human,—no kindly Ptas to open the *rhmei* to him and make him welcome.

He came down to them, and they took him by the arms and led him down and across the courtyard to the open gate of the Afen compound, barring it again behind them.

Then they forced him up against the wall and had their revenge, expertly, without leaving a visible mark on him.

It was not likely that he would complain, both for the personal shame of it and because he and his friends were always in their reach: especially Kta,—who would count it a matter of honor to avenge his friend, even on the Methi's guard.

Kurt straightened himself as much as he could at the moment and t'Senife straightened his *ctan*, which had come awry, and took his arm again.

They brought him up a side entrance of the Afen, by stairs he had not used before. They they passed into familiar halls near the center of the building.

Another of their kind met them, a stripe-robed and braided young man, handsome as Bel, but with sullen, hateful eyes. To him these men showed great deference. Shan t'Tefur, they called him.

They discussed the betrothal, and how they had been too late.

"Then the Methi should have that news," concluded t'Tefur, and his narrow eyes shifted toward a room with a solid door. "It is empty. Hold him there until I have carried her that news."

They did so. Kurt sat on a hard chair by the barred slit of a window and so avoided the looks that pierced his back, giving them no excuse to repeat their treatment of him.

At last t'Tefur came back to say that the Methi would see him.

She would see him alone. T'Tefur protested with a violently angry look, but Djan stared back at him in such a way that t'Tefur bowed finally and left the room.

Then she turned that same angry look on Kurt.

"Entering the temple precincts was a mistake," she said. "If you had entered the temple itself I don't know if I could have saved you."

"I had that idea," he said.

"Who told you that you had the freedom to make contracts in Nephane—marrying that nemet?"

"I wasn't told I didn't. Nor was Elas told, or they wouldn't have allowed it. They are loyal to you. And they were not treated well, Djan."

"Not the least among the problems you've created for me, this disrespect of Elas." She walked over to the far side of the room, put back a panel that revealed a terrace walled with glass. It was night. They had a view of all the sea. She gazed out, leaving him watching her back, and she stayed that way for a long time. He thought he was the subject of her thoughts, he and Elas.

At last she turned and faced him. "Well," she said, "for Elas' inconvenience, I'm sorry. I shall send them word that you're safe. You haven't had dinner yet, have you?"

Appetite was the furthest thing from his mind. His stomach was both empty and racked with pain, and with an outright hear that her sudden shift in manner did nothing to ease. "You," he said, "frightened the wits out of my fiancée, made me a spectacle in the streets of Nephane, and all I particularly care about is—"

"I think," said Djan in a tone of finality, "that we had better save the talk. *I* am going to have dinner. If you want to argue the point, Shan can find you some secure room where you can think matters over. But you will leave the Afen—*if* you leave the Afen—when I please to send you out."

And she called a girl named Pai, who recieved her orders with a deep bow.

"She," said Djan when the girl had gone, "is *chan* to the Afen. I inherited her, it seems. She is very loyal and very silent, both virtues. Her family served the last Methi, a hundred years ago. Before that, Pai's family was still *chan* to methis, even before the human occupation and during it. There is nothing in Nephane that does not have roots, except the two of us. Forget your temper, my friend. I lost mine. I rarely do that. I am sorry."

"Then we will have out whatever you want to say and I will go back to Elas."

"I would think so," she agreed quietly, ignoring his anger. "Come out her. Sit down. I am too tired to stand up to argue with you."

He came, shrugging off his apprehensions. The terrace was dark. She left it so, and sat on the window ledge, watching the sea far below. It was indeed a spectacular view of Nephane, its lights winding down the crag below, the high dark rock a shadow against the moon. The moonlit surface of the sea was cut by the wake of a single ship heading out.

"If I were sensible," said Djan as he joined her and sat down on the ledge facing her, "if I were at all sensible I'd have you taken out and dropped about halfway. Unfortunately I decided against it. I wonder still what you would do in my place."

He had wondered that himself. "I would think of the same things that have occurred to you," he said.

"And reach the same answer?"

"I think so," he admitted. "I don't blame you."

She smiled, ironic amusement. "They maybe we will have a brighter future than other humans who have held Nephane. —They built this section of the Afen, you know. That's why there is no *rhmei*, no heart to the place. It's unique in that respect—the fortress without a heart, the building without a soul. Did Kta tell you what became of them?"

"Nemet drove them out, I know that."

"Humans ruled Nephane about twenty years. But they involved themselves with the nemet. The mistress of the base commander was of the great Indras family—of Irain. Humans were very cruel to the nemet, and they enjoyed humiliating the Great Families by that. But one night she let her brothers in and the whole of Nephane rose in rebellion against the humans on the night of a great celebration, when most of the humans were drunk on *telise*. So they lost their machines and fled south and became the Tamurlin in a generation or so—like animals. Only Pai's ancestor On t'Erefe defended the humans in the Afen, being *chan* and obliged to defend his human lord. The human Methi and On died together, out there in the hall. The other humans who died were killed in the courtyard, and those who were caught were brought back there and killed.

"Myself, I have read the records that went before their

fall. The supply ship failed them, never came back—probably after reporting to Aeolus; it was destroyed on its return trip, another war casualty, unnoticed. The years passed, and they had made the nemet here hate them. They had threatened them with the imminent return of the ship for twenty years and the threat was wearing thin. So they fell. But when we arrived, the nemet thought the threat had come true and that they were all to die. For all my crewmates cared, we might have destroyed Nephane to secure the base. I would not permit it. And when I had freed the nemet from the immediate threat of my companions, they made me methi. Some say I am sent by Fate; they think the same of you. For an Indras, nothing ever happens without logical purpose. Their universe is entirely rational. I admire that in them. There is a great deal in these people that was worth the cost. And I think you agree with me. You're evidently settled very comfortably into Elas."

"They are my friends," he said.

Djan leaned back, leaned on the sill and looked out over her shoulder. The ship was nearly to the breakwater. "This is a world of little haste and much deliberation. Can you imagine two ships like that headed for each other in battle? Our ships come in faster than the mind can think, from zero vision to alongside, attack and vanish. But those vessels with their sails and oars—by the time they came within range of each other—there would be abundant time for thought. There is a dreadful deliberateness about the nemet. They maneuver so slowly, but they do hold a course once they've taken it."

"You're not talking about ships."

"Do you know what lies across the sea?"

His heart leaped; he thought of Mim, and his first terrible thought was that Djan knew. But he let nothing of that reach his face. "Indresul," he said. "A city that is hostile to Nephane."

"Your friends of Elas are Indras. Did you know?"

"I had heard so, yes."

"So are most of the Great Families of Nephane. The Indras established this as a colony once, when they conquered the inland fortress of Chteftikan and began to build this fortress with Sufaki slaves taken in that war. Indresul has no love of the Nephanite Indras, but she had never forgotten that through them she has a claim on this city. She wants it. I am walking a narrow line, Kurt Morgan, and your Indras friends in Elas and your own meddling in nemet affairs are an embarrassment to me at a time when I can least afford embarrassment. I need quiet in this city. I will do what is necessary to secure that."

"I've done nothing," he said, "except inside Elas."

"Unfortunately," said Djan, "Elas does nothing without consequence in Nephane. That is the misfortune of wealth and power.—That ship out there—is bound for Indresul. The Methi of Indresul has eluded my every attempt to talk. You cannot imagine how they despise Sufaki and humans. Well, at last they are going to send an ambassador,—one Mor t'Uset ul Orm, a councillor who has high status in Indresul. He will come at the return of that ship. And this betrothal of yours, publicized in the market today, had better not come to the attention of t'Uset when he arrives."

"I have no desire to be noticed by anyone," he said.

The glance she gave him was ice. But at that moment Pai-lechan and another girl pattered into the hall cat-footed and brought tea and *telise* and a light supper, setting it on the low table by the ledge.

Djan dismissed them both, although strict formality dictated someone serve. The *chani* bowed themselves out.

"Join me," she said, "in tea or *telise,* if nothing else."

His appetite had returned somewhat. He picked at the food and then found himself hungry. He ate fully enough for his share, and demurred when she poured him *telise,* but she set the cup beside him. She carried the dishes out herself, returned and settled upon the ledge beside him. The ship had long since cleared the harbor, leaving its surface to the wind and the moon.

"It is late," he said. "I would like to go back to Elas."

"This nemet girl. What is her name?"

All at once the meal lay like lead at his stomach.

"What is her name?"

"Mim," he said, and reached for the *telise,* swallowed some of its vaporous fire.

"Did you compromise the girl? Is that the reason for this sudden marriage?"

The cup froze in his hand. He looked at her, and all at once he knew she had meant it just as he had heard it, and flushed with heat, not the *telise*.

"I am in love with her."

Djan's cool eyes rested on him, estimating. "The nemet are a beautiful people. They have a certain attraction. And I suppose nemet women have a certain—flattering appeal to a man of our kind. They always let their men be right."

"It will not trouble you," he said.

"I am sure it will not." She let the implied threat hang in the air a moment and then shrugged lightly. "I have nothing personal against the child. I don't expect I'll ever have to consider the problem. I trust your good sense for that. Marry her. Occasionally you will find, as I do, that nemet thoughts and looks and manners—and nemet prejudices— are too much for you. That fact moved me, I admit it, or you would be keeping company with the Tamurlin—or the fishes. I had rather think we were companions,—human and reasonably civilized. This person Mim, she is only *chan*; she does at least provide a certain respectability if you are careful. I suppose it is not such a bad choice, so I do not think this marriage will be such an inconvenience to me. And I think you understand me, Kurt."

The cup shook in his hand. He put it aside, lest his fingers crush the fragile crystal.

"You are gambling your neck, Djan. I won't be pushed."

"I do not push," she said, "more than will make me understood. And I think we understand each other plainly."

VII

The gray light of dawn was over Nephane, spreading through a mist that overlay all but the upper walls of the Afen. The cobbled street running down from the Afen gate was wet, and the few people who had business on the streets at that hour went muffled in cloaks.

Kurk stepped up to the front door of Elas, tried the handle in the quickly dashed hope that it would be unlocked, then knocked softly, not wanting to wake the whole house.

More quickly than he had expected, soft footsteps approached the door inside, hesitated. He stood squarely before the door to be surveyed from the peephole.

The bar flew back, the door was snatched inward, and Mim was there in her nightrobe. With a sob of relief she flung herself into his arms and hugged him tightly.

"Hush," he said, "it's all right; it's all right, Mim."

They were framed in the doorway. He brought her inside and closed and barred the heavy door. Mim stood wiping at her eyes with her wide sleeve.

"Is the house awake?" he whispered.

"Everyone finally went to bed. I came out again and waited in the *rhmei*. I hoped—I hoped you would come back. Are you all right, my lord?"

"I am well enough." He took her in his arm and walked with her to the warmth of the *rhmei*. There in the light her large eyes stared up at him and her hands pressed his, gentle as the touch of wind.

"You are shaking," she said. "Is it the cold?"

"It's cold and I'm tired." It was hard to slip back into Nechai after hours of human language. His accent crept out again.

"What did she want?"

"She asked me some questions. They held me all night—Mim, I just want to go upstairs and get some sleep. Don't worry. I am well, Mim."

"My lord," she said in a tear-choked voice, "before the *phusmeha* it is a great wrong to lie. Forgive me, but I know that you are lying."

"Leave me alone, Mim, please."

"It was not about the questions. If it was, look at me plainly and say that it was so."

He tried, and could not. Mim's dark eyes flooded with sadness.

"I am sorry," was all that he could say.

Her hands tightened on his. That terrible dark-eyed look would not let him go. "Do you wish to break the contract, or do you wish to keep it?"

"Do you?"

"If it is your wish."

With his chilled hand he smoothed the hair from her cheek and wiped at a streak of tears. "I do not love her," he said; and then, tribute to the honesty Mim herself used: "But I know how she feels, Mim. Sometimes I feel that way too. Sometimes all Elas is strange to me and I want to be human just for a little time. It is like that with her."

"She might give you children and you would be lord over all Nephane."

He crushed her against him, the faint perfume of *aluel* leaves about her clothing, a freshness about her skin, and remembered the synthetics-and-alcohol scent of Djan, human and, for the moment, pleasing. There was kindness in Djan; it made her dangerous, for it threatened her pride.

It threatened Elas.

"If it were in Djan's nature to marry, which it is not, I would still feel no differently, Mim. But I cannot say that this will be the last time I go to the Afen. If you cannot bear that, then tell me so now."

"I would be concubine and not first wife, if it was your wish."

"No," he said, realizing how she had heard it. "No, the only reason I would ever put you aside would be to protect you."

She leaned up on tiptoe and took his face between her two silken hands, kissed him with great tenderness. Then she drew back, hands still uplifted, as if unsure how he would react. She looked frightened.

"My lord husband," she said, which she was entitled to call him, being betrothed. The words had a strange sound between them. And she took liberties with him which he understood no honorable nemet lady would take with her betrothed, even in being alone with him. But she put all her manners aside to please him,—perhaps, he feared, to fight for him in her own desperate fashion.

He pressed her to him tightly and set her back again. "Mim, please. Go before someone wakes and sees you. I have to talk to Kta."

"Will you tell him what has happened?"

"I intend to."

"Please do not bring violence into this house."

"Go on, Mim."

She gave him an agonized look, but she did as he asked her.

He did not knock at Kta's door. There had already been too much noise in the sleeping house. Instead he opened it and slipped inside, crossed the floor and parted the curtain that screened the sleeping area before he spoke Kta's name.

The nemet came awake with a start and an oath, looked at Kurt with dazed eyes, then rolled out of bed and wrapped a kilt around himself. "Gods," he said, "you look deathly, friend. What happened? Are you all right? Is there some—?"

"I've just been put to explaining a situation to Mim," Kurt said, and found his limbs shaking under him, the delayed reaction to all that he had been through. "Kta, I need advice."

Kta showed him a chair. "Sit down, my friend. Compose your heart and I will help you if you can make me understand. Shall I find you something to drink?"

Kurt sat down and bowed his head, locked his fingers

behind his neck until he make himself remember the calm that belonged in Elas. The scent of incense, the dim light of the *phusa,* the sense of stillness, all this comforted him, and the panic left him though the fear did not.

"I am all right," he said. "No, do not bother about the drink."

"You only now came in?" Kta asked him, for the morning showed through the window.

Kurt nodded, looked him in the eyes, and Kta let the breath hiss slowly between his teeth.

"A personal matter?" Kta asked with admirable delicacy.

"The whole of Elas seemed to have read matters better than I did when I went up to the Afen. Was it that obvious? Does the whole of Nephane know by now, or is there any privacy in this city?"

"Mim knew, at least. Kurt, Kurt, light of heaven, there was no need to guess. When the Methi's men came back to assure us of your safety, it was clear enough, coupled with the Methi's reaction to the betrothal. My friend, do not be ashamed. We always knew that your life would be bound to that of the Methi. Nephane has taken it for granted from the day you came. It was the betrothal to Mim that shocked everyone—I am speaking plainly. I think the truth has its moment, eve if it is bitter. Yes, the whole of Nephane knows, and is by no means surprised."

Kurt swore, a raw and human oath, and gazed off at the window, unable to look at the nemet.

"Have you," said Kta, "love for the Methi?"

"No," he said harshly.

"You chose to go," Kta reminded him, "when Elas would have fought for you."

"Elas has no place in this."

"We have no honor if we let you protect us in this way. But it is not clear to us what your wishes are in this matter. Do you wish us to intervene?"

"I do not wish it," he answered.

"Is this the wish of your heart? Or do you still think to shield us? You owe us the plain truth, Kurt. Tell us yes or no and we will believe your word and do as you wish."

"I do not love the Methi," he said in a still voice, "but I do not want Elas involved between us."

"That tells me nothing."

"I expect," he said, finding it difficult to meet Kta's dark-eyed and gentle sympathy, "that it will not be the last time. I owe her, Kta. If my behavior offends the honor of Elas or of Mim, tell me. I have no wish to bring misery on this house, and least of all on Mim. Tell me what to do."

"Life," said Kta, "is a powerful urge. You protest you hate the Methi, and perhaps she hates you, but the urge to survive and perpetuate your kind—may be a sense of honor above every other honor. Mim has spoken to me of this."

He felt a deep sickness, thinking of that. At the moment he himself did not even wish to survive.

"Mim honors you," said Kta, "very much. If your heart toward her changed, still,—you are bound, my friend. I feared this; and Mim foreknew it. I beg you do not think of breaking this vow with Mim; it would dishonor her. *Ai*, my friend, my friend, we are a people that does not believe in sudden marriage, yet for once we were led by the heart, we were moved by the desire to make you and Mim happy. Now I hope that we have not been cruel instead. You cannot undo what you have done with Mim."

"I would not," Kurt said, "I would not change that."

"Then," said Kta, "all is well."

"I have to live in this city," said Kurt, "and how will people see this and how will it be for Mim?"

Kta shrugged. "This is the Methi's problem. It is common for a man to have obligations to more than one woman. One cannot, of course, have the Methi of Nephane for a common concubine. But it is for the woman's house to see to the proprieties and to obtain respectability. An honorable woman does so, as we have done for Mim. If a woman will not, or her family will not, matters are on her head, not yours. Though," he added, "a methi can do rather well as he or she pleases, and this has been a common difficulty with Methis, particularly with human ones,—and the late Tehal-methi of Indresul was notorious. Djan-methi is efficient. She is a good methi. The people have bread and peace, and as long as that lasts, you can only obtain honor by your association with her. I am only concerned that your feelings may turn again to human things, and Mim be only of a strange people that for a time entertained you."

"No."

"I beg your forgiveness if this would never happen."

"It would never happen."

"I have offended my friend," said Kta. "I know you have grown nemet, and this part of you I trust; but forgive me: I do not know how to understand the other."

"I would do anything to protect Mim—or Elas."

"Then," said Kta in great earnestness, "think as nemet, not as human. Do nothing without your family. Keep nothing from your family. The Families are sacred. Even the Methi is powerless to do you harm when you stand with us and we with you."

"Then you do not know Djan."

"There is the law, Kurt. So long as you have not taken arms against her or directly defied her, the law binds her. She must go through the Upei, and a dispute—forgive me—with her lover—is hardly the kind of matter she could lay before the Upei."

"She could simply assign you and *Tavi* to sail to the end of the known world. She has alternatives, Kta."

"If the Methi chooses a quarrel with Elas," said Kta, "she will have chosen unwisely. Elas was here before the Methi came, and before the first human set foot on this soil. We know our city and our people, our voice is heard in councils on both sides of the Dividing Sea. When Elas speaks in the Upei, the Great Families listen; and now of all times the Methi dares not have the Great Families at odds with her. Her position is not as secure as it seems, which she knows full well, my friend."

VIII

The ship from Indresul came into port late on the day scheduled, a bireme with a red sail—the international emblem, Kta explained as he stood with Kurt on the dock, of a ship claiming immunity from attack. It would be blasphemy against the gods either to attack a ship bearing that color or to claim immunity without just cause.

The Nephanite crowds were ominously silent as the ambassador left his ship and came ashore. Characteristic of the nemet, there was no wild outburst of hatred, but people took just long enough moving back to clear a path for the ambassador's escort to carry the point that he was not welcome in Nephane.

Mor t'Uset ul Orm, white-haired and grim of face, made his way on foot up the hill to the height of the Afen and paid no heed to the soft curses that followed at his back.

"The house of Uset," said Kta as he and Kurt made their way uphill in the crowd, "that house on this side of the Dividing Sea, will not stir out of doors this day. They will not go into the Upei for very shame."

"Shame before Mor t'Uset or before the people of Nephane?"

"Both. It is a terrible thing when a house is divided. The Guardians of Uset on both sides of the sea are in conflict. *Ei, ei*, fighting the Tamurlin is joyless enough; it is worse that two races have warred against each other over this land; but when one thinks of war against one's own family, where gods and Ancestors are shared, whose hearth once

75

burned with a common flame,—*ai*, heaven keep us from such a day."

"I do not think Djan will take this city to war. She knows too well where it leads."

"Neither side wants it," said Kta, "and the Indras-descended of Nephane want it least of all. Our quarrel with—"

Kta fell silent as they came to the place where the street narrowed to pass the gate in the lower defense wall. A man reaching the gate from the opposite direction was staring at them—tall, powerful, wearing the braid and striped robe that was not uncommon in the lower town and among the Methi's guard.

All at once Kurt knew him. Shan t'Tefur. Hate seemed in permanent residence in t'Tefur's narrow eyes. For a moment Kurt's heart pounded and his muscles tensed, for t'Tefur had stopped in the gate and seemed about to bar their way.

Kta jostled against Kurt, purposefully, clamped his arm in a hard grip unseen beneath the fold of the *ctan* and edged him through the gate, making it clear he should not stop.

"That man," said Kurt, resisting the urge to look back, for Kta's grip remained hard, warning him. "That man is from the Afen."

"Keep moving," Kta said.

They did not stop until they reached the high street, that area near the Afen which belonged to the mansions of the Families, great, rambling things, among which Elas was one of the most prominent. Here Kta seemed easier, and slowed his pace as they headed toward the door of Elas.

"That man," Kurt said then, "came where I was being held in the Afen. He brought me into the Methi's rooms. His name is t'Tefur."

"I know his name."

"He seems to have a dislike for humans."

"Hardly," said Kta. "It is a personal dislike. He has no fondness for either of us. He is Sufaki."

"I noticed—the braid, the robes,—that is not the dress of the Methi's guard, then?"

"No. It is Sufak."

"Osanef—Osanef is Sufaki. Han t'Osanef and Bel do not wear—"

"No. Osanef is Sufaki, but the *jafikn*, that long hair braided in the back, that is an ancient custom: the warrior's braid. No one has done it since the Conquest. It was forbidden the Sufaki then. But in recent years the rebel spirits have revived the custom—and the Robes of Color, which distinguish their houses. There are three Sufak houses of the ancient aristocracy surviving, and t'Tefur is of one. He is a dangerous man. His name is Shan t'Tefur u Tlekef, or as he prefers to be known—Tlekefu Shan Tefur. He is Elas' bitter enemy, and he is yours, not alone for the sake of Elas."

"Because I'm human? But I understood Sufaki had no particular hate for—" And it dawned on him, with a sudden heat of the face.

"Yes," said Kta, "he has been the Methi's lover for many months."

"What—does your custom say he and I should do about it?"

"Sufak custom says he may try to make you fight him. And you must not. Absolutely you must not."

"Kta, I may be helpless in most things nemet, but if he wants to press a fight, that is something I can understand. Do you mean a fight, or do you mean a fight to the death? I am not that anxious to kill him over her, but neither am I going to be—"

"Listen. Hear what I am saying to you. You must avoid a fight with him. I do not question your courage or your ability. I am asking this for the sake of Elas. Shan t'Tefur is dangerous."

"Do you expect me to allow myself to be killed? Is he dangerous in that sense, or how?"

"He is a power among the Sufaki. He sought more power, which the Methi could give him. You have made him lose honor and you have threatened his position of leadership. You are resident with Elas, and we are of the Indras-descended. Until now, the Methi has inclined toward the Sufaki, ever since she dispensed with me as an interpreter. She has been surrounded by Sufaki, chosen friends of Shan t'Tefur, and has drawn much of her power from them, so much so that the Great Families are uneasy. But of a sudden Shan t'Tefur finds his footing unsteady."

They walked in silence for a moment. Increasingly bitter and embarrassed thoughts reared up. Kurt glanced at the nemet. "You pulled me from the harbor. You saved my life. You gave me everything I have—by Djan's leave. You went to her and asked for me, and if not for that—I would be—I would certainly not be walking the streets free. So do not misunderstand what I ask you. But you said that from the time I arrived in Nephane, people knew that I would become involved with the Methi. Was I pushed toward that, Kta? Was I aimed at her,—an Indras weapon—against Shan t'Tefur?"

And to his distress, Kta did not answer at once.

"Is it the truth, then?" Kurt asked.

"Kurt, you have married within my house."

"Is it true?" he insisted.

"I do not know how a human hears things," Kta protested. "Or whether you attribute to me motives no nemet would have, or fail to think what would be obvious to a nemet. Gods, Kurt—"

"Answer me."

"When I first saw you—I thought—He is the Methi's kind. Is that not most obvious? Is there offense in that? And I thought: He ought to be treated kindly, since he is a gentle being, and since one day he may be more than he seems now. And then an unworthy thought came to me: It would be profitable to your house, Kta t'Elas. And there is offense in that. At the time you were only human to me; and to a nemet, that does not oblige one to deal morally. I do offend you. I cause you pain. But that is the way it was. I think differently now. I am ashamed."

"So Elas took me in,—to use."

"No," said Kta quickly. "We would never have opened—"

His words died as Kurt kept staring at him. "Go ahead," said Kurt. "Or do I already understand?"

Kta met his eyes directly, contrition in a nemet. "Elas is holy to us. I owe you a truth. We would never have opened our doors to you—to anyone—Very well, I will say it: it is unthinkable that I would have exposed my hearth to human influence, whatever the advantage is promised with the Methi.

Our hospitality is sacred, and not for sale for any favor. But I made a mistake—in my anxiousness to win your favor, I gave you my word; and the word of Elas is sacred too. So I accepted you. My friend, let our friendship survive this truth: when the other Families reproached Elas for taking a human into its *rhmei,* we argued simply that it was better for a human to be within an Indras house than that you be sent to the Sufaki instead, for the influence of the Sufaki is already dangerously powerful. And I think another consideration influenced Djan-methi in hearing me: that your life would have been in constant danger in a Sufak house, because of the honor of Shan t'Tefur,—although I dared not say it in words. So she sent you to Elas. I think she feared t'Tefur's reaction even if you remained in the Afen."

"I understand," said Kurt, because it seemed proper to say something. The words hurt. He did not trust himself to say much.

"Elas loves and honors you," said Kta, and when Kurt still failed to answer him he looked down, and with what appeared much thought, he cautiously extended his hand to take his arm, touching like Mim, with feather-softness. It was an unnatural gesture for the nemet; it was one studied, copied, offered now on the public street as an act of desperation.

Kurt stopped perforce, set his jaw against the tears which threatened.

"Avoid t'Tefur," Kta pleaded. "If the housefriend of Elas kills the heir of Tefur,—or if he kills you—killing will not stop there. He will provoke you if he can. Be wise. Do not let him do this."

"I understand. I have told you that."

Kta glanced down, gave the sketch of a bow. The hand dropped. They walked on, near to Elas.

"Have I a soul?" Kurt asked him suddenly, and looked at him.

The nemet's face was shocked, frightened.

"Have I a soul?" Kurt asked again.

"Yes," said Kta, which seemed difficult for him to say.

It was, Kurt thought, an admission which had already cost Kta some of his peace of mind.

*   *   *

The Upei, the council, met that day in the Afen and adjourned, as by law it must, as the sun set, to convene again at dawn.

Nym returned to the house at dusk, greeted lady Ptas and Hef at the door. When he came into the *rhmei* where the light was, the senator looked exhausted, utterly drained. Aimu hastened to bring water for washing, while Ptas prepared the tea.

There was no discussion of business during the meal. Such matters as Nym had on his mind were reserved for the rounds of tea that followed. Instead Nym asked politely after Mim's preparation for her wedding, and for Aimu's, for both were spending their days sewing, planning, discussing the coming weddings, keeping the house astir with their happy excitement and sometimes tears, and Aimu glanced down prettily and said that she had almost completed her own trousseau and that they were working together on Mim's things, for, Aimu thought, their beloved human was not likely to choose the long formal engagement such as she had had with Bel.

"I met our friend the elder t'Osanef," said Nym in answer to that, "and it is not unlikely, little Aimu, that we will advance the date of your own wedding."

"*Ei,*" murmured Aimu, her dark eyes suddenly wide. "How far, honored Father?"

"Perhaps within a month."

"Beloved husband," exclaimed Ptas in dismay, "such haste?"

"There speaks a mother," Nym said tenderly. "Aimu, child, do you and Mim go fetch another pot of tea. And then go to your sewing. There is business afoot hereafter."

"Shall I—?" asked Kurt, offering by gesture to depart.

"No, no, our guest. Please sit with us. This business concerns the house, and you are soon to be one of us."

The tea was brought and served with all formality. Then Mim and Aimu withdrew, leaving the men of the house and Ptas. Nym took a slow sip of tea and looked at his wife.

"You had a question, Ptas?"

"Who asked the date advanced? Osanef? Or was it you?"

"Ptas, I fear we are going to war." And in the stillness

that awful word made in the room he continued very softly: "If we wish this marriage I think we must hurry it on with all decent speed; a wedding between Sufaki and Indras may serve to heal the division between the Families and the sons of the east; that is still our hope. But it must be soon."

The lady of Elas wept quiet tears and blotted them with the edge of her scarf. "What will they do? It is not right, Nym, it is not right that they should have to bear such a weight on themselves."

"What would you? Break the engagement? That is impossible. For us to ask that—no. No. And if the marriage is to be, then there must be haste. With war threatening,—Bel would surely wish to leave a son to safeguard the name of Osanef. He is the last of his name. As you are, Kta, my son. I am above sixty years of age, and today it has occurred to me that I am not immortal. You should have laid a grandson at my feet years ago."

"Yes, sir," said Kta quietly.

"You cannot mourn the dead forever; and I wish you would make some choice for yourself, so that I would know how to please you. If there is any young woman of the Families who has touched your heart—"

Kta shrugged, looking at the floor.

"Perhaps," his father suggested gently, "the daughters of Rasim or of Irain . . ."

"Tai t'Isulan,—" said Kta.

"A lovely child," said Ptas, "and she will be a fine lady."

Again Kta shrugged. "A child, indeed. But I do at least know her, and I think I would not be unpleasing to her."

"She is—what?—seventeen?" asked Nym, and when Kta agreed: "Isulan is a fine religious house. I will think on it and perhaps I will talk with Ban t'Isulan, if in several days you still think the same.—My son, I am sorry to bring this matter upon you so suddenly, but you are my only son, and these are sudden times. Ptas, pour some *telise*."

She did so. The first few sips were drunk in silence. This was proper. Then Nym sighed softly.

"Home is very sweet, wife. May we abide as we are tonight."

"May it be so," reverently echoed Ptas, and Kta did the same.

"The matter in council," said Ptas then. "What was decided?"

Nym frowned and stared at nothing in particular. "T'Uset is not here to bring peace, only more demands of the Methi Ylith. Djan-methi was not in the Upei today; it did not seem wise. And I suspect—" His eyes wandered to Kurt, estimating; and Kurt's face went hot. Suddenly he gathered himself to leave, but Nym forbade that with a move of his hand, and he settled again, bowing low and not meeting Nym's eyes.

"Our words could offend you," said Nym. "I pray not."

"I have learned," said Kurt, "how little welcome my people have made for themselves among you."

"Friend of my son," said Nym gently, "your wise and peaceful attitude is an ornament to this house. I will not affront you by repeating t'Uset's words. Reason with him proved impossible: the Indras of the mother city hate humans, and they will not negotiate with Djan-methi. And that is not the end of our troubles." His eyes sought Ptas. "T'Tefur created bitter discussion, even before t'Uset was seated, demanding we not permit him to be present during the Invocation."

"Light of heaven," murmured Ptas. "In t'Uset's hearing?"

"He was at the door."

"We met the younger t'Tefur today," said Kta. "There were no words, but his manner was deliberate and provocative, aimed at Kurt."

"Is it so?" said Nym, concerned, and with a glance at Kurt: "Do not fall into his hands. Do not place yourself where you can become a cause, our friend."

"I am warned," said Kurt.

"Today," said Nym, "there was a curse spoken between the house of Tefur and the house of Elas, before the Upei, and we must all be on our guard. T'Tefur blasphemed, shouting down the Invocation, and I answered him as his behavior deserved. He calls it treason, that when we pray we still call on the name of Indresul the shining. This he said in t'Uset's hearing."

"And for the likes of this," said lady Ptas, "we must endure to be cursed from the hearthfire of Elas-in-Indresul, and have our name pronounced annually in infamy at the Shrine of Man."

"Mother," said Kta, bowing low, "not all Sufaki feel so. Bel would not feel this way. He would not."

"T'Tefur's number is growing," said Ptas, "that he dares to stand in the Upei and say such a thing."

Kurt looked from one to the other in bewilderment. It was Nym who undertook to explain to him. "We are Indras. A thousand years ago Nai-methi of Indresul launched colonies toward the Isles, south of this shore, then laid the foundations of Nephane as a fortress to guard the coast from Sufaki pirates. He destroyed Chteftikan, the capital of the Sufaki kingdom, and Indras colonists administered the new provinces from this citadel. For most of time we ruled the Sufaki. But the coming of humans cut our ties to Indresul, and when we came out of those dark years, we wiped out all the cruel laws that kept the Sufaki subject, accepted them into the Upei. For t'Tefur, that is not enough. There is great bitterness there."

"It is religion," said Ptas. "Sufaki have many gods, and believe in magic and worship demons. Not all. Bel's house is better educated. But Indras will not set foot in the precincts of the temple, the so-named Oracle of Phan. And it would be dangerous in these times even to be there in the wall-street after dark. We pray at our own hearths and invoke the Ancestors we have in common with the houses across the Dividing Sea. We do them no harm—we inflict nothing on them, but they resent this."

"But," said Kurt, "you do not agree with Indresul."

"It is impossible," said Nym. "We are of Nephane. We have lived among Sufaki; we have dealt with humans. We cannot unlearn the things we know for truth. We will fight if we must, against Indresul. The Sufaki seem not to believe that, but it is so."

"No," said Kurt, and with such passion that the nemet were hushed. "No. Do not go to war."

"It is excellent advice," said Nym after a moment. "But we may be helpless to guide our own affairs. When a man finds his affairs without resolution, his existence out of time with heaven and his very being a disturbance to the *yhia*, then he must choose to die for the sake of order. He does well if he does so without violence. In the eyes of heaven even nations are finally answerable to such logic, and even nations may sometimes be compelled to suicide. They have their methods,—being many minds and not one, they cannot proceed toward their fate with the dignity a single man can manage, but proceed they do."

"*Ei*, honored Father," said Kta, "I beg you not to say such things."

"Like Bel, do you believe in omens? I do not,—not, at least, that words, ill-thought or otherwise, have power over the future. The future already exists, in our hearts already, stored up and waiting to unfold when we reach our time and place. Our own nature is our fate. You are young, Kta. You deserve better than my age has given you."

There was silence in the *rhmei*. Suddenly Kurt bowed himself a degree lower, requesting, and Nym looked at him.

"You have a methi," said Kurt, "who is not willing to fight a war. Please. Trust me to go speak to her, as another human."

There was a stir of uneasiness. Kta opened his mouth as if he would protest, but Nym consented.

"Go," he said, nothing more.

Kurt rose and adjusted his *ctan,* pinning it securely. He bowed to them collectively and turned to leave. Someone hurried after; he thought it was Hef, whose duty it was to tend the door. It was Kta who overtook him in the outer hall.

"Be careful," Kta said. And when he opened the outer door into the dark: "Kurt, I will walk to the Afen with you."

"No," said Kurt. "Then you would have to wait there, and you would be obvious at this hour. Let us not make this more obvious than need be."

But there was, once the door was closed and he was on the street in the dark, an uneasy feeling about the night. It was quieter than usual. A man muffled in striped robes stood in the shadows of the house opposite. Kurt turned and walked quickly uphill.

Djan put her back to the window that overlooked the sea and leaned back against the ledge, a metallic form against the dark beyond the glass. Tonight she dressed as human, in a dark blue form-fitting synthetic that shimmered like powdered glass along the lines of her figure. It was a thing she would not dare wear among the modest nemet.

"The Indras ambassador sails tomorrow," she said. "Confound it, couldn't you have waited? I'm trying to keep humanity out of his sight and hearing as much as possible, and you have to be walking up and down the halls—He's staying on the floor just below. If one of his staff had come out—"

"This isn't a social call."

Djan expelled her breath slowly, nodded him toward a seat near her. "Elas and the business in the Upei. I heard. What did they send you to say?"

"They didn't send me. But if you have any means of controlling the situation, you'd better exert it,—fast."

Her cool green eyes measured him, centered soberly on his. "You're scared. What Elas said must have been considerable."

"Stop putting words in my mouth. There's going to be nothing left but Indresul to pick up the pieces if this goes on. There was some kind of balance here, Djan. There was stability. You blew it to—"

"Nym's words?"

"No. Listen to me."

"There was a balance of power, yes," Djan said. "A balance tilted in favor of the Indras and against the Sufaki. I have done nothing but use impartiality. The Indras are not used to that."

"Impartiality. Do you maintain that with Shan t'Tefur?"

Her head went back. Her eyes narrowed slightly, but then she grinned. She had a beautiful smile, even when there was no humor in it. "Ah," she said. "I should have told you. Now your feelings are ruffled."

"I'm sure I don't care," he said, started to add something more cutting still, and then regretted even what he had said. He had, after a fashion, cared; perhaps she had feelings for him also. There was anger in her eyes, but she did not let it fly.

"Shan," she said, "is a friend. His family were lords of this land once. He thinks he can bend me to his ambitions, which are probably considerable, and he is slowly learning he can't. He is angry about your presence, which is an anger that will heal. I believe him about as much as I believe you when your own interests are at stake. I weigh all that either of you says, and try to analyze where the bias lies."

"Being yourself perfect, of course."

"In this government there does not have to be a methi. Methis serve when it is useful to have one—In times of crisis, to bind civil and military authority into one swiftly-moving whole. My reason for being is somewhat different. I am Methi precisely because I am neither Sufaki nor Indras. Yes, the Sufaki support me. If I stepped down, the Indras would immediately appoint an Indras methi. The Upei is Indras: nobility is the qualification for membership, and there are only three noble houses of the Sufaki surviving. The others were massacred a thousand years ago. Now Elas is marrying a daughter into one—so Osanef too becomes a limb of the Families. The Upei makes the laws: and the Assembly may be Sufaki, but all they can do is vote yea or nay on what the Upei deigns to hand them. The Assembly hasn't rallied to veto anything since the day of its creation. So what else do the Sufaki have but the Methi? Oppose the Families by veto in the Assembly? Hardly likely, when the living of the Sufaki depends on big shipping companies like Irain and Ilev and Elas. A little frustration burst out today. It was regrettable. But if it makes the Families realize the seriousness of the situation, then perhaps it was well done."

"It was not well done," Kurt said. "Not when it was done, nor where it was done, nor against what it was done. The ambassador witnessed it. Did your informants tell you that detail? Djan, your selective blindness is going to make chaos out of this city. Listen to the Families. Call in their Fathers. Listen to them as you listen to Shan t'Tefur."

"Ah, so it does rankle."

He stood up. She resented his speaking to her. It had been on the edge of every word. It was in his mind to walk out, but that would let her forget everything he had said. Necessity overcame his pride. "Djan. I have nothing against you. In spite of—because of—what we did one night, I have a certain regard for you. I had some hope you might at least listen to me, for the sake of all concerned."

"I will look into it," she said. "I will do what I can." And when he turned to go: "I hear little from you. Are you happy in Elas?"

"He looked back, surprised by the gentleness of her asking. "I am happy," he said.

She smiled. "In some measure I do envy you."

"The same choices are open to you."

"No," she said. "Not by nemet law. Think of me and think of your little Mim, and you will know what I mean. I am Methi. I do as I please. Otherwise this world would put bonds on me that I couldn't live with. It would make your life miserable if you had to accept such terms as this world would offer me. I refuse."

"I understand," he said. "I wish you well, Djan."

She let the smile grow sad, and stared out at the lights of Nephane a moment, ignoring him.

"I am fond of few people," she said. "In your peculiar way you have gotten into my affections, —more than Shan, more than most who have their reason for using me. Get out of here, back to Elas, discreetly. Go on."

IX

The wedding Mim chose was a small and private one. The guests and witnesses were scarcely more numerous than what the law required. Of Osanef, there was Han t'Osanef u Mur, his wife Ia t'Nefak, and Bel. Of the house of Ilev there was Ulmar t'Ilev ul Imetan and his wife Tian t'Elas e Ben, cousin to Nym, and their son Cam and their new daughter-in-law, Yanu t'Pas. They were all people Mim knew well, and Osanef and Ilev, Kurt suspected, were among a very few nemet houses that could be found reconciled to the marriage on religious grounds.

If even these had scruples about the question, they had the grace still to smile and to love Mim and to treat her chosen husband with great courtesy.

The ceremony was in the *rhmei,* where Kurt first knelt before old Hef and swore that the first two sons of the union, if any, would be given the name h'Elas as *chani* to the house, so that Hef's line could continue.

And Kta swore also to the custom of *iquun,* by which Kta would see to the begetting of the promised heirs, if necessary.

Then Nym rose and with palms toward the light of the *phusmeha* invoked the guardian spirits of the Ancestors of Elas. The sun outside was only beginning to set. It was impossible to conduct a marriage-rite after Phan had left the land.

"Mim," said Nym, taking her hand, "called Mim-lechan h'Elas e Hef, you are *chan* to this house no longer, but become as a daughter of this house, well beloved, Mim

88

h'Elas e Hef. Are you willing to yield your first two sons to
Hef, your foster-father?"

"Yes, my lord of Elas."

"Are you consenting to all the terms of the marriage
contract?"

"Yes, my lord of Elas."

"Are you willing now, daughter to Elas, to bind yourself
by these final and irrevocable vows?"

"Yes, my lord of Elas."

"And you, Kurt Liam t'Morgan u Patrick Edward, are
you willing to bind yourself by these final and irrevocable
vows, to take this free woman Mim h'Elas e Hef for your
true and first wife, loving her before all others, commiting
your honor into her hands and your strength and fortune to
her protection?"

"Yes, my lord."

"Hef h'Elas," said Nym, "the blessing of this house and its
Guardians upon this union."

The old man came forward, and it was Hef who completed the ceremony, giving Mim's hand into Kurt's and
naming for each the final vows they made. Then, according
to custom, Ptas lit a torch from the great *phusmeha* and
gave it into Kurt's hands, and he into Mim's.

"In purity I have given," Kurt recited the ancient formula
in High Nechai, "in reverence preserve, Mim h'Elas e Hef
shu-Kurt, well-beloved, my wife."

"In purity I have received," she said softly, "in reverence
I will keep myself to thee to the death, Kurt Liam t'Morgan
u Patrick Edward, my lord, my husband."

And with Mim beside him, and to the ritual weeping of
the ladies and the congratulations of the men, Kurt left the
rhmei. Mim carried the light, walking behind him up the
stairs to the door of his room that now was hers.

He entered, and watched as she used the torch to light the
triangular bronze lamp, the *phusa,* which had been replaced
in its niche, and he heard her sigh softly with relief, for the
omen would have been terrible if the light had not taken.
The lamp of Phan burned with steady light, and she then
extinguished the torch with a prayer and knelt down before
the lamp as Kurt closed the door, knelt down and lifted her
hands before it.

"My Ancestors, I, Mim t'Nethim e Sel shu-Kurt, called by these my beloved friends Mim h'Elas, I, Mim, beg your forgiveness for marrying under a name not my own, and swear now by my own name to honor the vows I made under another. My Ancestors, behold this man, my husband Kurt t'Morgan, and whatever distant spirits are his, be at peace with them for my sake. Peace, I pray my Fathers, and let peace be with Elas on both sides of the Dividing Sea. *Ei*, let thoughts of war be put aside between our two lands. May love be in this house and upon us both forever. May the terrible Guardians of Nethim hear me and receive the vow I make. And may the great Guardians of Elas receive me kindly as you have ever done, for we are of this house now, and within your keeping."

She lowered her hands, finishing her prayer, and offered her right hand to Kurt, who drew her up.

"Mim t'Nethim," he said. "Then I had never heard your real name."

Her large eyes lifted to him. "Nethim has no house in Nephane, but in Indresul we are ancestral enemies to Elas. I have not burdened Kta with knowing my true name. He asked me, and I would not answer, so surely he suspects that I am of a hostile house; but if there is any harm in my silence, it is upon me only. And I have spoken your name before the Guardians of Nethim many times, and I have not felt that they are distressed at you, my lord Kurt."

He had started to take her in his arms, but hesitated now, held his hands a little apart from her, suddenly fearing Mim and her strangeness. Her gown was beautiful and had cost days of work which he had watched; he did not know how to undo it, or if this was expected of him. And Mim herself was as complex and unknowable, wrapped in customs for which Kta's instructions had not prepared him.

He remembered the frightened child that Kta had found among the Tamurlin, and feared that she would suddenly see him as human and loathe him, without the robes and the graces that made him—outwardly—nemet.

"Mim," he said. "I would never see any harm come to you."

"It is a strange thing to say, my lord."

"I am afraid for you," he said suddenly. "Mim, I do love you."

She smiled a little, then laughed, down-glancing. He treasured the gentle laugh: it was Mim at her prettiest. And she slipped her hands about his waist and hugged him tightly, her strong slim arms dispelling the fear that she would break.

"Kurt," she said, "Kta is a dear man, most honored of me. I know that you and he have spoken of me. Is this not so?"

"Yes," he said.

"Kta has spoken to me too: he fears for me. I honor his concern. It is for both of us. But I trust your heart where I do not know your ways; I know if ever you hurt me, it would be much against your will." She slipped her warm hands to him. "Let us have tea, my husband, a first warming of our hearth."

That was much against his will, but it pleased her. She lit the small room-stove, which also heated, and boiled water and made them tea, which they enjoyed sitting on the bed together.

He had little to say but much on his mind; neither did Mim, but she looked often at him.

"Is it not enough tea?" he asked finally, with the same patient courtesy he always used in Elas, which Kta had taught his unwilling spirit. But this time there was great earnestness in the question, which brought a sly smile from Mim.

"What is your custom now?" she asked of him.

"What is yours?" he asked.

"I do not know," she admitted, down-glancing and seeming distressed. Then for the first time he realized, and felt pained for his thoughtlessness: she had never been with a man of her own kind,—nor with any man of decency.

"Put up the teacups," he said, "and come here, Mim."

The light of morning came through the window and Kurt stirred in his sleep, his hand finding the smoothness of Mim beside him, and he opened his eyes and looked at her. Her eyes were closed, her lashes dark and heavy on her golden cheek, her full lips relaxed in dreams. A little scar marred her temple, as others not so slight marked her back and hips, and that anyone could have abused Mim was a thought he could not bear.

He moved, leaned on his arm across her and touched his lips to hers, smoothed aside the dark and shining veil of hair that flowed across her and across the pillows, and she stirred, responding sweetly to his morning kiss.

"Mim," he said, "good morning."

Her arms went around his neck. She pulled herself up and kissed him back. Then she blinked back tears, which he made haste to wipe away.

"Mim?" he questioned her, much troubled; but she smiled at him and even laughed.

"Dear Kurt," she said, holding his face between her hands. And then, breaking for the side of the bed, she began to wriggle free. "*Ei, ei,* my lord, I must hurry,—you must hurry—the sun is up. The guests will be waiting"

"Guests?" he echoed, dismayed. "Mim—"

But she was already slipping into her dressing gown, then pattering away into the bath. He heard her putting wood into the stove.

"It is custom," she said, putting her head back through the doorway of the bath. "They come back at dawn to breakfast with us.—Oh please, Kurt, please, hurry to be ready. They will be downstairs already, and if we are much past dawning, they will laugh."

It was the custom, Kurt resolved to himself, and nerved himself to face the chill air and the cold stone floor, when he had planned a far warmer and more pleasant morning.

He joined Mim in the bath and she washed his back for him, making clouds of comfortable steam with the warm water, laughing and not at all caring that the water soaked her dressing gown.

She was content with him.

At times the warmth in her eyes or the lingering touch of her fingers said she was more than content.

The hardest thing that faced them was to go down the stairs into the *rhmei*, at which Mim actually trembled. Kurt took her arm and would have brought her down with his support, but the idea shocked her. She shook free of him and walked like a proper nemet lady, independently behind him down the stairs.

The guests and family met them at the foot of the steps and brought them into the *rhmei* with much laughter and with ribald jokes that Kurt would not have believed possible from the modest nemet. He was almost angry, but when Mim laughed he knew that it was proper, and forgave them.

After the round of greetings, Aimu came and served the morning tea, hot and sweet, and the elders sat in chairs while the younger people—Kurt and Mim included, and Hef, who was *chan*,—sat upon rugs on the floor and drank their tea and listened to the elders talk. Kta played one haunting song for them on the *aos*, without words, but just for listening and for being still.

Mim would be honored in the house and exempt from duties for the next few days, after which time she would again take her share with Ptas and Aimu; she sat now and accepted the attentions and the compliments and the good wishes,—Mim, who had never expected to be more than a minor concubine to the lord of Elas, accepted with private vows and scant legitimacy—now she was the center of everything.

It was her hour.

Kurt begrudged her none of it, even the nemet humor. He looked down at her and saw her face alight with pride and happiness—and love, which she would have given with lesser vows had he insisted; and he smiled back and pressed her hand, which the others kindly did not elect to make joke of at that moment.

X

Ten days passed before the outside world intruded again into the house of Elas.

It came in the person of Bel t'Osanef u Han, who arrived, escorted by Mim, in the garden at the rear of the house, where Kta was instructing Kurt in the art of the *ypan*, the narrow curved longsword that was the Indras' favorite weapon and chief sport.

Kurt saw Bel come into the garden and turned his blade and held it in both hands to signal halt. Kta checked himself in mid-strike, and turned his head to see the reason of the pause. Then with the elaborate ritual that governed the friendly use of these edged weapons, Kta touched his left hand to his sword and bowed, which Kurt returned. The nemet believed such ritual was necessary to maintain balance of soul between friends who contended in sport, and distrusted the blades. In the houses of the Families resided the *ypai-sulim,* the Great Weapons which had been dedicated in awful ceremony to the house Guardians and bathed in blood. These were never drawn unless a man had determined to kill or to die, and could not be sheathed again until they had taken a life. Even these light foils must be handled carefully, lest the ever-watchful house spirits mistake someone's intent and cause blood to be drawn.

And once it had been death to the Sufaki to touch these lesser weapons, or even to look at the *ypai-sulim* where they hung at rest, so that fencing was an art the Sufaki had never employed: they were skilled with the spear and the bow—distance-weapons.

Bel waited at a respectful distance until the weapons were safely sheathed and laid aside, and then came forward and bowed.

"My lords," said Mim, "shall I bring tea?"

"Do so, Mim, please," said Kta. "Bel, my soon-to—be brother—"

"Kta," said Bel. "My business is somewhat urgent."

"Sit then," said Kta, puzzled. There were several stone benches about the garden. They took those nearest.

Then Aimu came from the house. She bowed modestly to her brother. "Bel," she said then, "you come into Elas without at least sending me greetings? What is the matter?"

"Kta," said Bel, "permission for your sister to sit with us."

"Granted," said Kta, a murmured formality, as thoughtless as "thank you." Aimu sank down on the seat near them. There were no further words. Tea had been asked; Bel's mood was distraught. There was no discussion proper until it had come, and it was not long. Mim brought it on a tray, a full service with extra cups.

Aimu rose up and helped her serve, and then both ladies settled on the same bench while the first several sips that courtesy demanded were drunk in silence and with appreciation.

"My friend Bel," said Kta, when ritual was satisfied, "is it unhappiness or anger or need that has brought you to this house?"

"May the spirits of our houses be at peace," said Bel. "I am here now because I trust you above all others save those born in Osanef. I am afraid there is going to be bloodshed in Nephane."

"T'Tefur," exclaimed Aimu with great bitterness.

"I beg you, Aimu, hear me to the end before you stop me."

"We listen," said Kta, "but, Bel, I suddenly fear this is a matter best discussed between our fathers."

"Our fathers' concern must be with Tlekef; Shan t'Tefur is beneath their notice—but he is the dangerous one, much more than Tlekef. Shan and I—we were friends. You know that. And you must realize how hard it is for me to come now to an Indras house and say what I am going to say. I am trusting you with my life."

"Bel," said Aimu in distress, "Elas will defend you."

"She is right," said Kta, "but Kurt—may not wish to hear this."

Kurt gathered himself to leave: it was Bel's willingness to have him stay that Kta questioned; he had been long enough in Elas to understand nemet subtleties. It was expected of Bel to demur.

"He must stay," said Bel, with more feeling than courtesy demanded. "He is involved."

Kurt settled down again, but Bel remained silent a time thereafter, staring fixedly at his own hands.

"Kta," he said finally, "I must speak now as Sufaki. There was a time, you know, when we ruled this land from the rock of Nephane to the Tamur and inland to the heart of Chteftikan and east to the Gray Sea. Nothing can ever bring back those days; we realize that. You have taken from us our land, our gods, our language, our customs,—you accept us as brothers only when we look like you and talk like you, and you despise us for savages when we are different. —It is true, Kta: look at me. Here am I, born a prince of the Osanef, and I cut my hair and wear Indras robes and speak with the clear round tones of Indresul, like a good civilized man, and I am accepted. Shan is braver. He does what many of us would do if we did not find life so comfortable on your terms. But Elas taught him a lesson I did not learn."

"He left us in anger. I have not forgotten the day. But you stayed."

"I was eleven; Shan was twelve. At that time we thought it a great thing—to be friends to an Indras, to be asked beneath the roof of one of the Great Families, to mingle with the Indras. I had come many times; but this day I brought Shan with me, and Ian t'Ilev chanced to be your guest also that day. Ian made it clear enough that he thought our manners quaint. Shan left on the instant; you prevented me, and persuaded me to stay, for we were closer friends, and longer friends. And from that day Shan t'Tefur and I had in more than that sense gone our separate ways. I could

not call him back. The next day when I met him I tried to
convince him to go back to you and speak with you,—but he
would not. He struck me in the face and cursed me from
him, and said that Osanef was fit for nothing but to be
servant to the Indras—he said it in cruder words—and that
he would not. He has not ceased to despise me."

"It was not well done," said Kta. "I had bitter words with
Ian over the matter, until he came to a better understanding
of courtesy, and my father went to Ilev's father. I assure you
it was done. I did not tell you so; there never seemed a
moment apt for it."

"Kta,—if I had been Indras, would you have found a
moment apt for it?"

Kta gave back a little, his face sobered and troubled. "Bel,
if you were Indras, your father would have come to Elas in
anger and I would have been dealt with by mine—most
harshly. I did not think it mattered, since your customs are
different. But times are changing. You will become marriage-
kin to Elas. Can you doubt that you would have justice from
us?"

"I do not question your friendship," he said, and looked
at Aimu. "Times change, when a Sufaki can marry an
Indras, where once Sufaki were not admitted to an Indras
rhmei where they could meet the daughters of a Family. But
there are still limitations, friend Kta. We try to be business-
men and we are constantly outmaneuvered and outbid by
the combines of wealthy Indras houses; information passes
from hearth to hearth along lines of communication we do
not share. When we go to sea, we sail under Indras captains, as I do for you, my friend,—because we have not the
wealth to maintain warships as a rule,—seldom ever merchantmen. A man like Shan, that makes himself different,
who wears the *jafikn,* who wears the Robes of Color, who
keeps his accent—you ridicule him with secret smiles, for
what was once unquestioned honor to a man of our people.
There is so little left to us of what we were. Do you know,
Kta, after all these years,—that I am not really Sufaki? Is
that a surprise to you? You have ruined us so completely
that you do not even know our real name. The people of
this coast are Sufaki, the ancient name of this province
when we ruled it, but the house of Osanef and the house of

Tefur are Chteftik, from the old capital. And my name, despite the way I have corrupted it to please Indras tongues, is not Bel t'Osanef u Han. It is Hanu Balaket Osanef, and nine hundred years ago we rivaled the Insu dynasty for power in Chteftikan. A thousand years ago, when you were struggling colonists, we were kings, and no man would dare approach us on his feet. Now I change my name to show I am civilized, and bear with you when your cultured accent mispronounces it. Kta, Kta, I am not bitter with you. I tell you these things so that you will understand, because I know that Elas is one Indras house who might listen. You Indras are not trusted. There is talk of some secret accommodation you may have made with your kinsmen of Indresul, —talk that all your vowing war is empty, that you only do this like fisherman at a market, to increase the price in your bargain with Indresul."

"Now hold up on that point," Kta broke in, and for the first time anger flashed in his eyes. "Since you have felt moved to honesty with me,—which I respect,—hear me, and I will return it. If Indresul attacks, we will fight. It has always been a fault in Sufaki reasoning that you assume Indresul loves us like its lost children; quite the contrary. We are yearly cursed in Indresul, by the very families you think we share. We share Ancestors up to a thousand years ago, but beyond that point we are two hearths, and two opposed sets of Ancestors, and we are Nephanite. By the very hearth-loyalty you fear so much, Nephanite, and by the light of heaven I swear to you there is no such conspiracy among the Families. We took your land, yes, and there were cruel laws, yes, but that is in the past, Bel. Would you have us abandon our ways and become Sufaki? We would die first. But I do not think we impose our ways on you. We do not force you to adopt our dress or to honor our customs save when you are under our roof. You yourselves give most honor to those who seem Indras. You hate each other too much to unite for trade as our great houses do. Shan t'Tefur himself admits that when he pleads with you to make companies and rival us for trade. By all means. It would improve the lot of your poor, who are a charge on us."

"And why, Kta? You assume that we can rise to your

level. But have you ever thought that we might not want to be like you?"

"Do you have another answer? Some urge it, like Shan, —to destroy all that is Indras. Will that solve matters?"

"No. We will never know what we might have been; our nation is gone, merged with yours. But I doubt we would like your ways, even if things were upside down and we were ruling you."

"Bel," exclaimed Aimu, "you cannot think these things: you are upset. Your mind will change."

"No, it has never been different. I have always known it is an Indras world, and that my sons and my sons' sons will grow more and more Indras, until they will not understand the mind of the likes of me. I love you, Aimu, and I do not repent my choice, but perhaps now you do. I do not think your well-bred Indras friends would think you disgraced if you broke our engagement. Most would be rather relieved you had come to your senses, I think."

Kta's back stiffened. "Have a care, Bel. My sister has not deserved your spite. Anything you may care to say or do with me—that is one matter; but you go too far when you speak that way to her."

"I beg pardon," Bel murmured, and glanced at Aimu. "We were friends before we were betrothed, Aimu; I think you know how to understand me, and I fear you may come to regret me and our agreement. A Sufaki house will be a strange enough place for you; I would not see you hurt."

"I hold by our agreement," said Aimu. Her face was pale, her breathing quick. "Kta, take no offense with him."

Kta lowered his eyes, made a sign of unwilling apology, then glanced up. "What do you want of me, Bel?"

"Your influence. Speak to your Indras friends; make them understand."

"Understand what? That they must cease to be Indras and imitate Sufaki ways? This is not the way the world is ordered, Bel. And as for violence, if it comes, it will not come from the Indras—that is not our way and it never has been. Persuasion is something you must use on your people."

"You have created a Shan Tefur," said Bel, "and he finds many others like him. Now we who have been friends of the Indras do not know what to do." Bel was trembling. He clasped his hands, elbows on his knees. "There is no more peace, Kta. But let no Indras answer violence with violence, or there will be blood flowing in the streets come the month of Nermotai and the holy days. —Your pardon, my friends." He rose, shaking out his robes. "I know the way out of Elas. You do not have to lead me. Do what you will with what I have told you."

"Bel," said Aimu, "Elas will not put you off for the sake of Shan t'Tefur's threats."

"But Osanef has to fear those threats. Do not expect me to be seen here again in the near future. I do not cease to regard you as my friends. I have faith in your honor and your good judgment, Kta. Do not fail my hopes."

"Let me go with him to the door," said Aimu, though what she asked violated all custom and modesty. "Kta, please."

"Go with him," said Kta. "Bel, my brother, we will do what we can. Be careful for yourself."

XI

Nephane was well named the city of mists. They rolled in and lasted for days as the weather grew warmer, making the cobbled streets slick with moisture. Ships crept carefully into harbor, the lonely sound of their bells occasionally drifting up the height of Nephane through the still air. Voices distantly called out in the streets, muted.

Kurt looked back, anxious, wondering if the sudden hush of footsteps that had been with him ever since the door of Elas meant an end of pursuit.

A shadow appeared near him. He stumbled off the edge of the unseen curb and caught his balance, fronted by several others who appeared, cloaked and anonymous, out of the grayness. He backed up and halted, warned by a scrape of leather on stone: others were behind him. His belly tightened, muscles braced.

One moved closer. The whole circle narrowed. He ducked, darted between two of them and ran. Soft laughter pursued him, nothing more. He did not stop running.

The Afen gate materialized out of the fog. He pushed the heavy gate inward. He had composed himself by the time he reached the main door. The guards stayed inside on this inclement day, and only looked up from their game, letting him pass,—alert enough, but, Sufaki-wise, careless of formalities. He shrugged the *ctan* back to its conventional position under his right arm and mounted the stairs. Here the guards came smartly to attention: Djan's alien sense of discipline: and they for once made to protest his entry.

He pushed past and opened the door, and one of them then hurried into the room and back into the private section of the apartments, presumably to announce his presence.

He had time enough to pace the floor, returning several times to the great window in the neighboring room. Fog-bound as the city was, he could scarcely make out anything but Haichema-tleke, Maiden Rock, the crag that rose over the harbor, against whose shoulder the Afen and the Great Families' houses were built. Gray and ghostly in a world of pallid white, it seemed the cloud-city's anchor to solid earth.

A door hissed upon the other room and he walked back. Djan was with him. She wore a silver-green suit, thin, body-clinging stuff. Her coppery hair was loose, silken and full of static. She had a morning look about her, satiated and full of sleep.

"It's near noon," he said.

"Ah," she murmured, and looked beyond him to the window. "So we're bound in again. Cursed fog. I hate it.— Like some breakfast?"

"No."

Djan shrugged and from utensils in the carved wood cabinet prepared tea, instantly heated. She offered him a cup: he accepted, nemet-schooled. It gave one something to do with the hands.

"I suppose," she said when they were seated, "that you didn't come here in this weather and wake me out of a sound sleep to wish me good morning."

"I almost didn't make it here; which is the situation I came to talk to you about. The neighborhood of Elas isn't safe even by day. There are Sufaki hanging about, who have no business there."

"The quarantine ordinances were repealed, you know. I can't forbid their being there."

"Are they your men? I'd be relieved if I thought they were. That is,—if yours and Shan t'Tefur's aren't one and the same, and I trust that isn't the case. For a long time it's been at night; since the first of Nermotai, it's been even by day."

"Have they hurt anyone?"

"Not yet. People in the neighborhood stay off the streets. Children don't go out. It's an ugly atmosphere. I don't know whether it's aimed at me in particular or Elas in general, but it's a matter of time before something happens."

"You haven't done anything to provoke this?"

"No. I assure you I haven't. But this is the third day of it. I finally decided to chance it. Are you going to do anything?"

"I'll have my people check it out, and if there's cause I'll have the people removed."

"Well, don't send Shan t'Tefur on the job."

"I said I would see to it. Don't ask favors and then turn sharp with me."

"I beg your pardon. But that's exactly what I'm afraid you'll do,—trust things to him."

"I am not blind, my friend. But you're not the only one with complaints. Shan's life has been threatened. I hear it from both sides."

"By whom?"

"I don't choose to give my sources. But you know the Indras houses and you know the hard-line conservatives. Make your own guess."

"The Indras are not a violent people. If they said it, it was more in the sense of a sober promise than a threat, and that in consideration of the actions he's been urging. You'll have riots in the streets if Shan t'Tefur has his way."

"I doubt it. See, I'm being perfectly honest with you: a bit of trust. Shan uses that apparent recklessness as a tactic; but he is an intelligent man, and his enemies would do well to reckon with that."

"And is he responsible for the late hours you've been keeping?"

Her eyes flashed suddenly, amused. "This morning, you mean?"

"Either you're naive or think he is. That is a dangerous man, Djan."

The humor died out of her eyes. "Well, you're one to talk about the dangers of involvement with the nemet."

"You're facing the danger of a foreign war and you need the goodwill of the Indras Families; but you keep company with a man who talks of killing Indras and burning the fleet."

"Words. If the Indras are concerned, good. I didn't create this situation: I walked into it as it is. I'm trying to hold this city together. There will be no war if it stays together. And it will stay together if the Indras come to their senses and give the Sufaki justice."

"They might, if Shan t'Tefur were out of it. Send him on a long voyage somewhere. If he stays in Nephane and kills someone, which is likely, sooner or later, then you're going to have to apply the law to him without mercy. And that will put you in a difficult position, won't it?"

"Kurt." She put down the cup. "Do you want fighting in this city? Then let's just start dealing like that with both sides, one ultimatum to Shan to get out, one to Nym, to be fair—and there won't be a stone standing in Nephane when the smoke clears."

"Try closing your bedroom to Shan t'Tefur," he said, "for a start. Your credibility among the Families is in rags as long as you're Shan t'Tefur's mistress."

It hurt her. He had thought it could not, and suddenly he perceived she was less armored than he had believed.

"You've given your advice," she said. "Go back to Elas."

"Djan—"

"Out."

"Djan, you talk about the sanctity of local culture, the balance of powers, but you seem to think you can pick and choose the rules you like. In some measure I don't blame Shan t'Tefur. You'll be the death of him before you're done, playing on his ambitions and his pride and then refusing to abide by the customs he knows. You know what you're doing to him? You know what it is to a man of the nemet that you take for a lover and then play politics with him?"

"I told him fairly that he had no claim on me. He chose."

"Do you think a nemet is really capable of believing that? And do you think that he believes now he had no just claim on the Methi's loyalty, whatever he does in your name? He'll push you someday to the point where you have to choose. He's not going to let you have your own way with him forever."

"He knows how things are."

"Then ask yourself why he comes running when you call him to your bed, and if you discover it's not your considerable personal attractions, don't say I didn't warn you. A nemet doesn't take that kind of treatment, not without some compelling reason. If this is your method of controlling the Sufaki, you're picked the wrong man."

"Nevertheless"—her voice acquired a tremor that she tried to suppress—"my mistakes are my choice."

"Will that undo someone's dying?"

"My choice," she insisted, with such intensity that it gave him pause.

"You're not in love with him?" It was question, and plea at once. "You're too sensible for that, Djan. You said yourself this world doesn't give you that choice. You'd kill him or he'd be the death of you sooner or later."

She shrugged, and the old cynical bitterness that he trusted was back." I was conceived to serve the state. Doing so is an unbreakable habit. Other people—like you, my friend, —normal people—serve themselves. Relationships like serving self, serving—others—are outside my experience. I thought I was selfish, but I begin to see there are other dimensions to that word. I find personal relations tedious, these games of me and thee. I enjoy companionship. I—love you. I love Shan. That is not the same as: I love Nephane. This city is mine; it is *mine*. Spare me your appeals to personal affection. I would destroy either of you if I were clearly convinced it was necessary to the survival of this city. Remember that."

"I am sorry for you," he said.

"Get out."

Tears gathered to her eyes, belying everything she had said. She struggled for dignity, lost; the tears spilled free, her lips trembling into sobs. She clenched her jaw, turned her face and gestured for him to go.

"I am sorry," he said, this time with compassion, at which she shook her head and kept her back to him until the spasm had passed.

He took her arms, trying to comfort her, and felt guilty because of Mim; but he felt guilty because of Djan too, and feared that she would not forgive him for witnessing this. She had been here longer, a good deal longer than he. He well knew the nightmare, waking in the night, finding that reality had turned to dreams and the dream itself was as real as the stranger beside him, looking into a face that was not human, perceiving ugliness where a moment before had been beauty.

"I am tired," she said, leaning against him. Her hair smelled of these exotic on this world, lab-born, like Djan—perfumes like home, from a thousand star-scattered worlds the nemet had never dreamed of. "Kurt, I work, I study, I try. I am tired to death."

"I would help you," he said, "if you would let me."

"You have loyalties elsewhere," she said finally. "I wish I'd never sent you to Elas, to learn to be nemet, to belong to them. You want things for your cause, he wants things for his. I know all that, and occasionally I want to forget it. It's a human weakness. Am I not allowed just one? You came here asking favors. I knew you would, sooner or later."

"I would never ask you deceitfully, to do you harm. I owe you, as I owe Elas."

She pushed back from him. "And I hate you most when you do that. Your concern is touching, but I don't trust it."

"Nephane is killing you."

"I can manage."

"Probably you can," he said. "But I would help you."

"Ah, as Shan helps me. But you don't like it when it's the opposition, do you? Blast you, I gave you leave to marry and you've done it, you've made your choice, however tempting it was to—"

She did not finish. He suddenly found reason for uneasiness in that omission. Djan was not one to let words fly carelessly.

"When I came here," he said, "whenever I come, I try to leave my relations with Elas at the door. You've never tried to make me go against them; and I do not use you, Djan."

"Your little Mim," said Djan. "What is she like? Typical nemet?"

"Not typical."

"Elas is using you," she said. "Whether you know it or not, that is so. I could still stop that. I could simply have you given quarters here in the Afen. No arrest decree has Upei review. *That* power of a methi is absolute."

She actually considered it. He went cold inside, realizing that she could and would do it, and knew suddenly that she meant this for petty revenge, taking his peace of mind in retaliation for her humiliation of a moment ago. Pride was important to her.

"Do you want me to ask you not to do that?" he asked.

"No," she said. "If I decide to do that, I will do it, and if I do not, I will not. What you ask has nothing to do with it. But I would advise you and Elas to remain quiet."

XII

The fog did not go out. It held the city the next morning, the faint sound of warning bells drifting up from the harbor. Kurt opened his eyes on the grayness outside the window, then looked toward the foot of the bed where Mim sat combing her long hair, black and silken and falling to her waist when unbound. She looked back at him and smiled, her alien and wonderfully lovely eyes soft with warmth.

"Good morning, my lord."

"Good morning," he murmured.

"The mist is still with us," she said. "Hear the harbor bells?"

"How long can this last?"

"Sometimes many days when the seasons are turning,— especially in the spring." She flicked several strands of hair apart and began with quick fingers to plait them into a thin braid. Then she would sweep most of her hair up to the crown of her head, fasten it with pins and combs, an intricate and fascinating ritual daily performed and nightly undone. He liked watching her. In a matter of moments she began the next braid.

"We say," Mim commented, "that the mist is a cloak of the *imiine*, the sky-sprite Nue, when she comes to visit earth and walk among men. She searches for her beloved, that she lost long ago in the days when godkings ruled. He was a mortal man who offended one of the godkings, a son of Yr whose name was Knyha;—and, poor man, he was slain by Knyha, and his body scattered over all the shore of Nephane so that Nue would not know what had become of him. She still searches and walks the land and the sea and haunts the rivers, especially in the springtime."

"Do you truly think that?" Kurt asked, not sarcastically: one could not be that with Mim. He was prepared to mark it down to be remembered with all his heart if she wished him to.

Mim smiled. "I do not, not truly. But it is a beautiful story, is it not, my lord? There are truths and there are truths, my lord Kta would say, and there is Truth itself, the *yhia*,—and since mortals cannot always reason all the way to Truth, we find little truths that are right enough on our own level. But you are very wise about things. I think you really might know what makes the mist come. Is it a cloud that sits down upon the sea, or is it born in some other way?"

"I think," said Kurt, "that I like Nue best. It sounds better than water vapor."

"You think I am silly and you cannot make me understand."

"Would it make you wiser if you knew where fog comes from?"

"I wish that I could talk to you about all the things that matter to you."

He frowned, realizing that she was in earnest. "You matter. This place, this world matters to me, Mim."

"I know so very little."

"What do you want to know?"

"Everything."

"Well, you owe me breakfast first."

Mim flashed a smile, put in the last combs and finished her hair with a pat. She slipped on the *chatem*, the overdress with the four-paneled split skirt which fitted over the gossamer drapery of the *pelan*, the underdress. The *chatem* high-collared and long-sleeved, tight and restraining in the bodice, —rose and beige brocade, over a rose *pelan*. There were many buttons up either wrist and up the bodice to the collar. She patiently began the series of buttons.

"I will have tea ready by the time you can be downstairs," she said. "I think Aimu will have been—"

There was a deep hollow boom over the city, and Kurt glanced toward the window with an involuntary oath. It was the sighing note of a distant gong.

"*Ai,*" said Mim. "*Intaem-Inta.* That is the great temple. It is the beginning of Cadmisan."

The gong moaned forth again through the fog-stilled air, measured, four times more. Then it was, the last echoes dying.

"It is the fourth of Nermotai," said Mim, "the first of the Sufak holy days. The temple will sound the *Inta* every morning and every evening for the next seven days, and the Sufaki will make prayers and invoke the *Intain,* the spirits of their gods."

"What is done there?" Kurt asked.

"It is the old religion which was here before the Families. I am not really sure what is done, and I do not care to know. I have heard that they even invoke the names of godkings in Phan's own temple; but we do not go there, ever. There were old gods in Chteftikan, old and evil gods from the First Days, and once a year the Sufaki call their names and pay them honor, to appease their anger at losing this land to Phan. These are beings we Indras do not name."

"Bel said," Kurt recalled, "that there could be trouble during the holy days."

Mim frowned. "Kurt, I would that you take special care for your safety, and do not come and go at night during this time."

It hit hard. Mim surely spoke without reference to the Methi, at least without bitterness: if Mim accused, he knew well that Mim would say so plainly. "I do not plan to come and go at night," he said. "Last night—"

"It is always dangerous," she said with perfect dignity, before he would finish, "to walk abroad at night during Cadmisan. The Sufak gods are earth-spirits, Yr-bred and monstrous. There is wild behavior and much drunkenness."

"I will take your advice," he said.

She came and touched her fingers to his lips and to his brow, but she took her hand from him when he reached for it, smiling. It was a game they played.

"I must be downstairs attending my duties," she said. "Dear my husband, you will make me a reputation for a licentious woman in the household if you keep making us late for breakfast.—No!—dear my lord, I shall see you downstairs at morning tea."

*   *   *

"Where do you think you are going?"

Mim paused in the dimly lit entry hall, her hands for a moment suspending the veil over her head as she turned. Then she settled it carefully over her hair and tossed the end over her shoulder.

"To market, my husband."

"Alone?"

She smiled and shrugged. "Unless you wish to fast this evening. I am buying a few things for dinner. Look you, the fog has cleared, the sun is bright, and those men who were hanging about across the street have been gone since yesterday."

"You are not going alone."

"Kurt, Kurt, for Bel's doom-saying? Dear light of heaven, there are children playing outside, do you not hear? And should I fear to walk my own street in bright afternoon? After dark is one thing, but I think you take our warnings much too seriously."

"I have my reasons, Mim."

She looked up at him in most labored patience. "And shall we starve? Or will you and my lord Kta march me to market with drawn weapons?"

"No, but I will walk you there and back again." He opened the door for her, and Mim went out and waited for him, her basket on her arm, most obviously embarrassed.

Kurt nervously scanned the street, the recesses where of nights t'Tefur's men were wont to linger. They were indeed gone. Indras children played at tag. There was no threat—no presence of the Methi's guards either, but Djan never did move obviously: he had no difficulty returning to Elas late, probably, he thought with relief, she had taken measures.

"Are you sure," he asked Mim, "that the market will be open on a holiday?"

She looked up at him curiously as they started off together. "Of course, and busy. I put off going, you see, these several days with the fog and the trouble on the streets, and I am sorry to cause you this trouble, Kurt, but we really are running out of things and there could be the fog again tomorrow, so it is really better to go today. I have some sense, after all."

"You know I could quite easily walk down there and buy what you need for supper, and you would not need to go at all."

"*Ai*, but Cadmisan is such a grand time in the market, with all the country people coming in, and the artists, and the musicians—besides," she added, when his face remained unhappy, "dear husband, you would not know what you were buying or what to pay. I do not think you have ever handled our coin. And the other women would laugh at me and wonder what kind of wife I am to make my husband do my work, or else they would think I am such a loose woman that my husband would not trust me out of his sight."

"They can mind their own business," he said, disregarding her attempt at levity; and her small face took on a determined look.

"If you go alone," she said, "the fact is that folk will guess Elas is afraid, and this will lend courage to the enemies of Elas."

He understood her reasoning, though it comforted him not at all. He watched carefully as their downhill walk began to take them out of the small section of aristocratic houses surrounding the Afen and the temple complex. But here in the Sufaki section of town, people were going about business as usual. There were some men in the Robes of Color, but they walked together in casual fashion and gave them not a passing glance.

"You see," said Mim, "I would have been quite safe."

"I wish I was that confident."

"Look you, Kurt, I know these people. There is lady Yafes, and that little boy is Edu t'Rachik u Gyon—the Rachik house is very large. They have so many children it is a joke in Nephane. The old man on the curb is t'Pamchen. He fancies himself a scholar. He says he is reviving the old Sufak writing and that he can read the ancient stones. His brother is a priest, but he does not approve of the old man. There is no harm in these people. They are my neighbors. You let t'Tefur's little band of pirates trouble you too much. T'Tefur would be delighted to know he upset you. That is the only victory he dares to seek as long as you give him no opportunity to challenge you."

"I suppose," Kurt said, unconvinced.

The street approached the lower town by a series of low steps down a winding course to the defense wall and the gate. Thereafter the road went among the poorer houses, the markets, the harborside. Several ships were in port, two broad-beamed merchant vessels and three sleek galleys, warships with oars run in or stripped from their locks, yards without sails, the sounds of carpentry coming loudly from their decks, one showing bright new wood on her hull.

Ships were being prepared against the eventuality of war. *Tavi*, Kta's ship, had been there; she had had her refitting and had been withdrawn to the outer harbor, a little bay on the other side of Haichema-tleke. That reminder of international unease, the steady hammering and sawing, underlay all the gaiety of the crowds that thronged the market.

"That is a ship of Ilev, is it not?" Kurt asked, pointing to the merchantman nearest, for he saw what appeared to be the white bird that was emblematic of that house as the figurehead.

"Yes," said Mim. "But the one beside it I do not recognize. Some houses exist only in the Isles. Lord Kta knows them all, even the houses of Indresul's many colonies. A captain must know these things. But of course they do not come to Nephane. This one must be a trader that rarely comes, perhaps from the north, near the Yvorst Ome, where the seas are ice."

The crowd was elbow-to-elbow among the booths. They lost sight of the harbor, and nearly of each other. Kurt seized Mim's arm, which she protested with a shocked look: even husband and wife did not touch publicly.

"Stay with me," he said, but he let her go. "Do not leave my sight."

Mim walked the maze of aisles a little in front of him, occasionally pausing to admire some gimcrack display of the tinsmiths, intrigued by the little fish of jointed scales that wiggled when the wind hit their fins.

"We did not come for this," Kurt said irritably. "Come, what would you do with such a thing?"

Mim sighed, a little piqued, and led him to that quarter of the market where the farmers were, countrymen with produce and cheeses and birds to sell, fishermen with the take from their nets, butchers with their booths decorated with whole carcasses hanging from hooks.

Mim deplored the poor quality of the fish that day, disappointed in her plans—selected from a vegetable seller some curious yellow corkscrews called *lat,* and some speckled orange ones called *gillybai.* She knew the vegetable seller's wife, who congratulated her on her recent marriage, marveled embarrassingly over Kurt—she seemed to shudder slightly, but showed brave politeness—then became involved in a long story about mutual acquaintance's daughter's child.

It was woman's talk. Kurt stood to one side, forgotten, and then, sure that Mim was safe among people she knew and not willing to seem utterly the tyrant,—withdrew a little. He looked at some of the other tables in the next booth, somewhat interested in the alien variety of the fish and the produce—some of which, he reflected with unease, he had undoubtedly eaten without knowing its uncooked appearance. Much of the seafood was not in the least appealing to Terran senses.

From the harbor there came the steady sound of hammering, reechoing off the walls in insane counterpoint to the noise of the many colored crowds.

Someone jostled him. He looked up into the unsmiling face of a Sufaki in Robes of Color. The man said nothing. Kurt made a slight bow of apology, unanswered, and turned about to go after Mim.

Another man blocked his way. Kurt tried to step around him. The Sufaki moved in front of him with sullen threat in his narrow eyes. Another appeared to his left, crowding him back to the right.

He moved suddenly, trying to slip past them. They cut him off from Mim. He could not see her any longer. The noisy crowds surged between. He dared not start something with Mim near, where she could be hurt.

They forced him continually in one direction, toward a gap between the booths where they jammed up against a warehouse. He saw the alley and broke for it.

Others met him at the turning ahead, pursuit hot behind. He had expected it and hit the opposition without hesitation. He avoided a knife and kicked its owner, who screamed in agony,—struck another in the face and a third in the groin before those behind overhauled him.

A blow landed between his shoulders and against his head, half blinding him. He fell under a weight of struggling bodies, pinned while more than one of them wrenched his arms back and tied his wrists.

He had broken one man's arm. He saw that with satisfaction as they hauled him to his feet and tried to aid their own injured.

Then they seized him by either arm and hurried him deeper into the alley.

The backways of Nephane were a maze of alien geometry, odd-shaped buildings jammed incredibly into the S-curve of the main street, fronting outward in decent order while their rear portions formed a labyrinthine tangle of narrow alleyways and contiguous walls. Kurt quickly lost track of the way they had come.

They reached the back door of a warehouse, thrust Kurt inside and entered the dark with him, closing the door so that all the light was from the little door aperture.

Kurt scrambled to escape into the shadows, sure now that he would be found some time later with his throat cut and no proof who his murderers had been.

They seized him before he could run more than a few steps, hurried him to the dusty floor and slipped a cord about his ankle. Finally, despite his kicking and heaving, they succeeded in lashing both his ankles together. Then they forced his jaws apart and thrust a choking wad of cloth into his mouth, tying it in place with a violence that cut his face.

"Get a light," one said.

The door opened before that was done. Their comrades had joined them, bringing the man with the broken arm. When the light was lit they attended to the setting of the arm, with screams they tried to muffle.

Kurt wriggled over against some bales of canvas, nerves raw to every outcry from the injured man. They would repay him for that, he was sure, before they disposed of him.

It was the human thing to do. In this respect he hoped they were different.

*   *   *

Hours passed. The injured man slept, after a drink they had given him. Kurt occupied himself with trying to work the knots loose. They were not fully within his reach. He tried instead to stretch the cords. His fingers swelled and passed the point of pain. The ache spread up his arms. His feet were numb. Breathing was an effort.

At least they did not touch him. They played at *bho,* a game of lots, and sat in the light, an unreal tableau suspended in the growing blackness. The light picked out only the edges of bales and crates.

From the distance of the hill came the deep tones of the *Intaem-Inta.* The gamers stopped, reverent of it, continued.

Outside Kurt heard the faint scuff of sandalled feet on stone. His hopes rose. He thought of Kta, searching for him.

Instead there came a bold rap on the door. The men admitted the newcomers, one in Indras dress, the others in Robes of Color; they wore daggers in their belts.

One was a man who had watched outside Elas.

"We will see to him now," the Indras-dressed one said, a small man with eyes so narrow he could only be Sufaki. "Put him on his feet."

Two men hauled Kurt up, cut the cords that bound his ankles. He could not stand without them holding him. They shook him and struck him to make him try, but when it was evident that he truly could not stand, they took him each by an arm and pulled him along with them in great haste, out into the mist and the dark, along the confusing turns of the alleys.

They tended constantly downhill, and Kurt was increasingly sure of their destination: the bay's dark waters would conceal his body with no evidence to accuse the Sufaki of his murder, no one to hear how he had vanished—no one but Mim, who might well be able to identify them.

That was the thought which most tormented him. Elas should have been turning Nephane upside down by now, if only Mim had reached them. But there was no indication of a search.

They turned a corner, cutting off the light from the lantern-carrier in front of them, which moved like a witchlight in the mist. The other two men were half carrying him. Though he had feeling in his feet again, he made it no easier for them.

They made haste to overtake the man with the lantern, and cursed him for his haste. At the same time they jerked cruelly on Kurt's arms, trying to force him to carry his own weight.

And suddenly he shouldered left, where steps led down into a doorway, toppling one of his guards with a startled cry. With the other one he pivoted, unable to free himself, held by the front of his robe and one arm.

Kurt jerked. Cloth tore. He hurled all his weight into a kick at the lantern-bearer.

The man sprawled, oil spilling, live flame springing up. The burned man screamed, snatching at his clothing, trying to strip it off. His friend's grip loosened, knife flashing in the glare. He rammed it for Kurt's belly.

Kurt spun, received the edge across his ribs instead, tore free, kneed the man as the burning man's flames reached something else flammable in the debris of the alley.

He was free. He pivoted and ran, in the mist and the dark that now was scented with the stench of burned flesh and fiber.

It was several turns of the alleys later when he first dared stop, and leaned against the wall close to fainting for want of air, for the gag obstructed his breathing.

At last, as quietly as possible, he knelt against the back steps of a warehouse, contorted his body so that he could use his fingers to search the debris in the corner. There was broken pottery in the heap: he found a shard keen-edged enough, leaned against the step with his heart pounding from exertion and his ears straining to hear despite the blood that roared in his head.

It took a long time to make any cut in the tight cords. At last a strand parted, and another, and he was able to unwind the rest. With deadened hands he rubbed the binding from the gag and spit the choking cloth from his mouth, able to breathe a welcome gasp of the chill foggy air.

Now he could move, and in the concealment of the night and the fog he had a chance. His way lay uphill—he had no choice in that. The gate would be the logical place for his enemies to lay their ambush. It was the only way through the defense wall that ringed the upper town.

When he reached the wall, he was greatly relieved. It was not difficult to find a place where illicit debris had piled up against the ancient fortification. Sheds and buildings proliferated here, crowding into narrow gap between the permitted buildings and the former defense of the high town. He scrambled by the roofs of three of them up to the crest and found the situation unhappily tidier on the other side. He walked the wall, dreading the jump; and in a place where the erosion of centuries had lessened the height perhaps five feet, he lowered himself over the edge and dropped a dizzying distance to the ground on the high town side.

The jolt did not knock him entirely unconscious, but it dazed him and left him scarcely able to crawl the little distance into the shadows. It was a time before he had recovered sufficiently to try to walk again, at times losing clear realization of how he had reached a particular place.

He reached the main street. It was deserted. Kurt took to it only as often as he must, finally broke into a run as he saw the door of Osanef. He darted into the friendly shadow of its porch.

No one answered. Light came through the fog indistinctly on the upper hill, a suffused glow from the temple or the Afen. He remembered the festival, and decided even Indras-influenced Osanef might be at the temple.

He took to the street running now, two blocks from Elas and trusting to speed, not daring even the other Indras houses. They had no love of humans; Kta had warned him so.

He was in the final sprint for Elas' door before he realized Elas might be watched, would logically be watched unless the Methi's guards were about. It was too late to stop. He reached its triangular arch and pounded furiously on the door, not even daring to look over his shoulder.

"Who is there?" Hef's voice asked faintly.

"Kurt. Let me in. Let me in, Hef."

The bolt shot back, the door opened, and Kurt slipped inside and leaned against the closed door, gasping for breath in the sudden warmth and light of Elas.

"Mim," said Hef. "Lord Kurt, what has happened? Where is Mim?"

"Not—not here?"

"No. We thought at least—whatever had happened—you were together."

Kurt caught his breath with a choking swallow of air and pushed himself square on his feet. "Call Kta."

"He is out with Ian t'Ilev and Val t'Ran, searching for you both. *Ai*, my lord, what can we do? I will call Nym—"

"Tell Nym—tell Nym I have gone to get the Methi's help. Give me a weapon,—anything—"

"I cannot, my lord, I cannot. My orders forbid—"

Kurt swore and jerked the door open again, ran for the street and the Afen gate.

When he reached the Afen wall, the great gates were closed and the wall-street that led to the temple compound was crowded with Sufaki—drunken, most of them. Kurt leaned on the bars and shouted for the guards to hear him and open them, but his voice was lost in the noise of the crowds, with all Sufak Nephane gathered into that square down the street and spilling over into the wall-street. Some, drunker than the rest, began also to shake at the bars of the gates to try to raise the guards. If there were any on duty to hear, they ignored the uproar.

Kurt caught his breath, exhausted, far from help of Kta or Djan. Then he remembered the other gate, the sally port in the far end of the wall where it touched Haichema-tleke, and opened onto the temple square. That would be the one for them to guard, that nearest the temple. They might hear him there, and open.

He raced along the wall, jostling Sufaki in his exhausted weaving and stumbling. A few drunk ones laughed and caught at his clothing. Others cursed him, trying to bar his way.

A cry began to go up, resentment for his presence. *Jafikn*-wearing Sufaki barred his path, turned him. Someone struck him from the side, nearly throwing him to the pavement.

He ran, but they would not let him escape the square, blocking his way out,—t'Tefur's men, armed with blades.

Authority, he thought, sensible authority would not let this happen. He broke to one side, racing for the temple steps, sending shrieking women and cursing men crowding out of his way.

Hands reached to stop him. He tore past them almost all the way to the very top of the long temple steps before enough of them seized him to hold him.

"Elas' doing!" a hysterical voice shrieked from below. "Kill the human!"

Kurt struggled around to see who had shouted, looked down on a sea of alien faces in the torchlight and the haze of thin mist. "Where is Shan t'Tefur?" Kurt screamed back at them. "Where has he taken my wife?"

The babble of voices almost hushed for a moment: the nemet held their women in great esteem. Kurt drew a great gasp of air and shouted across the gathering. "Shan t'Tefur! If you are here, come out and face me. Where is my wife? What have you done with her?"

There was a moment of shocked silence and then a rising murmur like thunder as an aged priest came from the upper steps through the men gathered there. He cleared the way with the emblem of his office, a vine-wreathed staff. The staff extended till it was almost touching Kurt, and the priest spat some unintelligible words at him.

There was utter silence now, drunken laughter coming distantly from the wall—street. In this gathering no one so much as stirred. Even Kurt was struck to silence,—the staff extended a degree further and with unreasoning loathing he shrank from it, not wanting to be touched by this mouthing priest with his drunken gods of earth. They held him, and the rough wood of the staff's tip trembled against his cheek.

"Blasphemer," said the priest, "sent by Elas to profane the rites. Liar. Cursed from the earth you will be, by the old gods, the ancient gods, the life-giving sons of Thael. Son of Yr to Phan united, Aem-descended, to the gods of ancient Chteftik,—cursed!"

"A curse on the lot of you," Kurt shouted in his face, "if you have any part in t'Tefur's plot! My wife Mim never harmed any of you, never harmed anyone. Where is she? You people,—you! that were in the market today—that walked away—Are you all in this? What did they do with her? Where did they take her?—Is she alive? By your own gods you can tell me that at least. Is she alive?"

"No one knows anything of the woman, human," said the aged priest. "And you were ill-advised to come here with your drunken ravings. Who would harm Mim h'Elas, a daughter of Sufak herself? You come here and profane the mysteries—taught no reverence in Elas, it is clear. Cursed be you, human, and if you do not leave now, we will wash the pollution of your feet from these stones with your blood. —Let him go, let go the human, and give him the chance to leave."

They released him, and Kurt swayed on the steps above the crowd, scanning the faces for one that was familiar. Of Osanef, of any friend, there was no sign. He looked back at the priest.

"She is lost in the city, hurt or dead," Kurt pleaded. "You are a religious man.—Do something!"

For a moment pity or conscience almost touched the stern old face. The cracked lips quavered on some answer. There was a hush over the crowd.

"It is Indras' doing!" a male voice shouted. "Elas is looking for some offense against the Sufaki—and now they try to create one! The human is Elas' creature!"

Kurt whirled about, saw a familiar face for the first time.

"He is one of them!" Kurt shouted. "That is one of the men who was in the market when my wife was taken. They tried to kill me and they have my wife—"

"Liar," shouted another man. "Ver has been at the temple since the ringing of the *Inta*. I saw him myself. The human is trying to accuse an innocent man."

"Kill him!" someone else shouted, and others throughout the crowd took up the cry, surging forward, young men, wearing the Robes of Color. T'Tefur's men.

"No," cried the old priest, pounding his staff for attention. "No, take him out of here, take him far from the temple precincts."

Kurt backed away as men swarmed about him, nearly crushed in the press, jerked bodily off his feet, limbs strained as they passed him off the steps and down into the crowd.

He fought, gasping for breath and trying to free hands or even a foot to defend himself as he was borne across the courtyard toward the wall-street.

And the gate was open, and men of the Methi's guard

were there, dimly outlined in the mist and the flaring torches, but about them was the flash of metal, and bronze helmets glittered under the murky firelight, ominous and warlike.

"Give him to us," said their leader.

"Traitors," cried one to the young men.

"Give him to us," the officer repeated. It was t'Senife.

In anger they flung Kurt at the guardsmen, threw him sprawling on the stones, and the guards in their haste were no more gentle, snatching him up again, half dragging him through the sally port into the Afen grounds.

Hysterical outcries came from the crowd as they closed the door, barring the multitude outside. Something heavy struck the door, a barrage of missiles like the patter of hail for a moment. The shrieking rose and died away.

The Methi's guard gathered him up, hauling his bruised arms, pulling him along with them until they were sure that he would walk as rapidly as they.

They took him by the back stairs and up.

XIII

"Sit down," Djan snapped.

Kurt let himself into the nearest chair, although Djan continued to stand. She looked over his head toward the guards who waited.

"Are things under control?"

"They would not enter the Afen grounds."

"Wake the day guard. Double watch on every post, especially the sally port. T'Lised, bring h'Elas here."

Kurt glanced up. "Mim—"

"Yes, Mim." Djan dismissed the guard with a wave of her hand and swept her silk and brocade skirts aside to take a chair. No flicker of sympathy touched her face as Kurt lifted a shaking hand to wipe his face and tried to collect his shattered nerves.

"Is she all right?" he asked.

"She will mend. Nym reported you missing when you failed to return; my men found her wandering the dock. I couldn't get sense out of her; she kept demanding to go to Elas, until I finally got through to her the fact that you were missing too. Then Kta came here saying you'd come back to Elas and then left again to find me; he was able to pass the gate in company with some of my men or I doubt he'd have made it through, given the mood of the people out there. So I sent Kta home again under guard and told him to wait there,—and I hope he did. After the riot you created in the temple square, finding you was simple."

Kurt bowed his head, glad enough to know Mim was safe, too tired to argue.

"Do you even remotely realize what trouble you caused? My men are in danger of being killed out there because of you."

"I'm sorry."

"What happened to you?"

"T'Tefur's men hauled me out of the market, held me in some warehouse until dark and took me out—I suppose to dispose of me in the harbor. I escaped. I—may have killed one or two of them."

Djan swore under her breath. "What else?"

"Those who were taking me from the temple, if your men recognized them—one was in the market. T'Tefur's men. One was a man I told you used to watch Elas—"

"Shall I call Shan here? If you repeat those things to his face—"

"I'll kill him."

"You will do nothing of the sort," Djan shouted, suddenly at the end of per patience. "You caused me trouble enough, you and your precious little native wife. I know well enough your stubbornness, but I promise you this: if you cause me any more trouble, I'll hold you and all Elas directly responsible."

"What am I supposed to do, wait for the next time? Is my wife going to have to go into hiding for fear of them and I not be able to do anything or lay a hand on the men I know are responsible?"

"You chose to live here, you begged me for the privilege, and you chose all the problems of living in a nemet house and having a nemet wife. Now enjoy it."

"I'm asking you to do something."

"And I'm telling you I've had enough problems from you. You're becoming a liability to me."

The door opened cautiously and Mim entered the room, stood transfixed as Kurt rose to his feet. Her face dissolved in tears and for a moment she did not move. Then she cast herself to her knees and fell upon her face before Djan.

Kurt went to her and drew her into his arms, smoothing her disordered hair, and she turned her face against him and wept. Her dress was torn open, buttons ripped to the waist, the *pelan* soiled with mud from the streets and with blood.

"You'd better do something," Kurt said, looking across at Djan. "Because if I meet any of them after this I'll kill them."

"If you doubt I'll do what I said, you're mistaken."

"What kind of place is this when this can happen to her? What do I owe your law when this can happen and they can get away with it?"

"H'Elas," said Djan, ignoring him, "have you remembered who did this to you?"

"Please," said Mim, "do not shame my husband."

"You husband has eyes to see what happened to you. He is threatening to take matters into his own hands,—which will be unfortunate for Elas if he does, and for him too. So you had better find it convenient to remember, h'Elas."

"Methi,—I—only remember what I told you. They kept me wrapped in—in someone's cloak, I think, and I could hardly breathe. I saw no faces—and I remember—I remember being moved, and I tried to escape, but they—hit me—they—"

"Let be," Kurt said, holding her. "Let be, Djan."

"How long have you lived in Nephane, h'Elas?"

"F-four years, Methi."

"And never heard those voices, never saw a face you knew, even at the beginning?"

"No, Methi. Perhaps—perhaps they were from the country."

"Where were you held?"

"I do not know, Methi. I cannot remember clearly. It was dark,—a building, dark,—and I could not see. I do not know."

"They were t'Tefur's men," said Kurt. "Let her alone."

"There are more radical men than Shan t'Tefur, those who aim at creating complete havoc here—and you just gave them all the ammunition they need, killing two of them, defiling the temple."

"Let them come out into the open and accuse me. I don't think they're the kind. Or if they try me again,—"

"I've warned you, Kurt, in as plain words as I can use. Do *nothing*."

"I'll do what's necessary to protect my wife."

"Don't try me. Don't think your life or hers means more to me than this city."

"Next time," said Kurt, holding Mim tightly to his side, "I'm going to be armed. If you don't intend to afford me the protection of the law, then I'll take care of the matter, public or private, fair or foul."

"My lord," pleaded Mim, "please, please, do not quarrel with her."

"You'd better listen to her," said Djan. "Women have survived the like for thousands of years. She will. Honor's cold comfort for being dead, as the practicalities of the Tamur surely taught—"

"She understands!" Kurt cried, hugging Mim to him, and Djan silenced herself quickly. Mim trembled. Her hands were cold in his.

"You have leave to go, h'Elas," said Djan.

"I'll see her home," said Kurt.

"*You're* going nowhere tonight," Djan said, and shouted in Nechai for the guard, who appeared almost instantly, expecting orders.

"I'll take her home," Kurt repeated, "and I'll come back if you insist on it."

"No," said Djan. "I made a mistake ever putting you in Elas, and I warned you. As of this moment you're staying in the Afen, and it's going to take more than Kta's persuasions to change my mind on that. You've created a division in this city that words won't settle, and my patience is over, Kurt. —T'Udein, see h'Elas home."

"You'll have to use more than an order to keep me here," said Kurt.

Mim put her hand on his arm and looked up at him. "Please, no, no, I will go home. I am so very tired. I hurt, my lord. Please let me go home, and do not quarrel with the Methi for my sake. She is right: it is not safe for you or for Elas. It will never be safe for you. I do not want you to have any grief for my sake."

Kurt bent and touched his lips to her brow. "I'm coming home tonight, Mim. She only thinks otherwise. Go with t'Udein, then, and tell your father to keep that door locked."

"Yes, my lord Kurt," she said softly, her hands slipping

from his. "Do not be concerned for me. Do not be concerned."

She bowed once to the Methi, but Djan snapped her fingers when she would have made the full obeisance, dismissing her. Kurt waited until the door was securely closed, then fixed his eyes on Djan, trembling so with rage he did not trust himself.

"If you ever use words like that to my wife again—"

"She has more sense than you do. *She* would not have a war fought over her offended pride."

"You held her without so much as a word to Elas—"

"I sent word back when Kta came, and if you had stayed where you belonged, the matter would have been quietly and efficiently settled. Now I have to think of other matters besides your convenience and your feelings."

"Saving t'Tefur, you mean."

"Saving this city from the bloodbath you nearly started tonight. My men had rocks thrown at them—at a methi's guards! If they'll do that, they'll cut throats next."

"Ask your guards who those men were. Or are you afraid they'll tell you?"

"There are a lot of charges flying in the wind tonight, none of them substantiated."

"I'll substantiate them—before the Upei."

"Oh, no, you won't. You bring up that charge in the Upei and there are things about many people,—your little ex-slave wife included—that are going to be brought up too, dragged through public hearing under oath. When you start invoking the law, friend, the law keeps moving until the whole truth is out, and a case like that right now would tear Nephane apart. I won't stand for it. Your wife would suffer most of all, and I think she has come to understand that very clearly."

"You threatened her with that?"

"I explained things to her. I did not threaten. Those fellows won't admit to your charges, no, they'll have counterclaims that won't be pretty to hear. Mim's honor and Mim's history will be in question, and the fact that she went from the Tamurlin to a human marriage won't be to her credit or that of Elas. And believe me, I'd throw her or you to the Sufaki if it had to be done, so don't push me any further."

"T'Tefur's city isn't worth saving."

"Where do you think you're going?"

He had started for the door. He stopped and faced her. "I'm going to Elas, to my wife. When I'm sure she's all right, I'll come back and we can settle matters. But unless you want more people hurt or killed, you'd better give me an escort to get there."

She stared at him. He had never seen her angrier; but perhaps she could read on his face what he felt at the moment. Her expression grew calmer, guarded.

"Until morning," she said. "Make your peace there. My men will get you safely to Elas, but I am not sending them through the streets with you twice in one night, dragging you past the Sufaki like a lure to violence. So stay there till morning. And if you cause me more trouble tonight, Kurt, so help me you'll regret it."

Kurt pushed open the heavy door of Elas, taking it out of Hef's hands, closed it quickly upon the Methi's guards, then turned to Hef.

"Mim," said Kurt. "She is here, she is safe?"

Hef bowed. "Yes, my lord,—not a few moments ago she came in, also with the Methi's guard. I beg my lord, what—"

Kurt ignored his questions, hurried past him to the *rhmei* and found it empty, left it and raced upstairs to their room.

There was no light there but the *phusa*. That light drew his eyes as he opened the door, and before it knelt Mim. He let his breath go in a long sign of relief, slid to his knees and took her by the shoulders.

Her head fell back against him, her lips parted in shock, her face filmed with perspiration. Then he saw her hands at her heart and the dark wet stain on them.

"No," he cried, a shriek, and caught her as she slid aside, her hands slipping from the hilt of the dragon blade that was deep in her breast. She was not dead; the outrage of the metal in her flesh still moved with her shallow breathing, and he could not nerve himself to touch it. He pressed his lips to her cheek and heard the gentle intake of her breath. Her brows knit in pain and relaxed. Her eyes held a curious, childlike wonder.

"*Ei,* my lord," he heard her breathe.

And the breath passed softly from her lips and the light from her eyes. Mim was a weight, suddenly heavy, and he gave a strangled sob and held her against him, folded tightly into his arms.

Quick footsteps pounded up the stairs, and he knew it was Kta. The Nemet stopped in the doorway, and Kurt turned his tear-stained face toward him.

"*Ai*, light of heaven," Kta whispered.

Kurt let Mim very gently to the floor, closed her eyes and carefully drew forth the blade. He knew it then for the one he had once stolen and Mim had taken back. He held the thing in his hand like a living enemy, his whole arm trembling.

"Kurt!" Kta exclaimed, rushing to him. "Kurt, no! Give it to me. Give it to me."

Kurt staggered to his feet with the blade still in his hand, and Kta's hazy form wavered before him, hand outstretched in pleading. His eyes cleared. He looked down at Mim.

"Kurt, please, I beg you."

Kurt clenched his fingers once more on the hilt. "I have business," he said, "at the Afen."

"Then you must kill me to pass," said Kta, "because you will kill Elas if you attack the Methi, and I will not let you go."

Kta's family: Kurt saw the love and the fear in the nemet's eyes and could not blame him. Kta would try to stop him; he believed it, and he looked down at the blade, deprived of revenge, lacking the courage or the will or whatever impulse Mim had had to drive it to her heart.

"Kurt." Kta took his hand and pried the blade from his fingers. Nym was in the shadows behind him,—Nym, and Aimu and Hef—Hef weeping, unobtrusive even in his grief. Things were suspended in unreality.

"Come," Kta was saying gently, "come away."

"Don't touch her."

"We will take her down to the *rhmei*," said Kta. "Come, my friend, come."

Kurt shook his head, recovering himself a little. "I will carry her," he said. "She is my wife, Kta."

Kta let him go then, and Kurt knelt down and gathered up Mim's yielding form into his arms. She did not feel right any longer. It was not like Mim—loose, like a broken doll.

Silently the family gathered in the *rhmei*: Ptas and Nyn, Aimu and Kta and Hef, and Kurt laid down his burden at Ptas' feet. Ptas wept for her, and folded Mim's hands upon her breast. There was nothing heard in the *rhmei* but the sound of weeping, of the women and of Hef. Kurt could not shed more tears. When he looked into the face of Nym he met a grim and terrible anger.

"Who brought her to this?" asked Nym, so that Kurt trembled under the weight of his own guilt.

"I could not protect her," Kurt said. "I could not help her." He looked down at her, drew a shaken breath. "The Methi drove her to this."

Nym looked at him sorrowfully, then turned and walked to the light of the hearthfire. For a moment the lord of Elas stood with head bowed and then looked up, lifted his arms before the holy fire, a dark and powerful shadow before its golden light.

"Our Ancestors," he prayed, "received this soul, not born of our kindred; spirits of our Ancestors, receive her, Mim h'Elas. Take her gently among you, one with us, as birth-sharing, loving, beloved. Peace was upon her heart, this child of Elas, daughter of Minas, of Indras, of the far-shining city."

"Spirits of Elas," prayed Kta, holding his hands also toward the fire, "our Ancestors, wake and behold us. Guardians of Elas, see us, this wrong done against us; swift to vengeance, our Ancestors, wake and behold us."

Kurt looked on, lost, unable even to mourn for her as they mourned, alien even in the moment of her dying. And he watched as Ptas took from Kta's hands the dragon blade. She bent over Mim with that, and this was beyond bearing. Kurt cried out, but Ptas severed only a lock of Mim's dark hair and cast it into the blaze of the holy fire.

Aimu sobbed audibly. Kurt could take no more. He turned suddenly and fled the hall, out into the entryway.

"It is done." Kta knelt where he found him, crouched in the corner of the entry against the door. He set his hand on Kurt's shoulder. "It is over now. We will put her to rest. Will you wish to be present?"

Kurt shuddered and turned his face toward the wall. "I

can't," he said, lapsing into his native tongue. "I can't. I loved her, Kta. I can't go."

"Then we will care for her, my friend. We will care for her."

"I *loved* her," he insisted, and felt the pressure of Kta's fingers on his shoulder.

"Is there—some rite you would wish? Surely—surely our Ancestors would find no wrong in that."

"What could she have to do with my people?" Kurt swallowed painfully and shook his head. "Do it the way she would understand."

Kta arose and started to leave, then knelt again. "My friend,—come to my room first. I will give you something that will make you sleep."

"No," he said. "Leave me alone. Leave me."

"I am afraid for you."

"Take care of her. Do that for me."

Kta hesitated, then rose again and withdrew on silent feet.

Kurt sat listening for a moment. The family left the *rhmei* by the left-hand hall, their steps dying away into the far places of the house. Kurt rose then and opened the door quietly, shutting it quietly behind him in such a way that the inner bar fell into place.

The streets were deserted, as they had been since the Methi's guards had taken their places at the wall-street. He walked not toward the Afen, but downward, toward the harbor.

XIV

Daylight was finally beginning to break through the mists, lightening everything to gray, and there was the first stirring of wind that would disperse the fog.

Kurt skirted the outermost defense wall of Nephane, the rocking, skeletal outlines of ships ghostly in the gray dawn. No one watched this end of the harbor, where the ancient walls curved against Haichema-tleke's downslope, where the hill finally reached the water, where the walls towered sixty feet or more into the mist.

Here the city ended and the countryside began. A dirt track ran south, rutted with the wheels of hand-pulled carts, mired, thanks to the recent rains. Kurt ran beside the road and left it, heading across country.

He could not think clearly yet where he was bound. Elas was closed to him. If he set eyes on Djan or t'Tefur now he would kill them, with ruin to Elas. He ran, hoping only that it was t'Tefur who would pursue him, out beyond witnesses and law.

It would not bring back Mim. Mim was buried by now, cold in the earth. He could not imagine it, could not accept it, but it was true.

He was weary of tears. He ran, pushing himself to the point of collapse, until that pain was more than the pain for Mim, and exhaustion tumbled him into the wet grass all but senseless.

When he began to think again, his mind was curiously clear. He realized for the first time that he was bleeding from an open wound—had been all night, since the assassin's blade had passed his ribs. It began to hurt. He found it ot deep, but as long as his hand. He had no means to bandage it. The bleeding was not something he would die of. His bruises were more painful: his cord-cut wrists and ankles hurt to bend. He was almost relieved to feel these things, to exchange these miseries for the deep one of Mim's loss, which had no limit. He put Mim away in his mind, rose up and began to walk again, steps weaving at first, steadier as he chose his direction.

He wanted nothing to do with the villages. He avoided the dirt track that sometimes crossed his way. As the day wore on and the warmth increased he walked more surely, choosing his southerly course by the sun.

Sometimes he crossed cultivated fields, where the crops were only now sprouting, and the earliest trees were in bloom and not yet fruited. Root-crops like *stas* were stored away in the safety of barns, not to be had in the fields.

By twilight he was feeling faint with hunger, for he had not eaten—he reckoned back to breakfast a day ago. He did not know the land, dared not try the wild plants. He knew then that he must think of stealing or starve to death, and he was sorry for that, because the country folk were generally both decent and poor.

The bitter thought occurred to him that among the innocent of this world his presence had brought nothing but grief. It was only his enemies that he could never harm.

Mim stayed with him. He could not so much as look at the stars overhead without hearing the names she gave them: Ysime the pole star, mother of the north wind; blue Lineth, the star that heralded the spring, sister of Phan. His grief had settled into a quieter misery, one with everything.

In the dark, there came to his nostrils the scent of woodsmoke, borne on the northwest wind.

He turned toward it, smelled other things as he drew nearer, animal scents and the delicious aroma of cooking. He crept silently, carefully toward the fold of hills that concealed the place.

There was no house, but a campfire tended by two men and a youth, country folk, keepers of flocks, *cachiren*. He heard the soft calling of their wool-bearing animals from somewhere beyond a brush barricade on the other side of the fire.

A snarled warning cut the night. The shaggy *tilof* that guarded the *cachin* lifted its head, his hackles rising, alerting the *cachiren*, they who scrambled up, weapons in hand, and the beast raced for the intruder.

Kurt fled, seeking a pile of rock that had tumbled from the hillside, and tried to find a place of refuge. The beast's teeth seized his ankle, tore as he jerked free and scrambled higher.

"Come down!" shouted the youth, spear poised for the throwing. "Come down from there."

"Hold the creature off," Kurt shouted back. "I will gladly come down if you will only call him off."

Two of them kept spears aimed at him, while the youth went higher and dragged the snarling and spitting guard-beast down again by his shaggy ruff.

Kurt clambered down gingerly and spoke to them gently and courteously, for they prodded him with their spears, forcing him in the direction of the firelight, and he feared what they would do when they saw his human face.

When he reached the light he kept his head down, and knelt by the fireside and sat back on his heels in an at-home posture. The keen point of a spearblade touched beneath his shoulder. The other two men circled to the front to look him over.

"Human," one exclaimed, and point the point pressed deeper and made him wince.

"Where are the rest of you?" the white-haired elder asked.

"I am not Tamurlin," said Kurt, and I am alone. I beg you, I need food. I am of the Methi's people."

"He is lying," said the boy behind him.

"He might be," said the elder, "but he talks manlike."

"You do not need to give me hospitality," said Kurt, for the sharing of bread and fire created a religious bond forever unless otherwise agreed upon from the beginning. "But I do ask you for food and drink. It is the second day since I have eaten."

"Where did you come from?" asked the elder.

"From Nephane."

"He is lying," the boy insisted. "The Methi killed the others."

"Unless one escaped."

"Or more than one," said the elder.

"May the light of Phan fall gently on thee," Kurt said, the common blessing. "I swear I have not lied to you, and I am no enemy."

"It is, at least, no Tamurlin," said the second man. "Are you house-friend to the Methi, stranger?"

"To Elas," said Kurt.

"To Elas," echoed the elder in amazement. "To the sons of storm,—a human for a house-friend? This is hard to believe. The Indras-descended are too proud for that."

"If you honor the name of Elas," said Kurt, "or of Osanef, which is our friend,—give me something to eat. I am about to faint from hunger."

The elder considered again and finally extended an arm in invitation to the meal they had left cooking beside their fire. "Not in hospitality, stranger, since we do not know you, but there is food and drink. We are poor men. Take sparingly, but be free of it, if you are as hungry as you say. May the light of Phan fall upon thee in blessing or in curse according to what you deserve."

Kurt moved carefully, for the spear was surely still at his back. He knelt down by the rock where the food was warming and took one of the three meal cakes, breaking off half; and a little crumb of the soft cheese that lay on a greasy leather wrap beside them. But he used the fine manners of Elas, not daring to do otherwise with their critical eyes on him and the spear ready.

When he was done he rose up and bowed his thanks. "I will go my way now," he said.

"No, stranger," said the second man. "I think you ought to stay with us and go to our village in the morning. In this district we see few travelers from Nephane, and I think you would be safer with us. Someone might take you for Tamurlin and put a spear through you before he realized his mistake. That would be sad for both of you."

"I have business elsewhere," said Kurt, playing out the farce with the rules they set and bowing politely. "And I thank you for your concern, but I will go on now."

The elder man brought his spear crosswise in both hands. "I think my son is right. You have run from somewhere, that much is certain, and I am not sure that you are house-friend to Elas. No, it is more likely the Methi simply missed killing you with the others, and we well know in the country what humans are."

"If I do come from Djan-methi, you will not win her thanks by delaying me on my mission."

"What, does the Methi send out her servants without provisions?"

"I had an accident," he said. "My mission is urgent; I had no time to go back. I counted on the hospitality of the country folk to help me on my way."

"Stranger, you are not only a liar, you are a bad liar. We will take you to our village and see what the Afen has to say about you."

Kurt ran, plunged in a wild vault over the brush barricade and in among the startled *cachin,* creating panic as their woolly bodies scattered and herded first to the rocks and then back toward the barricade, breaking it down in their mad rush to escape. The *tilof*'s sharp cries resounded in the rocks. The beast and the men had work enough at the moment.

Kurt climbed, fingers and sandalled toes seeking purchase in the crevices of the rocks, sending stones cascading down the hillside. He cleared the crest, found a level, brushy ground and ran, desperate, trusting pursuit would be at least delayed.

But word would go back to Nephane and to Djan, and she would be sure now the way he had fled. Ships could outrace him down the coast.

If he did not reach his own abandoned ship and secure the means to live, he was finished in this land. Djan would have guessed it already, and now she could lay her ambush with assurance.

If she knew the precise location of his ship, he could not hope to avoid it.

The sun rose over the same grassy rangeland that had surrounded him for the last several days, dry grass and wind and dust.

Kurt leaned on his staff, a twisted branch from which he had stripped the twigs, and looked toward the south. There was not a sign of the ship. Nothing. Another day of walking, of the tormenting heat and the infection's throbbing fever in his wound. He started moving again, relying on the staff, every step a jarring and constant pain, his mouth so dry that swallowing hurt.

Sometimes he rested, and thought of lying down and ceasing to struggle against the thirst; sometimes he would do that, but eventually misery and the habit of life would bring him to his feet and set him walking.

Phan was a terrible presence in these lands, wrathfully blinding in the day, deserting the land at night to a biting cold. Kurt rubbed blistered skin from his nose, his hands. His bare legs and especially his knees were swollen with sunburn, tiny blisters which many times formed and burst, making a crack-line that oozed and bled.

The thirst was beyond bearing as the sun reached the zenith. There was no water, had been none since the small stream the day before—or the day before that. Time blurred since he had entered this land. He began to wonder if he had already missed the ship, bypassing it over one of the gently rolling hills. That would be irony: to live by the skills of pinpointing a ship from one star to another and to die by missing a point over a hill.

He turned west finally, toward the sea, thinking that he could not fail at least to find that, hoping that the lower country would have fresh water. The changing of the seasons had confused him. He remembered green around the ship, green in winter. Had it been so far south? The sailing—he could not remember how many days it had taken.

By afternoon he ceased to care what direction he was moving in and knew that he was killing himself, and did not care. He started down a hillside, too tired to take the safer slope, and slipped on the dusty grass. He slid, opening the lacerations on his hands and knees, grass and stone stripping sunburned skin and blisters from his exposed flesh as he rolled down the slope.

The pain grew less finally, or he adjusted to it, he knew not which. He found himself walking and did not remember getting to his feet. It was not important any more, the ship, the sea, life or death. He moved and so lived, and therefore moved.

The sun dipped horizonward into dusk, a beacon that lit
the sky with red, and Kurt locked onto it, a reference point,
a guidance star in this void of grass. It led him downcountry,
where there were trees and the land looked more familiar.

Night fell, and he stood on the broad shoulder of a hill,
leaning on his staff, fearing if he sat down now he would not
have the strength in his burn-swollen legs to get up again.
He started the long descent toward the dark of the woods.

A light gleamed off across the wide valley, a light like a
campfire. Kurt paused, rubbed his eyes to be sure it was
there. It was a pinpoint like a very faint star, that flickered,
but stayed discernible in all that distance and desolation.

He headed for it, driven now by feverish hope, nerved to
kill if need be to obtain food and water.

It gleamed nearer, just when he feared he had lost it in
his descent. He saw it through the brush. Men's voices—
nemet voices—were audible, soft, quiet in conversation.

Then silence. Brush moved. The fire continued to gleam.
He hesitated, feeling momentary panic, a sense of being
stalked in turn.

Brush crashed near him and strong arm took him from
behind about the throat, bent him back. He fell, pulled
down by two mean, weighted with a knee on his right arm,
another hand pinning his left. A knife whispered from its
sheath and rested across his throat.

The man on his left checked the other hand on his wrist.
Kurt ceased to struggle, trying only to breathe.

"It is t'Morgan," said a whisper. Gentle hands searched
his belt for weapons, found nothing, tugged his arms free of
those who held him and drew him up, those who had lately
threatening him handling him carefully, lifting him to his
feet, aiding him to stand.

"Are you alone?" one asked of him.

"Yes," Kurt tried to say. They almost had to carry him,
bringing him into the circle of firelight. Other nemet joined
them from the shadows.

Kta was among them. Kurt saw his face among the others
and felt his sanity had left him. He tried to go toward him,
shaking free of the others.

He fell. When he managed to get his arms beneath him
and tried again to sit up, Kta was beside him. The nemet

washed his burning face from a waterskin, offered it to his lips and took it away before he could make himself sick with it.

"How did you come here?" Kurt found his own voice unrecognizable.

"Looking for you," said Kta. "I thought you might understand a beacon fire, which drew me once to you. And you did see it, thank the gods. I planned to reach your ship and wait for you there, but I have not been able to find it. But gods, no one walks cross-country. You are mad."

"It was a hard walk," Kurt agreed. Kta smoothed his filthy hair aside, woman-tender, his fingers careful of burned skin, pouring water to cool his face.

"Your skin," said Kta, "is cooked. Merciful spirits of heaven, look at you."

Kurt rubbed at the stubble that protected his lower face, aware how bestial he must be in the eyes of the nemet, for the nemet had very little facial hair, very little elsewhere. He struggled to sit, and bending his legs made it feel like the sunburned skin of his knees would split. "Food," he pleaded, and someone gave him a bit of cheese. He could not eat much of it, but he washed it down with a welcome swallow of *telise* from Kta's flask.

Then it was as if the strength that was left poured out of him. He lay down again and the nemet made him as comfortable as they could with their cloaks, washed the ugly wound across his ribs with water and then—which made him cry aloud—with fiery *telise*.

"Forgive me, forgive me," Kta murmured through the haze of his delirium. "My poor friend, it is done, it will mend."

He slept then, conscious of nothing.

The camp began to stir again toward dawn, and Kurt wakened as one of the men added wood to the fire. Kta was already sitting up, watching him anxiously.

Kurt groaned and sat up, dragging himself to a cross-legged posture despite his knees. "A drink, please, Kta."

Kta nodded to the boy Pan, who hastened to bring Kurt a waterskin and *stas*, which had been baked last night. It was cold, but with salt it went very well, washed down with *telise*. He ate it to the last, but dared not force the second one offered on his shrunken stomach.

"Are you feeling better?" asked Kta.

"I am all right," he said. "You should not have come after me."

And then a second, terrible thought hit him: "Or did Djan send you to bring me back?"

Kta's face went thin-lipped, a killing anger that turned Kurt cold. "No," he said. "I am outlawed. The Methi has killed my father and mother."

"No." Kurt shook his head furiously, as if that could unsay the truth of it. "Oh, no, Kta." But it was true. The nemet's face was calm and terrible. "*I* caused it," Kurt said. "*I* caused it."

"She killed them," said Kta, "as she killed Mim. We know Mim's tale from Djan-methi's own lips, spoken to my father. My people will not live without honor, and so my parents died. My father confronted the Methi in the Upei for Mim's death and for the Methi's other crimes—and she cast him from the Upei, which was her right. My father and my mother chose death, which was their right. And Hef with them. He would not let them go unattended into the shadows."

"Aimu?" Kurt asked, dreading to know.

"I gave her to Bel as his wife. What else could I do, what other hope for her? Elas is no more in Nephane. Its fire is extinguished. I am in exile. I will not serve the Methi any longer, but I live to honor my father and my mother and Hef and Mim. They are my charges now. I am all that is left, now that Aimu can no longer invoke the Guardians of Elas."

Kta's lips trembled. Kurt ached for him no less than for his family, for it was unbecoming for a man of the Indras to shed tears. It would shame him terribly to break.

"If," said Kurt, "you want to discharge your debt to me you have discharged it. I can live in this green land if you only give me weapons and food and water. Kta, I would not blame you if you never wanted to look at me again; I would not blame you if you killed me."

"I came for you," said Kta. "You are also of Elas, though you cannot continue our rites or perpetuate our blood.

When the Methi struck at you, she struck at us. We are of one house, you and I. Until one or the other of us is dead, we are left hand and right. You have no leave to go your way. I do not give it."

He spoke as lord of Elas, which was his right now. The bond Mim had forged reasserted itself. Kurt bowed his head in respect.

"Where shall we go now?" Kurt asked. "And what shall we do?"

"We go north," said Kta. "Light of heaven, I knew at once where you must go, and I am sure the Methi does; but it would have been more convenient if you had brought your ship to earth in the far north. The Ome Sin is a closed bottle in which the Methi's ships can hunt us at their pleasure. If we cannot escape its neck and reach the northern seas, you and I are done, my friend, and all these brave friends who have come with me."

"Is Bel here?" Kurt asked, for about him he saw many familiar faces, but he feared greatly for t'Osanef and Aimu if they had elected to stay in Nephane. T'Tefur might carry revenge even to them.

"No," said Kta. "Bel is Sufaki, and his father needs him desperately just now. For all of us that have come, there is no way back, not as long as Djan rules. But she has no heir, and being human—there is no dynasty. We are prepared to wait."

Kurt hoped silently that he had not given her one. That would be the ultimate bitterness, to ruin these good men by that, when he had brought them all to this pass.

"Break camp," said Kta. "We start—"

Something hissed and struck against flesh, and all the camp exploded into chaos.

"Kta!" a man cried warning, and went down with a feathered shaft in his throat. About them in the dawn-dim clearing poured a horde of howling creatures that Kurt knew for his own kind. One of the nemet pitched to the ground almost at his feet with his face a bloody smear, and in the next moment a crushing blow across the back brought Kurt down across him.

Rough hands jerked him up, and his shock-dazed eyes looked at a bearded human face. The man seemed no less surprised, stayed the blow of his ax, then bellowed an order to his men.

The killing stopped, the noise faded.

The human put out his bloody hand and touched Kurt's face, his hair-shrouded eyes dull and mused with confusion. "What band?" he asked.

"I came by ship," Kurt answered him. "By starship."

The Tamurlin's blue eyes clouded, and with a snarl he took the front of Kurt's nemet garb and ripped it off his shoulder, as though the nemet dress gave the lie to his claim. But then there was a cry of awe from the humans gathered around. One took his sun-browned arm and held it up against Kurt's pale shoulder and turned to his comrades, seeking their opinion.

"A man from shelters," he cried, "a ship-dweller."

"He came in the ship," another shouted, "in the ship, the ship."

They all shouted the ship, the ship, over and over again, and danced around and flashed their weapons. Kurt looked around at the carnage they had made in the clearing, his heart pounding with dread at seeing one and another man he knew lying there. He prayed Kta had escaped: some had dived for the brush.

He had not. Kta lay on his face by the fire, unconscious—his breathing was visible.

"Kill the others," said the leader of the Tamurlin. "We keep the human."

"*No!*" Kurt cried, and jerked ineffectually to free his arms. His mind snatched at the first argument he could find. "One of them is a nemet lord. He can bring you something of value."

"Point him out."

"There," Kurt said, jerking his head to show him. "Nearest the fire."

"Let's take all the live ones," said another of the Tamurlin, with a look in his eyes that boded no good for the nemet. "Let's deal with them tonight at the camp—"

"*Ya!*" howled the others, agreeing, and the chief snarled a reluctant order, for it had not been his idea. He took command of the situation with a sweep of his arm. "Pick them all up, all the live ones, and bring them. We'll see if this man really is from the ship. If he isn't, we'll find out what he really is."

The others shouted agreement and turned their attention to the fallen nemet, Kta first. Him they shook and slapped until he began to fight them again, and then they twisted his hands behind him and tied him.

Two other nemet they found not seriously hurt and treated in similar fashion. A third man they made walk a few paces, but he could not do so, for his leg was pierced with a shaft. One of them kicked his good leg from under him and smashed his skull with an ax.

Kurt twisted away, chanced to look on Kta's face, and the look in the nemet's eyes was terrible. Two more of his men they killed in the same way, and at each fall of the ax Kta winced, but his gaze remained fixed. By his look they could as well have killed him.

XV

The ship rested as Kurt remembered it, tilted, the port still open. About it now were camped a hundred of the Tamurlin, hide-clothed and mostly naked, their huts of grass and sticks and hides encircling the shining alloy landing struts.

They came running to see the prizes their party had brought, these savage men and women and few starveling children. They shouted obscene threats at the nemet, but shied away, murmuring together when they realized Kurt was human. One of the young men advanced cautiously—though Kurt's hands were tied—and others ventured after him. One pushed at Kurt, then hit him across the face, but the chief snatched him back, protective of his property.

"What band is he from?" one of them asked.

"Not from us," said the chief. "None of ours."

"He is human," several of the others argued the obvious.

The chief took Kurt by the collar and pulled, taking his *pel* down to the waist, pushed him forward into their midst. "He's not ours, whatever he is. Not of the tribes."

Their reaction was near to panic, babbling excitement. They put out their filthy hands, comparing themselves with him, for their hides were sun-browned and creased with premature wrinkles from weather and wind, with dirt and grease ground into the crevices. They prodded at Kurt with leathery fingers, pulled at his clothing, ran their hands over his skin and howled with amusement when he cursed and kicked at them.

144

It was a game, with them running in to touch him and out again when he tried to defend himself; but when he tired of it and let them, that spoiled it and angered them. They hit, and this time it was in earnest. One of them in a fit of offended arrogance pushed him down and kicked him repeatedly in the side, and the lot of them roared with laughter at that, even more so when a little boy darted in and did the same. Kurt twisted onto his knees and tried to rise, and the chief seized him by the arm and hauled him up.

"Where from?" the chief asked.

"Offworld," said Kurt from bloodied lips. He saw the ship beyond the chief's shoulder, a sanctuary out of his own time that he could not reach. He burned with shame for their treatment of him, and for the nemet's eyes on these his brothers, these shaggy, mindless, onetime lords of the earth. "That ship brought me here."

"The Ship," the others took it up. "The holy Ship! The Starship!"

"This is *not* the Ship," the chief shouted them down and pointed at it, his hand trembling with passion. "The curse-sign on it—this man is not what the Articles say."

The Alliance emblem. Kurt had forgotten the sunburst emblem of the Alliance that was blazoned on the ship. They were Hanan. He followed the chief's pointing finger, wondering with a sickness at the pit of his stomach how much of the war these savages recalled.

"A starman!" one of the young men shouted defiantly. "A starman! The Ship is coming!"

And the others took up the howl with wild-eyed fervor, the same ones who had lately thrown him in the dust.

"The ship, ya, the Ship, the Ship, the machines and the armies!"

"They are coming!"

"Indresul Indresul! The waiting is over!"

The chief backhanded Kurt to the ground, kicked him to show his contempt, and there was a cry of resentment from the people. A youth ran in—for what purpose was never known. The chief dropped the boy with a single blow of his fist and rounded on the leaders of the dissent.

"And I am still captain here," he roared, "and I know the

Articles and the Writings, and who will come and argue them with me?"

One of the men looked as if he might, but when the captain came closer to him, he ducked his head and sidled off. The rebellion died into sullen resentment.

"You've seen the sign," said the captain. "Maybe the Ship is near. But this little thing isn't what the Writings predict." He looked down at Kurt with threat in his eyes. "Where are the machines, the Ship as large as a mountain, the armies from the starworlds that will take us to Indresul?"

"Not far away," said Kurt, setting his face to lie, which was never a skill of his. "I was sent out from Aeolus to find you. Is this how you welcome me? That will be the last you ever see of Ships if you kill me."

The captain was taken aback by that answer.

"Mother Aeolus," cried one of the men, though he called it Elus, "the great Mother. He has seen the Great Mother of All Men."

The captain looked at Kurt from under one brow, hating, just the least part uncertain. "Then," he said, "what did she say to you?"

The lie closed in on him, complex beyond his own understanding. Aeolus—homeworld—confounded with the nemet's Mother Isoi, Mother of Men: nemet religion and human hopes confused into reverence for a promised Ship. "She— lost you," he said, gathering himself to his feet. They personified her: he hoped he understood that aright. "Her messenger was lost on the way hundreds of years ago, and she was angry, blaming you. But she has decided to send again, and now the Ship is coming, if my report to her is good."

"How can her messenger wear the mark of Phan?" the captain asked. "You are a liar."

The sunburst emblem of the ship. Kurt resisted the impulse to lose his dignity by looking where the captain pointed. "I am not a liar," said Kurt. "And if you don't listen to me, you'll never see her."

"You come from Phan," the captain snarled, "from Phan, to lie to us and turn us over to the nemet."

"I am human. Are you blind?"

"You camped with the earthpeople. You were no prisoner in that camp."

Kurt straightened his shoulders and looked the man in the eyes, lying with great offense in his tone. "We thought you men were supposed to have these nemet under control. That's what you were left here to do, after all, and you've had three hundred years to do that. So I had no real fear of the nemet and they were able to surprise me some time ago and take my weapons. It took me this long to escape from Nephane and come south. They hunted me down, with orders to bring me back to Nephane alive, so naturally they did me no harm in that camp, but that doesn't mean the relationship was friendly. I don't particularly like the nemet, but I'd advise you to save these three alive. When my captain comes down here, as he will, he's going to want to question a few of the nemet, and these will do very well for that purpose."

The captain bit his lip and gnawed his mustache. He looked at the three nemet with burning hatred and spit out an obscenity that had not much changed in several hundred years. "We kill them."

"No," Kurt said. "There's need of them live and healthy."

"Three nemet?" the captain snarled. "One. One we keep. You choose which one."

"All three," Kurt insisted, though the captain brandished his ax. It took all his self-possession not to flinch as the weapon made a pass at him.

Then the captain whirled the weapon in a glittering arc at the nemet, purposely defying him. The humans murmured, eyes glittering like the metal itself. The ax passed within an inch of Kta and of the next man.

"Choose!" the captain cried. "You choose, starman. One nemet. We take the other two."

The howling began to be a moan. One of the little boys shrieked in glee and ran in, striking all three nemet with a stick.

"Which one?" the captain asked again.

Kurt kept his sickness from his face, saw Kta look at him, saw the nemet's eyes sending a desperate and angry message to him, which he ignored, looking at the captain.

"The one on the left," Kurt said. "That one. Their leader."

*   *   *

One of the two nemet died before nightfall. The execution was in the center of camp, and there was no way Kurt could avoid watching from beginning to end, for the captain's narrow eyes were on him more than on the nemet, watching his least reaction. Kurt kept his own eyes unfocused as much as possible, and his arms folded, so that his trembling was not evident.

The nemet was a brave man, and his last reasoned act was a glance at Kta—not desperate, but seeking approval of him. Kta was standing, hands bound: the lord of Elas gave the man a steadfast look, as if he had given him an order on the deck of their own ship; and the nemet died with what dignity the Tamurlin afforded him. They made a butchery of it, and the Tamurlin howled with excitement until the man no longer reacted to any torment. Then they finished him with an ax. As the blade came down, Kta's self-control came near to breaking. He wept, his face as impassive as ever, and the Tamurlin pointed at him and laughed.

After that the captain ordered Kurt taken to his own shelter. There he questioned him, threatening him with not quite the conviction to make good the threats, accusing him over and over of lying. The captain was a shrewd man. At times there would come a light of cunning into his hair-shrouded eyes, and he doggedly refused to be led off on a tangent. Constantly he dragged the questioning back to the essential points, quoting from the versified Articles and the Writings of the Founders to argue against Kurt's claims.

His name was Renols, or something which closely resembled that common Hanan name, and he was the only educated man in the camp. His power was his knowledge, and the moment Renols ceased to believe, or ceased to fear, then Renols could dispose of Kurt with lies of his own. The captain was a pragmatist, capable of it; Kurt was well certain he was capable of it.

The tent reeked of fire, of sweat, of the curious pungent leaf the Tamurlin chewed. One of his women lay in the corner against the wall, taking the leaves one by one. Her eyes had a fevered look. Sometimes the captain reached for one of the slim gray leaves and chewed at it half-heartedly.

It perfumed the breath. Sweat began to bead on his temples. He grew calmer.

He offered the bowl of leaves to Kurt, insisting. At last Kurt took one, judiciously tucked it in his cheek, whole and unbruised. Even so, it burned his mouth and spread a numbness that began to frighten him.

If he became drunk with it, he could say something he would not say: his capacity for the drug might be far less than Renols'.

"When," asked Renols, "will the Ship come?"

"I told you. There's machinery in my own ship. Let me in there and I can call my captain."

Renols chewed and stared at him with his thick brows contracted. A dangerous look smoldered in his eyes. But he took another leaf and held out the bowl to Kurt a second time. His hands were stubby-fingered, the nails broken, the knuckles ridged with cut-scars.

Kurt took a second leaf and carefully eased that to the same place as the first.

The calculating look remained in Renols' eyes. "What sort of man is he, this captain?"

The understanding began to come through. If a ship came, if Mother Aeolus did send it and all points of his prisoner's tale proved true, then Renols would be faced with someone of greater authority than himself. He would perhaps become a little man. Renols must dread the Ship; it was in his own selfish interests that there not be one.

But it was also remotely possible that his prisoner would be an important man in the near future, so Renols must fear him. Kurt reckoned that too, and reckoned uneasily that familiarity might well overcome Renols' fear, when Aeolus' messenger turned out to be only mortal.

"My captain," said Kurt, embroidering the tale, "is named Ason, and Aeolus has given him all the weapons that you need. He will give them to you and show you their use before he returns to Aeolus to report."

The answer evidently pleased Renols more than Renols had expected. He grunted, half a laugh, as if he took pleasure in the anticipation.

Then he gave orders to one of the sallow-faced women who sat nearby. She laid the child she had been nursing in the lap of the nearest woman, who slept in the after-effects of the leaf, and went out and brought them food. She offered first to Renols, then to Kurt.

Kurt took the greasy joint in his fingers and hesitated, suddenly fearing the Tamurlin might not be above cannibalism. He looked it over, relieved to find no comparison between this joint and human or nemet anatomy. Starvation and Renols' suspicious stare overcame his other scruples and he ate the unidentified meat, careful with each bite not to swallow the leaves tucked in his cheek. The meat, despite the strong medicinal taste of the leaves, had a musty, mildewed flavor that almost made him retch. He held his breath and tried not to taste it, and wiped his hands on the earthen floor when he was done.

The captain offered him a second piece, and stopped in the act.

From outside there came a disturbance. Laughter. Someone shrieked in pain.

Renols put down the platter of meat and went out to speak with the man at the entry to the shelter.

"You swore," said Kurt when he came back.

"We're keeping yours," said Renols. "The other one is ours."

The confusion outside grew louder. Renols looked torn between annoyance at the interruption and desire to see what was passing outside. Abruptly he called in the man at the entry, tersely bidding him take Kurt to confinement.

The commotion sank away into silence. Kurt listened, teeth clamped tight against the heaving of his stomach. He had spit out the leaves there in the darkness of the shelter where they had left him, hands tied around one of the two support posts. He twisted until he could dig with his fingers in the hard dirt floor and bury the rejected leaves.

There was a bitter taste in his mouth now. His vision blurred, his pulse raced, his heart crashed against his ribs. He began to be hazy-minded, and slept a time.

Footsteps in the dust outside aroused him. Shadows entered the moonlight-striped shelter, pulling a loose-limbed body with them. It was Kta. They tied the semiconscious nemet to the other post and left him.

After a time Kta lifted his head and leaned it back against the post. He did not speak or look at Kurt, only stared off into the dark, his face and body oddly patterned with moonlight through the woven-work.

"Kta," said Kurt finally. "Are you all right?"

Kta made no reply.

"Kta," Kurt pleaded, reading anger in the set of the nemet's jaw.

"Is it to you," Kta's hoarse voice replied, "is it to you that I owe my life? Do I understand that correctly? Or do I believe instead the tale you tell to the *umani*?"

"I am doing all I can."

"What is it you want from me?"

"I am trying to save our lives," Kurt said. "I am trying to get you out of here. You know me, Kta. Can you take seriously any of the things I have told them?"

There was a long silence. "Please," said Kta in a broken voice, "please spare me your help from now on."

"Listen to me. There are weapons in the ship if I can convince them to let me in there. If I can fire its engines I can burn this nest out."

"I will forgive you," said Kta, "when you do that."

"Are you," Kurt asked after a moment, "much hurt?"

"I am alive," Kta answered. "Does that not satisfy you?— Shall I tell you what they did to the boy, honored friend?"

"I could not stop it,—Kta, look at me. Listen. Is there any hope at all from *Tavi?* If we could get free, could we find out way there?"

There was no answer.

"Kta,—where is your ship anchored?"

"Why? So you can buy our lives with that too?"

"Do you think I mean to tell—"

"They are your kind, human. It would be possible to survive,—if you could buy your life. I will not give you *Tavi*."

Against such bitterness there was no answer. Kurt swallowed at the resentment and the hurt that rose in his throat; he held his peace after that. He wanted no more truth from Kta.

The silence wore on, two-sided. At last it was Kta who turned his head. "What are you fighting for?" he asked.

"I thought you had drawn your conclusion."

"I am asking. What are you trying to do?"

"To save your life. And mine."

"What use is that to either of us under these terms?"

Kurt twisted toward him. "What use is it to give in to them? Is it sense to let them kill you and do nothing to help yourself?"

"Stop protecting me. I am better dead."

"Like *they* died? Like that?"

"Show me," said Kta, his voice shaking, "show me what you can do against these creatures. Put a weapon in my hands or even get my hands free and I will die well enough. But what dignity is there in living like this? Give me a reason. Tell me something I could have told the men they killed, why I have to live, when I should have died before them."

"Kta, tell me, is there any possible chance of reaching *Tavi*?"

"The coast is leagues away. They would overtake us. This ship of yours. Is it true what you said, that you could burn them out?"

"Everyone would die,—you too, Kta."

"You know how much that means to me. Light of heaven, what manner of world is yours? Why did you have to interfere?"

"I did the best I knew to do."

"You were wrong," said Kta.

Kurt turned away and let the nemet alone, as he so evidently wanted to be. Kta had reason enough to hate humanity. Almost all he had ever loved was dead at the hands of humans, his home lost, his hearth dead, now even the few friends he had left slaughtered before his eyes. His parents,—Hef,—Mim,—himself. Elas was dying. To this had human friendship brought the lord of Elas, and most of it was his own friend's doing.

In time, Kta seemed to sleep, his head sunk on his breast, his breathing heavy.

A shadow crept across the slatting outside, a ripple of darkness that bent at the door, crept inside the shelter. Kurt woke, moved, began a cry of warning. The shadow plum-

meted, holding him, clamping a rough, calloused hand over
his mouth.

The movement wakened Kta, who jerked, and a knife
flashed in the dim light as the intruder drove for Kta's
throat.

Kurt twisted, kicked furiously and threw the would-be
assassin tumbling. He righted himself, and a feral human
face stared at both of them, panting, the knife still clenched
for use.

The human advanced the knife, demonstrating it to them,
ready. "Quiet," he hissed. "Stay quiet."

Kurt shivered, reaction to the near-slaughter of Kta. The
nemet was unharmed, breathing hard, his eyes also fixed on
the wild-haired human.

"What do you want?" Kurt whispered.

The human crept close to him, tested the cords on his
wrists. "I'm Garet," said the man. "Listen. I will help you."

"Help me?" Kurt echoed, still shuddering, for he thought
the man might be mad. The leaf-smell was about him.
Feverish hands sought his shoulders. The man leaned close
to whisper yet more softly.

"You can't trust Renols, he hates the thought of the Ship.
He'll find a way to kill you. He isn't sure yet, but he'll find a
way. I could get you into your ship tonight. I could do
that."

"Cut me free," Kurt replied, snatching at any chance.

"I *could* do that."

"What do you want, then?"

"You'll have the weapons in the little ship. You can kill
Renols then. *I* will help you. *I* will be second and I will go
on helping you."

"You want to be captain?"

"You can make me that, if I help you."

"It's a deal," said Kurt, and held his breath while the man
made a final consideration. He dared not ask Kta's freedom
too. He dared not turn on Garet and take the knife. The
slim chance there was in the situation kept him from risking
it; in silence, once inside the ship, he could handle Garet
and stand off Renols.

The knife haggled at the cords, parting the tough fiber
and sending the blood excruciatingly back to his hands. He

rose up carefully, for Garet held the knife ready against him if he moved suddenly.

Then Garet's eyes swept toward Kta. He bent toward him, blade extended.

Kurt caught his arm, fronted instantly by Garet's bewildered suspicion, and for a moment fear robbed Kurt of any sense to explain.

"He is mine," Kurt said.

"We can catch a lot of nemet," said Garet. "What's this one to you?"

"I know him," said Kurt. "And I can get cooperation out of him. He's not about to cry out, because he knows he'd die; he knows I'm his only chance of staying alive, so eventually he'll tell me all I ask of him."

Kta looked up at both of them, well able to understand. Whether it was consummate acting or fear of Garet or fear of human treachery, he looked frightened. He was among aliens. Perhaps it even occurred to him that he could have been long deceived.

Garet glowered, but he thrust the knife into his belt and led the way out into the tangle of huts outside.

"Sentries?" Kurt breathed into his ear.

Garet shook his head, drew him further through the village, up to the landing struts, the extended ladder. A sentry did stand there. Garet poised to throw, knife balanced between his fingertips. He drew back—

—the hiss and *chunk!* of an arrow toppled him, clawing at the ground. The sentry crouched and whirled, and men poured out of the dark. Kurt went down under a triple assault, struggling and kicking as they hauled him where they would take him, up to the ladder.

Renols was there, ax in hand. He prodded Kurt in the belly with it. His ugly face contorted further in a snarl of anger.

"Why?" he asked.

"He came," said Kurt, "threatened to kill me if I didn't come at once. Then he told me you were planning to kill me. I didn't know what to believe. But this one had a knife, so I kept quiet."

"Sentries are dead," another man reported. "Six men are

dead, throats cut. One of our scouts hasn't come back either."

"Garet's brothers," Renols said, and looked at the men who surrounded him. "His folk's doing. Find his women and his brats. Give them to the dead men's families, whatever they like."

"Captain," said that man, biting his lip nervously. "Captain, the Garets are a big family. Their kin is in the Red band too. If they get to them with some story—"

"Get them," said Renols. "Now."

The men separated. Those who held Kurt remained. Renols looked up at the entry to the ship, thought silently, then nodded to his men, who brought Kurt away as they walked through the camp. They were quiet. Not a sound came from the encampment. Kurt walked obediently enough, although the men made it harder for him out of spite.

They came to the hut from which he had escaped. Renols stooped and looked inside, where Kta was still tied.

He straightened again. "The nemet is still alive," he said. Then he looked at Kurt from under one brow. "Why didn't Garet kill him?"

Kurt shrugged. "Garet hit him. I guess he was in a hurry."

Renols' scowl deepened. "That isn't like Garet."

"How should I know? Maybe Garet thought he might fail tonight and didn't want a dead nemet for proof of his visit."

Renols thought that over. "So. How did he know you wouldn't raise an alarm?"

"He didn't. But it makes sense I'd keep quiet. How am I to know whose story to believe?"

Renols snorted. "Put him inside. We'll catch one of the Garets alive and then we'll see about it."

The human left. Kurt tested the strength of the new cords, which were unnecessarily tight and rapidly numbed his hands—a petty measure of their irritation with him. He sighed and leaned his head back against the post, ignoring Kta's staring at him.

There was no chance to discuss matters. Kta seemed to sense it, for he said nothing. Someone stood not far from the hut, visible through the matting.

Quite probably, Kurt thought, the nemet had added things

up for himself. Whether he had then reached the right conclusion was another matter.

Eventually first light began to bring a little detail to the hut. Kta finally slept. Kurt did not.

Then a stir was made in the camp, men running in the direction of Renols' hut. Distant voices were discussing something urgently. The commotion spread, until people were stirring about in some alarm.

And Renols' lieutenants came to fetch them both, handling them both harshly as they hurried them toward Renols' shelter.

"We found Garet's brothers," Renols said, confronting Kurt.

Kurt stared at him, neither comforted nor alarmed by that news. "Garet's brothers are nothing to me."

"We found them dead. All of them. Throats cut. There were tracks of nemet—sandal-wearing."

Kurt glanced at Kta, not needing to feign shock.

"Two of our searchers haven't come back," said Renols. "You say this one is a chief among the nemet. A lord. Probably they're his. Ask him."

"You understood," Kurt said in Nechai. "Say something."

Kta set his jaw. "If you think to buy time by giving them anything from me, you are mistaken."

"He has nothing to say," said Kurt to Renols.

Renols did not look surprised. "He will find something to say," he promised. "Astin, get a guard doubled out there. No women to go out of camp today. Raf, bring the nemet to the main circle."

It would be possible, Kurt realized with a cold sickness at the heart, it would be possible to play out the game to the end. Kta would not betray him any more than he would betray the men of *Tavi*. To let Kta die might buy him the hour or so needed to hope for rescue. Possibly Kta would not even blame him. It was always hard to know what Kta would consider a reasonable action.

He followed along after those who took Kta—Kta with his spine stiff and every line of him braced to resist, but making not a sound. Kurt himself went docilely, his eyes scanning the hostile crowd that gathered in ominous silence.

He let it continue to the very circle, where the sand was

still dark-spotted with the blood of the night before. He feared he would not have the courage to commit so senseless an act, giving up both their lives. But when they tried to put Kta to the ground, he scarcely thought. He tore loose, hit one man, stooped, jerked the ax from his startled hand and swung it toward those who held Kta.

The nemet reacted with amazing agility, swung one man into the path of the ax, kneed the other, snatched a dagger and applied it with the blinding speed he could use with the *ypan*. The men clutched spurting wounds and went down howling and writhing.

"Archers!" Renols bellowed. There was a great clear space about the area. Kurt and Kta stood back to back, men crowding each other to get out of the way. Renols was closest.

Kurt charged him, ax swinging. Renols went down with his side open, rolling in the dust. Other men scrambled out of the way as he kept swinging. Kta stayed with him. Their area changed. People fled from them screaming.

"Shoot them!" someone else shrieked.

Then all chaos broke loose, a hoarse cry from the rear of the crowd. Some of the Tamurlin turned screaming in panic, their cries swiftly drowned in the sounds of battle in the center of the crowd.

Kta jerked at Kurt's arm and pointed—both of them for the moment stunned by the appearance of nemet among the Tamurlin, the flash of bright-edged swords in the sunlight. No Tamurlin offered them fight any more: the humans were trying more to escape than to fight, and soon there were only nemet around them. The humans had vanished into the brush.

Now with Kurt behind him, Kta stood in the clear, with dagger in hand and the dead at his feet, and the nemet band raised a cheer.

"Lord Kta!" they cried over and over. "Lord Kta!" And they came to him, bloody swords in hand, and knelt down in the dust before their almost-naked and much-battered lord. Kta held out his hand to them, dropping the blade, and turned palm upward to heaven, to the cleansing light of the sun.

"*Ei*, my friends," he said, "my friends, well done."

Val t'Ran, the officer next in command after Bel t'Osanef,
rose from his knees and looked as if he would gladly have
embraced Kta, if such impulses belonged to nemet. Tears
shone in his eyes. "I thank heaven we were in time, Kta-
ifhan, and I would have reckoned we could not be."

"It was you who killed the humans outside the camp, was
it not?"

"Aye, my lord, and we feared they had spoiled our ambush. We thought we might have been discovered by that.
We were very careful stalking the camp, after that."

"It was well done," said Kta again, with great feeling, and
held out his hand to the boy Pan, who had come with the
rescuers. "Pan, it was you who brought them?"

"Yes, sir," said the youth. "I had to run, sir, I had to. I
hated to leave you. Tas and I—we thought we could do
more by getting to the ship—but he died of his wound on
the way."

Kta swallowed heavily. "I am sorry, Pan. May the Guardians of your house receive him kindly.—Let us go. Let us be
out of this foul place."

Kurt saw them prepare to move out, looked down at what
weight was clenched in his numb hand, saw the ax and his
arm bloodstained to the shoulder. He let it fall, suddenly
shaking in every limb. He stumbled aside from all of them,
bent over in the lee of a hut and was sick for some few
minutes until everything had emptied out of his belly, drugs,
Tamurlin food. But the sights that stayed in his mind were
something over which he had no such power. He took dust
and rubbed at the blood until his skin stung with the sandy
dirt and the spots were gone. In a deserted hut he found a
gourd of water and drank and washed his face. The place
stank of leaf. He stumbled out again into the sunlight.

"Lord Kurt," said one of the seamen, astonished to find
him. "Kta-ifhan is frantic. Come. Hurry. Come, please."

The nemet looked strange to him, alien, the language
jarring on his ears. Human dead lay around. The nemet
were leaving. He felt no urge to go among them.

"Sir."

Fire roared near him; a wave of heat brought him to
alertness. They were setting fire to the village. He stared
about him like a man waking from a dream.

He had pulled a trigger, pressed a button and killed, remotely, instantly. He had helped to fire a world, though his post was noncombat. They had been minute, statistical targets.

Renols' astonished look hung before him. It had been Mim's.

He lay in the dust, with its taste in his mouth and his lips cut and his cheek bruised. He did not remember falling. Gentle alien hands lifted him, turned him, smoothed his face.

"He is fevered," Pan's clear voice said out of the blaze of the sun. "The burns, sir—the sun, the long walk—"

"Help him," said Kta's voice. "Carry him if you must. We must get clear of this place. There are other tribes."

The journey was a haze of brown and green, of sometime drafts of skin-stale water. At times he walked, hardly knowing anything but to follow the man in front of him. Toward the last, as their way began to descend to the sea and the day cooled, he began to take note of his surroundings again. Losing the contents of his stomach a second time, beside the trail, made him weak, but he was free of the nausea and his head was clearer afterwards. He drank *telise*, the kindly seaman who offered it bidding him keep the flask; it only occurred to him later that using something a sick human had used would be repugnant to the man. It did not matter; he was touched that the man had given it up for his sake.

He shook off their offered help thereafter. He had his legs again, though they shook under him, and he was self-possessed enough to remember his ship and the equipment they had abandoned; he had been too dazed and the nemet, the nemet with their distrust of machines, had abandoned everything.

"We have to go back," he told Kta, trying to reason with him.

"No," said the nemet. "No. No more lives of my men. We are already racing the chance that other tribes may be alerted by now."

It was the end of the matter.

And toward evening, with the coast before them and *Tavi* lying off-shore, most welcome of sights—there came a seaman racing up across the sand, stumbling and hard-breathing.

He saw Kta and his eyes widened, and he sketched a staggering bow before his lord and gasped out his message.

"Methi's ship," he said, "upcoast. Lookout saw them from the point there. They are searching every inlet on this shore—almost—almost we would have had to pull away—but without enough rowers. Thank heaven you made it, sir."

"Let us hurry," said Kta, and they began to plunge down the sandy slope to the beach itself.

"My lord," hissed the seaman. "I think the ship is *Edrif.* The sail is green."

"*Edrif.*" Kta gazed toward the point with fury in every line of him. "Yeknis take them!—Kurt, Tefur's *Edrif,* do you hear?"

"I hear," Kurt echoed. The longing for revenge churned inside him, when a few moments before he would never have looked to fight again. He shivered in the cold sea wind, wrapped his borrowed *ctan* about him and followed Kta downslope as fast as his trembling legs would take him.

"We have not crew enough to take him now," Kta muttered beneath his breath. "Would that I did! We would send that son of Yr's abominations down to Kalyt's green halls—amusement for Kalyt's scaly daughters. Light of heaven! If I had the whole of us this moment,—"

He did not, and fell silent with a grimness that had the pain of tears behind it. Kurt heard the nemet's voice shake, and feared for him before the witness of the men.

XVI

Tavi's dark blue sail billowed out and filled with the night wind, and Val t'Ran called out a hoarse order to the rowers to hold oars. The rhythm of wood and water cadenced to a halt, forty oars poised level over the water. Then with a direction from Val they came inboard with a single grate of wood, locked into place by the sweating rowers who rested at the benches.

Somewhere *Edrif* still prowled the coast, but the Sufaki vessel had the disadvantage of having to seek, and the lower coast was rough, with many inlets that were possible for *Tavi*, a sleek, shallow-drafted longship—while *Edrif*, greater in oarage, must keep to slightly deeper waters.

Now *Tavi* caught the wind, with the water sloughing rapidly under her hull. On her starboard side rose a great jagged spire against the night sky, sea-worn rock, warning of other rocks in the black waters. The waves lapped audibly at the crag, but they skimmed past and skirted one on the left by a similarly scant margin.

These were waters Kta knew. The crew stayed at the benches, ready but unfrightened by the closeness of the channel they ran.

"Get below," Kta told Kurt. "You have been on your feet too long. I do not want to have to pull you a second time out of the sea. Get back from the rail."

"Are we clear now?"

"There is a straight course through these rocks and the wind is bearing us well down the center of it. Heaven favors

161

us. Here, you are getting the spray where you are standing. Lun, take this man below before he perishes."

The cabin was warm and close, and there was light, well-shielded from outside view. The old seaman guided him to the cot and bade him lie down. The heaving of the ship disoriented him in a way the sea had never done before. He fell into the cot, rousing himself only when Lun propped him up to set a mug of soup to his lips. He could not even manage it without shaking. Lun held it patiently, and the warmth of the soup filled his belly and spread to his limbs, pouring strength into him.

He bade Lun prop his shoulders with blankets and give him a second cup. He was able to sit then partially erect, his hands cradling the steaming mug. He did not particularly want to drink it; it was the warmth he cherished, and the knowledge that it was there. He was careful not to fall asleep and spill it. From time to time he sipped at it. Lun sat nodding in the corner.

The door opened with a gust of cold wind and Kta came in, shook the salt water from his cloak and gave it to Lun.

"Soup here, sir," said Lun, prepared and gave him a cup of it, and Kta thanked him and sank down on the cot on the opposite side of the little cabin. Lun departed and closed the door quietly.

Kurt stared for a long time at the wall, without the will left to face another round with Kta. At last Kta moved enough to drink, and let go his breath in a soft sigh of weariness.

"Are you all right?" Kta asked him finally. He put gentleness in his question, which had been long absent from his voice.

"I am all right."

"The night is in our favor. I think we can clear this shore before *Edrif* realizes it."

"Do we still go north?"

"Yes. And with t'Tefur no doubt hard behind us."

"Is there any chance we could take him?"

"We have ten benches empty and no reliefs. Or do you expect me to kill the rest of my men?"

Kurt flinched, a lowering of his eyes. He could not face

an accounting now. He did not want the fight. He stared off elsewhere and took a sip of the soup to cover it.

"I did not mean that against you," Kta said. "Kurt, these men left everything for my sake, left families and hearths with no hope of returning. They came to me in the night and begged me—begged me—to let them take me from Nephane, or I would have ended my life that night in spite of my father's wishes. Now I have left twelve of them dead on this shore.—I am responsible for them, Kurt. My men are dead and I am alive. Of all of them, *I* survived."

"I saved *each* of them," Kurt protested, "as long as I could. I did what I knew to do, Kta."

Kta drank the rest of the soup as if he tasted nothing at all and set the cup aside. Then he sat quietly, his jaw knotted with muscle and his lips quivering. It passed.

"My poor friend," said Kta at last. "I know. I know. There was a time I was not sure. I am sorry. Go to sleep."

"Upon that?"

"What would you that I say?"

"I wish I knew," Kurt said, and set his cup aside and laid his head on the blankets again. The warmth had settled into his bones now, and the aches began, the fever of burned skin, the fatigue of ravaged nerves.

"*Yhia* eludes me," Kta said then. "Kurt, there must be reasons. I should have died; but they—who were in no danger of dying—they died. My hearth is dead and I should have died with it; but they—That is my anger, Kurt. I do not know why."

From a human Kurt would have dismissed it as nonsensical; but from Kta, it was no little thing—not to know. It struck at everything the nemet believed. He looked at Kta, greatly pitying him.

"You went among humans," said Kurt. "We are a chaotic people."

"No," said Kta. "The whole of creation is patterned. We live in patterns. And I do not like the pattern I see now."

"What is that?"

"Death upon death, dying upon dead. None of us are safe save the dead. But what will become of us—is still in front of us."

"You are too tired. Do your thinking in the morning, Kta. Things will seem better then."

"What, and in the morning will they all be alive again? Will Indresul make peace with my nation and Elas be unharmed in Nephane? No. Tomorrow the same things will be true."

"So may better things. Go to bed, Kta."

Kta rose up suddenly, went and lit the prayer-light of the small bronze *phusa* that sat in its wood-and-bronze niche. The light of Phan illuminated the corner with its golden radiance and Kta knelt, sat on his heels and lifted his open palms.

In a low voice he began the invocation of his Ancestors, and soon his voice faded and he rested with his hands in his lap. Just now it was an ability Kurt envied the religious nemet—like Kta, like Mim, no longer to feel physical pain. The mind utterly concentrated first upon the focus of the light and then beyond, reaching for what no man ever truly attained, but reaching.

The stillness that had been in Elas came over the little cabin. There was the groaning of the timbers, the rush of water past the hull, the rocking of the sea. The quiet seeped inward. Kurt found it possible at last to close his eyes.

He had slept some little time. He stirred, waking from some forgotten dream, and saw the prayer-light flickering on the last of its oil.

Kta still sat as he had before.

A chill struck him. He thought of Mim, dead before the *phusa,* and Kta's state of mind, and he sprang from bed. Kta's face and half-naked body glistened with sweat, though it was not even warm in the room. His eyes were closed, his hands loose in his lap, though every muscle in his body looked rigid.

"Kta," Kurt called. Interruption of meditation was no trifling matter to a nemet, but he seized Kta's shoulders nonetheless.

Kta shuddered and drew an audible breath.

"Kta. Are you all right?"

Kta let the breath go. His eyes opened. "Yes," he murmured thickly, tried to move and failed. "Help me up, Kurt."

Kurt drew him up, steadied him on his deadened legs. After a moment the nemet ran a hand through his sweat-damp hair and straightened his shoulders.

He did not speak further, only stumbled to his cot and fell in, eyes closed, as relaxed as a sleeping child. Kurt stood there staring down at him in some concern, and at last concluded that he was all right. He pulled a blanket over Kta, put out the main light, but left the prayer-light to flicker out on its remaining oil. If it must be extinguished there were prayers which had to be said, he knew them from hearing Mim say them; but it would be hypocrisy to speak them and offensive to Kta to omit them.

He sought the refuge of his own bed and lay staring at the nemet's face in the almost-dark, remembering the invocation Kta had made of the Guardians of Elas, those mysterious and now angry spirits that protected the house. He did not believe in them, and yet felt a heaviness in the air when they had been invoked, and he wondered with what Kta's consciousness or subconscious had been in contact.

He remembered the oracular computers of Alliance central command which analyzed, predicted, made policy, —prophesied; and he wondered if those machines and the nemet did not perceive some reason beyond rationality, if the machines men had built functioned because the nemet were right, because there was a pattern and the nemet came close to knowing it.

He looked at Kta's face, peaceful and composed, and felt an irrational terror of him and his outraged Ancestors, as if whatever watched Elas was still alive and still powerful, beyond the power of men to control.

But Kta slept with the face of innocence.

Kurt braced himself as Lun heaved a bucket of seawater over him—cold, stinging with salt in his wounds, but a comfort to the soul. He was clean again, shaved, civilized. The man handed him a blanket and Kurt wrapped in it gratefully, not minding its rough texture next to his abused skin. Kta, leaning with his back against the rail, gave him a pitying look, his own bronze skin able to absorb Phan's burning rays without apparent harm, even the bruises he had suffered at the hands of the Tamurlin muted by his dusky complexion, his straight black hair drying in the wind to fall into its customary order, while Kurt's—lighter, sun-bleached now, was entirely unruly. Kta looked godlike and serenely undamaged, renewed by the morning's light, like a snake newly molted.

"It looks terribly sensitive," Kta said, grimacing at the sunburn that bled at Kurt's knees and wrists and ankles. "Oil would help."

"I will try some in a little while," Kurt said. He took his clothing and dressed, an offense to his fevered skin: he went clad this day only in the *ctan*. When there were no women present it was enough.

"How long will it take us to reach the Isles?" Kurt asked of Kta, for Kta had given that as their first destination.

Kta shrugged. "Another day, granted the favor of heaven and the ladies of the winds. There are dangers in these waters besides *Edrif;* Indresul has a colony to the west— Sidur Mel; with a fleet based there,—a danger I do not care to wake. And even in the Isles, the great colony of Smethisan is dominated by the house of Lur, trade-rivals of Elas, and I would not trust them. But the Isle of Acturi is ruled by house-friends: I hope for port there."

The canvas snapped overhead and Kta cast a look up at the sail, waved a signal back to Val. *Tavi*'s crew hurried into action.

"The gray ladies," said Kta, meaning the sky-sprites, "may not favor us for long. Sailors should speak respectfully of heaven and never take it for granted."

"A change in the weather?"

"For the worse." Kta wore a worried look, indicated a faint grayness at the very edge of the northern sky. "I had hoped to reach the Isles before that. Spring winds are uncertain, and that one blows right off the ice of the Yvorst Ome. We may feel the edge of it before the day is done."

By midmorning *Tavi*'s sail filled and hung slack by turns, Kta's ethereal ladies turning fickle; By noon the ship had taken on a queasy motion, almost without wind to stir her sail. Canvas snapped. Val bellowed orders to the deck crew, while Kta stood near the bow and looked balefully at the advancing bank of cloud.

"You had better find heavier clothing," said Kta. "When the wind shifts, you will feel it in your bones."

The clouds took on an ominous look now that they were closer. They came like a veil over the heavens, black-bottomed.

"It will drive us back," Kurt observed.

"We will gain what distance we can and fight to hold our position. You are not experienced in this; you have seen no storms such as the spring winds bring. You ought not to be on deck when it hits."

By afternoon the northwest sky was utterly black, showing flashes of lightning out of it, and the wind was picking up in little puffs, uncertain at first, from this quarter and that.

Kta looked at it and swore with feeling. "I think," he said, "that the demons of old Chteftikan sent it down on us for spite. Sufak is to leeward, with its hidden rocks. The only comfort is that Shan t'Tefur is nearer them, and if we go aground, he will have gone before us.—*Hya*, you, man! Tkel! Take another hitch in that! Wish you to climb after it in the storm? I shall send you up after it."

Tkel grinned, waved his understanding and caught quickly at the line to which he was clinging, for *Tavi* was suddenly beginning to experience heavy seas.

"Kurt," said Kta, "be careful. This deck will be awash soon, and a wave could carry you overboard."

"How do your men keep their footing?"

"They do not move without need. You are no seaman, my friend. I wish you would go below. I would not have you entertaining Kalyt's green-eyed daughters tonight. I know not what their feelings may be about humans."

Kurt knew the legend. Drowned sailors were held in the domain of Kalyt the sea father until proper rites could release their souls from bondage to the lustful seasprites and send them to their ancestral hearths.

He took Kta's warning, but it was advice, not order, and he was not willing to go below. He walked off aft and suddenly a great swell made him lose his balance. He caught at the mast in time to save himself from pitching headlong into the rowers' pit. He refused to look back at Kta, humiliated enough. He found his balance again and walked carefully toward the low prominence of the cabin, taking refuge against its wall.

Tavi was soon hard-put to maintain her course against the seas. Her bow rose on the swells and her deck pitched alarmingly as she rode them down. Overhead the sky turned to premature twilight, and the wind carried the scent of rain.

Then a great gust of wind scoured the sea and hit the ship. The spray kicked up, the bow awash as water broke over the ship's bronze-shod ram. Kurt wiped the stinging water from his eyes as sea and sky tilted insanely. He kept tight grip on the safety line. *Tavi* became a fragile wooden shell shrunk to miniature proportions against the waves that this morning had run so smoothly under her bow.

Wood and rigging groaned as if the vessel was straining to hold together, and a torrent of water nearly swept Kurt off his feet. Rain and salt water mixed in a ceaseless, blinding mist. In the shadowy sky lightning flashed and thunder boomed directly after, and Kurt flinched against the cabin wall, constantly expecting the ship not to surface after the next pitch downward or the breaking of spray across her deck. Thunder ripped overhead—lightning seemed close enough to take the very mast. His heart was in his throat already; at every crash of thunder he simply shut his eyes and expected to die. He had ridden out combat a dozen times. The fury of this little landbound sea was more awesome. He clung, half drowned, and shivered in the howling wind, and Kta's green-eyed seasprites seemed real and malevolently threatening, the depths yawning open and deadly, alternate with the sky beyond the rail. He could almost hear them singing in the wind.

It was a measureless time before the rain ceased, but at last the clouds broke and the winds abated. To starboard through the haze of rain land appeared, the land they so much wanted to leave behind,—a dim gray line, the stark cliffs and headlands of Sufak. Kta turned the helm over to Tkel and stood looking toward the east, wiping the rain from his face. The water streamed from his hair.

"How much have we lost?" Kurt asked.

Kta shrugged. "Considerable. Considerable. We must fight contrary winds, at least for the present. Spring is a constant struggle between southwind and north, and eventually south must win. It is a question of time and heaven's good favor."

"Heaven's good favor would have prevented that storm," said Kurt. Cold limbs and exhaustion made him more acid than he was lately wont to be with Kta, but Kta was well-armored this day: he merely shrugged off the human cynicism.

"How are we to know? Maybe we were going toward trouble and the wind blew us back to safety. Maybe the storm had nothing to do with us. A man should not be too conceited."

Kurt gave him a peculiar look, and caught his balance as the sea's ebbing violence lifted *Tavi*'s bow and lowered it again. It pleased him, even so, to find Kta straight-facedly laughing at him: so it had been in Elas, on evenings when they talked together, making light of their serious differences. It was good to know they could still do that.

"Hya!" Val cried, "My lord Kta! Ship astern!"

There was, amid the gray haze, a tiny object that was not a part of the sea or the shore. Kta swore.

"They cannot help but overhaul us, my lord!"

"That much is sure," said Kta, and then lifted his voice to the crew. "Men, if that is *Edrif* astern, we have a fight coming. Arm yourselves and check your gear; we may not have time later. Kurt, my friend,—" Kta turned and faced him, "When they close, as I fear they will, keep away from exposed areas. The Sufaki are quite accurate bowmen. If we are rammed, jump and try to find a bit of wood to cling to. Use sword or ax, whatever you wish, but I do not plan to be boarding or boarded if I can prevent it. Badly as we both want Shan t'Tefur, we dare not risk it."

The intervening space closed slowly. Nearer view confirmed the ship as *Edrif*, a sixty-oared longship, and *Tavi*, though of newer and swifter design, had ten of her fifty benches vacant. At the moment only twenty oars were working.

"Ei," said Kta to the men in the rowers' pits on either side of him—the other twenty also seated and ready, six of the deck crew taking vacant posts to bring *Tavi*'s oarage closer to normal strength. *"Ei,* now, keep the pace, you rowers, as you are, and listen to me. *Edrif* is stalking us, and we will have to begin to move. Let none of us make a

mistake or hesitate; we have no margin and no relief. Skill must save us, skill and discipline and experience; no Sufak ship can match us in that—Now, now, run out the rest of the oars. Hold, you other men, hold!"

The cadence halted briefly, *Tavi*'s twenty working oars poised creaking and dripping until the other twenty-six were run out and ready. Kta gave the count himself, a moderate pace. *Edrif* gained steadily, her sixty oars beating the sea. Figures were now discernible on her deck.

Kurt made a quick descent to seize a blade from a rack in the companionway, and on second thought exchanged it for a short-handled ax, such as was properly designed for freeing shattered rigging, not for combat. He did not estimate that his lessons with Kta had made him a fencer equal to a nemet who had handled the *ypan* all his life, and he did not trust that all Sufaki shunned the *ypan* in favor of the bow and the knife.

He delayed long enough to dress too, to slip on a *pel* beneath the *ctan* and belt it, for the wind was bitter, and the prospect of entering a fight all but naked did not appeal to him.

When he had returned to the deck, even after so brief a time, *Edrif* had closed the gap further, so that her green dragon figurehead was clear to be seen above the water that boiled about her metal-shod ram. A stripe-robed officer stood at her bows, shouting back orders, but the wind carried his voice away.

"Prepare to turn full about," Kta shouted to his own crew. "Quick turn, starboard bank—stand by—Turn! Hard about,—*hard!*"

Tavi changed course with speed that made her timbers groan, oars and helm bringing her about three-quarters to the wind, and Kta was already shouting an order to Pan.

The dark blue sail with the lightning emblem of Elas billowed down from the yard and filled, deck crew hauling to sheet it home. *Tavi* came alive in the water, suddenly bearing down on *Edrif* with the driving power of the wind and her forty-six oars.

Frenzied activity erupted on the other deck. *Edrif* began to turn, full broadside for a moment, continuing until she was nearly stern on. Her dark green sail spread, but she could not turn with graceful *Tavi*'s speed, and her crew hesitated, taken by surprise. *Tavi* had the wind in her own sail, stealing it from theirs.

"Portside oars!" Kta roared over the thunder of the rowing. "Stand by to ship oars portside!—*Hya*, Val!"

"Aye!" Val shouted back. "Understood, my lord!"

A shout of panic went up from *Edrif* as *Tavi* closed, and Kta shouted to the portside bank as they headed for collision. *Tavi*'s two banks lifted from the water, and with frantic haste the men portside shipped oars while the starboard rowers held their poised level.

With the final force of wind and gathered speed, *Tavi* brushed the side of *Edrif*, the Sufak vessel's starboard oars splintering as shouts of pain and panic came from her pits. Sufaki rowers deserted their benches and scrambled for very life, their officers cursing at them in vain.

"Take in sail!" Kta shouted, and *Tavi*'s blue sail began to come in. Quickly she lost the force of the wind and glided under momentum.

"Helm!" Kta shouted. "Starboard oars—in water—and *pull!*"

Tavi was already beginning to turn about under her helm, and the one-sided blue of her oars took her hard about again, timbers groaning. There was a crack like a shot and a scream: one of the long sweeps had snapped under the strain and tumbled a man bleeding into the next bench—the next man leaned to let him fall, but kept the pace, and one of the deck crew ran to aid him, dragging him from the pit. Arrows hissed across the deck—Sufaki archers.

"Portside oars!" Kta shouted, as those men, well-drilled, had already run out their oars to be ready. "All hold! In water—and pull!"

Forty-five oars hit the water together, muscles rippled across glistening backs—stroke—and stroke—and stroke, and *Edrif* astern and helpless with half her oarage hanging in ruin and her deck littered with splinter-wounded men. The arrows fell short now, impotent. The breathing of *Tavi*'s men was in unison and loud, like the ship drawing wind, as if all the crew and the ship they sailed had become one living entity as she drove herself northward, widening the distance.

"First shift," Kta shouted. "Up oars!"

With a single clash of wood the oars came up and held level, dipping and rising slightly with the give of the sea and the oarsmen's panting bodies.

"Ship oars and secure. Second shift,—hold for new pace. Take your beat—Now—two—three—"

They accepted the more leisurely pace, and Kta let go a great sigh and looked down at his men. The first shift still leaned over the wooden shafts, heaving with the effort to breathe. Some coughed rackingly, striving with clumsy hands to pull their discarded cloaks up over their drenched shoulders.

"Well done, my friends," said Kta. "It was very well done."

Lun and several others lifted a hand and signaled a wordless salute, without breath to speak.

"*Hya,* Pan,—you men. It was as fine a job as I have seen. —Get coverings for all those men in the pits. A sip of water too. Kurt, help there, will you?"

Kurt moved, glad at last to find himself useful, and took a pitcher of water to the side of the pit. Two of the men were overcome with exhaustion and had to be lifted out and laid on the deck beside the man whose splintered oar had gashed his belly. It proved an ugly wound, but the belly cavity was not pierced. The man was vowing he would be fit for duty in a day, but Kta ordered otherwise.

Edrif was far astern now, a mere speck, not attempting to follow them. Val gave the helm to Pan and walked forward to join Kta and Kurt.

"The hull took it well," Val reported. "Chal just came up from checking it. But *Edrif* will be a while mending."

"Shan t'Tefur has a mighty hate for us," said Kta, "not lessened by this humiliation. As soon as they can bind up their wounds and fit new oars, they will follow."

"It was bloody chaos on her deck," said Val with satisfaction. "I had a clear view of it. Shan t'Tefur has reason to chase us, but those Sufaki seamen may decide they have had enough. They ought to know we could have sunk them if we had wished."

"The thought may occur to them, but I doubt it will win us their gratitude. We will win as much time as we can." He scanned the pits. "I have not pulled an oar in several years, but it will do me no harm. And you, friend Kurt, you are due gentler care after what you have endured, but we need you."

Kurt shrugged cheerfully enough. "I will learn."

"Go bandage your hands," said Kta. "You have little whole skin left. You are due to lose what remains."

XVII

The clouds had gone by morning and Phan shed his light over a dead calm sea. *Tavi* rolled with a lazy motion, all but dead in the water, her crew lying over the deck where they could find space, wrapped in their cloaks.

Kurt walked to the stern, rubbing his eyes to keep awake. His companion on watch, Pan, stood at the helm. The youth's eyes were closed. He swayed on his feet.

"Pan," said Kurt gently, and Pan came awake with a jerk, his face flushing with consternation.

"Forgive me, Kurt-ifhan."

"I saw you nod," Kurt said, "only an instant ago. Go lie down and I will stand by the helm. In such a sea, it needs no skill."

"I ought not, my lord, I—"

The youth's eyes suddenly fixed on the sky in hope, and Kurt felt it too, the first effects of a gentle southern breeze. it stirred their hair and their cloaks, touched their faces lightly and ruffled the placid waters.

"*Hya!*" Pan shrieked, and all across the deck men sat up. "The wind, the south wind!"

Men were on their feet, and Kta appeared in the doorway of the cabin and waved his hand in signal to Val, who shouted an order for the men to get moving and set the sail.

In a moment the night-blue sail billowed out full. *Tavi* came to run before the wind. A cheer went up from the crew as they felt it.

"*Ei*, my friends," Kta grinned, "full rations this morning,

174

and permission to indulge,—but moderately. I want no head-aches. That wind will bear *Edrif* along too, so keep a sharp eye on all quarters, you men on watch. You rowers, enjoy yourselves."

The wind continued fair and the battered men of *Tavi* were utterly content to sleep in the sun, to massage heated oil into aching limbs and blistered hands, to lie still and talk, employing their hands as they did so with many small tasks that kept *Tavi* in running order.

Toward evening Kta ordered a course change and *Tavi* bore abruptly northwest, coming in toward the Isles. A ship was on the western horizon at sunset, creating momentary alarm, but the sail soon identified her as a merchant vessel of the house of Ilev, the white bird emblem of that house shining like a thing alive on the black sail before the sun.

The merchantman passed astern and faded into the shadowing east, which did not worry them. Ilev was a friend.

Soon there were visible the evening lights on the shores of a little island. Now the men ran out the oars with a will and bent to them as *Tavi* drew toward that light-jeweled strand: Acturi, home port of Hnes, a powerful Isles-based family of the Indras-descended.

"Gan t'Hnes," said Kta as *Tavi* slipped into the harbor of Acturi, "will not be moved by threats of the Sufaki. We will be safe here for the night."

A bell began to toll on shore, men with torches running to the landing as *Tavi* glided in and ran in her oars.

"*Hya!*" a voice ashore hailed them. "What ship are you?"

"*Tavi*, out of Nephane. Tell Gan t'Hnes that Elas asks his hospitality."

"Make fast, *Tavi*, make fast and come ashore. We are friends here. No need to ask."

"Are you sure of them?" Kurt wondered quietly, as the mooring lines were cast out and made secure. "What if some ship of the Methi made it in first?" He nervously scanned the other ships down the little wharf, sails furled and anonymous in the dark. "Hnes might be forced—"

"No, if Gan t'Hnes will not honor house-friendship, then the sun will rise in the west tomorrow dawn. I have known this man since I was a boy at his feet, and Hnes and Elas

have been friends for a thousand years—well, at least for
nine hundred, which is as far as Hnes can count."

"And if that was not t'Hnes' word you were just given?"

"Peace, suspicious human, peace. If Acturi had been
taken from Hnes' control, the shock would have been felt
from shore to shore of the Ome Sin.—*Hya,* Val, run out the
gangplank and Kurt and I will go ashore. Stay with the ship
and hold the men until I have Gan's leave to bring our crew
in."

Gan t'Hnes was a venerable old man and, looking at him,
Kurt found reason that Kta should trust him. He was solidly
Indras, this patriarch of Acturi's trading empire. His house
on the hill was wealthy and proper, the hearthfire tended by
lady Na t'Ilev e Ben sh'Kma, wife to the eldest of Gan's
three sons, who himself was well into years. Lord Gan was a
widower,—the oldest nemet Kurt had seen, and to consider
that nemet lived long and very scarcely showed age, he must
be ancient.

Of course formalities preceded any discussion of business,
all the nemet rituals. There was a young woman, grand-
daughter to the *chan* of Hnes. She made the tea and served
it—and seeing her from the back, her graceful carriage and
the lustrous darkness of her hair, Kurt thought of Mim: she
even looked a little like her in the face, and when she knelt
down and offered him a cup of tea he stared, and felt a pain
that brought tears to his eyes.

The girl bowed her head, cheeks flushing at being gazed
at by a man, and Kurt took the cup, and looked down and
drank his tea, thoughts returning in the quiet and peace of
this Indras home that had not touched him since that night
in Nephane. It was like coming home, for he had never
expected to set foot in a friendly house again; and yet home
was Elas, and Mim, and both were gone.

Hnes was a large family, ruled of course by Gan, and by
Kma, his eldest, and lady Na; and there were others of the
house too, one son being away at sea. There was the aged
chan, Dek, his two daughters and several grandchildren;
Gan's second son Lel and his wife Pym and concubine Tekje
h'Hnes; Lel's daughter Imue, a charming child of about
twelve, who might be the daughter of either of his two

wives: she had Tekje's Sufak-tilted eyes, but sat beside Pym and treated both her mothers with respectful affection; and there were two small boys, both sons of Lel.

The first round of tea was passed with quiet conversation. The nemet were curious about Kurt, the children actually frightened; but the elders smoothed matters over with courtesy.

Then came the second round, and the ladies left with the children, all but lady Na, the first lady of Hnes, whose opinion was of equal weight with that of the elder men.

"Kta," began the lord of Hnes cautiously, "how long are you out from Nephane?"

"Nigh to fifteen days."

"Then," said the old man, "you were there to be part of the sad tale which has reached us."

"Elas no longer exists in Nephane, my lord, and I am exiled. My parents and the *chan* are dead."

"You are in the house of friends," said Gan t'Hnes. "*Ai*, that I should have lived to see such a day. I loved your father as my great friend, Kta, and I love you as if you were one of my own. Name the ones to blame for this."

"The names are too high to curse, my lord."

"No one is beyond the reach of heaven."

"I would not have all Nephane cursed for my sake. The ones responsible are the Methi Djan and her Sufaki lover Shan t'Tefur u Tlekef. I have sworn undying enmity between Elas and the Chosen of Heaven, and a bloodfeud between Elas and the house of Tefur, but I chose exile. If I had intended war, I could have raised war that night in the streets of Nephane. So might my father, and chose to die rather than that. I honor his self-restraint."

Gan bowed his head in thoughtful sorrow. "A ship came two days ago," he said. "*Dkelis* of Irain in Nephane. Her word was from the Chosen of Heaven herself, that Elas had offended against her and had chosen to remove itself from her sight.—That the—true author of the offense was—forgive me, my guests—a human who did murder against citizens of Nephane while under the guardianship of Elas."

"I killed some of t'Tefur's men," said Kurt, sick at heart. He looked at Kta. "Was that it? Was that what caused it?"

"You know there were other reasons," said Kta grimly.

"This was only her public excuse, a means to pass blame.—My lord Gan, was that the sum of the message?"

"In sum," said Gan, "that Elas is outlawed in all holdings of Nephane; that all citizens must treat you as enemies; that you, Kta, and all with you, are to be killed,—excepting lord Kurt, who must be returned alive and unharmed to the Methi's justice."

"Surely," said Kta, "Hnes will not comply."

"Indeed not. Irain knew that; I doubt even they would execute that order, brought face to face with you."

"What will you, sir? Had you rather we spent the night elsewhere? Say it without offense. I am anxious to cause you no inconvenience."

"Son of my friend," said Gan fiercely, "there are laws older than Nephane, than even the shining city itself, and there is justice higher than what is writ in the Methi's decree. No. Let her study how to enforce that decree. Stay in Acturi. I will make this whole island a fortress against them if they want a fight of it."

"My friend, no, no, that would be a terrible thing for your people. We ask at the most supplies and water, in containers that bear no mark of Hnes. *Tavi* will clear your harbor at dawn. No one saw us come save only Ilev, and they are house-friends to us both. And I do not plan that any should see us go. Elas has fallen. That is grief enough. I would not leave a wake of disaster to my friends where I pass."

"Whatever you need is yours,—harbor, supplies, an escort of galleys if you wish it. But stay, let me persuade you, Kta,—I am not so old I would not fight for my friends. All Acturi's strength is at your command. I do not think that with war against Indresul imminent, the Methi will dare alienate one of her possessions in the Isles."

"I did not think she would dare what she did against Elas, sir, and Shan t'Tefur is likely hard behind us at the moment. We have met him once, and he would act against you without hesitation. I know not what authority the Methi has given him, but even if she would hesitate, as you say, an attack might be an accomplished fact before she heard about it. No, sir."

"It is your decision," said Gan regretfully. "But I think even so, we might hold them."

"Provisions and weapons only. That is all I ask."

"Then see to it, my sons, quickly. Provide *Tavi* with all she needs, and have the hands start loading at once."

The two sons of Hnes rose and bowed their respects all around, then went off quickly to carry out their orders.

"These supplies," said Gan, "are a parting gift from Hnes. There is nothing I can send with you to equal the affection I bear you, Kta, my almost-son. Have you men enough? Some of mine would sail with you."

"I would not risk them."

"Then you are short-handed?"

"I would not risk them."

"Where will you go, Kta?"

"To the Yvorst Ome,—beyond the reach of the Methi and the law."

"Hard lands ring that sea, but Hnes ships come and go there. You will meet them from time to time. Let them carry word between us. *Ai,* what days these are. My sight is longer than that of most men, but I see nothing that gives me comfort now. If I were young, I think I would sail with you, Kta, because I have no courage to see what will happen here."

"No, my lord, I know you. I think were you as young as I, you would sail to Nephane and meet the trouble head-on as my father did. As I would do, but I had Aimu's life to consider, and their souls in my charge."

"Little Aimu. I hesitated to ask. I feared more bad news."

"No, thank heaven. I gave her to a husband, and on his life and honor he swore to me he would protect her."

"What is her name now?" asked lady Na.

"My lady, she is Aimu t'Elas e Nym sh'Bel t'Osanef."

"T'Osanef," murmured Gan, in that tone which said: *Ei, Sufaki,* but with pity.

"They have loved each other from childhood," said Kta. "It was my father's will, and mine."

"Then it was well done," said Gan. "May the light of heaven fall gently on them both." And from an Indras of orthodoxy, it was much. "He is a brave man, this t'Osanef, to be husband to our Aimu now."

"It is true," said Kta, and to the lady Na: "Pray for her, my lady. They have much need of it."

"I shall, and for you, and for all who sail with you," she answered, and included Kurt with a glance of her lovely eyes, to which Kurt bowed in deep reverence.

"Thank you," said Kta. "Your house will be in my thoughts too."

"I wish," said Gan, "that you would change your mind and stay. But perhaps you are right. Perhaps someday things will be different, since the Methi is mateless. Someday it may be possible to return."

"It is possible," said Kta, "if she does not appoint a Sufaki successor. We do not much speak of it, but we fear there will be no return—not for our generation."

Gan's jaw tightened. "Acturi will send ships out tonight, I think."

"Do not fight t'Tefur," Kta pleaded.

"They will sail, I say, and provide at least a warning to *Edrif.*"

"When Djan-methi knows of it—"

"Then she will learn the temper of the Isles," said Gan, "and the Chosen of Heaven will perhaps restrain her ambition with sense."

"Ai," murmured Kta. "I do not want this, Gan."

"This is Hnes' choice. Elas has its own honor to consider. I have mine."

"Friend of my father, these waters are too close to Indresul's. You know not what you could let loose. It is a dangerous act."

"It is," said Gan again, "Hnes' choice."

Kta bowed his head, bound to silence under Gan's roof, but that night he spent long in meditation and lay wakeful on his bed in the room he shared with Kurt.

Kurt watched him, and ventured no question into his unrest. He had enough of his own that evening, beginning to fit together the pieces of what Kta had never explained to him, the probable scene in the Upei as Nym demanded justice for Mim's death, while the Methi had in the actions of Elas' own guest the pretext she needed to destroy Elas.

So Nym had died, and Elas had fallen.

And Djan could claim he had made it all inevitable, his

marriage with Mim and his loyalty to Elas being the origin of all her troubles.

—*Excepting lord Kurt, who must be returned alive and unharmed to the Methi's justice.*

Hanan justice.

The justice of a personal anger, where the charges were nothing she would dare present in the Upei. She would destroy all he loved, but she would not let him go. Being Hanan, she believed in nothing after. She would not grant him quick oblivion.

He lay upon the soft down mattress of Hnes' luxury and stared into the dark, and slept only the hours just before dawn, troubled by dreams he could not clearly remember.

The wind bore fair for the north now, warm from the Tamur Basin. The blue sail drew taut and *Tavi*'s bow lanced through the waves, cutting their burning blue to white foam.

Still Kta looked often astern, and whether his concern was more for Gan t'Hnes or for t'Tefur, Kurt was not sure.

"It is out of our hands," Kurt said finally.

"It is out of our hands," Kta agreed with yet another look aft. There was nothing. He bit at his lip. *"Ei, ei,* at least he will not be with us through the Thiad."

"The Necklace. The Lesser Isles," Kurt knew them by repute, barren crags strung across the Ome Sin's narrowest waters, between Indresul and Nephane and claimed by neither side successfully. They were a maze by fair weather, a killer of ships in storms. "Do we go through it or around?"

"Through if the weather favors us. To Nephane's side—wider waters there—if the seas are rough. I do not treat Indresul's waters with the familiarity the Isles-folk use. Well, well, but past that barrier we are free, my friend, free as the north seas and their miserable ports allow us."

"I have heard," Kurt offered, "that there is some civilization there, some cities of size."

"There are two towns, and those are primitive,—*ei* well, one might be called a city, Haithen. It is a city of wood, of frozen streets. Yvesta the mother of snows never looses those lands. There are no farms, only desolate flats, and impossible mountains, and frozen rivers,—ice masses float in the Yvorst Ome that can crush ships, and there are great sea beasts the like of which do not visit these blue waters. *Ai,* it is nothing like Nephane."

"Are you regretting," Kurt asked softly, "that you have chosen as you have?"

"It is a strange place we go," said Kta, "and yet shame to Elas is worse. I think Haithen may be preferable to the Methi's law. It pains me to say it, but Haithen may be infinitely preferable to the Methi's Nephane. Only when we are passing by the coast of Nephane, I shall think of Aimu, and of Bel, and wish that I had news of them. That is the hardest thing, to realize that there is nothing I can do. Elas is not accustomed to helplessness."

En t'Siran, captain of *Rimaris,* swung onto the deck of the courier ship *Kadese,* beneath the furled red sails. Such was his haste that he did not even sit and take tea with the captain of *Kadese* before he delivered his message; he took the ritual sip of tea standing, and scarcely caught his breath before he passed the cup back to the captain's man and bowed his courtesy to the senior officer.

"T'Siran," said the courier captain, "you signaled urgent news."

"A confrontation," said t'Siran, "between Isles ships and a ship of their own kind."

"Indeed." The captain put his own cup aside, signaled a scribe, who began to write. "What happened? Could you identify any of the houses?"

"Easily on the one side. They bore the moon of Acturi on their sails—Gan t'Hnes' sons, I am well sure of it. The other was a strange sail, dark green with a gold dragon."

"I do not know that emblem," said the captain. "It must be one of those Sufak designs."

"Surely," agreed t'Siran, for the dragon Yr was not one of the lucky symbols for an Indras ship. "It may be a methi's ship."

"A confrontation, you say. With what result?"

"A long wait. Then dragon-sail turned aside, toward the coast of Sufak."

"And the men of Acturi?"

"Held their position some little time. Then they went back into the Isles. We drew off quickly. We had no orders to provoke combat with the Isles. That is the sum of my report."

"It is," said the captain of *Kadese*, "a report worth carrying."

"My lord." En t'Siran acknowledged the unusual tribute from a courier captain, bowed his head and, as the captain returned the parting courtesy, left.

The captain of *Kadese* hardly delayed to see *Rimaris* spread sail and take her leave before he shouted an order to his own crew and bade them put about for Indresul.

The thing predicted was beginning. Nephane had come to a point of division. The Methi of Indresul had direct interest in this evidence, which might affect policies up and down the Ome Sin and bring Nephane nearer its day of reckoning.

From now on, *Kadese*'s captain thought to himself, the Methi Ylith would begin to listen to her captains, who urged that there would be no better time than this. Heaven favored it.

"Rowers to the benches," he bade his second, "reliefs at the minimum interval, all available crew."

With four shifts and a hundred and ten oars, the slim *Kadese* was equipped to go the full distance. The wind was fair behind her. Her double red sail was bellied out full, and there was nothing faster on either side of the Ome Sin.

There were scattered clouds, small wisps of white with gray undersides that grew larger in the east as the hours passed. The crew of *Tavi* kept a nervous watch on the skies, dreading the shift of wind that could mean delay in these dangerous waters.

In the west, near at hand, rose the grim jagged spires of the Thiad. The sun declined toward the horizon, threading color into the scant clouds which touched that side of the sky.

The waves splashed and rocked at them as *Tavi* came dangerously close to a rock that only scarcely broke the surface. One barren island was to starboard, a long spine of jagged rocks.

It was the last of the feared islets.

"We are through," exulted Mnek as it fell behind them. "We are for the Yvorst Ome."

Then sail appeared in the dusky east.

Val t'Ran, normally harsh-spoken, did not even swear when it was reported. He put the helm over for the west, cutting dangerously near the fringe rocks of the north Thiad, and sent Pan running to take orders from Kta, who was coming toward the stern as rapidly as Kta ever moved on *Tavi*'s deck.

"To the benches!" Kta was shouting, rousing everyone who had been off duty. Men scrambled before him.

He strode up to the helm and gave Val the order to maintain their present westerly heading.

"Tkel!" he called up to the rigging. "What sail?"

"I cannot tell, my lord," Tkel's voice drifted down from the yard, where the man swung precariously on the foot-rope. "The distance is too great."

"We shall keep it so," Kta muttered, and eyed mistrust-fully the great spires and deadlier rough water which lay to port. "Gently to starboard, Val. Even for good reason, this is too close."

"Aye, sir," said Val, and the ship came a few degrees over.

"They are following," Tkel shouted down after a little time had passed. "They must think we are out of Indresul, my lord."

"The lad is too free with his supposings," Val said between his teeth.

"Nevertheless," said Kta, "that is probably the answer."

"I will join the deck crew," Kurt offered. "Or serve as relief at the benches."

"You are considered of Elas," said Kta. "It makes the men uneasy when you show haste or concern. But if work will relieve your nerves, indulge yourself. Go to the benches."

Kta himself was frightened. It was likely that Kta himself would gladly have taken a hand with the oars, with the rigging, with anything that would have materially sped *Tavi* on her way; Kurt knew the nemet well enough to read it in his eyes, though his face was calm. He burned to do some-thing. They had fenced together: Kurt knew the nemet's impatient nature. The Ancestors, Kta had told him once, were rash men. That was the character of Elas.

In the jolted, moving vision of Kta that Kurt had from the

rowers' pit, his own mind numbed by the beat of the oars and the need to breathe, the nemet still stood serenely beside Val at the helm, arms folded, staring out to the horizon.

Then Tkel's shrill voice called down so loudly it rose even over the thunder of the oars.

"Sails off the port bow!"

Tavi altered course. Deck crews ran to the sheets, the oars shuddered a little at the unexpectedly deep bite of the blades, lifted. Chal upon the catwalk called out a faster beat. Breath came harder. Vision blurred.

"They are three sails!" Tkel's voice floated down.

It was tribute to *Tavi*'s discipline that no one broke time to look. Kta looked, and then walked down among the rowers along the main deck so they could see him clearly.

"Well," he said, "we bear due north. Those are ships of Indresul ahead of us. If we can hold our present course and they take interest in the other ship, all will be well.—*Hya*, Chal, ease off the beat. Make it one which will last. We may be at this no little time."

The cadence of the oars took a slower beat. Kta went back to his place at the helm, looking constantly to that threatened horizon. Whatever the Indras ships were doing was something outside the world of the pits: the pace maintained itself, mind lost, no glances at anything but the sweat-drenched back of the man in front, his shoulders, clearing the sweep in back only scarcely, bend and breathe and stretch and pull.

"They are in pursuit," said Sten, whose bench was aftmost port.

The candence did not falter.

"They are triremes intercepting us," Kta said at last, shouting so all could hear. "We cannot outrun them. Hard starboard. We are going back to Nephane's side."

At least two hundred and ten oars each, double sail.

As *Tavi* bore to starboard, Kurt had his first view of what pursued them, through the oarport: two-masted, a greater and a lesser sail, three banks of oars on a side lifting and falling like the wings of some sea-skimming bird. They seemed to move effortlessly despite their ponderous bulk, gaining with every stroke of their oars, where men would have reliefs from the benches.

Tavi had none. It was impossible to hold this pace long. Vision hazed. Kurt drew air that seemed tainted with blood.

"We must come about," Val cried from the helm. "We must come about, my lord, and surrender."

Kta cast a look back. So, from his vantage point, did Kurt, saw the first of the three Indras triremes pull out to the fore of the others, her gold and white sail taut with the wind. The beat of her oars suddenly doubled, at maximum speed.

"Up the beat," Kta ordered Chal, and Chal shouted over the grate and thunder of the oars, quickening the time to the limit of endurance.

And the wind fell.

The breath of heaven left the sail and had immediate effect on the speed of *Tavi*. A soft groan went up from the crew. They did not slacken the pace.

The leading trireme grew closer, outmatching them in oarage.

"Hold!" Kta shouted hoarsely, and walked to the front of the pits. "Hold! Up oars!"

The rhythm ceased, oars at level, men leaning over them and using their bodies' weight to counter the length of the sweeps, their breathing raucous and cut with hacking coughs.

"Pan! Tkel!" Kta shouted aloft. "Strike sail!"

Now a murmur of dismay came from the men, and the crew hesitated, torn between the habit of obedience and an order they did not want.

"Move!" Kta shouted at them furiously. "Strike sail! You men in the pits, ship oars and get out of there! Plague take it, do not spoil our friendship with mutiny! Get out of there!"

Lun, pit captain, give a miserable shake of his head, then ran in his oar with abrupt violence, and the others followed suit. Pan and Mnek and Chal and others scrambled to the rigging, and quickly a " 'ware below!" rang out and the sail plummeted, tumbling down with a shrill singing of ropes.

Kurt scrambled from the pit with the others, found the strength to gain his feet and staggered back to join Kta on the quarterdeck.

Kta took the helm himself, put the rudder over hard, depriving *Tavi* of what momentum she had left.

The leading ship veered a little in its course, no longer coming directly at them, and tension ebbed perceptibly among *Tavi*'s men.

Then light flashed a rapid signal from the deck of the rearmost trireme and the lead ship changed course again, near enough now that men could be clearly seen on her lofty deck. The tempo of her oars increased sharply, churning up the water.

"Gods!" Val murmured incredulously. "My lord Kta, they are going to ram!"

"Abandon ship!" Kta shouted. "Val,—go—go, man! And you, Kurt—"

There was no time left. The dark bow of the Indras trireme rushed at *Tavi*'s side, the water foaming white around the gleaming bronze of the vessel's double ram. With a grinding shock of wood *Tavi*'s rail and deck splintered and the very ship rose and slid sideways in the water, lifted and pushed into ruin by the towering prow of the trireme.

Kurt flung an arm around the far rail and clung to it, shaken off his feet by the tilting of the deck. With a second tilting toward normal and a grating sound, the trireme began to back water and disengage herself as *Tavi*'s wreckage fell away. Dead were littered across the deck. Men screamed. Blood and water washed over the splintered planking.

"Kurt," Kta screamed at him, "jump!"

Kurt turned and stared helplessly at the nemet, fearing the sea as much as enemy weapons. Behind him the second of the triremes was coming up on the undamaged side of the listing ship, her oars churning up the bloodied waters. Some of the survivors in the water were struck by the blades, trying desperately to cling to them. The gliding hull rode them under.

Kta seized him by the arm and pushed him over the rail. Kurt twisted desperately in midair, hit the water hard and choked, fighting his way to the surface with the desperation of instinct.

His head broke surface and he gasped in air, sinking again as he swallowed water in the chop, his hand groping for anything that might float. A heavy body exploded into the dark water beside him and he managed to get his head above water again as Kta surfaced beside him.

"Go limp," Kta gasped. "I can hold you if you do not struggle."

Kurt obeyed as Kta's arm encircled his neck, went under, and then felt the nemet's hand under his chin lift his face to air again. He breathed, a great gulp of air, lost the surface again. Kta's strong, sure strokes carried them both, but the rough water washed over them. Of a sudden he thought that Kta had lost him, and panicked as Kta let him go: but the nemet shifted his grip and dragged him against a floating section of timber.

Kurt threw both arms over it, coughing and choking for air.

"Hold on!" Kta snapped at him, and Kurt obediently tightened his chilled arms, looking at the nemet across the narrow bit of debris. Wind hit them, the first droplets of rain. Lightning flashed in the murky sky.

Behind them the galley was coming about. Someone on deck was pointing at them.

"Behind you," Kurt said to Kta. "They have us in sight— for something."

Kurt lifted himself from his face on the deck of the trireme, rose to his knees and knelt beside Kta's sodden body. The nemet was still breathing, blood from a head wound washing as a crimson film across the rain-spattered deck. In another moment he began to try to rise, still fighting.

Kurt took him by the arm, cast a look at the Indras officer who stood among the surrounding crew. Receiving no word from him, he lifted Kta so that he could rise to his knees, and Kta wiped the blood from his eyes and leaned over on his hands, coughing.

"On your feet," said the Indras captain.

Kta would not be helped. He shook off Kurt's hand and completed the effort himself, braced his feet and straightened.

"Your name," said the officer.

"Kta t'Elas u Nym."

"T'Elas," the man echoed with a nod of satisfaction.

"Aye, I was sure we had a prize.—Put them both in irons. Then put about for Indresul."

Kta gave Kurt a spiritless look, and in truth there was nothing to do but submit. They were taken together into the hold, the trireme having far more room belowdecks than little *Tavi*—and in that darkness and cold they were put into chains and left on the bare planking without so much as a blanket for comfort.

"What now?" Kurt asked, clenching his teeth against the spasms of chill.

"I do not know," said Kta. "But it would surely have been better for us if we had drowned with the rest."

XVIII

Indresul the shining was set deep within a bay, a great and ancient city. Her white, triangle-arched buildings spread well beyond her high walls, permanent and secure. Warships and merchantmen were moored at her docks. The harbor and the broad streets that fanned up into the city itself were busy with traffic. In the high center of the city, at the crest of the hill around which it was built, rose a second great ring-wall, encircling large buildings of gleaming white stone, an enormous fortress-temple complex, the Indume, heart and center of Indresul. There would be the temple, the shrine that all Indras-descended revered as the very hearthfire of the universe.

"The home of my people," said Kta as they stood on the deck waiting for their guards to take them off. "Our land, which we call on in all our prayers. I am glad that I have seen it, but I do not think we will have a long view of it, my friend."

Kurt did not answer him. No word could improve matters. In the three days they had been chained in the hold, he had had time to speak with Kta, to talk as they once had talked in Elas, long, inconsequential talks—sometimes even to laugh, though the laughter had the taste of ashes. But the one thing Kta had never said was what was likely to happen to Kurt, only that he himself would be taken in charge by the house of Elas-in-Indresul. Kta undoubtedly did suspect and would not say. Perhaps too he knew what would likely

190

become of a human among these most orthodox of Indras:
Kurt did not want to foreknow it.

The mournful echo of sealing doors rolled through the
vaulted hall, and through the haze of lamps and incense in
the triangular hall burned the brighter glare of the holy
fire,—the *rhmei* and the *phusmeha* of the Indume-fortress.
Kurt paused involuntarily as Kta did, confused by the light
and the profusion of faces.

From some doorway hidden by the haze and the light
from the hearthfire, there appeared a woman, a shadow in
brocade flanked by the more massive figures of armed men.

The guards who had brought them from the trireme moved
them forward with the urging of their spear shafts. The
woman did not move. Her face was clearer as they drew
near her: she was goddess-like, tall, willowy. The shining
darkness of her hair was crowned with a headdress that
fitted beside her face like the plates of a helm, and shimmered when she moved with the swaying of fine gold chains
from the wide wings of it. She was nemet, and of incredible
beauty: Ylith t'Erinas ev Tehal, Methi of Indresul.

Her dark eyes turned full on them, and Kta fell on his
face before her, full length on the polished stone of the
floor. Her gaze did not so much as flicker; this was the
obeisance due her. Kurt fell to his knees also, and on his
face, and did not look up.

"Nemet," she said, "look at me."

Kta stirred then and sat up, but did not stand.

"Your name," she asked him. Her voice had a peculiar
stillness, clear and delicate.

"Methi, I am Kta t'Elas u Nym."

"Elas. Elas of Nephane. How fares your house there,
t'Elas?"

"The Methi may have heard. I am the last."

"What, Elas fallen?"

"So Fate and the Methi of Nephane willed it."

"Indeed.—And how is this, that a man of Indras descent
is companioned by a human?"

"He is of my house, Methi, and he is my friend."

"You are an offense, t'Elas, an affront to my eyes and to
the pure light of heaven. Let t'Elas be given to the examina-

tion of the house he has defiled, and let their recommendation be made known to me."

She clapped her hands: the guards moved, in a clash of metal and hauled Kta up. Kurt injudiciously flung himself to his knees, halted suddenly with the point of a spear in his side. Kta looked down at him with the face of a man who knew his fate was sealed, and then yielded and went with them.

Kurt flashed a glance at Ylith, anger swelling in his throat.

The staff of the spear across his neck brought him half stunned to the marble floor, and he expected it to be through his back in the next instant, but the blow did not come.

"Human." There was no love in that word. "Sit up."

Kurt moved his arms and found purchase against the floor. He did not move quickly, and one of his guards jerked him up by the arm and let him go again.

"Do you have a name, human?"

"My name," he answered with deliberate insolence, "is Kurt Liam t'Morgan u Patrick Edward."

Ylith's eyes traveled over him and fixed last on his face. "Morgan. This would be your own alien house."

He made no response. Her tone invited none.

"Never have I looked upon a living human," Ylith said softly. "Indeed,—this seems more intelligent than the Tamurlin, is it not so, Lhe?"

"I do not believe," said the slender man at her left, "that he is Tamurlin, Methi."

"He is still of their blood." A frown darkened her eyes. "It is an outrage against nature. One would take him for nemet but for that unwholesome coloration,—and until one saw his face. Have him stand. I would take a closer look at him."

Kurt had both his arms seized, and he was pulled roughly and abruptly to his feet, his face hot with shame and anger. But if there was one act that would seal the doom of all Nephane, friends and enemies alike, it was for the friend of Elas-in-Nephane to attack this woman. He stubbornly turned his face away, until the flat of a spear blade against his cheek turned his head back and he met her eyes.

"Like one of the *inim*-born," the Methi observed. "So one would imagine them, the children of the upper air,

—somewhat birdlike, the madness of eye, the sharpness of features. But there is some intelligence there too. Lhe, I would save this human a little time and study him."

"As the Methi wills it."

"Put him under restraint, and when I find the time I will deal with the matter." Ylith started to turn away, but paused instead for another look, as if the very reality of Kurt was incredible to her. "Keep him in reasonable comfort. He is able to understand, so let him know that he may expect less comfort if he proves troublesome."

Reasonable comfort, as Lhe interpreted it, was austere indeed. Kurt sat against the wall on a straw filled pallet that was the only thing between him and the bare stones of the floor, and shivered in the draft under the door. There was a rounded circlet of iron around his ankle, secured by a chain to a ringbolt in the stones of the wall, and it was beyond his strength to tear free. There was nowhere to go if he could.

He straightened his leg, dragging the chain along the floor with him, and stretched out face down on the pallet, doubling his chilled arms under him for warmth.

Nothing the Tamurlin had done to him could equal the humiliation of this; the worst beating he had ever taken was no shame at all compared to the look with which Ylith t'Erinas had touched him. They had insisted on washing him, which he would gladly have done, for he was filthy from his confinement in the hold, but they leveled spears at him, forced him to stand against a wall and remove what little clothing he still wore, then scrub himself repeatedly with strong soap. Then they hit him with a bucketful of cold water, and gave him nothing with which to dry his skin. There was a linen breechclout, not even the decency of a *ctan*; that and an iron ring and a cup of water from which to drink: that was the consideration Lhe afforded him.

Hours passed, and the oil lamp on the ledge burned out, leaving only the light that came through the small barred-window from the outer hall. He managed to sleep a little, turning from side to side, warming first his arms and then his back against the mattress.

Then, without warning or explanation, men invaded his cell and forced him from the room under heavy guard, hastening him along the dim halls, the ring on his ankle band a constant, metallic sound at every other step.

Upstairs was their destination, a small room somewhere in the main building, warmed by an ordinary fire in a common hearth. A single pillar supported its level ceiling.

To this they chained his hands, passing the chain behind him around the pillar; then they left him, and he was alone for a great time. It was no hardship: it was warm in this room. He absorbed the heat gratefully and sank down at the base of this pillar, leaning against it and bowing his head, willing even to sleep.

"Human."

He brought his head up, blinking in the dim light. Ylith had come into the room. She sat down upon the ledge beneath the slit of a window and regarded him curiously. She was without the crown now, and her massive braids coiled on either side of her head gave her a strangely fragile grace.

"You are one of the human woman's companions," she said, "that she missed killing."

"No," he said, "I came independently."

"You are an *educated* human, as she is."

"As educated as you are, Methi."

Ylith's eyes registered offense, and, it was possible,— amusement. "You are not a civilized human, however, and you are therefore demonstrating your lack of manners."

"My civilization," he said, "is some twelve thousand years old. And I am still looking for evidence of yours in this city."

The Methi laughed outright. "I have never met such answers. You hope to die, I take it. Well, human, look at me. Look up."

He did so.

"It is difficult to accustom myself to your face," she said. "But you do reason. I perceive that.—What is the origin of humans, do you know?"

It was, religiously, a dangerous question. "We are," he said, "children of one of the brothers of the earth, at least as old as the nemet."

"But not light-born," said Ylith, which was to say, unholy

and lawless. "Tell me this, wise human: does Phan light your land too?"

"No. One of Phan's brothers lights our world."

Her brows lifted. "Indeed. *Another* sun?"

He saw the snare of a sudden, realized that the Indras of the shining city were not so liberal and cosmic in their concept of the universe as human-dominated Nephane.

"Phan," she said, "has no equals."

He did not attempt to answer her. She did not rage at him, only kept staring, her face deeply troubled. Not naive, was Ylith of Indresul: she seemed to think deeply, and seemed to find no answer that pleased her. "You seem to me," she said, "precisely what I would expect from Nephane. The Sufaki think such things."

"The *yhia*," he said, venturing dangerously, "is beyond man's grasp, is that not so, Methi? And when man seeks to understand, being man and not god, he seeks within mortal limits, and understands his truth in simple terms and under the guise of familiar words that do not expand his mortal senses beyond his capacity to understand. This is what I have heard. We all—being mortal—deal in models of reality, in oversimplifications."

It was such a thesis as Nym had posed him once over tea, in the peace of the *rhmei* of Elas, when conversation came to serious things, to religion, and humanity. They had argued, and disagreed, and they had been able then to smile and reconcile themselves in reason. The nemet loved debating. Each evening at teatime there was a question posed if there was no business at hand, and they would talk the topic to exhaustion.

"You interest me," said Ylith. "I think I shall hand you over to the priests and let them hear this wonder,—a human that reasons."

"We are," he said, "reasoning beings."

"Are you of the same source as Djan-methi?"

"Of the same kind, not the same politics or beliefs."

"Indeed."

"We have disagreed."

Ylith considered him in some interest. "Tell me, is the color of her hair truly like that of metal?"

"Like copper."

"You were her lover."

Heat flashed to his face. He looked suddenly and resentfully into her eyes. "You are well-informed. Where do you plant your spies?"

"Does the question offend you? Do humans truly possess a sense of modesty?"

"And any other feeling known to the nemet," he returned. "I had *loved* your people. Is this what your philosophy comes to, hating me because I disturb your ideas, because you cannot account for me?"

He would never have said such a thing outside Elas; the nemet themselves were too self-contained, although he could have said it to Kta. He was exhausted; the hour was late. He came close to tears, and felt shamed at his own outburst.

But Ylith tilted her head to one side, a little frown creasing her wide-set brows. "You are certainly unlike the truth I have heard of humans." And after a moment she rose and opened the door, where an elderly man waited,—a whitehaired man whose hair flowed to his shoulders, and whose *ctan* and *pel* were gold-bordered white.

The old man made a profound obeisance to Ylith, but he did not kneel: by this it was evident that she knew of his presence there, that they had agreed before hand.

"Priest," she said, "look on this creature and tell me what you see."

The priest straightened and turned his watery eyes on Kurt. "Stand," he urged gently. Kurt gathered his almost paralyzed limbs beneath him and struggled awkwardly to his feet. Of a sudden he hoped; he did not know why this alien priest should inspire that in him, but the voice was soft and the dark eyes like a benediction.

"Priest," urged the Methi.

"Great Methi," answered the priest, "this is no easy matter. Whether this is a man as we understand the word, I cannot say. But he is not Tamurlin. Let the Methi do as seems just in her own eyes, but it is possible that she is dealing with a feeling and reasoning being, whether or not it is a man."

"Is this creature good or evil, priest?"

"What is man, great Methi?"

"Man," snapped the Methi impatiently, "is the child of Nae. Whose child is he, priest?"

"I do not know, great Methi."

Ylith lowered her eyes then, flicked a glance toward Kurt and down and back again. "Priest, I charge you, debate this matter within the college of priests and return me an answer. Take him with you if it will be needful."

"Methi, I will consult with them, and we will send for him if his presence seems helpful."

"Then you are dismissed," she said, and let the priest go.

Then she left too, and Kurt sank down again against his pillar, confused and mortally tired and embarrassed. He was alone and glad to be alone, so he did not have to be so treated before friends or familiar enemies.

He slumped against his aching joints and tried to will himself to sleep. In sleep the time passed. In sleep he did not need to think.

In sleep sometimes he remembered Mim, and thought himself in Elas, and that the morning bells would never ring.

Doors opened, boomed shut. People stirred around him, shuffling here and there, forcing him back to wakefulness.

The Methi had come back.

This time they brought Kta.

Kta saw him—relief touched his eyes—but he could say nothing. The Methi's presence demanded his attention. Kta came and knelt before her, and went full to his face. His movements were not easy. He appeared to have been hard-used.

And she ignored him, looking above his prostrate form to the tall, stern man who bowed stiffly to his knees and rose again.

"Vel t'Elas," said Ylith, "what has Elas-in-Indresul determined concerning this man Kta?"

Kta's distant kinsman bowed again, straightened. He was of immense dignity, a man reminiscent of Nym. "We deliver him to the Methi for judgment, for life or for death."

"How do you find concerning his dealings with Elas?"

"Let the Methi be gracious: he has kept our law and still honors our Ancestors, except in the offense for which we deliver him up to you: his dealings with this human, and that he is of Nephane."

"Kta t'Elas u Nym," said Ylith.

Kta lifted his face and sat back on his heels.

"Kta t'Elas, your people have chosen an alien to rule them. Why?"

"She was chosen by heaven, Methi, not by men; and it was a fair choosing, by the oracles."

"Confirmed in proper fashion by the Upei and the Families?"

"Yes, Methi."

"Then," she said, looking about at the officers who had come into the room, "heaven has decided to deliver Nephane into our hands once more.—And you, u Nym, who were born Indras,—where is your allegiance now?"

"In my father's land, Ylith-methi, and with my house-friends."

"Do you then reject all allegiance to *this* house of Elas, which was father to your Ancestors?"

"Great Methi," said Kta, and his voice broke, "I reverence you and the home of my Ancestors, but I am bound to Nephane by ties equally strong. I cannot dishonor myself and the Ancestors of Elas by turning against the city that gave me birth. Elas-in-Indresul would not understand me if I did so."

"You equivocate."

"No, Methi. It is my belief."

"What was your mother's name, u Nym? Was she Sufaki or was she Indras?"

"Methi, she was the lady Ptas t'Lei e Met sh'Nym."

"Most honorable, the house of Lei. Then in both lines you are Indras and well descended,—surely of an orthodox house. Yet you choose the company of Sufaki and humans. I find this exceedingly difficult of understanding, Kta t'Elas u Nym."

Kta bowed his head and gave no answer.

"Vel t'Elas," said the Methi, "is this son of your house in any way a follower of the Sufak heresy?"

"Great Methi, Elas finds that he has been educated into the use of alien knowledge and errors, but his upbringing is orthodox."

"Kta t'Elas," said the Methi, "what is the origin of humans?"

"I do not know, Methi."

"Do you say that they are possessed of a soul, and that they are equal to nemet?"

Kta lifted his head. "Yes, Methi," he said firmly, "I believe so."

"Indeed, indeed." Ylith frowned deeply and rose from her place, smoothing the panels of her *chatem*. Then she shot a hard look at the guards. "Lhe,—take these prisoners both to the upper prisons and provide what is needful to their comfort. But confine them separately and allow them no communication with each other. None, Lhe."

"Methi." He acknowledged the order with a bow.

Her eyes lingered distastefully on Kurt. "This," she said, "is nemetlike. It is proper that he be decently clothed. Insofar as he thinks he is nemet, treat him as such."

Light flared.

Kurt blinked and rubbed his eyes as the opening of his door and the intrusion of men with torches brought him out of a sound sleep into panic. Faceless shadows moved in on him.

He threw off the blanket and scrambled up from the cot his new quarters provided him—not to fight, not to fight: it was the worst thing for him and for Kta.

"You must come," said Lhe's voice out of the glare.

Kurt schooled himself to bow in courtesy, instincts otherwise. "Yes, sir," he said, and began to put on his clothing. When he was done, one guard laid hands on him.

"My lord," he appealed to Lhe, a look of reproach on his face. And Lhe, dignified, elegant Lhe, was the gentleman Kurt suspected; he was too much nemet and too Indras to ignore the rituals of courtesy when they were offered.

"I think that he will come of his own accord," said Lhe to his companions, and they reluctantly let him free.

"Thank you," said Kurt, bowing slightly. "Can you tell me where or why—?"

"No, human," said Lhe. "We do not know, except that you are summoned to the justice hall."

"Do you hold trials at *night*?" Kurt asked, honestly

shocked. Even in liberal Nephane, no legal business could be done after Phan's light had left the land.

"You cannot be tried," said Lhe. "You are human."

In some part it did not surprise him, but he had not clearly considered the legalities of his status. Perhaps, he thought, his dismay showed on his face, for Lhe looked uncomfortable, shrugged and made a helpless gesture.

"You must come," Lhe repeated.

Kurt went with them unrestrained, through plain halls and down several turns of stairs, until they came to an enormous pair of bivalve doors and passed through them into a hall of ancient stonework.

The beamed ceiling here was scarcely visible in the light of the solitary torch, which burned in a wall socket. The only furniture was a long tribunal and its chairs.

A ringbolt was in the floor, already provided with chain. Lhe courteously—with immense courtesy—asked him to stand there, and one of the men locked the chain through the ring on his ankle.

He stared up at Lhe, rude, angry, and Lhe avoided his eyes.

"Come," said Lhe to his men. "We are not bidden to remain." And to Kurt: "Human,—you will win far more by humble words than by pride."

He might have meant it in kindness; he might have been laughing. Kurt stared at their retreating backs, shaking all over with rage and fright.

Of a sudden he cried out, kicked at the restraint in a fit of fury, jerked at it again and again, willing even to break his ankle if it would make them see him, that he was not to be treated like this.

All that he succeeded in doing was in losing his balance, for there was not enough chain to do more than rip the skin around his ankle. He sprawled on the bruising stone and picked himself up, on hands and knees, head hanging.

"Are you satisfied?" asked the Methi.

He spun on one knee toward the voice beyond the torchlight. Softly a door closed unseen, and she came into the circle of light. She wore a robe that was almost a mere *pelan*, gauzy blue, and her dark hair was like a cloud of night, held by a silver circlet around her temples. She stopped at the edge of the tribunal, her short tilted brows lifted in an expression of amusement.

"This is not," she said, "the behavior of an intelligent being."

He gathered himself to sit, nemet-fashion, on feet and ankles, hands palm up in his lap, the most correct posture of a visitor at another's hearth.

"This is not," he answered, "the welcome I was accorded in Nephane, and some of them were my enemies. I am sorry if I have offended you, Methi."

"This is not," she said, "Nephane. And I am not Djan." She sat down in the last of the chairs of the tribunal and faced him so, her long-nailed hands folded before her on the bar. "If you were to strike one of my people,—"

He bowed slightly. "They have been kind to me. I have no intention of striking anyone."

"*Ai*," she said, "now you are trying to impress us."

"I am of a house," he answered, hoping that he was not causing Kta worse difficulty by that claim. "I was taught courtesy. I was taught that the honor of that house is best served by courtesy."

"It is," she said, "a fair answer."

It was the first grace she had granted him. He looked up at her with a little relaxing of his defenses. "Why," he asked, "did you call me here?"

"You troubled my dreams," she said. "I saw fit to trouble yours." And then she frowned thoughtfully. "Do you dream?"

It was not humor, he realized; it was, for a nemet, a religiously reasonable question.

"Yes," he said, and she thought about that for a time.

"The priests cannot tell me what you are," she said finally. "Some urge that you be put to death quite simply; others urge that you be killed by *atia*. Do you know what that means, t'Morgan?"

"No," he said, perceiving it was not threat but question.

"It means," she said, "that they think you have escaped the nether regions and that you should be returned there with such pains and curses as will bind you there. That is a measure of their distress at you. *Atia* has not been done in centuries. Someone would have to research the rites before they could be performed. I think some priests are doing that now.—But Kta t'Elas insists you have a soul, though he could lose his own for that heresy."

"Kta," said Kurt with difficulty through his own fear, "is a gentle and religious man. He—"

"T'Morgan," she said, "you are my concern at the moment, what you are."

"You do not want to know. You will ask until you get the answer that agrees with what you want to hear, that is all."

"You have the look," she said, "of a bird,—a bird of prey. Other humans I have seen had the faces of beasts. I have never seen one alive or clean. Tell me, if you had not that chain, what would you do?"

"I would like to get off my knees," he said. "This floor is cold."

It was rash impudence. It chanced to amuse her. Her laugh held even a little gentleness. "You are appealing. And if you were nemet, I could not tolerate that attitude in you. But what things really pass in your mind? What would you, if you were free?"

He shrugged, stared off into the dark. "I—would ask for Kta's freedom," he said. "And we would leave Indresul and go wherever we could find a harbor."

"You are loyal to him."

"Kta is my friend. I am of Elas."

"You are human. Like Djan, like the Tamurlin."

"No," he said, "like neither."

"Wherein lies the difference?"

"We are of different nations."

"You were her lover, t'Morgan. *Where* do you come from?"

"I do not know."

"Do not know?"

"I am lost. I do not know where I am or where home is."

She considered him, her beautiful face more than usually unhuman with the light falling on it at that angle, like a slightly abstract work of art. "The hearthfire of your kind —assuming you are civilized—lies far distant. It would be terrible to die among strangers, to be buried with rites not your own, with no one to call you by your right name."

Kurt bowed his head, of a sudden seeing another darkened room, Mim lying before the hearthfire of Elas, Mim

without her own name for her burying in Nephane: alien
words and alien gods, and the helplessness he had felt. He
was afraid suddenly with a fear she had put a name to, and
he thought of himself dead and being touched by them and
committed to burial in the name of gods not his and rites he
did not understand. Almost he wished they would throw
him in the sea and give him to the fish and to Kalyt's
green-haired daughters.

"Have I touched on something painful?" Ylith asked softly.
"Did you find the Guardians of Elas did somewhat resent
your presence,—or did you imagine that you were nemet?"

"Elas," he said, "was home to me."

"You married there."

He looked up, startled, surprised into reaction.

"Did she consent," she asked, "or was she given?"

"Who—told you of that?"

"Elas-in-Indresul examined Kta t'Elas on the matter. I
ask you: did she consent freely?"

"She consented." He put away his anger and assumed
humility for Mim's sake, made a bow of request. "Methi,
she was one of your own people, born on Indresul's side.
Her name was Mim t'Nethim e Sel."

Ylith's brows lifted in dismay. "Have you spoken with
Lhe of this?"

"Methi?"

"He is of Nethim. Lhe t'Nethim e Kma, second-son to the
lord Kma; and Nethim is of no great friendship to Elas.
T'Elas did not mention the house name of the lady Mim."

"He never knew it. Methi, she was buried without her
right name. It would be a kindness if you would tell the lord
Kma that she is dead, so they could make prayers for her. I
do not think they would want to hear that request from
me."

"They will ask who is responsible for her death."

"Shan t'Tefur u Tlekef and Djan of Nephane."

"Not Kurt t'Morgan?"

"No." He looked down, unwilling to give way in her
sight. The nightmare remembrances he had crowded out of
his mind in the daylight were back again, the dark and the
fire, and Nym standing before the hearthfire calling upon
his Ancestors with Mim dead at his feet. Nym could tell

them his grievances in person now. Nym and Ptas—Hef. They had walked and breathed that night and now they had gone to join her. Shadows now, all of them.

"I will speak to Kma t'Nethim and to Lhe," she said.

"Maybe," Kurt said, "you ought to omit to tell them that she married a human."

Ylith was silent a moment. "I think," she said, "that you grieve over her very much. Our law teaches that you have no soul, and that she would have sinned very greatly in consenting to such a union."

"She is dead. Leave it at that."

"If," she continued, relentless in the pursuit of her thought, *"if* I admitted that this was not so,—then it would mean that many wise men have been wrong, that our priests are wrong, that our state has made centuries of error. I would have to admit that in an ordered universe there are creatures which do not fit the order, I should have to admit that this world is not the only one, that Phan is not the only god. I should have to admit things for which men have been condemned to death for heresy. Look up at me, human. Look at me."

He did as she asked, terrified, for he suddenly realized what she was saying. She suspected the truth. There was no hope in argument. It was not politically or religiously expedient to have the truth published.

"You insist," she said, "that there are two universes, mine and yours, and that somehow you have passed into mine. By my rules you are an animal: I reason that even an animal could possess the outward attributes of speech and upright bearing. But in other things you are nemetlike. I dreamed, t'Morgan. I dreamed, and you were dead in my dream, and I looked upon your face and it troubled me exceedingly. I thought then that you had been alive and that you had loved a nemet, and that therefore you must have a soul. And I woke, and was still troubled—exceedingly."

"Kta," he said, "did nothing other than you have done. He was troubled. He helped me. He ought to be set free."

"You do not understand. He is nemet. The law applies to him. You—can be kept. On him, I must pronounce sentence. Would you choose to die with Kta, rather than enjoy your life in confinement? You could be made comfortable. It would not be that hard a life."

He found surprisingly little difficult about the answer. At the moment he was not even afraid. "I owe Kta," he said. "He never objected to my company, living. And that, among nemet, seems to have been a rare friendship."

Ylith seemed a little surprised. "Well," she said, rising and smoothing her skirts. "I will let you return to your sleep, t'Morgan. I will honor some of your requests. Nethim will give her honor at my request."

"I am grateful for that, at least, Methi."

"Do you want for anything?"

"To speak with Kta," he said, "that most of all."

"That," she said, "will not be permitted."

XIX

Keys rattled. Kurt stirred out of the torpor of long waiting. Suddenly he realized it was not breakfast. Too many people were in the hall: he heard their moving, the insertion of the key. Another of the moods of Ylith-methi, he reckoned.

Or it was an execution detail, and he was about to learn what had become of Kta.

Lhe led them, Lhe with fatigue-marks under his eyes and his normally impeccable hair disarranged. A *tai*, a short sword, was through his belt.

"Wait down the hall," he said to the others.

They did not want to go. He repeated the order, this time with wildness in his voice, and they almost fled his presence.

No! Kurt started to protest, rising off his cot, but they were gone. Lhe closed the door and stood with his hand clenched on the hilt of the *tai*.

"I am t'Nethim," said Lhe. "My father's business is with Vel t'Elas. Mine is with you. Mim t'Nethim was my cousin."

Kurt recovered his dignity and bowed slightly, ignoring the threat of the fury that trembled in Lhe's nostrils. After such a point, there was little else to do. "I honored her," he said, "very much."

"No," said Lhe. "That you did not."

"Please. Say the rites for her."

"We have said rites, with many prayers for the welfare of her soul. Because of Mim t'Nethim we have spoken well of Elas to our Guardians for the first time in centuries: even in ignorance, they sheltered her. But other things we will not forgive. There is no peace between the Guardians of Nethim and you, human. They do not accept this disgrace."

"Mim thought them in harmony with her choice," said Kurt. "There was peace in Mim. She loved Nethim and she loved Elas."

It did not greatly please Lhe, but it affected him greatly. His lips became a hard line. His brows came as near to meeting as a nemet's might.

"She was consenting?" he asked. "Elas did not command this of her, giving her to you?"

"At first they opposed it, but I asked Mim's consent before I asked Elas. I wished her happy, t'Nethim. If you are not offended to hear it,—I loved her."

A vein beat ceaselessly at Lhe's temple. He was silent a moment, as if gathering the self-control to speak. "We are offended. But it is clear she trusted you, since she gave you her true name in the house of her enemies. She trusted you more than Elas."

"No. She knew I would keep that to myself; but it was not fear of Elas. She honored Elas too much to burden their honor with knowing the name of her house."

"I thank you, that you confessed her true name to the Methi so we could comfort her soul. It is a great deal," he added coldly, "that we *thank* a human."

"I know it is," said Kurt, and bowed, courtesy second nature by now. He lifted his eyes cautiously to Lhe's face; there was no yielding there.

Scurrying footsteps approached the door. With a timid knock, a lesser guardsman cracked the door and awkwardly bowed his apology. "Sir. Sir. The Methi is waiting for this human. Please, sir, she has sent t'Iren to ask about the delay."

"Out," Lhe snapped. The head vanished out of the doorway. Lhe stood for a moment, fingers white on the hilt of the *tai*. Then he gestured abruptly to the door. "Human. You are not mine to deal with. Out."

The summons this time was to the fortress *rhmei*, into a gathering of the lords of Indresul, shadowy figures in the firelit hall of state. Ylith waited beside the hearthfire itself, wearing again the wide-winged crown, a slender form of

color and light in the dim hall, her gown the color of flame
and the light glancing from the metal around her face.

Kurt went down to his knees and on his face without
being forced, despite that a guard held him there with the
butt of a spear in his back.

"Let him sit," said Ylith. "He may look at me."

Kurt sat back on his heels, amid a great murmuring of the
Indras lords, and he realized to his hurt that they murmured
against that permission. He was not fit to meet their Methi
as even a humble *chan* might, making a quick and dignified
obeisance and rising. He laced his hands in his lap, proper
for a man who had been given no courtesy of welcome, and
kept his head bowed despite the permission. He did not
want to stir their anger. There was nowhere to begin with
them, to whom he was an animal; there was no protest and
no action that would make any difference to them.

"T'Morgan," Ylith insisted softly.

He would not, even for her. She let him alone after that,
and quietly asked someone to fetch Kta.

It did not take long. Kta came of his own volition, as far
as the place where Kurt knelt, and there he too went to his
knees and bowed his head, but he did not make the full
prostration and no one insisted on it. He was at least without the humiliation of the iron band that Kurt still wore on
his ankle.

If they were to die, Kurt thought wildly, irrationally, he
would ask them to remove it. He did not know why it
mattered, but it did: it offended his pride more than the
other indignities, to have something locked on his person
against which he had no power. He loathed it.

"T'Elas," said the Methi, "you have had a full day to
reconsider your decision."

"Great Methi," said Kta in a voice faint but steady, "I
have given you the only answer I will ever give."

"For love of Nephane?"

"Yes."

"And for love of the one who destroyed your hearth?"

"No. But for Nephane."

"Kta t'Elas," said the Methi, "I have spoken at length
with Vel t'Elas. They would take you to the hearth of your

Ancestors, and I would permit that, if you would remember that you are Indras."

He hesitated long over that. Kurt felt the anxiety in him; but he would not offend Kta's dignity by turning to urge him one way or the other.

"I belong to Nephane," said Kta.

"Will you then refuse me, will you *directly refuse me,* t'Elas, knowing the meaning of that refusal?"

"Methi," pleaded Kta, "let me be, let me alone in peace. Do not make me answer you."

"Then you were brought up in reverence of Indras law and the Ind."

"Yes, Methi."

"And you admit that I have the authority to require your obedience? That I can curse you from hearth and from city, from all holy rites, even that of burial? That I have the power to consign your undying soul to perdition to all eternity?"

"Yes," said Kta, and his voice was no more than a whisper in that deathly silence.

"Then, t'Elas,—I am sending you and the human t'Morgan to the priests. Consider, consider well the answers you will give them."

The temple lay across a wide courtyard, still within the walls of the Indume, a cube of white marble, vast beyond all expectation. The very base of its door was as high as the shoulder of a man, and within the triangular *rhmei* of the temple blazed the *phusmeha* of the greatest of all shrines, the hearthfire of all mankind.

Kta stopped at the threshold of the inner shrine, that awful golden light bathing his sweating face and reflecting in his eyes. He had an expression of terror on his face such as Kurt had never seen in him. He faltered and would not go on, and the guards took him by the arms and led him forward into the shrine, where the roar of the fire drowned the sound of their steps.

Kurt started to follow him, in haste. A spearshaft slammed across his belly, doubling him over with a cry of pain, swallowed in the noise.

When he straightened in the hands of the guards, barred

from that holy place, he saw Kta at the side of the hearthfire fall to his face on the stone floor. The guards with him bowed and touched hands to lips in reverence, bowed again and withdrew as white-robed priests entered the hall from beyond the fire.

One was the elderly priest who had defended him to the Methi, the only one of all of them in whom Kurt had hope.

He jerked free, cried out to the priest, the shout also swallowed in the roar; Kta had risen and vanished with the priests into the light.

His guards recovered Kurt, snatching him back with violence he was almost beyond feeling.

"The priest," he kept telling them. "That priest, the white-haired one,—I want to speak with him. Can I not speak with him?"

"Observe silence here," one said harshly. "We do not know the priest you mean."

"That priest!" Kurt cried, and jerked loose, threw a man skidding on the polished floor and ran into the *rhmei,* flinging himself facedown so close to the great fire bowl that the heat scorched his skin.

How long he lay there was not certain. He almost fainted, and for a long time everything was red-hazed and the air was too hot to breathe; but he had claimed sanctuary, as Mother Isoi had claimed it first in the Song of the Ind, when Phan came to kill mankind.

White-robed priests stood around him, and finally an aged and blue-veined hand reached down to him, and he looked up into the face he had hoped to find.

He wept, unashamed. "Priest," he said, not knowing how to address the man with honor, "please help us."

"A human," said the priest, "ought not to claim sanctuary. It is not lawful. You are a pollution on these holy stones. Are you of our religion?"

"No, sir," Kurt said.

The old man's lips trembled. It might have been the effect of age, but his watery eyes were frightened.

"We must purify this place," he said, and one of the younger priests said, "Who will go and tell this thing to the Methi?"

"Please," Kurt pleaded, "please give us refuge here."

"He means Kta t'Elas," said one of the others, as if it was a matter of great wonder to them.

"He is house-friend to Elas," said the old man.

"Light of heaven," breathed the younger. "Elas—with *this?*"

"Nethim," said the old man, "is also involved."

"Ai," another murmured.

And together they gathered Kurt up and brought him with them, talking together, their steps beginning to echo now that they were away from the noise of the fire.

Ylith turned slowly, the fine chains of her headdress gently swaying and sparkling against her hair, and the light of the hearthfire of the fortress leaped flickering across her face. With a glance at the priest she settled into her chair and sat leaning back, looking down at Kurt.

"Priest," she said at last, "you have reached some conclusion, surely, after holding them both so long a time."

"Great Methi, the College is divided in its opinion."

"Which is to say it has reached no conclusion, after three days of questioning and deliberation."

"It has reached several conclusions, however—"

"Priest," exclaimed the Methi in irritation, "yea or nay?"

The old priest bowed very low. "Methi, some think that the humans are what we once called the godkings, the children of the great earth-snake Yr and of the wrath of Phan when he was the enemy of mankind, begetting monsters to destroy the world."

"This is an old, old theory, and the godkings were long ago, and capable of mixing blood with man. Has there ever been a mixing of human blood and nemet?"

"None proved, great Methi. But we do not know the origin of the Tamurlin, and he is most evidently of their kind; now you are asking us to resolve, as it were, the Tamurlin question immediately, and we do not have sufficient knowledge to do so, great Methi."

"You have *him*. I sent him to you for you to examine. Does he tell you nothing?"

"What he tells us is unacceptable."

"Does he lie? Surely if he lies, you can trap him."

"We have tried, great Methi, and he will not be moved

from what he says. He speaks of another world and another sun. I think he believes these things."

"And do you believe them, priest?"

The old man bowed his head, clenching his aged hands. "Let the Methi be gracious: these matters are difficult or you would not have consulted the College. We wonder this: if he is not nemet, what could be his origin? Our ships have ranged far over all the seas, and never found his like. When humans will to do it, they come to us, bringing machines and forces our knowledge does not understand. If he is not from somewhere within our knowledge, then,—forgive my simplicity—he must still be from somewhere. He calls it another earth. Perhaps it is a failure of language, a misunderstanding,—but where in all the lands we know could have been his home?"

"What if there was another? How would our religion encompass it?"

The priest turned his watery eyes on Kurt, kneeling beside him. "I do not know," he said.

"Give me an answer, priest. I will make you commit yourself. Give me an answer."

"I—had rather believe him mortal than immortal, and I cannot quite accept that he is an animal. Forgive me, great Methi, what may be heresy to wonder,—but Phan was not the eldest born of Ib. There were other beings, whose nature is unclear. Perhaps there were others of Phan's kind. And were there a thousand others, it makes the *yhia* no less true."

"This is heresy, priest."

"It is," confessed the priest. "But I do not know an answer otherwise."

"Priest, when I look at him, I see neither reason nor logic. I question what should not be questioned. If this is Phan's world, and there is another,—then what does this foretell, this—intrusion—of humans into ours? There is power above Phan's, yes; but what can have made it necessary that nature be so upset, so inside-out? Where are these events tending, priest?"

"I do not know. But if it is Fate against which we struggle, then our struggle will ruin us."

"Does not the *yhia* bid us accept things only within the limits of our own natures?"

"It is impossible to do otherwise, Methi."

"And therefore does not nature sometimes command us to resist?"

"It has been so reasoned, Methi, although not all the College is in agreement on that."

"And if we resist fate, we must perish?"

"That is doubtless so, Methi."

"And someday it might be our fate to perish?"

"That is possible, Methi."

She slammed her hand down on the arm of her chair. "I refuse to bow to such a possibility. I refuse to perish, priest, or to lead men to perish. In sum, the College does not know the answer."

"No, Methi, we must admit we do not."

"I have a certain spiritual authority myself."

"You are the viceroy of Phan on earth."

"Will the priests respect that?"

"The priests," said the old man, "are not anxious to have this matter cast back into their hands. They will welcome your intervention in the matter of the origin of humans, Methi."

"It is," she said, "dangerous to the people that such thoughts as these be heard outside this room. You will not repeat the reasoning we have made together. On your life, priest, and on your soul, you will not repeat what I have said to you."

The old priest turned his head and gave Kurt a furtive, troubled look. "Let the Methi be gracious: this being is not deserving of punishment for any wrong."

"He invaded the *Rhmei* of Man."

"He sought sanctuary."

"Did you give it?"

"No," the priest admitted.

"That is well," said Ylith. "You are dismissed, priest."

The old man made a deeper bow and withdrew, backing away. The heavy tread and metal clash of armed men accompanied the opening of the door: and the armed men remained after it was closed. Kurt heard and knew they were there, but he must not turn to look: time was short.

He did not want to hasten it. The Methi still looked down on him, the tiny chains swaying, her dark face soberly thoughtful.

"You create difficulties wherever you go," she said softly.

"Where is Kta, Methi? They would not tell me. Where is he?"

"They returned him to us a day ago."

"Is he—?"

"I have not given sentence." She said it with a shrug, then bent those dark eyes full upon him. "I do not really wish to kill him. He could be valuable to me. He knows it. I could hold him up to the other Indras-descended of Nephane and say: look, we are merciful, we are forgiving, we are your people. Do not fight against us."

Kurt looked up at her, for a moment lost in that dark gaze, believing as many a hearer would believe Ylith t'Erinas: hope rose irrationally in him, on the tone of her gentle voice, her skill to reach for the greatest hopes. And good or evil, he did not know clearly which she was.

She was not like Djan, familiar and human and wielding power like a general. Ylith was a methi as the office must have been: a goddess-on-earth, doing things for a goddess' reasons and with amoral morality, creating truth.

Rewriting things as they should be.

He felt an awe of her that he had felt of nothing mortal, believed indeed that she could erase the both of them as if they had never been. He had been within the *Rhmei* of Man, had been beside the fire: the skin on his arms was still painful. When Ylith spoke to him he felt the roaring silence of that fire drowning him.

He was fevered. He was fatigued. He saw the signs in himself, and feared instead his own weakness.

"Kta would be valuable to you," he said, "even unwilling." He felt guilty, knowing Kta's stubborn pride. "Elas was the victim of one methi; it would impress Nephane's families if another methi showed him mercy."

"You have a certain logic on your side. And what of you? What shall I do with you?"

"I am willing to live," he said.

She smiled that goddess-smile at him, her eyes alone alive. "You existence is a trouble; but if I am rid of you, it will not solve matters. You would still have existed. What should I write at your death? That this day we destroyed a creature which could not possibly exist, and so restored order to the universe?"

"Some," he said, "are urging you to do that."

She leaned back, curling her bejeweled fingers about the carved fishes of the chair arms. "If, on the other hand, we admit you exist, then where do you exist? We have always despised the Sufaki for accepting humans and nemet as one state: herein began the heresies with which they pervert pure religion, heresies which we will not tolerate."

"Will you kill them? That will not change them."

"Heresy may not live. If we believed otherwise, we should deny our own religion."

"They have not crossed the sea to trouble you."

Ylith's hand came down sharply on the chair arm. "You are treading near the brink, human."

Kurt bowed his head.

"You are ignorant," she said. "This is understandable. I know of report that Djan-methi is—highly approachable. I have warned you before. I am not as she is."

"I ask you—to listen. Just for a moment,—to listen."

"First convince me that you are wise in nemet affairs."

He bowed his head once more, unwilling to dispute with her to no advantage.

"What," she said after a moment, "would you have to say that is worth my time? You have my attention, briefly. Speak."

"Methi," he said quietly, "what I would have said, were answers to questions your priests did not know how to ask me. My people are very old now, thousands and thousands of years of mistakes behind us that you do not have to make. But maybe I am wrong, maybe it is—what you call *yhia,* that I have intruded where I have no business to be and you will not listen because you cannot listen. But I could tell you more than you want to hear, I could tell you the future, where your precious little war with Nephane could lead you. I could tell you that my native world does not exist any longer, that Djan's does not,—all for a war grown so large and so long that it ruins whole worlds as yours sinks ships."

"You blaspheme!"

He had begun; she wished him silent. He poured out what he had to say in a rush, though guards ran for him.

"If you kill every last Sufaki you will still find differences to fight over. You will run out of people on this earth before you run out of differences.—Methi,—listen, to me! You know—if you have any sense you know what I am telling you. You can listen to me or you can do the whole thing over again, and your descendants will be sitting where I am."

Lhe had him, dragged him backward, trying to force him to stand. Ylith was on her feet, beside her chair.

"Be silent!" Lhe hissed at him, his hard fingers clamped into Kurt's arm.

"Take him from here," said Ylith. "Put him with t'Elas. They are both mad. Let them comfort one another in their madness."

"Methi," Kurt cried.

Lhe had help now: they brought him to his feet, forced him from the hall and into the corridor, and there, finally, clear sense returned to him and he ceased to fight them.

"You were so near to life," Lhe said.

"It is all right, t'Nethim," Kurt said. "You will not be cheated."

They went back to the upper prisons. Kurt knew the way, and, when they had come to the proper door, Lhe dismissed the reluctant guards out of earshot. "You are truly mad," he said, fitting the key in the lock. "Both of you. She would give t'Elas honor, which he refuses. He has attempted suicide: we had to prevent him. It was our duty to do this. He was being taken from the temple: he meant to cast himself to the pavement, but we pushed him back, so that he fell instead on the steps. We have provided comforts, which he will not use."

He dared look Lhe in the eyes, saw both anger and trouble there. Lhe t'Nethim was asking something of him: for a moment he was not sure what, and then he thought that the Methi would not be pleased if Kta evaded her justice. Elas had once hazarded its honor and its existence on receiving a prisoner in trust: and had lost. Methi's law. Elas had risked it because of a promise unwittingly false.

Nethim was involved: the priest had said it. The honor of

Nethim was in grave danger. Both Elas and the Methi had touched it.

The door opened. Lhe gestured him to go in, and locked the door behind him.

There were two cots within, a table, beneath a high barred window. Kta lay fully clothed, covered with dust and dried blood. They had brought him back the day before; in all that time, they had not cared for him, nor he for himself. Kurt exploded inwardly with fury at all nemet, even with Kta.

"Kta." Kurt bent over him, and saw Kta blink and stare chillingly nothingward. There was vacancy there. Kurt did not ask consent: he went to the table where there was the usual washing bowl and urn. Clean clothes were laid there, and cloths, and a flask of *telise*. Lhe had not lied. It was Kta's choice.

Kurt spread everything on the floor beside Kta's cot, unstopped the *telise* and slipped his arm beneath Kta's head, putting the flask to his lips.

Kta swallowed a little of the potent liquid, choked over it and swallowed again. Kurt stopped the flask and set it aside, then soaked a cloth in water and began to wipe the mingled sweat and blood and dirt off the nemet's face. Kta shivered when the cloth touched his neck; the water was cold.

"Kta," said Kurt, "what happened?"

"Nothing," said the nemet, not even looking at him. "They brought—they brought me back—"

Kurt regarded him sorrowfully. "Listen, friend, I am trying as best I know. But if you need better care, if there are things broken, tell me. They will send for it. I will ask them for it."

"They are only scratches." The threat of outsiders seemed to lend Kta strength. He struggled to rise, leaning on an elbow that was painfully torn. Kurt helped him. The *telise* was having effect, although the sense of well-being would be brief, Kta did not move as if he was seriously hurt. Kurt put a pillow into place at the corner of the wall, and Kta leaned back on it with a grimace and a sigh,—looked down at his badly lacerated knee and shin, flexed the knee experimentally.

"I fell," Kta said.

"So I heard." Kurt refolded the stained cloth and started blotting at the dirt on the injured knee.

It needed some time to clean the day-old injuries, and necessarily it hurt. From time to time Kurt insisted Kta take a sip of *telise*, though it was only toward the end that Kta evidenced any great discomfort. Through it all Kta spoke little. When the injuries were clean and there was nothing more to be done, Kurt sat and looked at him helplessly. In Kta's face the fatigue was evident. It seemed far more than sleeplessness or wounds,—something inward and deadly.

Kurt settled him flat again with a pillow under his head. Considering that he himself had been without sleep the better part of three days, he thought that weariness might be a major part of it: but Kta's eyes were fixed again on infinity.

"Kta."

The nemet did not respond and Kurt shook him. Kta did no more than blink.

"Kta, you heard me and I know it. Stop this and look at me. Who are you punishing? Me?"

There was no response, and Kurt struck Kta's face lightly, then enough that it would sting. Kta's lips trembled and Kurt looked at him in instant remorse, for it was as if he had added the little burden more than the nemet could bear. The threatened collapse terrified him.

Tired beyond endurance, Kurt sank down on his heels and looked at Kta helplessly. He wanted to go over to his own cot and sleep, he could not think any longer, except that Kta wanted to die and that he did not know what to do.

"Kurt." The voice was weak, so distant Kta's lips hardly seemed to move.

"Tell me how to help you."

Kta blinked, turned his head, seeming for the moment to have his mind focused. "Kurt,—my friend, they—"

"What have they done, Kta? What did they do?"

"They want my help and—if I will not,—I lose my life, my soul. She will curse me from the earth,—to the old gods—the—" He choked, shut his eyes and forced a calm over himself that was more like Kta. "I am afraid, my friend, mortally afraid. For all eternity,—But how can I do what she asks?"

"What difference can your help make against Nephane?" Kurt asked. "Man, what pitiful little difference can it make one way or the other? Djan has weapons enough; Ylith has ships enough. Let others settle it. What are you? She has offered you life and your freedom, and that is better than you had of Djan."

"I could not accept Djan-methi's conditions either."

"Is it worth this, Kta? Look at you! Look at you, and tell me it is worth it. Listen, I would not blame you; all Nephane knows how you were treated there. Who in Nephane would blame you if you turned to Indresul?"

"I will not hear your arguments," Kta cried.

"They are sensible." Kurt seized his arm and kept him from turning his face to the wall again. "They are sensible arguments, Kta, and you know it."

"I do not understand reason any longer. The temple and the Methi will condemn my soul for doing what I know is right. Kurt, I could understand dying, but this—this is not justice. How can a reasonable heaven put a man to a choice like this?"

"Just do what they want, Kta. It doesn't cost anyone much, and if you are only alive, you can worry about the right and the wrong of it later."

"I should have died with my ship," the nemet murmured. "That is where I was wrong. Heaven gave me the chance to die—in Nephane, in the camp of the Tamurlin, with *Tavi* I would have peace and honor then. But there was always you. You are the disruption in my fate. Or its agent. You are always there—to make the difference."

Kurt found his hand trembling as he adjusted the blanket over the raving nemet, trying to soothe him, taking for nothing the words that hurt. "Please," he said. "Rest, Kta."

"Not your fault. It is possible to reason—One must always reason—to know—"

"Be still."

"If," Kta persisted with fevered intensity, "if—I had died in Nephane with my father, then my friends, my crew—would have avenged me. Is that not so?"

"Yes," Kurt conceded, reckoning the temper of men like Val and Tkel and their company. "Yes, they would have killed Shan t'Tefur."

"And that," said Kta, "would have cast Nephane into

chaos, and they would have died, and come to join Elas in the shadows. Now they are dead,—as they would have died—but I am alive. Now I, Elas—"

"Rest. Stop this."

"—Elas was shaped to the ruin of Nephane—to bring down the city in its fall. I am the last of Elas. If I had died before this I would have died innocent of my city's blood. The crime would have been on Djan-methi's hands. Then my soul would have had rest with theirs, whatever became of Nephane. Instead, I lived,—and for that I deserve to be where I am."

"Kta,—hush. Sleep. You have a belly full of *telise* and no food to settle it. It has unbalanced your mind. Please. Rest."

"It is true," said Kta, "I was born to ruin my people. It is just—what they try to make me do—"

"Blame me for it," said Kurt. "I had rather hear that than this sick rambling. Answer me what I am, or admit that you cannot foretell the future."

"It is logical," said Kta, "that human fate brought you here to deal with human fate."

"You are drunk, Kta."

"You came for Djan-methi," said Kta. "You are for her."

Kta's dark eyes closed—rolled back, helplessly. Kurt moved at last, realizing the knot at his belly, the sickly gathering of fear, dread of Guardians and Ancestors and the nemet's reasoning.

Kta at last slept. For a long time Kurt stood staring down at him, then went to his own side of the room and lay down upon the cot, not to sleep, not daring to, only to rest his aching back. He feared to leave Kta unwatched, but at some time his eyes grew heavy, and he closed them only for a moment.

He jerked awake, panicked by a sound and simultaneously by the realization that he had slept.

The room was almost in darkness, but the faintest light came from the barred window over the table. Kta was on his feet, naked despite the chill, and had set the water bucket on the table, standing where a channel in the stone floor made a drain beneath the wall, beginning to wash himself.

Kurt looked to the window, amazed to find the light was

that of dawn. That Kta had become concerned about his appearance seemed a good sign. Methodically Kta dipped up water and washed, and when he had done what he could by that means, he took the bucket and poured water slowly over himself, letting it complete the task.

Then he returned to his cot and wrapped in the blanket. He leaned against the wall, eyes closed, lips moving silently. Gradually he slipped into the state of meditation and rested unmoving, the morning sun beginning to bring detail to his face. He looked at peace, and remained so for about half an hour.

The day broke full, a shaft of light finding its way through the barred window. Kurt bestirred himself and straightened his clothing that his restless sleeping had twisted in knots.

Kta rose and dressed also, in his own hard-used clothing, refusing the Methi's gifts. He looked in Kurt's direction with a bleak and yet reassuring smile.

"Are you all right?" Kurt asked him.

"Well enough, considering," said Kta. "It comes to me that I said things I would not have said."

"It was the *telise*. I do not take them for intended."

"I honor you," said Kta, "as my brother."

"You know," said Kurt, "that I honor you in the same way."

He thought that Kta had spoken as he did because there were hurrying footsteps in the hall. He made haste to answer, for fear that it would pass unsaid. He wanted above all that Kta understand it.

The steps reached their door. A key turned in the lock.

XX

This time it was not Lhe who had charge of them, but another man with strangers around him, that had charge of them and they were taken not to the *rhmei*, but out of the fortress.

When they came into the courtyard and turned not toward the temple again, but toward the outer gate of the Indume complex, Kta cast Kurt a frightened glance that carried an unwilling understanding.

"We are bound for the harbor," he said.

"Those are our orders," said the captain of the detachment, "since the Methi is there and the fleet is sailing. Move on, t'Elas, or will you be taken through the streets in chains?"

Kta's head came up. For the least moment the look of Nym t'Elas flared in his dark eyes. "What is your name?"

The guard looked suddenly regretful of his words. "Speak me no curse, t'Elas. I repeated the Methi's words. She did not think chains necessary."

"No," said Kta, "they are not necessary."

He bowed his head again and matched pace with the guards, Kurt beside him. The nemet was a pitiable figure in the hard, uncompromising light of day, his clothing filthy, his face unshaved—which in the nemet needed a long time to show.

Through the streets, with people stopping to stare at them, Kta looked neither to right nor to left. Knowing his pride, Kurt sensed the misery he felt, his shame in the eyes of these people; and he could not but think that Kta t'Elas would have attracted less comment in his misfortune had he not been laden with the added disgrace of a human companion. Some of the murmured comments came to Kurt's ears, and he was almost becoming inured to them: how ugly, how covered with hair, how almost-nemet, and caught with an Indras-descended, more the wonder—pity the house of Elas-in-Indresul to see one of its foreign sons in such a state and in such company!

The gangplank of the first trireme at the dock was run out, rowers and crew scurrying around making checks of equipment. Spread near its stern was a blue canopy upheld with gold-tipped poles, beneath which sat Ylith, working over some charts with Lhe t'Nethim and paying no attention to their approach.

When at last she did see fit to notice them kneeling before her, she dismissed Lhe back a pace with a gesture and turned herself to face them. Still she wore the crown of her office, and she was modestly attired in *chatem* and *pelan* of pale green silk, slim and delicate in this place of war. Her eyes rested on Kta without emotion, and Kta bowed down to his face at her feet, Kurt unwillingly imitating his action.

Ylith snapped her fingers. "It is permitted you both to sit," she said, and they straightened together. Ylith looked at them thoughtfully, most particularly at Kta.

"Ei, t'Elas," she said softly, "have you made your decision? Do you come to ask for clemency?"

"Methi," said Kta, "no."

"Kta," Kurt exclaimed, for he had hoped. "Don't—"

"If," said Ylith, "you seek in your barbaric tongue to advise the son of Elas against this choice, he would do well to listen to you."

"Methi," said Kta, "I have considered, and I cannot agree to what you ask."

Ylith looked down at him with anger gathering in her eyes. "Do you hope to make a gesture, and then I shall relent afterward and pardon you? Or do they teach such lack of religion across the Dividing Sea that the consequence is of little weight with you? Have you so far inclined toward the Sufak heresies that you are more at home with those dark spirits we do not name?"

"No, Methi," said Kta, his voice trembling. "Yet we of

Elas were a reverent house, and we do not receive justice from you."

"You say then that I am in error, t'Elas?"

Kta bowed his head, caught hopelessly between yea and nay, between committing blasphemy and admitting to it.

"T'Elas," said Ylith, "is it so overwhelmingly difficult to accept our wishes?"

"I have given the Methi my answer."

"And choose to die accursed." The Methi turned her face toward the open sea, opened her long-fingered hand in that direction. "A cold resting place at best, t'Elas, and cold the arms of Kalyt's daughters. A felon's grave, the sea,—a grave for those no house will claim, for those who have lived their lives so shamefully that there remains no one, not even their own house, to mourn them, to give them rest. Such a fate is for those so impious that they would defy a father or the Upei or dishonor their own kinswomen. But I, t'Elas, I am more than the Upei. If I curse,—I curse your soul not from hearth or from city only, but from all mankind, from among all who are born of this latter race of men. The lower halls of death will have you: Yeknis, those dark places where the shadows live, those unnameable first-born of Chaos. Do they still teach such things in Nephane, t'Elas?"

"Yes, Methi."

"Chaos is the just fate of a man who will not bow to the will of heaven. Do you say I am not just?"

"Methi," said Kta, "I believe that you are the Chosen of Heaven, and I reverence you and the home of my Ancestors-in-Indresul. Perhaps you are appointed by heaven for the destruction of my people, but if heaven will destroy my soul for refusing to help you, then heaven's decrees are unbelievably harsh. I honor you, Methi. I believe that you, like Fate itself, must somehow be just. So I will do as I think right, and I will not aid you."

Ylith regarded him furiously, then with a snap of her fingers and a gesture brought the guards to take them.

"Unfortunate man," she said. "Blind to necessity and gifted with the stubborn pride of Elas. I have been well-served by that quality in Elas until now, and it goes hard to find fault with that which I have best loved in your house. I truly pity you, Kta t'Elas. Go and consider again whether you have well chosen. There is a moment the gods lend us, to yield before going under. I still offer you life. *That* is heaven's justice.—Tryn, secure them both belowdecks. The son of Elas and his human friend are sailing with us, against Nephane."

The hatch banged open against the deck above and someone in silhouette came down the creaking steps into the hold.

"T'Elas. T'Morgan." It was Lhe t'Nethim, and in a moment the Indras officer had come near enough to them that his features were faintly discernible. "Have you all that you need?" he asked, and sank down on his heels a little beyond the reach of their chains.

Kta turned his face aside. Kurt, feeling somewhat a debt to this man's restraint, made a grudging bow of his head. "We are well enough," Kurt said, which they were, considering.

Lhe pressed his lips together. "I did not come to enjoy this sight. For that both of you—have done kindness to my house, I would give you what I can."

"You have generally done me kindness," said Kurt, yet careful of Kta's sensibilities. "That is enough."

"Elas and Nethim are enemies; that does not change. But human though you are—if Mim could choose you, of her own will—you are an exceptional human. And t'Elas," he said in a hard voice, "because you sheltered her, I thank you. We know the tale of her slavery among Tamurlin, —this through Elas-in-Indresul, through the Nethim. It is a bitter tale."

"She was dear to us," said Kta, looking toward him.

Lhe's face was grim. "Did you have her?"

"I did not," said Kta. "She was adopted of the *chan* of Elas. No man of my people treated her as other than an honorable woman, and I gave her at her own will to my friend, who tried with all his heart to treat her well. For Mim's sake, Elas is dead in Nephane. To this extent we defended her. We did not know that she was of Nethim. Because she was Mim, and of our hearth, Elas would have defended her even had she told us."

"She was loved," said Kurt, because he saw the pain in
Lhe's eyes, "and had no enemies in Nephane. It was mine
who killed her."

"Tell me the manner of it," said Lhe.

Kurt glanced down, unwilling: but Lhe was nemet—some
things would not make sense to him without all the truth.
"Enemies of mine stole her," he said, "and they took her;
the Methi of Nephane humiliated her. She died at her own
hand, Lhe t'Nethim. I blame myself also. If I had been
nemet enough to know what she was likely to do,—I would
not have let her be alone then."

Lhe's face was like graven stone. "No," he said. "Mim
chose well. If you were nemet you would know it. You
would have been wrong to stop her. Name the men who did
this."

"I cannot," he said. "Mim did not know their names."

"Were they Indras?"

"Sufaki," Kurt admitted. "Men of Shan t'Tefur u Tlekef."

"Then there is bloodfeud between that house and Nethim.
May the Guardians of Nethim deal with them as I shall if I
find them, and with Djan-methi of Nephane. What is the
emblem of Tefur?"

"It is the Great Snake Yr," said Kta. "Gold on green. I
wish you well in that bloodfeud, t'Nethim; you will avenge
Elas also, when I cannot."

"Obey the Methi," said Lhe.

"No," said Kta. "But Kurt may do as he pleases."

Lhe looked toward Kurt, and Kurt gave him nothing
better. Lhe made a gesture of exasperation.

"You must admit," said Lhe, "that the Methi has offered
you every chance; and it is a lasting wonder that you are not
sleeping tonight at the bottom of the sea."

"Nephane is my city," said Kta. "And as for your war,
your work will not be finished until you finish it with me, so
stop expecting me to obey your Methi. I will not."

"If you keep on as you are," said Lhe, "I will probably be
assigned as your executioner. In spite of the feud between
our houses, t'Elas, I shall not like that assignment; but I
shall obey her orders."

"For a son of Nethim," said Kta, "you are a fair-minded
man with us both. I would not have expected it."

"For a son of Elas," said Lhe, "you are fair-minded yourself. And," he added with a sideways glance at Kurt, "I cannot even fault you the guest of your house. I do not want to kill you. You and this human would haunt me."

"Your priests are not sure," said Kurt, "that I have a soul to do so."

Lhe bit his lip; he had come near heresy. And Kurt's heart went out to Lhe t'Nethim, for it was clear enough that in Lhe's eyes he was more than animal.

"T'Nethim," said Kta, "has the Methi sent you here?"

"No. My advice is from the heart, t'Elas. Yield."

"Tell your Methi I want to speak with her."

"Will you beg pardon of her? That is the only thing she will hear from you."

"Ask her," said Kta. "If she will or will not,—ought that not be her own choice?"

Lhe's eyes were frightened: they locked upon Kta's directly, without the bowing and the courtesy, as if he would drag something out of him. "I will ask her," said Lhe. "I already risk the anger of my father; the anger of the Methi is less quick, but I dread it more. If you go to her, you go with those chains. I will not risk the lives of Nethim on the asking of Elas."

"I consent to that," said Kta.

"Swear that you will do no violence."

"We both swear," said Kta, which as lord of Elas he could say.

"The word of a man about to lose his soul, and of a human who may not have one," declared Lhe in distress. "Light of heaven, I cannot make Nethim responsible for the likes of you."

And he rose up and fled the hold.

Ylith took a chair and settled comfortably before she acknowledged them. She had elected to receive them in her quarters, not on the windy deck. The golden light of swaying lamps shed an exquisite warmth after the cold and stench of betweendecks, thick rugs under their chilled bones.

"You may sit," she said, allowing them to straighten off their faces, and she received a cup of tea from a maid and sipped it. There was no cup for them. They were not there under the terms of hospitality, and might not speak until given permission. She finished the cup of tea slowly, looking at them, the ritual of mind-settling before touching a problem of delicacy. At last she returned the cup to the *chan* and faced them.

"T'Elas and t'Morgan. I do not know why I should trouble myself with you repeatedly when one of my own law-abiding citizens might have a much longer wait for an audience with me. But then, your future is likely to be shorter than theirs. Convince me quickly that you are worth my time."

"Methi," said Kta, "I came to plead for my city."

"Then you are making a useless effort, t'Elas. The time would be better spent if you were to plead for your life."

"Methi, please hear me. You are about to spend a number of lives of your own people. It is not necessary."

"What is? What have you to offer, t'Elas?"

"Reason."

"Reason. You love Nephane. Understandable. But they cast you out, murdered your house; I, on the other hand, would pardon you for your allegiance to them; I would take you as one of my own. Am I behaving as an enemy, Kta t'Elas?"

"You are the enemy of my people."

"Surely," said Ylith softly, "Nephane is cursed with madness, casting out such a man who loves her and honoring those who divide her. I would not need to destroy such a city, but I am forced. I want nothing of the things that happen there—of war, of human ways. I will not let the contagion spread." She lifted her eyes to the *chan* and dismissed the woman, then directed her attention to them again. "You are already at war," she told them. "I only intend to finish it."

"What—war?" asked Kta, though Kurt knew in his own heart then what must have happened and he was sure that Kta did. The Methi's answer was no surprise.

"Civil war," answered Ylith. "The inevitable conflict. Though I am sure our help is less than desired,—we are intervening, on the side of the Indras-descended."

"You do not desire to help the Families," said Kta. "You will treat them as you do us."

"I will treat them as I am trying to treat you. I would

welcome you as Indras, Kta t'Elas. I would make Elas-in-Nephane powerful again, as it ought to be, united with Elas-in-Indresul."

"My sister," said Kta, "is married to a Sufaki lord. My friend is a human. Many of the house-friends of Elas-in-Nephane have Sufaki blood. Will you command Elas-in-Indresul to honor our obligations?"

"A Methi," she said, "cannot command within the affairs of a house."

It was the legally correct answer.

"I could," she said, "guarantee you the lives of these people. A Methi may always intervene on the side of life."

"But you cannot command their acceptance."

"No," she said. "I could not do that."

"Nephane," said Kta, "is Indras and Sufaki and human."

"When I am done," said Ylith, "that problem will be resolved."

"Attack them," said Kta, "and they will unite against you."

"What, Sufaki join the Indras?"

"It has happened once before," said Kta, "when you hoped to take us."

"That," said Ylith, "was different. Then the Families were powerful, and wished greater freedom from the mother of cities. Now the Families have their power taken from them which I can offer all that will renounce the Sufak heresy. My honored father Tehal-methi was less mercifully inclined, but I am not my father. I have no wish to kill Indras."

Kta made a brief obeisance. "Methi, turn back these ships then, and I will be your man without reservation."

She set her hands on the arms of her chair and now her eyes went to Kurt and back again. "You do press me too far. You, t'Morgan, were born human, but you rise above that; I can almost love you for your determination—you try so hard to be nemet. But I do not understand the Sufaki, who were born nemet and deny the truth, who devote themselves to despoiling what we name as holy; and least of all"—her voice grew hard—"do I understand Indras-born such as you, t'Elas, who knowingly seek to save a way of life that aims at the destruction of Ind."

"They do not aim at destroying us."

"You will now tell me that the resurgence of old ways in Sufak is a false rumor, that the *jafikn* and the Robes of Color are not now common there, that prayers are not made in the Upei of Nephane that mention the cursed ones and blaspheme our religion. Mor t'Uset ul Orm is witness to these things. He saw one Nym t'Elas rise in the Upei to speak against the t'Tefuri and their blasphemies. Have you less than your father's courage—or do you dishonor his wishes, t'Elas?"

Kurt looked quickly at Kta, knowing how that would affect him, almost ready to hold him if he was about to do something rash; but Kta bowed his head, knuckles white on his laced hands.

"T'Elas?" asked Ylith.

"Trust me," said Kta, lifting his face again, composed, "to know my father's wishes. It is our belief, Methi, and we should not question the wisdom of heaven in settling two peoples on the Ome Sin; and so we do not seek to destroy the Sufaki. I am Indras; I believe that the will of heaven will win despite the action of men; and therefore I live my life quietly in the eyes of my Sufaki neighbors. I will not dishonor my beliefs by contending over them, as if they needed defense."

Ylith's dark eyes flamed with anger for a time, and then grew quiet, even sad. "No," she said, "no, t'Elas."

"Methi." Kta bowed—homage to a different necessity, and straightened, and there was a deep sadness in the air.

"T'Morgan," said the Methi softly, "will you still stay with this man? You are only a poor stranger among us. You are not bound to such as he."

"Can you not see," asked Kurt, "that he wishes greatly to be able to honor you, Methi?" He knew that he shamed Kta by that, but it was Kta's life at stake; and probably now, he realized, he had just thrown his own away too.

Ylith looked, for one of a few times, more woman than goddess, and sad and angry too. "I did not choose this war, this ultimate irrationality. My generals and my admirals urged it, but I was not willing. But I saw the danger growing. The humans return: the Sufaki begin to reassert their ancient ways; the humans encourage this, and encourage it finally to the point when the Families which kept Nephane safely Indras are powerless. I do what must be done. The woman Djan is threat enough to the peace; but she is holding her power by stripping away that of the Indras. And a Sufak Nephane armed with human weapons is a danger which cannot be tolerated."

"It is not all Sufaki who threaten you," Kurt urged. "One man. You are doing all of this for the destruction of one man, who is the real danger there."

"Yes, I know Shan t'Tefur and his late father.—*Ai*, you would not have heard. Tlekef t'Tefur is dead, killed in the violence."

"How?" asked Kta at once. "Who did so?"

"A certain t'Osanef."

"O gods," Kta breathed. The strength seemed to go out of him. His face went pale. "Which t'Osanef?"

"Han t'Osanef did the killing, but I have no further information. I do not blame you, t'Elas. If a sister of mine were involved, I would worry, I would indeed. Tell me this: why would Sufaki kill Sufaki? A contest for power? A personal feud?"

"A struggle," said Kta, "between those who love Nephane as Osanef does and those who want to bring her down, like t'Tefur. And you are doing excellently for t'Tefur's cause, Methi. If there is no Nephane, which is the likely result of your war, there will be another Chteftikan, and that war you cannot see the end of. There are Sufaki who have learned not to hate Indras; but there will be none left if you pursue this attack."

Ylith joined her hands together and meditated on some thought, then looked up again. "Lhe t'Nethim will return you to the hold," she said. "I am done. I have spared all the time I can afford today, for a man out of touch with reality. You are a brave man, Kta t'Elas; and you, Kurt t'Morgan, you are commendable in your attachment to this gentle madman. *Someone* should stay by him. It does you credit that you do not leave him."

XXI

"Kurt."

Kurt came awake with Kta shaking him by the shoulder and with the thunder of running feet on the deck overhead. He blinked in confusion. Someone on deck was shouting orders, a battle-ready.

"There is sail in sight," said Kta. "Nephane's fleet."

Kurt rubbed his face, tried to hear any clear words from overhead. "How much chance is there that Nephane can stop this here?"

Kta gave a laugh like a sob. "Gods, if the Methi's report is true, none. If there is civil war in the city, it will have crippled the fleet. Without the Sufaki, the Families could not even get the greater ships out of the harbor. It will be a slaughter up there."

Oars rumbled overhead. In a moment more the shouted order rang out and the oars splashed down in unison. The ship began to gather speed.

"We are going in," Kurt murmured, fighting down panic. A host of images assailed his mind. They could do nothing but ride it out, chained to the ship of the Methi. In space or on *Tavi*'s exposed deck, he had known fear in entering combat, but never such a feeling of helplessness.

"Edge back," Kta advised him, bracing his shoulder against the hull. He took his ankle chain in both hands. "If we ram, the shock could be considerable. Brace yourself and hold the chain. There is no advantage adding broken bones to our misery."

Kurt followed his example, casting a misgiving look at the mass of stored gear in the after part of the hold. If it was not well-secured, impact would send tons of weight down on them, and there was no shielding themselves against that.

The grating thunder of three hundred oars increased in tempo and held at a pace that no man could sustain over a long drive. Now even in the dark hold there was an undeniable sense of speed, with the beat of the oars and the rush of water against the hull.

Kurt braced himself harder against the timbers. What would happen if the trireme itself was rammed and a bronze Nephanite prow splintered in the midships area needed no imagination. He remembered *Tavi*'s ruin and the men ground to death in the collision, and tried not to think how thin was the hull at their shoulders.

The beat stopped, a deafening hush, then the portside oars ran inboard: the ship glided under momentum for an instant.

Wood began to splinter and the ship shuddered and rolled, grating and cracking wood all along her course. Thrown sprawling, Kurt and Kta held as best they could as the repeated shocks vibrated through the ship. Shouting came overhead, over the more distant screaming of men in pain and terror, suddenly overwhelmed by the sound of the oars being run out again.

The relentless cadence recommenced, the trireme recovering her momentum. All-encompassing was the crash and boom of the oars, pierced by the thin shouts of officers. Then the oars lifted clear with a great sucking of water, and held. The silence was so deep that they could hear their own harsh breathing, the give of the oars in their locks, the creak of timbers and the groan of rigging, and the sounds of battle far distant.

"This is the Methi's ship," Kta answered his anxious look. "It has doubtless broken the line and now waits. They will not risk this ship needlessly."

And for a long time they crouched against the hull, staring into the dark, straining for each sound that might tell them what was happening above.

New orders were given, too faintly to be understood. Men

ran across the deck in one direction and the other, and still the motion of the ship indicated they were scarcely moving.

Then the hatch crashed open and Lhe t'Nethim came down the steps into the hold, backed by three armed men.

"Do you suddenly need weapons?" asked Kta.

"T'Elas," said Lhe, "you are called to the deck."

Kta gathered himself to his feet, while one of the men bent and unlocked the chain that passed through the ring of the band at his ankle.

"Take me along with him," said Kurt, also on his feet.

"I have no orders about that," said Lhe.

"T'Nethim," Kurt pleaded, and Lhe considered an instant, gnawing his lip. Then he gestured to the man with the keys.

"Your word to do nothing violent," Lhe insisted.

"My word," said Kurt.

"Bring him too," said Lhe.

Kurt followed Kta up the steps into the light of day, so blinded by the unaccustomed glare that he nearly missed his footing on the final step. On the deck the hazy shapes of many men moved around them, and their guards guided them like blind men toward the stern of the ship.

Ylith sat beneath the blue canopy. There Kurt's sight began to clear. Kta went heavily to his knees, Kurt following his example, finding comfort in him. He began to understand Kta's offering of respect at such a moment: Kta did what he did with grace, paying honor like a gentleman, unmoved by threat or lack of it. His courage was contagious.

"You may sit," said Ylith softly. "T'Elas, if you will look to the starboard side, I believe you may see the reason we have called you."

Kta turned on one knee, and Kurt looked also. A ship was bearing toward them, slowly, relying on only part of its oarage. The black sail bore the white bird of Ilev, and the red immunity streamer floated from its mast.

"As you see," said the Methi, "we have offered the Families of Nephane the chance to talk before being driven under. I have also ordered my fleet to gather up survivors—without regard to nation; even Sufaki, if there be any. Now if your eloquence can persuade them to surrender, you will have won their lives."

"I have agreed to no such thing," Kta protested angrily.

"This is your opportunity, t'Elas. Present them my conditions, make them believe you,—or remain silent and watch these last ships try to stop us."

"What are your conditions?" Kta asked.

"Nephane will again become part of the empire or Nephane will burn. And if your Sufaki can accept being part of the empire,—well, I will deal with that wonder when it presents itself. I have never met a Sufaki, I confess it, as I had never met a human. I should be interested to do so,—on my terms. So persuade them for me, t'Elas, and save their lives."

"Give me your oath they will live," Kta said, and there was a stirring among the Methi's guards, hands laid on weapons.

But Kta remained as he was, humbly kneeling. "Give me your oath," he replied, "in plain words, life and freedom for the men of the fleet if they take terms. I know that with you, Ylith-methi, words are weapons, double-edged. But I would believe your given word."

A lifting of the Methi's fingers restrained her men from drawing, and she gazed at Kta with what seemed a curious, even loving, satisfaction.

"They have tried us in battle, t'Elas, and you have tried my patience. Look upon the pitiful wreckage floating out there, and the fact that you are still alive after disputing me with words, and decide for yourself upon which you had rather commit their lives."

"You are taking," said Kta, "what I swore I would not give."

Ylith lowered her eyes and lifted them again, which just failed of arrogance. "You are too reasonable," she said, "to destroy those men for your own pride's sake. You will try to save them."

"Then," said Kta in a still voice, "because the Methi is reasonable—she will allow me to go down to that ship. I can do more there than here, where they would be reluctant to speak with me in your presence."

She considered, nodded finally. "Strike the iron from him. From the human too.—If they kill you, t'Elas, you will be avenged." And, softening that arrogant humor: "In truth,

t'Elas, I am trying to avoid killing these men. Persuade
them of that, or be guilty of the consequences."

The Ilev longship bore the scars of fire and battle to such
an extent it was a wonder she could steer. Broken oars hung
in their locks. Her rail was shattered. She looked sadly
disreputable as she grappled onto the immaculate trireme of
the Methi, small next to that towering ship.

Kta nodded to Kurt as soon as she was made fast, and the
two of them descended on a ship's ladder thrown over the
trireme's side.

They landed one after the other, barefoot on the planks
like common seamen, filthy and unshaved, looking fit company for the men of the battered longship. Shock was on
familiar faces all about them: Ian t'Ilev among the foremost,
and men of Irain and Isulan.

Kta made a bow, which t'Ilev was slow to return.

"Gods," t'Ilev murmured then. "You keep strange company, Kta."

"*Tavi* went down off the Isles," said Kta. "Kurt and I
were picked up, the only survivors that I know of. Since that
time we have been detained by the Indras. Are you in
command here, Ian?"

"My father is dead. Since that moment, yes."

"May your Guardians receive him kindly," Kta said.

"The Ancestors of many houses have increased considera-
bly today." A muscle jerked slowly in t'Ilev's jaw. He
gestured his comrades to clear back a space, for they crowded
closely to hear. He set his face in a new hardness. "So do I
understand correctly that the Methi of Indresul is anxious to
clear us aside and proceed on, her way,—and that you are
here to urge that on us?"

"I have been told," said Kta, "that Nephane is in civil
war and that it cannot possibly resist. Is that true, Ian?"

There was a deathly silence.

"Let the Methi ask her own questions," t'Irain said harshly.
"We would have come to her deck."

And there were uglier words from others. Kta looked at
them, his face impassive. At that moment he looked much
like his father Nym, though his clothing was filthy and his

normally ordered hair blew in strings about his face. Tears glittered in his eyes.

"I did not surrender my ship," he said, "though gods know I would have been willing to; a dead crew is a bitter price for a house's pride, and one I would not have paid." His eyes swept the company. "I see no Sufaki among you."

The murmuring grew. "Quiet," said t'Ilev. "All of you. Will you let the men of Indresul see us quarrel?—Kta, say what she has sent you to say. Then you and t'Morgan may leave, unless you keep asking after things we do not care to share with the Methi of Indresul."

"Ian," said Kta, "we have been friends since we were children. Do as seems right to you. But if I have heard the truth,—if there is civil war in Nephane,—if there is no hope but time in your coming here, then let us try for conditions. That is better than going to the bottom."

"Why is she permitting this? Love of us? Confidence in you? Why does she send you down here?"

"I think," said Kta faintly, "I *think*—and am not sure— that she may offer better conditions than we can obtain from Shan t'Tefur. And I think she is permitting it because talk is cheaper than a fight, even for Indresul. It is worth trying, Ian, or I would not have agreed to come down here."

"We came to gain time. I think you know that. For us— crippled as we are—talk is much cheaper than a battle: but we are still prepared to fight too. Even taking the trouble to finish us can delay her. As for your question about Nephane's condition at the moment—"

The others wished him silent. Ian gave them a hard look. "T'Elas has eyes to see. The Sufaki are not here. They demanded command of the fleet. Some few—may their ancestors receive them kindly—tried to reason with Shan t'Tefur's men. Light of heaven, we had to *steal* the fleet by night, break out of harbor even to go out to defend the city. T'Tefur hopes for our defeat. What do you think the Methi's terms will be?"

There was quiet on the deck. For the moment the men were all listening, spirits and angers failing, all pretense laid aside. They only seemed afraid.

"Ian," said Kta, "I do not know. Tehal-methi was unyielding and bloody; Ylith is—I do not know. What she closes within her hand, I fear she will never release. But she is fair-minded, and she is Indras."

The silence persisted. For a moment there was only the creak of timbers, and the grinding of the longship against the side of the trireme as the sea carried them too close.

"He is right," said Lu t'Isulan.

"You are his house-friend," said a man of Nechis. "Kta sued for your cousin to marry."

"That would not blind me to the truth," said t'Isulan. "I agree with him. I am sick to death of t'Tefur and his threats and his ruffians."

"Aye," said his brother Toj. "Our houses had to be left almost defenseless to get enough men out here to man the fleet. And I am thinking they may be in greater danger at the moment from the Sufaki neighbors than from Indresul's fleet.—*Ei*," he said angrily when others objected to that, "clear your eyes and see, my friends. Isulan sent five men of the main hearth here and fifty from the lesser, and a third are lost. Only the sons of the *chan* are left to hold the door of Isulan against t'Tefur's pirates. I am not anxious to lose the rest of my brothers and cousins in an empty gesture. We will not die of hearing the terms, and if they are honorable, I for one would take them."

Ylith leaned back in her chair and accepted the respects of the small group of defeated men kneeling on her deck. "You may all rise," she said, which was generous under the circumstances. "T'Elas, t'Morgan,—I am glad you have returned safely.—Who heads this delegation?"

T'Ilev bowed slightly. "Ian t'Ilev uv Ulmar," he identified himself. "Lord of Ilev." And there was sadness in that assumption of the title, raw and recent. "I am not eldest, but the fleet chose me for my father's sake."

"Do you ask conditions?" asked Ylith.

"We will hear conditions," said t'Ilev.

"I will be brief," said Ylith. "We intend to enter Nephane, with your consent or without it. I will not leave the woman Djan in authority; I will not deal with her or negotiate with those who represent her. I will have order restored in Nephane and a government installed in which I have confidence. The city will thereafter remain in full and constant communication with the mother of cities. However, I will negotiate the extent of the bond between our cities. Have you any comment, t'Ilev?"

"We are the fleet, not the Upei, and we are not able to negotiate anything but our own actions. But I know the Families will not accept any solution which does not promise us our essential freedoms."

"And neither," Kta interjected unbidden, "will the Sufaki."

Ylith's eyes went to him: behind her, I he t'Nethim laid hand uneasily on the hilt of his *ypan*. Ylith's wit and Ylith's power were sufficient to deliver Kta an answer, and Kurt clenched his hands, hoping Kta would not be humiliated before these men. Then of a sudden he saw what game Kta was playing with his life and went cold inside: the Methi too was before witnesses, whose offense now could mean a battle, one ugly and, for the Methi's forces, honorless.

Her lips smiled. She looked him slowly up and down, finally acknowledged him by looking at him directly. "I have studied your city, t'Elas. I have gathered information from most unlikely sources, even you and my human, t'Morgan."

"And what," Kta asked softly, "has the Methi concluded?"

"That a wise person does not contest reality. Sufaki—are a reality. Annihilation of all Sufaki is hardly practical, since they are the population of the entire coast of Sufak. T'Morgan has told me a fable—of human wars. I considered the prospect of dead villages, wasted fields. Somehow this did not seem profitable. *Therefore*, although I do not think the sons of the east will ever be other than trouble to us, I consider that they are less trouble where they are, in Nephane and in their villages, rather than scattered and shooting arrows at my occupation forces. Religiously, I will yield nothing. But I had rather have a city than a ruin, a province than a desolation, and considering that it is your city and your land in question,—you may perhaps agree with me."

"We might," said Ian t'Ilev when she looked aside at him. "If not for that phrase *occupation forces*. The Families rule Nephane."

"*Ai*, no word of Sufaki? Well, but you know the law, t'Ilev. A methi does not reach within families. The question of precedence would be between your two hearths. How you resolve it is not mine to say. But I cannot foresee that Ilev-in-Indresul would be eager to cross the sea to intervene in the affairs of Ilev-in-Nephane. I do not think occupation would prove necessary."

"Your word on that?" asked Kta.

The Methi gave a curious look to him, a smile of faint irony. Then she opened both palms to the sky. "So let the holy light of heaven regard me: I do not mislead you." She leaned back then, stretched her hands along the arms of her chair, her lovely face suddenly grave and businesslike. "Terms: removal of Djan, the dissolution of the t'Tefuri's party, the death of t'Tefur himself, the allegiance of the Families to Indresul and to me. That is the limit of what I demand."

"And the fleet?" asked Ian t'Ilev.

"You can make Nephane in a day, I think. By this time tomorrow you could reach port. You will have a day further to accomplish what I have named or find us among you by force."

"You mean we are to conquer Nephane for you?" t'Ilev exclaimed. "Gods,—no."

"Peace, control of your own city,—or war. If we enter, we will not be bound by these terms."

"Give us a little time," t'Ilev pleaded. "Let us bear these proposals to the rest of the fleet. We cannot agree alone."

"Do that, t'Ilev. We shall give you a day's start toward Nephane whatever you decide. If you use that day's grace to prepare your city to resist us, we will not negotiate again until we meet in the ruins of your city. We are not twice generous, t'Ilev."

T'Ilev bowed, gathered the three of the crew who had come with him, and the gathered crew of the trireme parted widely to let them pass.

"Methi," said Kta.

"Would you go with them?"

"By your leave, Methi."

"It is permitted. Make them believe you, t'Elas. You have your chance,—one day to make your city exist. I hope you succeed. I shall be sorry if I learn you have failed. Will you go with him, t'Morgan? I shall be sorry to part with you."

"Yes," Kurt said. "By your leave."

"Look," she said. "Look up at me." And when he had

done so, he had the feeling that she studied him as a curiosity she might not see again. Her dark eyes held a little of fascinated fear. "You are," she said, "like Djan-methi."

"We are of one kind."

"Bring me Djan," she said. "But not as Methi of Nephane."

And her gesture had dismissed them. They gave back a pace. But then Lhe t'Nethim bowed at her feet, head to the deck, as one who asked a great favor.

"Methi," he said when she acknowledged him, "let me go with this ship. I have business in Nephane, with t'Tefur."

"You are valuable to me, Lhe," she said in great distress.

"Methi, it is hearth business, and you must let me go."

"Must? They will kill you before you reach Nephane, and where will your debt be honored then, t'Nethim, and how will I answer your father, that I let his son do this thing?"

"It is family," he said.

The Methi pressed her lips together. "If they kill you," she said, "then we will know how they will regard any pact with us.—T'Elas, be witness. Treat him honorably, however you decide, for his life or for his death. You will answer to me for this."

T'Nethim bowed a final, heartfelt thanks, and sprang up and hurried after them, among the men of Ilev's party who had delayed also to hear what passed.

"Someone *will* cut his throat," t'Ilev hissed at Kta, before they went over the rail. "What is he to you?"

"Mim's cousin."

"Gods! How long have you been of Indresul, Kta?"

"Trust me. If otherwise, let us at least clear this deck. I beg you, Ian."

T'Ilev bit his lip, then made haste to seek the ladder. "Gods help us," he murmured. "Gods help us,—I will keep silent on it. Burden me with nothing else, Kta."

And he disappeared over the side first and quickly descended to the longship, where his anxious crew waited.

The Ilev vessel glided in among the wrecked fleet with the white assembly streamer flying beside the red, and other captains gathered to her deck as quickly as possible: Eta t'Nechis, Pan t'Ranek, Camit t'Ilev, cousin of Ian—others,

young men, whose captaincies now told of tragedies at sea
or at home.

"Is that it?" shouted Eta t'Nechis when he had heard the
terms, and looked at t'Ilev as if other words failed him.
"Great gods, t'Ilev, did you decide for all of us? Or have
you handed command over to Elas and its company,—to
Elas, who ruined us in the first place, with its human guest.
And now they bring us an overseas house-friend!"

"Argue it later," said Kta. "Whether you want to fight or
negotiate at Nephane, put the fleet about for home now.
Every moment we waste will be badly needed."

"We have men still adrift out there!" cried t'Ranek, "men
the Indras will not let us reach."

"They are being picked up," said Ian. "That is better
than we can do for them. Kta is right. Put about."

"Give the Methi back her man," said t'Nechis, "all three
of them,—t'Elas, human and foreigner."

T'Nethim was pale, but he kept his dignity behind the
shelter Ian t'Ilev gave the three of them: voices were raised,
weapons all but drawn; and finally Ian settled the matter by
ordering his ship put about for Nephane with the fleet
streamer flying beside the others.

Then they were underway, and the sight of the Methi's
fleet dropping astern with no visible evidence of pursuit
greatly heartened the men and silenced some of the demands for vengeance.

"What need of them to pursue," asked t'Nechis, "if we
do their work for them? Gods, gods, this is wrong!"

And once again there was talk of throat-cutting, of throwing the three of them into the sea with Lhe t'Nethim cut in
pieces, until the t'Ilevi together put themselves bodily between the t'Nechisen and Kta t'Elas.

"Stop this," said Ian, and for all that he was a young man
and beneath the age of some of the men who quarreled, he
put such anger into his voice that there was a silence made,
if only a breath of one.

"It is shameful," said Lu t'Isulan with great feeling. "We
disgrace ourselves under the eyes of this Indras stranger.
Bring tea. It is a long distance to Nephane. If we cannot
make a well-thought decision in that length of time, then we
deserve our misery. Let us be still and think for a time."

"We will not share fire and drink with a man of Indresul," said t'Nechis. "Put him in irons."

T'Nethim drew himself back with great dignity. "I will go apart from you," he said, the first words they had listened for him to say. "And I will not interfere. I will still be on this ship if you decide for war."

And with a bow of courtesy, he walked away to the bow, a figure of loneliness among so many enemies. His dignity made a silence among them.

"If you will," said Kurt, "I will go there too."

"You are of Elas," said Kta fiercely, "Stand your ground."

There were hard looks at that. It came to Kurt then that Elas had lost a great deal with *Tavi*, not alone a ship, but brave men, staunch friends of Elas. And those who surrounded them now, with the exception of Irain, Ilev and Isulan, were Families which sympathized less with Elas.

And even among those, there were some who hated humans. Such, even, was Ian t'Ilev; it radiated from him, a little shiver of aversion whenever eyes chanced to meet.

Only Lu and Toj t'Isulan, house-friends to Elas, elected to sit by Kta at the sharing of drink: and they sat on Kta's left, Kurt on the right.

Kurt accepted the cup into his fingers gratefully and sipped at the hot sweet liquid. It held its own memories of home and Elas, of sanity and reason as if there was no power on earth that could change or threaten this little amenity, this odd tribute of the Indras to hearth and civilized order.

Yet everything, their lives and Nephane itself, was as fragile at the moment as the china cup in his fingers.

One round passed in silence. So did most of the second. It was, as the nemet would say, a third-round problem, a matter so disturbing that no one felt calm enough to speak until they had waited through a third series of courtesies and ceremony.

"It is certain," said Ian at last, "that the Methi's word is good so far. We are not pursued. We have to consider that she is indeed a methi of our own people, and it is unthinkable that she would lie."

"Granted," said t'Nechis. "But then what does the truth leave us?"

"With Nephane standing," said Kta very softly. "And I

do love the city, t'Nechis. Even if you hate me, believe that."

"I believe it," said t'Nechis. "Only I suggest that you have perhaps loved honors the Methi promised you—more than is becoming."

"She gave him nothing," said Ian. "And you have my word on that."

"It may be so," conceded t'Nechis, and yet with an uneasy look at Kurt, as if any nemet who consorted with humans was suspect. Kurt lowered his head and stared at a spot on the deck.

"How bad," asked Kta, "have things in Nephane become?"

"T'Elas," said the younger son of Uset-in-Nephane, "we are sorry for the misfortunes of Elas. But that was only the beginning of troubles. In some houses—in Nechis, in Ranek—men are dead: *ypai-sulim* have been drawn. Be careful how you speak to them. Understand the temper of their Guardians."

The Great Weapons, drawn only for killing and never resheathed without it. Kta made a little bow of deference individually to t'Nechis and to t'Ranek, and a gesture with hand to brow that Kurt did not understand: the other men reciprocated. There was silence, and a little easier feeling for that.

"Then," said Kta finally, "there would seem to be question whether there is a city to save. I—have heard a bitter rumor concerning Osanef. Can anyone tell me? Details were sparse."

"It is bad news, Kta," said Ian. "Han t'Osanef killed Tlekef t'Tefur. The house of Osanef was burned by the Tefur partisans, an example to other Sufaki not to remain friendly to us. The vandals struck at night, while the family slept, invaded the house and overthrew the fire to set the house ablaze. The lady Ia, Han's honored wife,—died in the fire."

"And Aimu," Kta broke in. "Bel and my sister?"

"Bel himself was badly beaten; but your lady sister was hurried to safety by the *chan* of Osanef. Both Bel and Aimu are safe, at last report, sheltered in Isulan with your father's sister."

"How did Han die?"

"He chose to die after avenging lady Ia. His funeral was the cause of much bloodletting.—Kta, I am sorry," he added, for Kta's face was pale and he looked suddenly weak.

"This is not all," said Toj t'Isulan. "The whole city is full of such funerals. Han and his lady were not the first or the last to lose their lives to t'Tefur's men."

"He is a madman," T'Nechis said. "He threatened to burn the fleet—to burn the fleet!—rather than let it sail with Indras captains. They talk of burning Nephane itself and drawing back to their ancestral hills of Chteftikan."

"Aye," said young t'Irain, "and I for my part would gladly have the city in Indresul's hands rather than t'Tefur's."

And that sentiment was approved by a sullen muttering among many of the others. T'Nechis scowled, but even he did not seem to be in total disagreement.

"Sirs," said Kurt, startling everyone. "Sirs, what has Djanmethi done in the situation? Has she—can she do—anything to restore peace in the city?"

"She has the power," said t'Ranek. "She refuses to control t'Tefur. This war is of her creation. She knew *we* would never turn on Indresul, so she puts power in the hands of those who would, those who support her ambition. And that does not respect her office, but neither does she."

"I do not know," said the youngest t'Nechis, "why we answer questions from the Methi's leman."

Kta moved, and if the elder t'Nechis had not imposed his own discipline on his cousin with a sharp gesture, there would have been trouble.

"My apologies," said t'Nechis, words that seemed like gall in his mouth.

"I understand," said Kurt, "that humans have won no love in Nephane or elsewhere. But bear with me. I have a thing to say."

"Say it," said t'Nechis. "We will not deny you that."

"You would do well," he said, "to approach her with a clear request for action and concessions for the Sufaki who are not with t'Tefur."

"You seem to favor her," said t'Ranek, "and to have a great deal of confidence in her. I think we were wrong to sympathize with you for the death of Mim h'Elas."

Kurt threw out a hand to stop Kta, and himself stared at

t'Ranek with such coldness that all the nemet grew silent. "My wife," he said, "was as much a victim of you as of Djan-methi, though I swear I tried to feel loyalty to the Families since I was part of Elas. I am human. I was not welcome and you made me know it as you made Djan-methi know it, and the Sufaki before her. If that were not the nature of Nephane, my wife would not be dead."

And before any could object, he sprang up and walked away, to t'Nethim's lonely station at the bow.

Lhe regarded him curiously, then even with pity, which from the enemy was like salt in the wound.

Soon, as Kurt had known, there came someone sent from Kta to try to persuade him back, to persuade him to bow his head and swallow his humanity and his pride and submit in silence.

He heard the footsteps coming behind him, pointedly ignored the approach until he heard the man call his name.

Then he turned and saw that it was t'Ranek himself.

"Kta t'Elas has threatened bloodfeud," said t'Ranek. "Please accept my apologies, t'Morgan. I am no friend of Elas, but I do not want a fight, and I acknowledge that it was not a worthy thing to say."

"Kta would fight over that?"

"It is his honor," said t'Ranek. "He says that you are of Elas. He also," t'Ranek added, with an uneasy glance at Lhe t'Nethim, "has asked t'Nethim to return. He has explained somewhat of the lady Mim h'Elas. Please accept my apology, Kurt t'Morgan."

It was not easy for the man. Kurt gave a stiff bow in acknowledgment, then looked at Lhe t'Nethim. The three of them returned to their places in the circle in utter silence. Kurt took his place beside Kta, t'Ranek with his brother, and Lhe t'Nethim stood nervously in the center until Kta abruptly gestured to him and bade him sit: t'Nethim settled at Kta's feet, thin-lipped and with eyes downcast.

"You have among you," said Kta in that hush, "my brother Kurt, and Lhe t'Nethim, who is under the protection of Elas."

Like the effect of wind over grass, the men in the circle made slight bows.

"I was speaking," Kurt said then, evenly and softly in that

stillness. "And I will say one other thing, and then I will not trouble you further. There are weapons in the Afen: if Djan-methi has not used them, it is because Djan-methi has chosen not to use them. Once you have threatened her, you will have to reckon with the possibility that she will use them. You are wrong in some of your suppositions. She could destroy not only Nephane but Indresul also if she chose. You are hazarding your lives on her forbearance."

The silence persisted. It was no longer one of hate, but of fear. Even Kta looked at him as a stranger.

"I am telling the truth," he said, for Kta.

"T'Morgan," said Ian t'Ilev. "Do you have a suggestion what to do?"

It was quietly, even humbly posed; and to his shame he was helpless to answer it. "I will tell you this," he said, "that if Djan-methi still controls the Afen when Ylith-methi sails into that harbor,—you are much more likely to see those weapons used. And worse,—if Shan t'Tefur should gain possession of them.—She does not want to arm him, or she would have: but she might lose her power to prevent him,—or abdicate it. I should suggest, gentlemen, that you make any peace you must with the Sufaki who will have peace: give them reasonable alternatives, and do all you can to get the Afen out of Djan-methi's hands and out of t'Tefur's."

"The Afen," protested t'Ranek, "has only fallen to treachery, never to attack by nemet. Haichema-tleke is too high, our streets too steep, and the human weapons would make it impossible."

"Our alternative," said Kta, "would seem to be to take the whole fleet and run for the north sea, saving ourselves. And I do not think we are of a mind to do that."

"No," said t'Nechis. "We are not."

"Then we attack the Afen."

XXII

The smoke over Nephane was visible even from a distance. It rolled up until the west wind caught it and spread it over the city like one of its frequent sea fogs, but blacker and thicker, darkening the morning light and overshadowing the harbor.

The men who stood on *Sidek*'s bow as the Ilev longship put into harbor at the head of the fleet watched the shore in silence. The smoke appeared to come from high up the hill, but no one ventured to surmise what was burning.

At last Kta turned his face from the sight with a gesture of anger. "Kurt," he said, "keep close by me. Gods know what we are going into."

Oars eased *Sidek* in and let her glide, a brave man of Ilev first ashore with the mooring cable. Other ships came into dock in quick succession.

Crowds poured from the gate, gathering on the dockside, all Sufaki, not a few of them in Robes of Color, young and menacing, but there were elders and women with children, clamoring and pleading for news, looking with frightened eyes at the tattered rigging of the ships. Some seamen who had not sailed with their Indras crewmates ran down to the side of them and began to curse and invoke the gods for grief at what had happened to them, seeking news of shipmates.

And swiftly the rumor was running the crowd that the fleet had turned back the Methi, even while Ian t'Ilev and other captains gave quick orders to run out the gangplanks.

The plans and alternate plans had been drilled into the ships' crews in exhortations of captains and family heads and what practice the narrow decks permitted. Now the Indras-descended moved smartly, with such decision and certainty that the Sufaki, confused by the false rumor of victory, gave back.

A young revolutionary charged forward, shrieking hate and trying to inflame the crowd, but Indras discipline held, though he struck one of the t'Nechisen half senseless. And suddenly the rebel gave back and ran, for no one had followed him. The Indras-descended kept swords in sheaths, gently making way for themselves at no greater speed than the bewildered crowd could give them. They did not try to pass the gates: they took their stand on the dock, and t'Isulan, who had the loudest voice in the fleet, held up his arms for silence.

News was what the crowd cried for: now that it was offered, they compelled each other to silence to hear it.

"We have held them a little while," shouted t'Isulan. "We are still in danger.—Where is the Methi to be found? Still in the Afen?"

People attempted to answer in the affirmative, but the replies and the questions drowned one another out. Women began screaming, everyone talking at once.

"Listen," t'Isulan roared above the noise. "Pull back and fortify the wall. Get your women to the houses and barricade the gates to the sea!"

The tumult began anew, and Kta, well to the center of the lines of Indras, seized Kurt by the arm and drew him to the inside as they started to move, t'Nethim staying close by them.

Kurt had his head muffled in his *ctan*. Among so many injured it was not conspicuous, and exposure had darkened his skin almost to the hue of the nemet—he was terrified, nonetheless, that the sight of his human face might bring disaster to the whole plan and put him in the hands of a mob. There had been talk of leaving him on the ship: Kta had argued otherwise.

The Indras-descended began to pass the outer-wall gates, filing peacefully upward toward their homes, toward their own hearths. It was supreme bluff. T'Isulan had hedged the truth with a skill uncommon to that tall, gruff breed that were his Family. It was their hope—to organize the Sufaki to work, and so keep the Sufaki out of the way of the Families.

And at the inner gate, the rebels waited.

There were jeers. Daggers were out. Rocks flew. Two Indras-descended fell, immediately gathered up by their kinsmen. T'Nethim staggered as a rock hit him. Kta hurried him further, half carrying him. The head of the column forced the gate bare-handed, with sheer weight of numbers and recklessness: it was sworn among them that they would not draw weapons, not until a point of extremity.

There was blood on the cobbles as they passed, and smeared on the post of the gate, but the Indras-descended let none of their own fall. They gained the winding Street of the Families, and their final rush panicked the rebels, who scattered before them, disordered and undisciplined.

Then the cause of the smoke became evident. Houses at the rising of the hill were aflame, Sufaki milling in the streets at the scene. Women snatched up screaming children and crowded back, caught between the fires and the rush of fleeing rebels and advancing Indras. A young mother clutched her two children to her and shrank against the side of a house, sobbing in terror as they passed her.

It was the area where the wealthiest Sufak houses joined the Street of the Families, and where the road took the final bend toward the Afen. Two Sufak houses, Rachik and Pamchen, were ablaze, and the blasphemous paint-splashed triangle of Phan gave evidence of the religious bitterness that had brought it on. Trapped Sufaki ran in panic between the roiling smoke of the fire and the sudden charge of the Indras.

"Spread out!" t'Isulan roared, waving his arm to indicate a barrier across the street. "Close off this area and secure it!"

A feathered shaft impacted into the chest of the man next to him; Tis t'Nechis fell with red dying his robes. A second and a third shaft sped, one felling an Indras and the other a Sufaki bystander who happened to be in the line of fire.

"Up there!" Kta shouted, pointing to the rooftop of Dleve.

"Get the man, t'Ranek! You men, spread out!—this side, this side, quickly,—"

The Indras moved, their rush to shelter terrifying the Sufaki who chanced to have sought the same protected side: but the Indras dislodged no one. A terrified boy started to dart out: an Indras seized him, struggling and kicking though he was, and pushed him into the hands of his kin.

"Neighbors!" Kta shouted to the house of Rachik. "We are not here to harm you. Gods, lady shu-t'Rachik, get those children back into the alley! Keep close to the wall."

There were a few grins, for the first lady t'Rachik with her brood was very like a frightened *cachin* with a half dozen of her children about her; other Rachiken were there too, both women and men, and the old father too. They were glad enough to escape the area, and the old man gave a sketchy bow to Kta t'Elas, gratitude. Though his house was burning, his children were safe.

"Shelter near Elas," said Kta. "No Indras will harm you. Put the Pamcheni there too, Gyan t'Rachik."

A cry rang out overhead and a body toppled from the roof to bounce off a porch and onto the stones of the street. The dead Sufaki archer lay with arrows scattered like straws about his corpse.

A girl of Dleve screamed, belatedly, hysterically.

"Throw a defense around this whole section," Kta directed his men. "Ian! Camit!—take the wall-street by Irain and set a guard there.—You Sufaki citizens! get these fires under control: buckets and pikes, quickly! You, t'Hsnet, join t'Ranek, you and all your cousins!"

Men scattered in all directions at his orders, and pushed their way through smoke and frightened Sufaki; but the Sufaki who remained on the street, elders and children, huddled together in pitiful confusion, afraid to move in any direction.

Then from the houses up the street came others of the Indras-descended, and the *chani,* such as had stayed behind to guard the houses when the fleet sailed. Sufaki women screamed at the sight of them, men armed with the deadly *ypai.*

Kta stood free of the wall, taking a chance, for t'Ranek's men were not yet in position to defend the street from archers. He lifted his sword arm aloft in signal to the Indras who were running up, weapons in hand.

"Hold off!" he shouted. "We have things under control. These poor citizens are not to blame. Help us secure the area and put out the fires."

"The Sufaki set them, in Sufak houses," shouted the old *chan* of Irain. "Let the Sufaki put them out!"

"No matter who started them," Kta returned furiously, his face purpling at being fronted by a *chan* of a friendly house. "Help put them out. The fires are burning and they will take our houses too. They must be stopped."

That *chan* seemed suddenly to realize who it was he had challenged, for he came to a sudden halt; and another man shouted:

"Kta t'Elas! *Ei,* t'Elas, t'Elas!"

"Aye," shouted Kta, "still alive, t'Kales! Well met! Give us help here."

"These people," panted t'Kales, reaching him and giving the indication of a bow, "these people deserve no pity. We tried to defend them. They shield t'Tefur's men, even when the fires strike their own houses."

"All Nephane has lost its mind," said Kta, "and there is no time to argue blame. Help us or stand aside. The Indras fleet is a day out of Nephane and we either collect ourselves a people or see Nephane burn."

"Gods," breathed t'Kales. "Then the fleet—"

"Defeated. We must organize the city."

"We cannot do it, Kta. None of these people will listen to reason. We have been beseiged in our own houses."

"Kta!" Kurt exclaimed, for another man was running down the street.

It was Bel t'Osanef. One of the Indras-descended barred his way with drawn *ypan* and nearly ran him through, but t'Osanef avoided it with desperate agility.

"Light of heaven!" Kta cried. "Hold, t'Idur! Let him pass!"

The seaman dropped his point and Bel began running again, reached the place where they stood.

"Kta,—ye gods, Kta!" Bel was close to collapse with his race to get through, and the words choked from him. "I had no hope—"

"You are mad to be on the street," said Kta. "Where is Aimu?"

"Safe. We shelter in Irain. Kta—"

"I have heard, I have heard, my poor friend."

"Then please,—Kta,—these people—these people of mine, they are innocent of the fires. Whatever—whatever your people say,—they try to make us out responsible—but it is a lie, a—"

"Calm yourself, Bel. Cast no words to the winds. I beg you, take charge of these people and get them to help or get them out of this area. The Indras fleet is coming down on Nephane and we have only a little time to restore order here and prepare ourselves."

"I will try," said Bel, and cast a despairing look at the frightened people milling about, at the dead men in the street. He went to the archer who lay in the center of the cobbled street, knelt down and touched him, then looked up with a negative gesture and a sympathetic expression for someone in the crowd.

There came a young woman—the one who had screamed; she crept forward and knelt down in the street beside the dead man, sobbing and rocking in her misery. Bel spoke to her in words no one else could hear, though there was but for the fire's crackling a strange silence on the street and among the crowd. Then he picked up the dead youth's body himself, and stuggled with it toward the Sufaki side.

"Let us take our dead decently inside," he said. "You men who can,—put the fires out."

"The Indras set them," one of the young women said.

"Udafi Kafurtin," said Bel in a trembling voice, "in the chaos we have made of Nephane, there is really no knowing who started anything. Our only identifiable enemy is whoever will not put them out.—Kta—Kta! Have these men of yours put up their weapons. We have had enough of weapons and threats in this city. My people are not armed, and yours do not need to be."

"Yours shoot from ambush!" shouted one of the Indras.

"Do as he asks!" Kta shouted, and glared about him with such fury that men began to obey him.

Then Kta went and bowed very low before t'Nechis, who had a cousin to mourn, and quietly offered his help, though

Kurt winced inwardly and expected temper and hatred from the grieving t'Nechis.

But in extremity t'Nechis was Indras and a gentleman. He bowed in turn, in proper grace. "See to business, Kta t'Elas. The t'Nechisen will take him home. We will be with you as soon as we can send my cousin to his rest."

By noon the fires were out, and the Sufaki who had aided in fighting the blaze scattered to their homes to bar the doors and wait in silence.

Peace returned to the Street of the Families, with armed men of the fleet standing at either end of the street and on rooftops where they commanded a view of all that moved. The scars were visible now, hollow shells of buildings, pavement littered with rubble.

Kurt left Lhe t'Nethim sheltered in the hall of Elas, the Indras grim-faced and subdued to have set foot in a hostile house.

He found Kta standing out on the curb—Kta, like himself, was masked with soot and sweat and the dim red marks of burns from fire fighting.

"They have buried t'Nechis," Kta said hollowly, without looking around. They had been so much together it was possible to feel the other's presence without looking. He knew Kta's face without seeing it, that it was tired and shadow-eyed and drawn with pain.

"Get off the street," Kurt said. "You are a target."

"T'Ranek is on the roof. I do not think there is danger. Fully half of Nephane is in our hands now, thank the gods."

"You have done enough. Go over to Irain. Aimu will be anxious to see you."

"I do not wish to go to Irain," Kta said wearily. "Bel will be there and I do not wish to see him."

"You have to, sooner or later."

"What do I tell him? What do I say to him when he asks me what will happen now?—Forgive me, brother, but I have made a compact with the Indras, and I swore once that was impossible; forgive me, brother, but I have surrendered your home to my foreign cousins;—I am sorry, my brother, but I have sold you into slavery for your own preservation."

"At least," said Kurt grimly, "the Sufaki will have the

same chance a human has among Indras; and that is better than dying, Kta, it is infinitely better than dying."

"I hope," said Kta, "that Bel sees it that way. I am afraid for this city—tonight. There has been too little resistance. They are saving something back. And there is a report t'Tefur is in the Afen."

Kurt let the breath hiss slowly between his teeth and glanced uphill, toward the Afen gate.

"If we are fortunate," he said, "Djan will keep control of the weapons."

"You seem to have some peculiar confidence she will not hand him that power."

"She will not do it," Kurt said. "Not willingly. I could be wrong,—but I think I know Djan's mind. She would suffer a great deal before she would let those machines be loosed on nemet."

Kta looked back at him, anger on his face. "She was capable of things you seem to have forgotten. Humanness blinds you, my friend; and I fear you have buried Mim more deeply than earth can put her. I do not understand that. Or perhaps I do."

"Some things," Kurt said, with a sudden and soul-deep coldness, "you still do not know me well enough to say."

And he walked back into Elas, ignoring t'Nethim, retreating into its deep shadows, into the *rhmei,* where the fire was dead, the ashes cold. He knelt there on the rugs as he had done so many evenings, and stared into the dark.

Lhe t'Nethim's quiet step dared the silent *rhmei.* It was a rash and brave act for an orthodox Indras. He bowed himself in respect before the dead firebowl and knelt on the bare floor.

He only waited, as he had waited constantly, attending them in silence.

"What do you want of me?" Kurt asked in vexation.

"I owe you," said Lhe t'Nethim, "for the care of my cousin's soul. I have come because it is right that a kinsman see the hearth she honored. When I have seen her avenged, I will be free again."

It was understandable. Kurt could imagine Kta doing so reckless a thing for Aimu.

Even for him.

He had used rudeness to Kta. Even justified, it pained him. He was glad to hear Kta's familiar step in the entry, like a ghost of things that belonged to Elas, disturbing its sleep.

Kta silently came and knelt down on the rug nearest Kurt.

"I was wrong," said Kurt. "I owe you an accounting."

"No," said Kta gently. "The words flew amiss. You are a stranger sometimes. I feared—you were remembering—human debts. And you have found no *yhia* since losing Mim. She lies at the heart of everything for you. A man without *yhia* toward such a great loss cannot remember things clearly, cannot reason. He is dangerous to all around him. I fear you. I fear for you. Even you do not know what you are likely to do."

He was silent for a long time. Kurt did not break the silence.

"Let us wash," said Kta at last. "And when I have cleansed my hands of blood I mean to light the hearth of Elas again, and return some feeling of life to these halls. If you dread to go upstairs, use my room, and welcome."

"No," said Kurt, and gathered himself to his feet. "I will go up, Kta. Do not worry for it."

The room that had been his and Mim's looked little different. The stained rug was gone, but all else was the same, the bed, the holy *phusa* before which she had knelt and prayed.

He had thought that being here would be difficult. He could scarcely remember the sound of Mim's voice. That had been the first memory to flee. The one most persistent was that still shape of shadow beneath the glaring hearth-fire, Nym's arms uplifted, invoking ruin, waking the vengeance of his gods.

But now his eyes traveled to the dressing table, where still rested the pins and combs that Mim had used, and when he opened the drawer there were the scarves that carried the gentle scent of *aluel*. For the first time in a long time he did remember her in daylight, her gentle touch, the light in her eyes when she laughed, the sound of her voice bidding him good morning, my lord. Tears came to his eyes. He took one of the scarves, light as a dream in his oar-callused hands, and folded it and put it back again. Elas was home for him again, and he could exist here, and think of her and not mourn any longer.

T'Nethim, his peculiar shadow, hovered uncertainly out on the landing. Kurt heard him, looked and bade him come in. The Indras uncertainly trod the fine carpeting, bowed in reverence before the dead *phusa*.

"There are clean clothes," Kurt said to him, flinging wide the closet which held all that had been his. "Take what you need."

He put off his own filthy garments and went into the bath, washed and shaved with cold water and dressed again in a change of clothing while Lhe t'Nethim did the same for himself. Kurt found himself changed, browner, leaner, ribs crossed by several ridged scars that were still sensitive: those misfortunes were far away, shut out by the friendly wall of this house.

There was only t'Nethim, who followed, silent, to remind him that war hovered about them.

When they had both finished, they went downstairs to the *rhmei* to find Kta.

Kta had relit the holy fire, and the warm light of it leaped up and touched their faces and chased the shadows into the deeper recesses of the high ceiling and the spaces behind the pillars of the hall. Elas was alive again in Nephane.

T'Nethim would not enter here now, but returned to the threshold of Elas, to take his place in the shadows, sword detached and laid before him like a self-appointed sentinel, as in ancient times the *chan* was stationed.

But Kurt went to join Kta in the *rhmei* and listened while Kta lifted hands to the fire and spoke a prayer to the Guardians for their blessing.

"Spirits of my Ancestors," he ended, "of Elas, my fathers, my father, fate had led me here and led me home again. My father, my mother, my friends who wait below, there is no peace yet in Elas. Aid me now to find it. Receive us home again and give us welcome, and also bear the presence of Lhe t'Nethim u Kma, who sits at our gate, a suppliant. Shadow of Mim, one of your own has come. Be at peace."

For a moment he remained still, then let fall his hands

and looked back at Kurt. "It is a better feeling," he said quietly. "But still there is a heaviness. I am stifling, Kurt. Do you feel it?"

Kurt shivered involuntarily, and the human part of him insisted it was a cold draft through the halls, blowing the fire's warmth in the other direction.

But all of a sudden he knew what Kta meant of ill feelings. An ancestral enemy sat at their threshold. Unease rippled through the air, disquiet hovered thickly there. T'Nethim existed, t'Nethim waited, in a city where he ought not to have come, in a house that was his enemy.

A piece of the *yhia* out of place, waiting.

Let us bid him go wait in some other house, Kurt almost suggested; but he was embarrassed to do it; and, it was to himself that t'Nethim attached, his own heels the man of Indras dogged.

A pounding came at the front door of Elas. They hurried out, taking weapons left by the doorway of the *rhmei,* and gave a nod of assent to t'Nethim's questioning look. T'Nethim slipped the bar and opened the door.

A man and a woman were there in the light: Aimu, with Bel t'Osanef.

She folded her hands upon her breast and bowed, and Kta bowed deeply to her. When she lifted her face she was crying, tears flooding over her face.

"Aimu," said Kta. "Bel,—welcome."

"Am I truly?" Aimu asked. "My brother, I have waited so long this afternoon, so patiently,—and you would not come to Irain."

"Ei, Aimu, Aimu, you were my first thought in coming home—how not, my sister? You are all Kurt and I have left. How can you think I do not care?"

Aimu looked into his face and her hurt became a troubled expression, as if suddenly she read something in Kta that she feared, knowing him. "Dear my brother," she said, "there is no woman in the house. Receive us as your guests and let me make this house home for you again."

"It would be welcome," he said. "It would very welcome, my sister."

She bowed a little and went her way into the women's part of the house. Kta looked back to Bel, hardly able to do otherwise, and the Sufaki's eyes were full sober. They demanded an answer.

"Bel," said Kta, "this house bids you welcome. Whether it is still a welcome you want to accept,—"

"You can tell me that, Kta."

"I am going to finish the quarrel between us and Tefur, Bel." Kta then gave Lhe t'Nethim a direct look, so the Indras knew he was earnestly not wanted; and Lhe retreated down the hall toward the darkness, still not daring the *rhmei.*

"He is a stranger," said Bel. "Is he of the Isles?"

"He is Indras," Kta admitted. "Forget him, Bel. Come into the *rhmei.* We will talk."

"I will talk here," said Bel. "I want to know what you are planning. Revenge on t'Tefur—in that I will gladly join you. I have a debt of blood there too. But why is the street still sealed? What is this silence in Irain? And why have you not come there?"

"Bel, do not press me like this. I will explain."

"You have made some private agreement with the Indras forces. That is the only conclusion that makes sense. I want you to tell me that I am wrong. I want you to account for how you return with the fleet,—for who this stranger is in Elas,—for a great many things, Kta."

"Bel, we were defeated. We have bought time."

"How?"

"Bel,—if you walk out of here now and rouse your people against us, you will be blood-guilty. We lost the battle. The Methi Ylith will not destroy the city if we fulfill her conditions. —Walk out of here if you choose, betray that confidence, —and you will have lives of your people on your conscience."

Bel paused with his hand on the door.

"What would you do to stop me?"

"I would let you go," said Kta. "I would not stop you. But your people will die if they fight, and they will throw away everything we have tried to win for them. Ylith-methi will not destroy the Sufaki, Bel. We would never have agreed to that. I am struggling with her to win your freedom. I think I can,—if the Sufaki themselves do not undo it all."

Bel's eyes were cold, a muscle slowly knotting in his jaw.

"You are surrendering," he said at last. "Did you not tell me once how the Indras-descended would fight to the death before they would let Nephane fall? Are these your promises? Is this the value of your honor?"

"I want this city to live, Bel."

"I know you, my friend. Kta t'Elas took good thought that it was honorable. And when Indras talk of honor, we always lose."

"I understand your bitterness; I do not blame you. But I won you as much as I could win."

"I know," said Bel. "I know it for the truth. If I did not believe it, I would help them collect your head,—Gods, my friend, my kinsman-by-marriage,—of all our enemies, it has to be you to come tell me you have sold us out,—for friendship's sake. Honorably. Because it was fated. *Ai*, Kta—"

"I am sorry, Bel."

Bel laughed shortly, a sound of weeping. "Gods, they killed my house for staying by Elas. My people—I tried to persuade to reason, to the middle course. I argued with great eloquence, *ai*, yes, and most bitter of all, I knew—I knew when I heard the fleet had returned—I knew as sure as instinct what the Indras must have done to come back so soon. It was the reasonable course, was it not, the logical, the expedient, the conservative thing to do? But I did not know until you failed to come to Irain that you had been the one to do it to us."

"T'Osanef," said Kurt, "times change things, even in Indresul. No human would have left Tehal-methi's hands alive. I was freed."

"Have you met with Ylith-methi face to face?"

"Yes," said Kta.

Bel shot him a yet more uneasy look. "Gods, I could almost believe—Did you run straight from here to Indresul? Was t'Tefur right about you?"

"Is that the rumor in the city?"

"A rumor I have denied until now."

"Shan t'Tefur knows where we were," said Kurt. "He tried to sink us in the vicinity of the Isles, but we were captured after that by the Indras, and that is the truth. Kta risked his life for your sake, t'Osanef. You could at least afford him the time to hear all the truth."

Bel considered a moment. "I suppose I can do that," he said. "There is little else I can do, is there?"

"Will you have more tea, gentlemen?" Aimu asked, when the silence lasted overlong among them.

"No," said Bel at last, and gave his cup to her. He looked once more at Kta and Kurt. "Kta,—I am at least able to understand. I am sorry—for the suffering you had."

"You are saying what is in your mind," said Kta, "not what is in your heart."

"I have listened to what you had to say. I do not blame you. What could you do? You are Indras. You chose the survival of your people and the destruction of mine. Is that so unnatural?"

"I will not let them harm the Sufaki," Kta insisted, while Bel stared at him with that hard-eyed pain which would not admit of tears.

"Would you defy Ylith-methi for us," asked Bel, "as you defied Djan?"

"Yes. You know I would."

"Yes," said Bel, "because Indras are madly honorable. You would die for me. That would satisfy your conscience. But you have already made the choice that matters. Gods, Kta, Kta, I love you as a brother; I understand you, and it hurts, Kta."

"It grieves me too," said Kta, "because I knew that it would hurt you personally. But I am doing what I can to prevent bloodshed among your people. I do not ask your help—only your silence."

"I cannot promise that."

"Bel," Kurt said sharply when t'Osanef made to rise. "Listen to *me*. A people can still hope, so long as they live; even mine, low as they have fallen on this world. You can survive this."

"As slaves again."

'Even so,—Sufaki ways would survive; and if that survives, little by little, you gain. Fight them, spend lives, fall; in the end, the same result: Sufaki ways seep in among the Indras and theirs among you. Bow to good sense. Be patient."

"My people would curse me for a traitor."

"It is too late to do otherwise," said Kurt.

"Are the Families agreed?" Bel asked Kta.

"A vote was taken in the fleet. Enough houses were present to bind the Families to the decision; the Upei's vote would be a formality."

"That is not unusual," said Bel, and suddenly looked at Aimu, who sat listening to everything, pained and silent. "Aimu,—do you have counsel for me?"

"No," she said. "No counsel. Only that you do what you think best. If your honored father were here,—my lord, he surely would have advice for you, being Sufaki, being elder. What could I tell you?"

Bel bowed his head and thought a time, and made a gesture of deep distress. "It is a fair answer, Aimu," he said at last. "I only hate the choice. Tonight—tonight, when it is possible to move without having my throat cut by one of your men, my brother Kta, I will go to what men of my father's persuasion I can reach. I leave t'Tefur to you. I will not kill Sufaki. I assume you are going to try to take the Afen?"

Kta was slow to answer, and Bel's look was one of bitter humor, as if challenging his trust. "Yes," said Kta.

"Then we go our separate ways this evening. I hope your men will exercise the sense to stay off the harbor-front. Or is it a night attack Indresul plans?"

"If that should happen," said Kta, "you will know that we of the Families have been deceived. I tell you the truth, Bel: I do not anticipate that."

Men came to the door of Elas from time to time as the day sank toward evening,—representatives of the houses, reporting decisions, urging actions. Ian t'Ilev came, to report the street at last under firm control all along the wall of the Afen gate. He brought too the unwelcome news that Res t'Benit had been wounded from ambush at the lower end of the street, grim forecast of trouble to come, when night made the Families' position vulnerable.

"Where did it happen?" asked Kta.

"At Imas," said Ian. It was the house that faced the Sufaki district. "But the assassin ran and we could not follow him into the—"

He stopped cold as he saw Bel standing in the triangular arch of the *rhmei*.

Bel walked forward. "Do you think me the enemy, Ian t'Ilev?"

"T'Osanef." Ian covered his confusion with a courteous bow. "No, I was only surprised to find you here."

"That is strange. Most of my people would not be."

"Bel," Kta reproved him.

"You and I know how things stand," said Bel. "If you will pardon me, I see things are getting down to business and the sun is sinking. I think it is time for me to leave."

"Bel, be careful. Wait until it is securely dark."

"I will be careful," he said, a little warmth returning to his voice. "Kta, take care for Aimu."

"Gods, are you leaving this moment? What am I to tell her?"

"I have said to her what I need to say." Bel delayed a moment more, his hand upon the door, and looked back. "She was your best argument; I remain grateful you did not stoop to that. I will omit to wish you success, Kta. Do not be surprised if some of my people choose to die rather than agree with you. I will not even pray for t'Tefur's death, when it may be the last the world will see of the nation we were. The name, my Indras friends, was Chtelek, not Sufak. But that probably will not matter hereafter."

"Bel," said Kta, "at least arm yourself."

"Against whom? Yours—or mine? Thank you, no, Kta. I will see you at the harbor—or be in it tomorrow morning, whichever fortune brings me."

The heavy door closed behind him, echoing through the empty halls, and Kta looked at Ian with a troubled expression.

"Do you trust him that far?" Ian t'Ilev asked.

"Begin no action against the Sufaki beyond Imas. I insist on that, Ian."

"Is everything still according to original plan?"

"I will be there at nightfall. But one thing you can do: take Aimu with you and put her safely in a defended house. Elas will be no protection to her tonight."

"She will be safe in Ilev. There will be men left to guard it, as many as we can spare: Uset's women will be there too."

"That will ease my mind greatly," said Kta.

*   *   *

Aimu wept at the parting, as she had already been crying and trying not to. Before she did leave the house, she went to the *phusmeha* and cast into the holy fire her silken scarf. It exploded into brief flame, and she held out her hands in prayer. Then she came and put herself in the charge of Ian t'Ilev.

Kurt felt deeply sorry for her and found it hard to think Kta would not make some special farewell, but he bowed to her and she to him with the same formality that had always been between them.

"Heaven guard you, my brother," she said softly.

"The Guardians of Elas watch over thee, my little sister, once of this house."

It was all. Ian opened the door for her and shepherded her out into the street, casting an anxious eye across and up where the guards still stood on the rooftops, a reassuring presence. Kta closed the door again.

"How much longer?" Kurt asked. "It's near dark. Shan t'Tefur undoubtedly has ideas of his own."

"We are about to leave."—T'Nethim appeared silently among the shadows of the further hall. Kta gave a jerk of his head and t'Nethim came forward to join them. "Stay by the threshold," he ordered t'Nethim. "And be still. What I have yet to do does not involve you. I forbid you to invoke your Guardians in this house."

T'Nethim looked uneasy, but bowed and assumed his accustomed place by the door, laying his sword on the floor before him.

Kta with Kurt walked into the firelit *rhmei*, and Kurt realized then the nature of Kta's warning to t'Nethim, for he walked to the left wall of the *rhmei*, where hung the Sword of Elas, Isthain. The *ypan-sul* had hung undisturbed for nine generations, untouched since the expulsion of the humans from Nephane, but for the sometime attention that kept its metal bright and its leather-wrapped hilt in good repair. The *ypai-sulim,* the Great Weapons, were unique to their houses and full of the history of them. Isthain, forged in Indresul when Nephane was still a colony, nearly a thousand years before, had been dedicated in the blood of a Sufaki captive in the barbaric past, carried into battle by eleven men before.

Kta's hand hesitated at taking the age-dark hilt of it, but then he lifted it down, sheath and all, and went to the hearthfire. There he knelt and laid the great Sword on the floor, hands outstretched over it.

"Guardians of Elas," he said, "waken, waken and hear me, all ye spirits who have ever known me or wielded this blade. I, Kta t'Elas u Nym, last of this house, invoke ye; know my presence and that of Kurt Liam t'Morgan u Patrick Edward, friend to this house. Know that at our threshold sits Lhe t'Nethim u Kma. Let your powers shield my friend and myself, and do no harm to him at our door. We take Isthain against Shan t'Tefur u Tlekef, and the cause of it you well know.—And you, Isthain, you shall have t'Tefur's blood or mine. Against t'Tefur direct your anger and against no others. Long have you slept undisturbed, my dread sister, and I know the tribute due you when you are wakened. It will be paid by morning's light, and after that time you will sleep again. Judge me, ye Guardians, and if my cause is just, give me strength. Bring peace again to Elas, by t'Tefur's death or mine."

So saying he took up the sheathed blade and drew it, the holy light running up and down the length of it as it came forth in his hand. Etched in its shining surface was the lightning emblem of the house, seeming to flash to life in the darkness of the *rhmei*. In both hands he lifted the blade to the light and rose, lifted it heavenward and brought it down again, then recovered the sheath and made it fast in his belt.

"It is done," he said to Kurt. "Have a care of me now, though your human soul has its doubts of such powers. Isthain last drank of human life, and she is an evil creature, hard to put to sleep once wakened. She is eldest of the *Sulim* in Nephane, and self-willed."

Kurt nodded and answered nothing. Whatever the temper of the spirit that lived in the metal, he knew the one which lived in Kta t'Elas. Gentle Kta had prepared himself to kill and, in truth, he did not want to stand too near, or to find any friend in Kta's path.

And when they came to the threshold where t'Nethim waited, Lhe t'Nethim bowed his face to the stone floor and let Kta pass the door before he would rise; but when Kurt delayed to close the door of Elas and secure it, t'Nethim gathered himself up and crept out into the gathering dark, the look on his perspiring face that of a man who had indeed been brushed by something that sought his life.

"He has prayed your safety," Kurt ventured to tell him.

"Sometimes," said Lhe t'Nethim, "that is not enough. Go ahead, t'Morgan,—but be careful of him. It is the dead of Elas who live in that thing. Mim my cousin—"

He ceased with a shiver, and Kurt put the nemet superstition out of mind with a horror that Mim's name could be entangled in the bloody history of Isthain.

He ran to overtake Kta, and knew that Lhe t'Nethim, at a safe distance, was still behind them.

XXIII

"There" said Ian t'Ilev, nodding at the iron gate of the Afen. "They have several archers stationed inside. We are bound to take a few arrows. You and Kurt must have most care: they will be directly facing you for a few moments."

Kta studied the situation from the vantage point in the door of Irain. It was dark, and there were only ill-defined shapes to be seen, the wall and the Afen a hulking mass. "We cannot help that. Let us go. Now."

Ian t'Ilev bowed shortly, then broke from cover, darting across the street.

In an instant came a heart-stopping shriek, and from the main street poured a force of men bearing torches and weapons: the Indras-descended came in direct attack against the iron gate of the Afen, bearing a ram with them.

White light illuminated the court of the Afen, blinding, and there was an answering Sufak ululation from inside the wall. The blows of the ram began to resound against the iron bars.

Kurt and Kta held a moment, while men from Isulan poured around them. Then Kta broke forth and they followed him to the shadow of the wall. Scaling-poles went up.

The first man took with him the line that would aid their descent on the other side. He gained the top and rolled over, the line jerking taut in the hands of those who secured it on the hitherside.

The next man swarmed up to the top and then it was Kurt's turn. Floodlights swung over to them now, spotting them, arrows beginning to fly in their direction. One hissed over Kurt's head. He hooked a leg over the wall, flung himself over and slid for the bottom, stripping skin from his hands on the knotted line.

The man behind him made it, but the next came plummeting to earth, knocking the other man to the ground. There was no time to help either. Kta landed on his feet beside him, broke the securing thong and ripped Isthain from its sheath. Kurt drew his own *ypan* as they ran, trying to dodge clear of the tracking floodlight.

The wall of the Afen itself provided them shelter, and there they regrouped. Of the twenty-four who had begun, at least six were missing.

T'Nethim was the last into shelter. They were nineteen.

Kta gestured toward the door of the Afen itself, and they slipped along the wall toward it, the place where the Methi's guard had taken their stand. Men, they knew those, but there was no mercy in the arrows which had already taken toll of them, and none in the plans they had laid. The door must be forced.

With a crash of iron the wall-gate gave way and the Indras under Ian t'Ilev surged forward in a frontal assault on the door to the Afen,—the Sufaki archers, standing and kneeling, firing as rapidly as they could; and Kta's small force hit the bowmen from the flank, creating precious seconds of diversion. Isthain struck without mercy, and Kurt wielded his own blade with less skill but no less determination.

The swordless archers gave up the bows at such unexpected short range and resorted to long daggers, but they had no chance against the *ypai*, cut down and overrushed. The charge of the Indras carried to the very door, over the bodies of the Methi's valiant guard, bringing the ram's metal-spiked weight to bear with slow and shattering force against the bronze-plated wood.

From inside, over all the booming and shouting, came a brief piercing whine. Kurt knew it, froze inside, caught Kta by the shoulder and pulled him back, shouting for the others to drop, but few heard him.

The Afen door dissolved in a sheet of flame and the ram and the men who wielded it were slag and ashes in the same instant. The Indras still standing were paralyzed with shock or they might have fled; and there came the click and whine as the alien field-piece in the inner hall built up power for the next burst of fire.

Kurt flung himself through the smoking doorway, to the wall inside and out of the line of fire. The gunners swung the barrel about on its tripod to aim at him against the wall, and he dropped, sliding as it moved, the beam passing over his head with a crackle of energy and a breath of heat.

The wall shattered, the support beams turning to ash in that instant; and Kurt scrambled up now with a shout as wild as that of the Indras, several seconds his before the weapon could fire again.

He took the gunner with a sweep of his blade, his ears hurting as the unmanned gun gathered force again, a wild scream of energy. A second man tried to turn it on the Indras who were pouring through the door.

Kurt ran him through, ignoring the man who was thrusting a pike at his own side. The hot edge of metal raked his back and he fell, rolled for protection. The Sufaki above him was aiming the next thrust for his heart. Desperately he parried with his blade crosswise and deflected the point up—the iron head raked his shoulder and grated on the stone floor.

In the next instant the Sufaki went down with Isthain through his ribs, and Kta paused amid the rush to give Kurt his hand and help him up.

"Get back to safety," Kta advised him.

"I am all right,—*No!*" he cried as he saw the Indras preparing to topple the live gun to the flooring. He staggered to the weapon that still hummed with readiness and swung it to where the Indras were pressing forward against the next barred doorway, trying vainly to batter it with shoulders and blades. Behind him the shattered wall and dust and chips of stone sifting down from the ceiling warned how close the area was to collapse. There was need of caution. He controlled the mishandled weapon to a tighter, less powerful beam.

"Have a care," Kta said. "I do not trust that thing."

"Clear your men back," said Kurt, and Kta shouted at them. When they realized what he was about, they scrambled to obey.

The doorway dissolved, the edges of the blasted wood charred and blackened, and Kurt powered down while the Indras surged forward again and opened the ruined doors.

The inner Afen stood open to them now, the lower halls vacant of defenders. For a moment there was silence. There were the stairs leading up to the Methi's apartments, to the human section, which other weapons would guard.

"She has given her weapons to the Sufaki," Kurt said. "There is no knowing what the situation is up there. We have to take the upper level. Help me. We need this weapon."

"Here," said Ben t'Irain, a heavyset man who was house-friend to Elas. He took the thing on his broad shoulder and gestured for one of his cousins to take its base as Kurt kicked the tripod and collapsed it.

"If we meet trouble," Kurt told him, "drop to your knee and hold this end straight toward the target. Leave the rest to me."

"I understand," said the man calmly, which was bravery for a nemet, much as they hated machines. Kurt gave the man a nod of respect and motioned the men to try the stairway.

They went quickly and carefully now, ready for ambush at any turn. Kurt privately feared a mine, but that was something he did not tell them: they had no other way.

The door at the top of the stairs was closed, as Kurt had known it must be; and with Ben to steady the gun, he blasted the wood to cinders, etching the outline of the stone arch on the wall across the hall. The weapon started to gather power again, beginning that sinister whine, and Kurt let it, dangerous as it was to move it when charged: it had to be ready.

They entered the hall leading to the human section of the Afen. There remained only the door of Djan's apartments.

Kurt held up a hand signaling caution, for there must be opposition here as nowhere else.

He waited. Kta caught his eye and looked impatient, out of breath as he was.

With Djan to reckon with, underestimation could be fatal to all of them. "Ben," he said, "this may be worth your life and mine."

"What will you?" Ben t'Irain asked him calmly enough,

though he was panting from the exertion of the climb. Kurt
nodded toward the door.

T'Irain went with him and took up position, kneeling.
Kurt threw the beam dead center, fired.

The door ceased to exist, and in the reeking opening was
framed a heap of twisted metal, the shapes of two men in
pale silhouette against the cindered wall beyond, where
their bodies and the gun they had manned had absorbed the
energy.

A movement to the right drew Kurt's attention. There
was a burst of light as he turned and Ben t'Irain gasped in
pain and collapsed beneath the gun.

T'Tefur. The Sufaki swung the pistol left at Kurt and Kurt
dropped, the beam raking the wall where he had been. In
that instant two of the Indras rushed the Sufaki leader, one
shot down, and Kta, the other one, grazed by the bolt.

Kta vaulted the table between them and Isthain swept in
an invisible downstroke that cleaved the Sufaki's skull. The
pistol discharged undirected and Kta staggered, raked across
the leg as t'Tefur's dying hands caught at him and missed.
Then Kta pulled himself erect and leaned on Isthain as he
turned and looked back at the others.

Kurt edged over to the whining gun and shut it down,
then touched t'Irain's neck to find that there was no heart-
beat. T'Tefur's first shot had been true.

He gathered his shaking limbs under him and rose, leaning on the charred doorframe; the heat made him jerk back,
and he staggered over to join Kta, past Ian t'Ilev's sprawled
body, for he was the other man t'Tefur had shot down
before dying.

Kta had not moved. He still stood by t'Tefur, both his
hands on Isthain's pommel. Then Kurt bent down and took
the gun from Shan t'Tefur's dead fingers, with no sense of
triumph in the action, no satisfaction in the name of Mim or
the other dead the man had sent before him.

It was a way of life they had killed, the last of a great
house. He had died well. The Indras themselves were silent,
Kta most of all.

A small silken form burst from cover behind the couch
and fled for the open door. T'Ranek stopped her, swept her
struggling off her feet and set her down again.

"It is the *chan* of the Methi," said Kta, for it was indeed the girl Pai t'Erefe, Sufaki, Djan's companion. Released, she fell sobbing to her knees, a small, and shaken figure in that gathering of warlike men: but she was also of the Afen, so when she had made the necessary obeisance to her conquerors, she sat back with her little back stiff and her head erect.

"Where is the Methi?" Kta asked her, and Pai set her lips and would not answer. One of the men reached down and gripped her arm cruelly.

"No," Kurt asked of him, and dropped to one knee, fronting Pai. "Pai, Pai, speak quickly. There is a chance she may live if you tell me."

Pai's large eyes reckoned him, inside and out. "Do not harm her," she pleaded.

"Where is she?"

"The temple—" When he rose she sprang to her feet, holding him, compelling his attention. "My lord, t'Tefur wanted her greater weapons. She would not give them. She refused him. My lord Kurt, my lord, do not kill her."

"The *chan* is probably lying," said t'Ranek, "to gain time for the Methi to prepare worse than this welcome."

"I am not lying," Pai sobbed, gripping Kurt's arm shamelessly rather than be ignored. "Lord Kurt, you know her. I am not lying."

"Come on." Kurt took her by the arm and looked at the rest of them, at Kta most particularly, whose face was pale and drawn with the shock of his wound. "Hold here," he told Kta. "I am going to the temple."

"It is suicide," said Kta. "Kurt, you cannot enter there. Even we dare not come after her there, no Indras—"

"Pai is Sufaki and I am human," said Kurt, "and no worse pollution there than Djan herself. Hold the Afen. You have won, if only you do not throw it away now."

"Then take men with you," Kta pleaded with him, and when he ignored the plea: "Kurt, Elas wants you back."

"I will remember it."

He hurried Pai with him, past t'Irain's corpse at the door and down the hall to the inner stairs. He kept one hand on her arm and held the pistol in the other, forcing the *chan* along at a breathless pace.

Pai sobbed, pattering along with small resisting steps, tripping in her skirts on the stairs, though she tried to hold them with her free hand. He shook her as they came to the landing, not caring that he hurt.

"If they reach her first," he said, "they will kill her, Pai. As you love her, move."

And after that, Pai's slippered feet hurried with more sureness, and she had swallowed down her tears, for the brave little *chan* had not needed to trip so often. She hurried now under her own power.

They came into the main hall, through the rest of the Indras, and men stared, but they did not challenge him; everyone knew Elas' human. Pai stared about her with fear-mad eyes, but he hastened her through, beneath the threatening ceiling at the main gate and to the outside, past the carnage that littered the entrance. Pai gave a startled gasp and stopped. He drew her past quickly, not much blaming the girl.

The night wind touched them, cold and clean after the stench of burning flesh in the Afen. Across the floodlit courtyard rose the dark side of Haichema-tleke, and beneath it the wall and the small gate that led out into the temple courtyard.

They raced across the lighted area, fearful of some last archer, and reached the gate out of breath.

"You," Kurt told Pai, "had better be telling the truth."

"I am," said Pai, and her large eyes widened, fixed over his shoulder. "Lord! Someone comes!"

"Come," he said, and, blasting the lock, shouldered the heavy gate open. "Hurry."

The temple doors stood ajar, far up the steps past the three triangular pylons. The golden light of Nephane's hearthfire threw light over all the square and hazed the sky above the roof-opening.

Kurt drew a deep breath and raced upward, dragging Pai with him, she stumbling now from exhaustion. He put his arm about her and half-carried her, for he would not leave her alone to face whatever pursued them. Behind them he could hear shouting rise anew from the main gate, renewed resistance—cheers for victory—he did not pause to know.

Within, the great hearthfire came in view, roaring up

from its circular pit to the *gelos,* the aperture in the ceiling, the smoke boiling darkly up toward the black stones.

Kurt kept his grip on Pai and entered cautiously, keeping near the wall, edging his way around it, surveying all the shadowed recesses. The fire's burning drowned his own footsteps and its glare hid whatever might lie directly across it. The first he might know of Djan's presence could be a darting bolt of fire deadlier than the fire that burned for Phan.

"Human."

Pai shrieked even as he whirled, throwing her aside, and he held his finger still on the trigger. The aged priest, the one who had so nearly consigned him to die, stood in a side hall, staff in hand, and behind him appeared other priests.

Kurt backed away uneasily, darted a nervous glance further left, right again toward the fire.

"Kurt," said Djan's voice from the shadows at his far right.

He turned slowly, knowing she would be armed.

She waited, her coppery hair bright in the shadows, bright as the bronze of the helmeted men who waited behind her; and the weapon he had expected was in her hand. She wore her own uniform now, that he had never seen her wear, green that shimmered with synthetic unreality in this time and place.

"I knew," she said, "when you ran, that you would be back."

He cast the gun to the ground, demonstrating both hands empty. "I'll get you out. It's too late to save anything, Djan. Give up. Come with me."

"What, have you forgiven, and has Elas? They sent you here because they won't come here. They fear this place. And Pai, for shame, Pai,—"

"Methi," wailed Pai, who had fallen on her face in misery, "Methi, I am sorry."

"I do not blame you. I have expected him for days." She spoke now in Nechai. "And Shan t'Tefur?"

"He is dead," said Kurt.

There was no grief, only a slight flicker of the eyes. "I could no longer reason with him. He saw things that could not exist, that never had existed. So others found their own solutions, they tell me. They say the Families have gone over to Ylith of Indresul."

"To save their city."

"And will it?"

"I think it has a chance at least."

"I thought," she said, "of making them listen. I had the firepower to do it—to show them where we came from."

"I am thankful," he said, "that you didn't."

"You made this attack calculating that I wouldn't."

"You know the object lesson would be pointless. And you have too keen a sense of responsibility to get these men killed defending you. I'll help you get out, into the hills. There are people in the villages who would help you. You can make your peace with Ylith-methi later."

She smiled sadly. "With a world between us, how did we manage to do it? Ylith will not let it rest. And neither will Kta t'Elas."

"Let me help you."

Djan moved the gun she had held steadily on him, killed the power with a pressure of her thumb. "Go," she told her two companions. "Take Pai to safety."

"Methi," one protested. It was t'Senife. "We will not leave you with him."

"Go," she said, but when they would not, she simply held out her hand to Kurt and started with him to the door, the white-robed priests melting back before them to clear the way.

Then a shadow rose up before them.

T'Nethim.

A blade flashed. Kurt froze, foreseeing the move of Djan's hand, whipping up the pistol. "Don't!" he cried out to them both.

The *ypan* arced down.

A cry of outrage roared in his ears. He seized t'Nethim's arm, thrown sprawling as the Sufaki guards went for the man. Blades lifted, fell almost simultaneously. T'Nethim sprawled down the steps, over the edge, leaving a dark trail behind him.

Kurt struggled to his knees, saw the awful ruin of Djan's shoulder and knew, though she still breathed, that she was finished. His stomach knotted in panic. He thought that her eyes pitied him.

Then they lost the look of life, the firelight from the doorway flickering across their surface. When he gathered her up against him she was loose, lifeless.

"Let her go," someone ordered.

He ignored the command, though it was in his mind that in the next moment a Sufak dagger could be through his back. He cradled Djan against him, aware of Pai sobbing nearby. He did not shed tears. They were stopped up in him, one with the terror that rested in his belly. He wished they would end it.

A deafening vibration filled the air, moaning deeply with a sighing voice of bronze, the striking of the *Inta,* the notes shaking and chilling the night. It went on and on, time brought to a halt, and Kurt knelt and held her dead weight against his shoulder until at last one of the younger priests came and knelt, holding out his hands in entreaty.

"Human," said the priest, "please, for decency's sake, —let us take her from this holy place."

"Does she pollute your shrine?" he asked, suddenly trembling with outrage. "She could have killed every living thing on the shores of the Ome Sin. She could not even kill one man."

"Human," said t'Senife, half kneeling beside him. "Human, let them have her. They will treat her honorably."

He looked up into the narrow Sufaki eyes and saw grief there. The priests pulled Djan from him gently, and he made the effort to rise, his clothes soaked with her blood. He shook so that he almost fell, and turned dazed eyes upon the temple square, where a line of Indras guards had ranged themselves. Still the *Inta* sounded, numbing the very air and in small groups men came moving slowly toward the shrine.

They were Sufaki.

He was suddenly aware that all around him were Sufaki, save for the distant line of Indras swordsmen who stood screening the approach to the temple.

He looked back, realizing they had taken Djan. She was gone, the last human face of his own universe that he would ever see. He heard Pai crying desolately, and almost absently bent and drew her to her feet, passing her into t'Senife's care.

"Come with me," he bade t'Senife. "Please. The Indras will not attack. I will get you both to safety. There should be no more killing in this place."

T'Senife yielded, nodded to his companion, tired men, both of them, with tired, sorrowful faces.

They came down the long steps. Indras turned, ready to take the three Sufaki, the men and the *chan* Pai, in charge, but Kurt put himself between.

"No," he said. "There is no need. We have lost t'Nethim; they have lost a methi. She is dead. Let them be."

One was t'Nechis, who heard that news soberly and bowed and prevented his men. "If you look for Kta t'Elas," said t'Nechis, "seek him toward the wall."

"Go your way," Kurt bade the Sufaki, "or stay with me if you will."

"I will stay with you," said t'Senife, "until I know what the Indras plan to do with Nephane." There was cynicism in his voice, but it surely masked a certain fear, and the methi's guards walked with him as he walked behind the Indras line in search of Kta.

He found Kta among the men of Isulan, with his leg bandaged and with Isthain now secure at his belt. Kta looked up in shock—joy damped by fear. Kurt looked down at his bloody hand and found it trembling and his knees likely to give out.

"Djan is dead," said Kurt.

"Are you all right?" Kta asked.

Kurt nodded, and jerked his head toward the Sufaki. "They were her guards. They deserve honor of that."

Kta considered them, inclined his head in respect. "T'Senife,—help us. Stand by us for a time, so that your people may see that we mean them no harm. We want the fighting stopped."

The rumor was spreading among the people that the Methi was dead. The *Inta* had not ceased to sound. The crowd in the square increased steadily.

"It is Bel t'Osanef," said Toj t'Isulan.

It was in truth Bel, coming slowly through the crowd, pausing to speak a word, exchange a glance with one he knew. Among some his presence evoked hard looks and muttering, but he was not alone. Men came with him, men whose years made the crowd part for them, murmuring in wonder: the elders of the Sufaki.

Kta raised a hand to draw his attention, Kurt beside him, though it occurred to him what vulnerable targets they both were.

"Kta," Bel said, "Kta, is it true,—the Methi is dead?"

"Yes," said Kta, and to the elders, who expressed their grief in soft murmurings: "That was not planned. I beg you, come into the Afen. I will swear on my life you will be safe."

"I have already sworn on mine," said Bel. "They will hear you. We Sufaki are accustomed to listen, and you Indras to making laws. This time the decision will favor us both, my friend, or we will not listen."

"We could please some in Indresul," said Kta, "by disavowing you. But we will not do that. We will meet Ylith-methi as one city."

"If we can unite to surrender," said one elder, "we can to fight."

Then it came to Kurt, like an incredibly bad dream: the human weapons in the citadel.

He fled, startling Kta, startling the Indras, so that the guard at the gate nearly ran him through before he recognized him in the dark.

But Elas' human had leave to go where he would.

Heart near to bursting, Kurt raced through the battlefield of the court, up the stairs, into the heights of the Afen.

Even those on watch in the Methi's hall did not challenge him until he ordered them sharply from the room and drew his *ypan* and threatened them. They yielded before his wild frenzy, hysterical as he was, and fled out.

"Call t'Elas," a young son of Ilev urged the others. "He can deal with this madman."

Kurt slammed the door and locked it, overturned the table and wrestled it into position against the door, working with both hands now, barring it with yet more furniture. They struck it from the outside, but it was secure. Then they went away.

He sank down, trembling, too weary to move. In time he heard the voice of Kta, of Bel, even Pai pleading with him.

"What are you doing?" Kta cried through the door. "My friend, what do you plan to do?"

But it was a Sufaki's voice, not Bel's, that urged on him the inevitable.

"You hold the weapons that could destroy the Indras fleet, that could free our city. A curse on you if you will not help us!"

But only Kta and Bel did he answer, and then always the same: "Go away. I am staying here."

In time they did go away, and he relaxed somewhat, until he heard a gentle stirring at his barricade.

"Who is there?" he shouted out.

"My lord," said Pai's fearful voice from near the floor. "My lord, you will not use those weapons, will you?"

"No," he said, "I will not."

"They would have forced you. Not Kta. Not Bel. They would not harm you. But some would have forced you. They wanted to attack. Kta persuaded them not to. Please, may I come in?"

"No, Pai. I do not trust even you."

"I will watch here all night, my lord. I will tell you if they come."

"You do not blame me—because I will not do what they want?"

There was a long hesitation. "Djan also would not do what they wished. I honored her. I will watch for you, my lord. Rest. I will not sleep."

He sat down then on the only remaining chair, with his head leaning back, and though he did not intend to, he slept for little periods. Sometimes he would ask Pai whether she slept—but her voice was always there, faithful and calm.

Then came morning, through the glass of the window that overlooked the west. When he went to look out, the sullen light exposed the whole of a great war fleet moving into the harbor.

Ylith's fleet had come.

He waited for a long time after they had docked. There was no sign of fighting. Eventually he sent Pai downstairs to spy out what was happening.

"There are Indras lords in the lower hall," she reported, "strangers. But they have been told you are here. They are trying to decide whether to attack this door or not. My lord, I am afraid."

"Leave the door," he told her. But she did not. He still heard her stirring occasionally outside.

Then he went around the various centers of the section, wrecking machinery, smashing delicate circuits.

"What are you doing?" Pai cried, when she heard the noise.

He did not trouble to answer. He dismantled the power sources as far as he could, the few handweapons he found also, everything. Then he took away the barricade before the door.

She waited outside, her large eyes wide with fear and with wonder,—perhaps no little shock, for he was filthy and bloody and almost staggering with exhaustion.

"They have not threatened you?" he asked.

She bowed her head gravely. "No, lord. They feared to make you angry. They know the power of the weapons."

"Let us go to Elas."

"I am *chan* to methis," she said. "It is not proper for me to quit my station."

"I am afraid for you with conditions as they are. Visit Elas with me."

She bowed very deeply, straightened and walked beside him.

The shock of seeing him in the lower hall all but paralyzed the men of Indresul, who watched there with a few of the Indras of Nephane. The presence of Nephanites among the occupying forces heartened him somewhat.

"The weapons," he said, "are dismantled beyond my ability to repair them. I am going to Elas if you want to find me."

And to his own surprise they let him pass, and puzzled guards on the Street of the Families did also, for a man of Indresul walked after them, watching them, his presence guarding them.

"No harm must come to you," said that man at last. "This is the order of the Methi Ylith."

*   *   *

There was no Hef to tend the door of Elas. Kurt opened it for himself and with Pai behind him entered its shadows. He stopped at the door of the *rhmei,* for he had not washed from the fighting and he wished to bring no pollution into the peace of that hall.

Kta rose to his feet from the chair of Nym, his face touched with deep relief. By him on lesser chairs sat Bel, Aimu, elders of the Sufaki and a stranger,—Vel t'Elas-in-Indresul.

Kurt bowed, realizing he had interrupted something of great moment, that an Indras of the shining city sat at this hearth.

"I beg your leave," he said. "I have finished at the Afen. No human weapons threaten your peace any longer. Tell your Methi that, Vel t'Elas."

"I had assured Ylith-methi," said Kta, his voice even but full of controlled feeling, "that this would be your choice. Is that Pai t'Erefe with you?"

"She needed a place for a time," he said. "If Elas will accept her as a guest."

"Elas is honored," murmured Kta. "Go wash, and come and sit with us, friend Kurt. We are in the midst of serious business." But before he went upstairs, Kta left his guests and came to him in the hall.

"It was well done," said Kta softly. "My friend, my brother Kurt,—go and wash, and come down to us. We are solving matters. It is a three- and a four-round problem, but the Methi Ylith has vowed to stay in port until it is done. We will talk here; then we will go down to the port to tell her our decisions. There are others of our cousins of Indresul in their several houses at this moment, and each Indras house has taken Sufaki among them, to shelter them at the sanctity of their hearths until this matter is resolved. Not a Sufaki will be harmed, who accepts house-friendship and the peace of our roofs."

"Would they all come?"

"No,—not all, not all. But perhaps the violent ones have fled to their hills, or perhaps they will come down in peace when they see it possible. But on every door of Sufak some Indras Family has set its seal; there will be no plundering.

And at every hearth we have taken house-friends. This we did,—while you barricaded yourself behind the Afen door."

Kurt managed a smile. "And that," he said, "was well done too. Am I still welcome here?"

"You are of Elas," Kta exclaimed indignantly. *"Of* this hearth and not simply beside it. Go upstairs."

"I have to find t'Nethim's family," he protested.

"This has been done.—I need you," Kta insisted. *"I* need you. Elas does. When Ylith-methi knows what you have done, and she will, I have no doubt that she will wish to see you, and you cannot go like that, and you cannot go ignorant of the business of your hearth."

He nodded wearily, felt for the stairs.

"Kta," said Bel softly. "See to him if you wish, personally. We will keep peace at your hearth until you return— surely, my lord of Indresul. Perhaps we can even find some things to discuss while you are gone if my lady wife will bring us another round of tea."

Kta considered the two of them, grave old Vel and the young Sufaki of his own age. Then he gave them a bemused slight bow and guided Kurt toward the stairs.

"Come," he said. "You are home, my friend."

DAW

More Top-Flight Science Fiction and Fantasy from
C.J. CHERRYH

Merovingen Nights (Mri Wars period)
☐ ANGEL WITH THE SWORD   (UE2143—$3.50)

Merovingen Nights—Anthologies
☐ FESTIVAL MOON (#1)   (UE2192—$3.50)
☐ FEVER SEASON (#2)   (UE2224—$3.50)
☐ TROUBLED WATERS (#3)   (UE2271—$3.50)
☐ SMUGGLER'S GOLD (#4)   (UE2299—$3.50)

Other Science Fiction
☐ HESTIA   (UE2208—$2.95)
☐ WAVE WITHOUT A SHORE   (UE2101—$2.95)

Other Anthologies
☐ SUNFALL   (UE1881—$2.50)
☐ VISIBLE LIGHT   (UE2129—$3.50)

FANTASY
The Morgaine Cycle
☐ GATE OF IVREL (BOOK 1)   (UE2321—$3.95)
☐ WELLS OF SHIUAN (BOOK 2)   (UE2322—$3.95)
☐ FIRES OF AZEROTH (BOOK 3)   (UE2323—$3.95)
☐ EXILE'S GATE (BOOK 4)   (UE2254—$3.95)

The Ealdwood Novels
☐ THE DREAMSTONE   (UE2013—$2.95)
☐ THE TREE OF SWORDS AND JEWELS
     (UE1850—$2.95)

NEW AMERICAN LIBRARY
P.O. Box 999, Bergenfield, New Jersey 07621

Please send me the DAW BOOKS I have checked above. I am enclosing $_____
(check or money order—no currency or C.O.D.'s). Please include the list price
plus $1.00 per order to cover handling costs. Prices and numbers are subject to
change without notice.

Name _____

Address _____

City _____ State _____ Zip _____
Please allow 4-6 weeks for delivery.

DAW

Science Fiction Masterworks from

C.J. CHERRYH

THE ALLIANCE-UNION UNIVERSE

The Company Wars
☐ DOWNBELOW STATION　　　　　(UE2227—$3.95)

The Era of Rapprochement
☐ FORTY THOUSAND IN GEHENNA　(UE1952—$3.50)
☐ MERCHANTER'S LUCK　　　　　(UE2139—$3.50)

　The Chanur Novels
　☐ THE PRIDE OF CHANUR　　　(UE2292—$3.95)
　☐ CHANUR'S VENTURE　　　　　(UE2293—$3.95)
　☐ THE KIF STRIKE BACK　　　　(UE2184—$3.50)
　☐ CHANUR'S HOMECOMING　　　(UE2177—$3.95)

☐ VOYAGER IN NIGHT　　　　　　(UE2107—$2.95)
☐ PORT ETERNITY　　　　　　　　(UE2206—$2.95)

The Mri Wars
☐ THE FADED SUN: KESRITH　　　(UE1960—$3.50)
☐ THE FADED SUN: SHON'JIR　　　(UE1889—$2.95)
☐ THE FADED SUN: KUTATH　　　　(UE2133—$2.95)

☐ SERPENT'S REACH　　　　　　　(UE2088—$3.50)

The Age of Exploration
☐ CUCKOO'S EGG　　　　　　　　(UE2083—$3.50)

The Hanan Rebellion
☐ BROTHERS OF EARTH　　　　　(UE2209—$3.95)
☐ HUNTER OF WORLDS　　　　　　(UE2217—$2.95)

DAW

DAW PRESENTS THESE BESTSELLERS BY
MARION ZIMMER BRADLEY

THE DARKOVER NOVELS

The Founding

☐ DARKOVER LANDFALL   UE2234—$3.95

The Ages of Chaos

☐ HAWKMISTRESS!   UE2230 $3.05
☐ STORMQUEEN!   UE2092—$3.95

The Hundred Kingdoms

☐ TWO TO CONQUER   UE2174—$3.50

The Renunciates (Free Amazons)

☐ THE SHATTERED CHAIN   UE1961—$3.50
☐ THENDARA HOUSE   UE2240—$3.95
☐ CITY OF SORCERY   UE2122—$3.95

Against the Terrans: The First Age

☐ THE SPELL SWORD   UE2237—$3.95
☐ THE FORBIDDEN TOWER   UE2235—$3.95

Against the Terrans: The Second Age

☐ THE HERITAGE OF HASTUR   UE2238—$3.95
☐ SHARRA'S EXILE   UE1988—$3.95

THE DARKOVER ANTHOLOGIES
with The Friends of Darkover

☐ THE KEEPER'S PRICE   UE2236—$3.95
☐ SWORD OF CHAOS   UE2172—$3.50
☐ FREE AMAZONS OF DARKOVER   UE2096—$3.50
☐ THE OTHER SIDE OF THE MIRROR   UE2185—$3.50
☐ RED SUN OF DARKOVER   UE2230—$3.95

NEW AMERICAN LIBRARY
P.O. Box 999, Bergenfield, New Jersey 07621
Please send me the DAW BOOKS I have checked above. I am enclosing $_____
(check or money order—no currency or C.O.D.'s). Please include the list price plus
$1.00 per order to cover handling costs. Prices and numbers are subject to change
without notice.

Name _____

Address _____

City _____ State _____ Zip _____
Please allow 4-6 weeks for delivery.

DAW

DAW Presents the Fantastic Realms of

JO CLAYTON

☐ A BAIT OF DREAMS	(UE2276—$3.95)
☐ SHADOW OF THE WARMASTER	(UE2298—$3.95)
DRINKER OF SOULS SERIES	
☐ DRINKER OF SOULS (Book 1)	(UE2275—$3.95)
☐ BLUE MAGIC (Book 2)	(UE2270—$3.95)
THE SKEEN SERIES	
☐ SKEEN'S LEAP	(UE2304—$3.95)
☐ SKEEN'S RETURN	(UE2202—$3.50)
☐ SKEEN'S SEARCH	(UE2241—$3.50)
THE DIADEM SERIES	
☐ DIADEM FROM THE STARS (#1)	(UE1977—$2.50)
☐ LAMARCHOS (#2)	(UE1971—$2.50)
☐ IRSUD (#3)	(UE2126—$2.95)
☐ MAEVE (#4)	(UE1760—$2.25)
☐ STAR HUNTERS (#5)	(UE2219—$2.95)
☐ THE NOWHERE HUNT (#6)	(UE1874—$2.50)
☐ GHOSTHUNT (#7)	(UE2220—$2.95)
☐ THE SNARES OF IBEX (#8)	(UE1974—$2.95)
☐ QUESTER'S ENDGAME (#9)	(UE2138—$3.50)
THE DUEL OF SORCERY TRILOGY	
☐ MOONGATHER (#1)	(UE2072—$3.50)
☐ MOONSCATTER (#2)	(UE2071—$3.50)
☐ CHANGER'S MOON (#3)	(UE2065—$3.50)

DAW

NEW DIMENSIONS IN MILITARY SF

Timothy Zahn
THE BLACKCOLLAR NOVELS

The war drug—that was what Backlash was, the secret formula, so rumor said, which turned ordinary soldiers into the legendary Blackcollars, the super warriors who, decades after Earth's conquest by the alien Ryqril, remained humanity's one hope to regain Its freedom.

☐ THE BLACKCOLLAR (Book 1)   (UE2168—$3.50)
☐ THE BACKLASH MISSION (Book 2)   (UE2150—$3.50)

Charles Ingrid
THE SAND WARS

He was a soldier fighting against both mankind's alien foe and the evil at the heart of the human Dominion Empire, trapped in an alien-altered suit of armor which, if worn too long, could transform him into a sand warrior—a no-longer human berserker.

☐ SOLAR KILL (Book 1)   (UE2209—$3.50)
☐ LASERTOWN BLUES (Book 2)   (UE2260—$3.50)

John Steakley
☐ **ARMOR**

Impervious body armor had been devised for the commando forces who were to be dropped onto the poisonous surface of A-9, the home world of mankind's most implacable enemy. But what of the man inside the armor? This tale of cosmic combat will stand against the best of Gordon Dickson or Poul Anderson.
(UE1979—$3.95)

DAW

**THEY WERE THE ULTIMATE ENEMIES,
GENERALS OF STAR EMPIRES FOREVER OPPOSED—
AND WORLDS WOULD FALL
BEFORE THEIR PRIVATE WAR...**

IN CONQUEST BORN
C.S. FRIEDMAN

Braxi and Azea, two super-races fighting an endless campaign over a long forgotten cause. The Braxaná—created to become the ultimate warriors. The Azeans, raised to master the powers of the mind, using telepathy to penetrate where mere weapons cannot. Now the final phase of their war is approaching, when whole worlds will be set ablaze by the force of ancient hatred. Now Zatar and Anzha, the master generals, who have made this battle a personal vendetta, will use every power of body and mind to claim the vengeance of total conquest.

☐ **IN CONQUEST BORN**   (UE2198—$3.95)